To Stand Beside Her

B. Kristin McMichael

Lexia Press
P.O. Box 982
Worthington, OH 43085
www.lexiapress.com

Second Paperback Edition

ISBN: 1941745997
ISBN-13: 978-1-941745-99-1

Cover design: Wicked Cover Designs
Editors: Kat's Eye Editing, Morissa Schwartz, David Calver, and Eric Boler

CONTENTS

Prologue   1

Chapter One   4

Chapter Two   15

Chapter Three   28

Chapter Four   36

Chapter Five   46

Chapter Six   55

Chapter Seven   66

Chapter Eight   74

Chapter Nine   79

Chapter Ten   91

Chapter Eleven   102

Chapter Twelve   107

Chapter Thirteen   118

Chapter Fourteen   124

Chapter Fifteen   136

Chapter Sixteen   147

Chapter Seventeen   160

Chapter Eighteen   168

Chapter Nineteen   175

Chapter Twenty   187

Chapter Twenty-One   198

Chapter Twenty-Two   212

Chapter Twenty-Three   227

Chapter Twenty-Four   240

Chapter Twenty-Five   246

Chapter Twenty-Six   254

Chapter Twenty-Seven   266

Chapter Twenty-Eight   275

Chapter Twenty-Nine   282

Chapter Thirty   288

Chapter Thirty-One   297

Chapter Thirty-Two   304

Chapter Thirty-Three   311

Chapter Thirty-Four   318

Chapter Thirty-Five   325

Chapter Thirty-Six   332

Epilogue   336

Acknowledgments   336

About the Author   340

PROLOGUE

Kay slipped on the cold stone but kept running, her shoes clicked lightly on the hard marble floors. It was her first level-four assignment, and she had failed. When she had initially accepted it, she needed the money. Now, it didn't seem to matter. Kay looked down each hallway for a door or hiding place. The nobles' quarter in the palace of Lior was unfamiliar territory.

"Straight ahead." The young man directed the men following him. The young guard led the chase through the palace halls, fueled by his embarrassment. He hadn't noticed that the girl he had been questioning was a courier until she became flustered by his inquiry. The young lady with the wavy light-brown hair and blue eyes looked friendly enough at the time; she had even blushed when he searched her, and her smile was nice to look at.

Kay heard the men getting closer behind her. She needed a hiding place soon, but the large, bare hallways offered no help. Turning right at the next intersection, she continued down yet another unfamiliar hallway. Kay was lost.

"Hey, watch where you're going!" a dark-haired, widely-built man exclaimed as Kay bumped into him.

"So sorry," Kay replied. "I'm late to work." Kay had heard Leila, her best friend and the best courier in the business, use that reply many times before.

"Stop that girl!" The young guard was yelling from the

other end of the hallway.

Kay quickly moved to pass the dark-haired man, but he easily clasped her wrists between his thick fingers. Kay looked into his eyes and tried her best to put on a flirtatious smile.

"Mister, you want me to be late for work?" she asked innocently, batting her eyes. It always worked for Leila.

The man's grip didn't loosen. Leila was right again; this wasn't the business for Kay. Try as she might to mimic her best friend, nothing seemed to work. If only I were Leila, Kay thought, letting her mind wander while she waited for the guards to catch up. Leila was the best. Most of the neighboring counties had begun calling Leila the Ghost Courier, and the description was an exact fit. Leila could easily enter any heavily-guarded place and leave unnoticed with her assignment. Kay had watched her many times in action. Leila truly was a ghost.

"I'm so sorry," said the young guard. He bowed his head to the dark-haired man, who was still tightly holding Kay's wrists. "Lord Macarius, please accept my apologies." The boy didn't lift his head.

"What did she do?" Macarius asked.

"She was heading into the noble's quarters," the boy explained, still bowing. The boy handed Macarius the papers that he had confiscated from Kay.

"Lock her in the jail for now. King Nalick will deal with her later," Macarius replied.

Kay turned to the stout man, Macarius, who was now smiling as he strolled away. He knew the truth behind the papers. Leila is going to kill me, Kay thought. She had taken the assignment against her friend's warning. Leila was always right. Deep down, Kay knew that she wasn't really meant to be a courier.

When they arrived at the jail, the guard ushered Kay into the cell. Would Leila find her before the king tried her? Kay had heard horror stories from the locals that

King Nalick was a harsh man, known to order severe punishments. Kay moved to a bed in the corner of the room and stood on it to look out the tiny window. The sun was still rising, but Leila would begin to worry soon. Kay stepped off the bed and sat in the corner. Leila wasn't completely healed from her last trip. Leila and Kay's employer, Roger, would be upset. With a sigh, Kay huddled in the corner to wait. There was nothing else she could do. Kay was caught.

CHAPTER ONE

Benét Leila quietly sipped her tea at a table on the patio of Veila's Tea Shop. The quiet, demure character Leila portrayed was in stark contrast to her actual personality. Carefully, and in the most ladylike manner, she attempted to scratch her head. The black wig covering her naturally golden-red hair, and the scarf placed skillfully over it, were beginning to prove bothersome. Maybe it was the persistent heat of the city that Leila wasn't accustomed to, or maybe it was the bad feeling she had because her best friend Kay was over an hour late. It wasn't like Kay to be late for their meeting to go home to Kay's son. Leila sighed. They were losing their best chance to leave the city. Soon, the empty streets would be filled, and they would miss their opportunity to blend in and be lost from any trackers.

As the noon bell struck, people began to slowly leave their shops and trickle down the street. Shortly thereafter, the streets would bustle with citizens. Every day, as the sun reached its peak above the city, the city of Lexia would temporarily halt as the residents proceeded home for their midday meal. Leila sat quietly, impervious to the noise around her, sipping her tea as she waited impatiently. Out of the corner of one eye, she noticed the tea shop owner closing the shop doors.

"Just drop your money in the slot at the door before you leave, honey," the wrinkled old lady said to Leila as she locked the door and slowly shuffled down the street into the forming crowd.

Leila's eyes followed the old lady down the street. Leila sat alone on the patio of the tea shop, but across the street stood a young man, trying his best to stay hidden. His dark blond hair was noticeable, since he stood a full head above the people passing him by. Lexia was a city full of olive-skinned, black-haired residents, and this man was obviously not a native. Despite his attempts to go unnoticed, it was clear that he was following Leila. New trackers were easy to spot.

One, she thought to herself. *No, two*, she corrected.

Two doors down, a man was being unceremoniously pushed out of an adjoining shop as the owner tried to close for lunch. Leila had broken a cardinal rule: one must not stay in one place too long. She needed to keep moving.

"Great," she whispered under her breath. Not only was Kay over an hour late, now she had to lose the tails before she could go looking for her. Luckily for Leila, it wasn't her first trip into Lexia. The pay was always better when an assignment included a trip to the city. Over the years, she had been there so many times that it was beginning to feel like a second home.

Leila stood and methodically stretched. She had waited long enough; it was time to move on and find out what was keeping Kay. She walked over and slid two coins into the slot in the middle of the shop door before eyeing each of the men trailing her.

This should be easy, she thought, *newbies.*

Leila knew the city better than any local. If she moved quickly, she could use the stragglers as cover on her way back to the inn. Darting between streets, she took care to blend in with the crowds. Before long, she had lost both of the trackers.

That didn't take much, she smirked.

It was always fun to teach the new trackers a lesson; Leila wasn't worth their time. She was an expert courier.

She had been hand chosen six years earlier at the age of twelve; now at eighteen years of age, she was the best courier of any neighboring country. No one—man or woman—could keep up with her. Leila was a ghost to many and a legend to everyone else. Through her training, she had perfected the use of multiple identities so that she could travel from city to city, fulfilling even the most demanding assignments.

After changing clothes and packing her bags, Leila followed the map in her head to the gate nearest to the palace jail. Kay was too late by now. She had to have been caught. Leila surveyed the area and saw that only one guard was on patrol. She could easily sneak by, but if she was caught inside, it would draw unwanted attention. The guard paced between the gate and the gatehouse.

What is the best way to get into jail? she wondered.

"Excuse me," Leila said, as politely as possible. "I heard from my uncle's neighbor's best friend that my sister was thrown in jail for some silly misunderstanding," she lied to the young, confused guard.

He clearly wasn't accustomed to being addressed by people on the street.

Unaffected by his stunned silence, she continued her lie. "She's about this tall." She indicated with her hand to the height of her shoulder. "And she has long brown hair. She's traveling with my grandmother and me and stopped by to find an old friend of our grandmother's. From what we were told, some mean guard misunderstood her and threw her in jail without a single question, and now we're distraught on how to get her out. I left grandmother back at the inn and told her not to worry. But now I think I might be in over my head. I've walked around these gates for hours, and it doesn't seem like there's any way to get in to help her out. We're not from around here, and I'm afraid we'll run out of money paying for the inn before we can find out how to clear up this misunderstanding."

"I'm s-s-sorry," he sputtered out. The young guard was having trouble talking to such a beautiful woman. "If there's any way I can help," he quickly stammered.

"You can help me?" Leila acted as graciously as she could while hiding her smirk. "That would be great; I don't know how I can thank you. Grandmother will be so happy." Leila hugged the stunned guard.

"T-T-This... This... This way," he stuttered. The guard began unlocking the gate, but before he could finish his statement, the young, blond-haired tracker from earlier trapped Leila's arms behind her.

Leila had let down her guard, and the tracker had seized the moment. The young guard bowed his head in shock. "S-S-Sorry Anatolio," he apologized to the young man that held Leila's arms behind her.

"You're better than I made you out to be," Leila said to the young man.

Her capturer, Anatolio, made no reply, and began to walk her through the gates. It had been years since someone had caught her off guard, and she was enjoying the entertainment. Leila had lost him so easily in the streets that she assumed he wouldn't find her again so soon. *He must have been waiting here for me*, she thought.

Leila moved her arms a bit to see how tight the young man was holding onto her. Anatolio adjusted his grip and held on tighter as he began to push her through the doors to the palace compound. Leila wasn't foolish enough to run from him since he would lead her right to Kay. Leila slowed their pace a little, giving her time to look around and assess the corridors they were passing through. She had been inside the palace over a dozen times and knew where almost everything was, but it was always good to double-check for any new problems she might encounter. Anatolio led her through a new section of the palace.

"Nice place," she commented, viewing the possible exits and layout of the palace.

"Newly redone?" Leila asked, but she got no response from her captor. "The quiet, serious type I see." He still didn't reply.

"So I know where you're not leading me," Leila said, and she turned slightly to see his face in an effort to read his reaction. "We're not on our way to either the king or the jail." The man's expression didn't change.

"Is this the tour you give all the ladies you kidnap?" Leila asked, still trying to get a reaction. Anatolio just continued to push her through door after door. *Since we're not headed toward Kay, this would be the best time to leave him,* she thought, but her curiosity over where he was leading her made her continue.

Pushed through a doorway, Leila heard the lock of the door click behind her and felt Anatolio release his grip. From all the twists and turns to get here, she figured that they were close to the middle of the palace. Leila walked a few steps forward to evaluate the room she was in, but to her surprise she was no longer in a room; rather, she had been led to a garden.

This is definitely not the spot I want to try to escape from, she thought, viewing the forty-foot walls.

In the corner of the garden, near the door they had entered, stood the young man, Anatolio. Leila cautiously walked toward him and tried to catch his gaze, but he continued to look elsewhere. Approaching him, she studied him carefully. He was modestly dressed, with no specific garb to indicate his position within the palace. He didn't carry a weapon, so he was no threat in that way. He was taller than she was, but from his face she gathered that he was at least a year or two younger, which meant that he was much less experienced.

This should not be a challenge, she thought.

"Since you didn't bring me to jail or to your king, am I to assume you know who I am?" Leila asked. He continued to look elsewhere. Leila moved closer, right into his line of view, so that he couldn't avoid looking at her.

"Who gave you orders to bring me here?" Leila asked.

"I did, miss," a voice said from behind her.

Leila quickly spun around to notice an old man. He was sitting so still in the garden that she hadn't been aware of him before he spoke. Since they had entered the garden, Anatolio had been staring straight at the man. The old man had a long, white beard and matching hair that lay on his shoulders like a cascading waterfall. Dressed in a light blue robe, he should have stood out in the abundance of green in the garden. He was sitting between two flowering trees filled with small birds and had blended in so perfectly that even the birds were startled when he talked. He sat so still that only his mouth moved as he spoke.

"Since I know who you are, I'll ask you the same question. Do you know who I am?" His eyes twinkled as he asked. He moved his head slightly as Leila thought of her answer. "You may leave us, Anatolio."

Anatolio bowed, turned to the door, and gave two knocks.

The old man slowly returned his gaze to Leila in anticipation of her answer.

"I'll take a guess. You're the palace seer," Leila answered.

"The tales told of you do not disappoint, young lady," the man affirmed.

"I'm Gabor, and you are Leila," he said, gently standing without disturbing the birds that were in the trees next to him.

"Why do you think my name is Leila?" she asked. When traveling on assignments, she had never told anyone her real name. To know the real name of a courier was deadly; if this secret got out, Leila would never be able to work safely again. Only her allies knew her name, and she had never met this man before.

"Do not worry, child, for I'm the only one who knows who you are," Gabor reassured her. "Not even Anatolio knows. To him you were just a favor to an old man." He chuckled to himself.

"So why am I here?" she asked.

"Just as I've been told, always direct." Gabor smiled at her as he moved closer. Not knowing if he was a friend or foe yet, Leila took a step back. "It's all right, child, I will not hurt you." Gabor tried to reassure her.

"If you mean me no harm, why would you bring me here by force, and then keep me in a locked room?" Leila asked cautiously.

"You are free to leave at any time," Gabor assured her. "I merely requested your presence, and did not specify to Anatolio how to attain you." Leila stared at his eyes as he talked. He wasn't lying. Gabor tried to move closer again, and this time she didn't back away.

"Would you like me to look into your future?" he asked, while offering her his hand.

"No, thank you," she replied, without taking it. "I live only in the present." Gabor slowly withdrew his hand. Leila didn't want to offend the man, but she also had no desire to be told what she would do in the future.

Gabor returned to his seat on the bench between the two trees, disturbing the birds, which flew to other trees in the garden. "Child, do you know why anywhere you go there is always someone there to help you if you get into trouble?" Gabor motioned for her to sit beside him.

Somewhat guardedly, Leila moved closer and sat down.

Gabor continued, "You're special. To the trained eye, you're an easy one to spot. The aura around you is pure white, and it does not change. Most people's auras are different shades of color, and they change, depending on the purity of their action. Yours, though, does not. When people come in contact with you, their aura becomes whiter in color to match yours. You have the power to change the world."

"Then, you will help me leave?" Leila asked.

"I would not turn you down, but first I must ask you..." Gabor paused to look her in the eyes. "How long will you run? You continue to punish yourself with these incredibly difficult missions time and time again, but that will not bring him back. Isn't it about time you stopped running?"

Leila was tempted to look away. How did this man know everything about her? It had been two years since Erich died saving her, and yet it was a hard subject for Leila to hear spoken aloud. Had she been better at what she did, Erich wouldn't have died trying to save her from a jail.

"I'm not running," she lied.

"Just like you, child, I can tell when a person lies." The old man moved to pat her shoulder. Leila quickly stood up before he could touch her. Her quick movement caught the old man off guard. "You can lie to me, but how long can your continue to lie to your heart?" He motioned for her to sit back down. "I have no desire to read your future; I already know what it is."

But how? I did well not to come into contact with him. Leila examined herself to see if she could remember any part touching him.

"I know what can become of you. If only you..." Gabor started.

"I do not wish to know my future," Leila said harshly. "I only wish to know where my friend is being kept, and then we can be on our way home. Thank you for your explanation of everything, but now it's time for me to be on my way." Leila didn't like talking about herself, especially with a stranger.

Gabor slowly stood and walked to the door. He gave three knocks and the door opened. Anatolio stood before Gabor and bowed his head. "She wishes to be taken to the jail that is housing her friend Kay." Anatolio nodded and walked back over to Leila.

"Child, do not let your heart grow cold. The immense power you have in your innocence can be amplified a hundred times if you let yourself love again. Erich is gone. It's not your fault. You may think you're alone in your pain, but there is another who is in just as much pain from being without love. I just hope that the day you see him you can recognize that you're not alone." Gabor smiled kindly at Leila.

Anatolio moved behind her and grabbed her arms.

"I thought you weren't keeping me here," Leila asked suspiciously.

"I'm not, but in order for you to be brought into the jail, you must be a captive. No one, apart from the king, can walk into the jail with a guest and demand to see someone being held there," Gabor explained. "Anatolio will take you there and put you with your friend, but that's all he's allowed to do. Jail will give you some time to think over everything we talked about," Gabor said as he smiled at her. "May we meet again, child."

Anatolio pushed gently on her arms to force her to begin walking. This time, Leila didn't test his resolve. He would take her to exactly where she wanted to go. Leila took no notice, though, of the change in her guard's gentler mood. She was caught up in her own thoughts.

Why did he tell me these things? What does he know of my future? Can I really be happy again without Erich? Leila questioned herself. She tried to get their conversation out of her head. *I need to focus. Plan an escape. What does it mean?* Lelia's mind began to wander back over her discussion with the seer. *How did he know about Erich?*

"We're almost there," Anatolio said to Leila, breaking her thoughts. "I can get you into the same cell, but that's it. I don't have any more authority than that." Leila was shocked to hear him speak.

"There are two guards on shift inside the jail and two guards outside the gate," Anatolio explained. He let go of her arms, and she turned to face him. "The guards only change one at a time, so there's always someone here. Right now there's only your friend in the jail and no other prisoners." Gently, Anatolio turned Leila back around and took hold of her arms again. "Good luck," he whispered in her ear as they approached the guards at the gate.

"Open," Anatolio ordered. "I've this one here to be placed with the other prisoner." The gates opened. Two men immediately jumped up from their card game as Anatolio approached. The portly guard's mustache failed to hide the smile that crossed his face. He was always fond of having beautiful lady prisoners under his watch.

"She's to be housed with the other prisoner," Anatolio commanded.

"I'll take her there," the prison guard offered.

Anatolio replied, "I'll take her myself." He changed his grip to hold back Leila's arms with one hand. Leila played along, like she could easily be held with one hand. Anatolio took the keys and led her down the hallway. He approached a room and unlocked the door. Leila walked herself through.

"You're on your own now, so be careful," Anatolio warned, and he locked the door behind her.

Leila walked into the dim room. Though she hadn't noticed, it was already dusk. The room had no light in it except for the last rays of sunlight streaming in one window. *This is bad*, she thought, observing that they were not in the women's quarters of the jail. Through the dim light she surveyed the room. The room was sparsely furnished. There was one window, a bed with a blanket in one corner, and in the other corner, staring at Leila with a tear-streaked face propped on her knees, sat Kay.

CHAPTER TWO

Kay was happy to see Leila, but at the same time, she was disappointed in herself. Kay sat in the corner of the cell staring at her feet, ashamed that she had been captured after everything had been planned so well.

Kay had been just a child when she ran away from her home and wandered into Leila's family's vineyard. Kay's life changed forever when she met Leila. Leila's parents took her in to their home and raised her alongside Leila and her two older brothers. When Kay got married, Leila's father walked Kay down the aisle. When Kay had given birth to her son, it was Leila's mother who taught Kay how to calmly soothe the baby. The only person in the whole world that Kay feared disappointing was her best friend, who she considered a sister, Leila.

Leila sat down next to Kay. She studied her friend's face. Kay had been crying. Leila felt a strong need to protect her, and Kay, knowing this, became even more disappointed in herself. Kay hung her head.

"I'm sorry," Leila said, "if I had known the papers had been marked, I'd have thrown them away." Leila hugged her friend.

"It's all my fault. You told me not to take those papers," Kay blurted out while Leila hugged her.

"I've been doing this longer than you; I should have been better prepared." Leila took the blame again. Growing up together, they were always complete opposites.

This current mission was far beyond Kay's abilities,

but she had traded for the assignment without Leila's knowledge; the higher pay that came with a harder mission was too enticing to pass up. Kay had tried to leave undetected, but, being the better courier, Leila caught up with her before she reached Lexia. Kay begged and pleaded with Leila to let her finish the mission, and Leila only agreed after she promised to follow the exact plan Leila had made.

"So, now what do we do?" Kay asked, without looking Leila in the eyes.

"We leave and go home. I'll return in a couple weeks and finish everything then," Leila concluded.

"But this jail isn't how you described it," Kay commented.

"That's because we are not in the women's jail," Leila responded. She had been in these jails once, many years ago. They seemed to have upgraded everything since her last escape from the men's jail. "I was here once with Erich," she explained to Kay. Kay flinched noticeably at the sound of Erich's name. This was a very hard subject to talk about with Leila. For over a year after he died, Leila hadn't once said his name to anyone.

"This might be a bit tricky, but we have to leave separately." Leila walked over to the door and listened to the men outside. "Since we're the only people in the jail, if we both leave, they'll know right away. You will leave first, pretending to be sick, and wait for me outside the gate."

"Won't you have a harder time leaving if I'm escaping?" Kay asked.

"This place won't be hard to leave; I'll go right out that window there." Leila motioned to the window above the bed.

"But we're over four floors up," Kay said in disbelief.

"Yes, and they don't seem to have bars on the window." Leila laughed to herself. "We'll be heading home tonight."

Leila took one last look. "Now is as good of a time as any. Pretend you're really hurt."

Kay took the cue and gave out a blood-curdling scream that sent the guards running into the cell.

"What happened?" asked the younger man.

"I don't know," Leila replied. "We were just sitting here, and now she's screaming."

"Help me pick up this girl," the older guard demanded. The younger guard helped the older guard pick up Kay. She continued to howl in pain. "Stay here," he ordered the young guard.

Leila stood in the doorway of her cell and watched as the older guard carried Kay, still sobbing, out of the cell. The startled young guard turned around and looked at her. His pale face told Leila he wasn't one for taking care of sick people. He cautiously walked back over to Leila.

From what she could hear, Kay was in the infirmary, and they were going to try to treat her there. She quietly crept over to the bed and moved it slightly, so that she would be able to use it to easily reach the window. In the dimness of the moonlight, Leila pulled herself up into the window. Kay was right: they were four stories above the ground. She slowly lowered herself out the window. The nice thing about being so high up was that no one would notice if she climbed out the window. She searched the wall with her feet and found a small ledge.

For any male, the climb down would be extremely hard, if not impossible, but for Leila, with her much smaller feet, it would work just fine. It was slow going, but after fifteen minutes she was down to ground level. She decided that she preferred the women's jail after all; she'd do her best next time to not get thrown back into the men's jail. She quietly skirted from shadow to shadow until she was near the gate. After a quick look around, she ran to a cart that was loading up to leave and wedged herself tightly underneath it. Once the cart had been packed it began moving toward the gate.

The cart stopped at the gate. "Let us pass," a man said gruffly. "I found this girl climbing out the window by the servant's quarters and will be taking her to the king. She has to be the ghost courier."

Leila looked closely at the legs beside her. Kay had been caught again. The man holding Kay was the other novice tracker from the tea house. He must have been waiting outside the palace to catch Leila.

This is getting ridiculous, Leila told herself. *I'm never letting Roger put her on another mission again.*

The cart driver received his stamp from the gate guard and Leila waited for the cart to begin moving again. She watched as Kay was marched back inside the palace compound walls. When the cart was out of the sight of the palace, Leila slipped out of her hiding place beneath the cart. Leila walked briskly down the street toward the palace. She was back to the same position as before, but this time it was just a bit later during the night. The palace would not be so easy to escape a second time. Leila tried to decide whether to just return or be caught again. By now they must have noticed that Leila was gone, so she would not be able to return unnoticed. She would have to go directly in and figure things out from there. Leila marched to the gate. The young guard from before was gone, but another man stood in his place.

"Hello," Leila said to the gatekeeper, who ignored her. "I just escaped the palace jail but have decided I'd like to go back in," she told him honestly.

The gatekeeper laughed. "Little girl, go back home. Go around telling lies like that, and someone might actually believe you." He turned away from her. They must not yet have noticed she was no longer in the jail cell.

"I'm giving you the chance to be the hero here. They

soon will notice I'm gone, and when they do..." Leila trailed off. The guard still had no interest in her.

"Fine," Leila said. "I'll be sitting right here next to the wall. When you finally get the report that a girl has escaped from the men's jail, come over and get me."

Leila marched over to the wall, still within view of the guard, and sat down on the ground. She leaned up against the cool stone wall and closed her eyes. *It could be a while.* The older guard seemed like the type that would be too proud to quickly report that she had escaped. As the cool night air blew, she untied her hair and rolled her sleeves back down. In Lexia, the days were always hot and the nights always cool. It made her miss her mountain home even more. She closed her eyes and tried not to think about her frightened friend. Leila waited for over an hour before the gate guard came over to her. She looked up at him.

"Um," the gatekeeper stammered.

"Do you believe me now?" Leila asked.

"Miss, could you come this way with me," he asked, offering her his hand to help her stand up.

Leila took his hand and stood. It was then she noticed she was taller than the man. No one would believe he caught her, but it didn't seem like he was going to pretend. He led the way, and she followed behind him. As soon as Leila crossed through the gate, two more men, larger men, fell in behind the two of them.

"I'm not going anywhere," Leila commented to the two men. Neither replied.

"Is everyone in your city so serious?" she asked the guard that was leading the way.

"Yes," the guard replied. He began anxiously wringing his hands.

Great, a city filled with serious, nervous people, Leila observed, a bit disappointedly.

Leila remained silent and watched her surroundings,

hoping to get an idea about how to get Kay out. In her mind, she traced her steps through the palace on a map in her head that she had memorized years ago.

"This isn't the way to the jail," Leila commented. "Since I came back on my own, couldn't you just put me back in the jail? I promise to behave," she said, lying to the men escorting her, but none of them flinched or changed their course from the path that led to the judgment chamber of the king. Leila wasn't in the mood to deal with yet another king.

"If I'd known that I was to have a date with the king, I think I'd have just let myself back in," she remarked, not seeing the smiles on the faces of the men behind her.

"I wish you would have," the gate guard said under his breath.

They passed a line of people that had exited the judgment chamber throughout the day. Each person who departed was either in tears or pale as a ghost. King Nalick wasn't known for soft punishments. The only people who didn't seem to fear Nalick were walking behind her.

The doors opened as Leila approached the end of the hall. Down the long pathway and inside the ornately decorated room sat Kay, with her captor directly beside her. In front of Kay was the large table that King Nalick sat behind with a palace recorder on each side of him. Nalick was a large man, much more muscular and taller than the other men of Lexia. His size reminded her of the mountain men where she was from. Around Lexia, Leila stood a head taller than all the women, and eye-to-eye with more than half the men. It was a different case at home, where she was of average size in her community and all the men were taller than her. The only distinction that made Nalick different than the people of Leila's home country was his coloring. He had the same olive skin tone, black hair, and dark eyes of the people of Lexia.

Physically, he was the formidable warrior that everyone claimed. *I wonder if I could beat him in a one-on-one battle*, she mused to herself. The last time Leila met him, she had been tempted to find out. She had yet to find a man who could beat her in both weapons and hand-to-hand combat.

"Wait here," one of the men behind her directed to the gatekeeper.

"You, to the front," the same man said to her.

"You could at least ask politely," Leila responded. "There's no reason to be impolite. I kindly waited over an hour for them to let me back in." He remained silent and smiled at her remark.

Leila walked down the pathway between the empty rows of seats. The room was used once a week by King Nalick to hand out punishments to those breaking laws within the palace. After her miraculous escape, he demanded that once she was caught she was to be brought directly to him. King Nalick gazed at the woman in front of him. Though her hair and dress were a different color, he was sure this was the woman he met over a year ago, when he was in Dria visiting his father. Leila stood in front of the table as the king just stared at her. She waited patiently for him to begin the conversation. Like with hand-to-hand combat, a conversation with a king was like a duel to her. Over the last four years, Leila had met eight kings, and they didn't appreciate when she talked first. So, she stood and waited.

"My Lord," the tracker that sat next to Kay spoke, interrupting the silence. "Can we finish the matter of the ghost courier that I caught?" he asked impatiently. The new tracker obviously wanted to be congratulated for his catch and was looking for the king's approval.

"We would be finished, except you did not catch the ghost courier," Nalick corrected the man. "For I believe if you ask the woman standing before us now, she might have something to say."

"Nope," Leila responded. "I'm fine."

Your turn, she thought.

"Well then." He smiled at Leila. "If this woman here is the ghost courier, then she needs to be punished."

Good counter. "For what crimes?" Leila asked innocently.

"Crimes against the city of Lexia," the tracker declared.

"I think our new guest was asking about specifics," the king responded to his overzealous tracker. "I've been told the ghost courier is responsible for several items that are missing from nobles here in the palace, and possibly an item or two from my own treasury."

"Really?" Leila said, exaggerating her reply. "Do you know if those items were really property of the nobles in question, or could they just be covering up their own shortcomings? And where is the proof? Did you find any of those so-called items on this young woman?"

Nalick chuckled. The woman that stood before him didn't disappoint. "I'm not the one to decide that, but there's the matter that this woman was caught trying to sneak into the noble's quarters."

"How do you know that? Maybe she just lost her way," Leila suggested. "Do you punish people for losing their way?"

"In that case, should I not be punishing you, too?" he asked. "I have been told you lost your way and found yourself outside the palace when you should have been locked inside of it."

"I just can't keep my left and right straight," Leila lied. "I get lost all the time."

"I'm sure you do." Nalick smiled at her. Nalick didn't believe her, but he also didn't move to call out her lies in front of the people present.

"My Lord, I demand that the ghost courier be punished. If we lock her back up, she will just escape again." The tracker interrupted again, trying to get his reward for capturing Kay.

"Take her back to jail, but this time, find a cell without a window," Nalick ordered. The guards moved past the protesting tracker and grabbed Kay while the two guards from earlier fell into place behind Leila.

"And where should we put her, Nalick?" one of them asked. Leila was surprised to hear the man address Nalick so casually.

"Leave her here," he ordered.

"But, but..." The tracker sputtered. "If you just put my captive back in jail she will escape."

"Do not worry. She won't be going anywhere. She isn't the ghost courier," Nalick replied as Kay was escorted out of the room.

"Now, I'd like to be left alone with this one," Nalick said, referring to Leila.

"Bring the seer," he ordered. The men beside him rose and left the room. One of the men from earlier escorted the tracker out. The second man shut the door and stood at the back of the room.

"So *everyone out* didn't include him?" Leila asked. She had no chance of leaving if both men stayed in the room with Nalick and her. One, she could possibly overpower, but it would be foolish to challenge two of them.

Nalick rose and walked over to her. Leila stood her ground and didn't move. Nalick circled around her, inspecting her like a wolf getting ready to pounce on its prey. Leila knew what was coming next. She'd had this same encounter with five other kings before. Though, in her opinion, they were all lesser men than the man in front of her. Still, she didn't happily anticipate the next words out of his mouth. Leila stood in silence as he returned to his table and leaned against the tabletop. Just like all the other kings, he looked at her like she was a prize. Leila refused to be a trophy to any king. Like any man in power, Nalick had committed acts against innocent people. Intentionally or not, Leila didn't approve of hurting innocents. She had been in several battles over the last four years, and was lucky to have escaped with her life each time. Even so, she had never once killed anyone who attacked her. In her opinion, even those who would try to kill her didn't deserve to die.

The door in the back of the room opened and the seer, Gabor, walked in, escorted by the man who had just left. Leila stared blankly at Nalick, trying her best to read his expression.

"I really don't think you understand the word *alone*," she commented to Nalick sarcastically. When the door shut behind them there were now five people in the room.

Gabor walked past her and bowed his head slightly to the king. Nalick nodded his head, and Gabor returned to Leila. Extending his hand, Leila knew what he was planning to do. Trying to stay in control of the situation, Leila gave the old man her hand. Surprised, he stopped, held her hand, and closed his eyes. After a few moments, Gabor returned to the king's side. Nalick leaned over to the seer and asked him a question, but he spoke too quietly for Leila to hear.

"You don't need to be hushed about this since you're discussing me," Leila said before Gabor could respond. Nalick looked up at her. "I'm guessing I can answer your questions just as well as he could."

Nalick smiled. He had become the king when he was fourteen and then everything changed. Almost every person treated him differently, except for his two good friends who were standing in the room with him now. In his years as king, Nalick had yet to find a woman that would speak her mind to, or at, him. Here before him stood the woman who was a legend around the feast tables he shared with neighboring kings. All told of encountering a lady so beautiful she would take your breath away, and yet who was so cunning none could cage her long enough to make her into a wife. She was truly everything they talked about, and more. Nalick didn't need the seer's opinion to know that this was the woman he wanted to marry.

"Okay," Nalick responded, taking the bait. "Are you the woman that I should marry?"

"Probably, but it's not going to happen," Leila responded. Leila had reached marriageable age several years ago, but after Erich's death, marriage held no interest to her.

"And why not?" he inquired.

"Because in order to have a real marriage, both people need to be willing to marry each other." Leila looked him up and down. He was handsome, but he was also an arrogant jerk. "I'm not willing to marry you."

She turned on her heels and walked to the two men in the back of the room. She could see in their eyes that they were trying not to laugh. *It's more than likely*, Leila thought, *that Nalick has never been told "no" before. Well, there's a first time for everything.* She smiled sweetly at the two men.

"Now, if you could graciously escort me back to the jail, it would be appreciated. I've something I need to pick up before I leave Lexia. I'd not want to get lost on the way," she added, winking at the two grinning men.

"I don't think you understand," Nalick said harshly, coming up behind her. "As king, I do not need to ask... and the position you are in, you cannot exactly refuse."

"See, that's the thing about people like you." Leila turned to explain with disdain in her eyes. She didn't back away from the angry man, even though he was twice her size and only feet away from her. "You think you don't need to ask, when a person in your position, more than anyone else, should be asking, especially on a question like marriage."

Leila walked to the door and opened it herself. The two men quickly followed as she walked out, leaving a stunned Nalick to watch her walk away.

"This way," one of the men said.

"Where to now?" Leila asked. They weren't leading her to the jail.

"The jail is no place for a lady," the taller of the two men explained. He led her to a staircase and up three flights. Leila was in a part of the palace she had never seen before. The man walked to a door and unlocked a room. "By the way, I'm Theo, and this is Macarius," he indicated to the man next to him. "If you should need anything, knock on the door."

"Sorry, miss," the other man, Macarius, said as he began to wrap a chain around her waist. He almost seemed to blush, wrapping his arms around her. He then locked her wrists to the chain. "The king's orders," he apologized.

"So he's not as stupid as I thought," she responded. Both men smiled. "I suppose if I asked to have these chains removed that would not be part of the *anything* you could do for me?"

"No," Theo replied as he opened the door. "Your friend should be inside."

"Thank you." Leila smiled at the two men. They were just following orders and not to blame for her situation.

Leila prepared to be thrown into a windowless single cell, but the lavish suite was not at all what she expected. It was ornately decorated in hues of purple and gold. In the middle of the room was a set of couches and chairs covered in silk. Over in the left corner was a table with six chairs. Fresh fruit and baked goods were on the center of the table. On each side of the room there were doors.

The room to the right was a bathing room with, of course, no windows. She walked to the door on the left and found a bedroom. There, lying curled up on the bed, was Kay, who appeared to be in a deep sleep. Leila walked over and pulled the blanket up around Kay. Quietly, she began to rearrange the furniture in order to pile everything high enough so that she could see out the window. Though the windows would make a good escape, Leila knew that Kay didn't have the physical strength to scale the wall, and with the chains that had been affixed to her, neither could she. She would need another plan to get them out. Leila tested the chains while thinking as she sat up near the window. The fresh air blew in and reminded her that she was now a caged bird. Leila rested her head on the windowsill and gazed at the stars. *I'll only close my eyes for a brief moment*, she thought to herself.

CHAPTER THREE

"**M**iss," a voice called to Leila, and she felt a soft tug on her leg.

"Miss!" the voice called again.

Leila slowly opened her eyes. She gazed around. Her head was resting on a windowsill and she was balanced on a chair on top of a table. Gradually, everything came back to her. It wasn't a dream after all. From the window, she could see the whole northern section of the city of Lexia. Beyond the city's gates was home. As Leila looked out the window, she could see that the sun was partway up in the sky already. She looked down to see the man, Theo, who she had met the night before, staring up at her in anticipation of her reply. Leila glanced to the bed. Kay wasn't there. Quickly, Leila hopped down and stood face-to-face with Theo, startling the young man.

"Where is she?" Leila demanded.

"She's meeting with the priests," Theo assured Leila, hands up in surrender. "She's safe. I was sent here to wake you and also bring you to the priests."

"Why?" Leila asked.

"I don't know, my lady." Theo shrugged his shoulders. "Nalick ordered it, and I'm generally obliged to follow my king's orders."

"I am not," Leila responded, walking into the next room. Theo followed behind her. "If you'd be so kind to send my reply to him." She smiled at Theo. "It's *no*. I don't take too well to be given orders."

"Um, I'm not quite in a position to be telling the king

such things." Theo began to turn red.

"Well, in that case, just send him here to ask me himself. I've no problem telling him no. Maybe if a few more people would tell him no, he would learn to be a nicer person." Leila walked over to the table and grabbed an apple. Then she realized that her wrists were still locked to her waist. She set the apple back down. "This might a bit of a problem for me," she said to Theo, indicating at the chains. "Would you be so kind as to unlock these?" she asked sweetly.

"Well, I'm not supposed to remove those." Theo didn't want to tell her no either.

"Theo, I'm not going anywhere without Kay. Also, do you really think a few chains would stop me from leaving if I wanted to? Please, just unlock these so that I can eat and bathe. After that you can lock me back up if you choose. Besides, if you stay here with me, then technically I'm not alone," Leila bartered with him.

"Well..." Theo stared at her closely. "You promise not to run away? You will stay right here in this room?"

She nodded her head, *yes.*

Leila waited as Theo knocked on the door to open it. He stepped outside the room momentarily and then returned with a key to unlock her wrists and the chain around her waist. Leila briefly stood and stretched her arms before walking over to the bathing room. Theo looked like he didn't know if he should follow.

"There are no windows in this room," Leila reassured him, "But if you still don't think it's safe to leave me alone, by all means, come on in."

Leila had never been shy. In her line of work, one would use any way possible to accomplish an assignment, and the female body could be very persuasive. The hint of watching her bathe turned Theo an even darker shade of red.

This poor man, she thought to herself. *I hope I don't get him into too much trouble.* Leila walked into the bathing room and started the bath water. She left the door open a crack as she began to undress. She quietly slipped into the warm tub. After falling asleep, Leila didn't have a new plan to leave the palace, and the longer she stayed, the harder it would be to free her inexperienced friend.

Leila had been in the water for only a few minutes before she heard the door outside the main room unlock. She closed her eyes and smiled. She could hear Nalick questioning Theo just outside the door.

Maybe I'll be able to at least teach this king some manners before I get out of here, she thought.

"I'm in here," Leila said loudly while not opening her eyes. "I promised not to run away for the moment," she replied before Theo could answer Nalick's next question.

Leila heard the door open a bit more. "Yes?" she asked, turning her head to look at Nalick standing in the doorway. "Contrary to belief, I'm not a ghost. I, too, need to bathe and eat regularly. Although I can last about two days before I get hungry." She smiled at his face; he was shocked to actually find her bathing. Leila dipped back under the water to rinse the bubbles out of her hair. "I'll not be leaving your company quite yet, so I thought it would nice if I was able to clean up a bit, but if you need me to come right now..." Leila stood, allowing the bubbles from the bath to cover her body, but just barely.

Nalick had no response. He had been sure that she was planning her next escape and was stunned when he actually found her bathing. Embarrassed, he quickly turned his back to her.

"When you're done, Theo will take you to the priests," Nalick stated.

"No," Leila replied, reaching for a towel.

"What?" Nalick asked as he turned slightly. She was now wrapped in a towel but she wasn't much more presentable than she had been only a minute before.

"I don't think you have a hearing problem." She raised her eyebrows, daring him to counter. "Do you need me to repeat myself? I said no."

"I wasn't asking you a question." Nalick began to get frustrated with Leila, which made her smile.

"See, that was the problem," Leila explained, coming face-to-face with him while only in a towel.

"Then let me rephrase that. Would you please accompany Theo to the priests after you are done, my lady?" Nalick asked, adding a wink and a small bow.

"Sure." Leila listened to Nalick leave the room and heard the door lock again.

Leila promptly dried off. In the corner of the room was a closet. She walked over and looked through the clothes in it. Most of the clothes were her size, but nothing she would choose to wear normally. She pulled a random dress out and put it on.

"I'm so sorry," Leila apologized, as Kay entered the room only moments later. "I didn't know that that tracker was waiting for me. I ran into him and another tracker earlier yesterday morning, but easily lost them when I came looking for you." She hugged her friend and checked her over looking for any differences since she had last saw her. "I should have been there with you."

"If I had listened to you, he wouldn't have caught me." Kay sighed dejectedly and sat down in the living room. "I messed up again. When I got to the end of the tunnel, I didn't remember which way to turn. I chose wrong. I tried to get out the door, but it was guarded, so I went out the window." Kay shook her head. "I should not be doing this job. I'm no good at it."

"If you just stick to level one and level two assignments you will be fine," Leila reassured her. Kay finally hugged her back. "You have never failed any of those missions," she reminded her friend.

"Yeah, but the one time I fail, I put your freedom in

jeopardy." Kay looked like she was about to cry. "I'll never forgive myself if you spend the rest of your life caged up in chains like this." Kay picked up the chains on the table. "I woke up this morning and felt so guilty."

"So what did the priests say?" Leila asked, changing the subject and picking up an apple.

"Not good." Kay responded.

"At all?" Leila asked between bites, "Did the priests say they'll help us out?"

"Not exactly." Kay paused, seeing the anger start to boil within Leila. "I didn't understand much, but they said something about the seer."

Leila stood and started to pace. She had been thinking that the best way to get Kay out was with the help of the priests, but if they were unwilling to help, it would take much longer to get her out. This time the plan needed to be foolproof. This was going to be difficult for her to do alone.

"It seems there are certain rituals that have to be done to us. But everything was so confusing. There was all this talk about you and some white aura." Kay looked across the room at the opening door as she trailed off in thought.

"My lady," Theo said, entering the room and giving a little bow to Leila. "Would you please come with me?"

Leila stood up and turned back to Kay. "Stay right here, I should be back soon."

Theo walked over to the table and picked up the chains, and again wrapped one around Leila's waist. He tightly locked both her hands to the chain around her abdomen. Leila didn't mind the treatment, for she won the battle by getting the chains off while she was in the room. This escape would require that she escort Kay so that she had no chance of forgetting anything, and being free of the chains would be the key.

Theo led the way back down the stairs that they had

climbed the night before. At the end of the stairway was Macarius who joined Leila and Theo.

"He really doesn't trust that I can walk to another place in the palace alone?" Leila asked the two men. "I do know my way around."

"Do you blame him?" Macarius asked.

Leila thought a second. "No, I suppose not." She paused, and then told the men, "but I'm not yet ready with all my plans to leave." Both men laughed at her last comment. "What? I was telling the truth, which I suppose I don't do too often."

"So we've been told," Macarius added. "Did you really walk out the front door of King Jahangir's palace?"

"Yes, and why not? It was the way I came in; I thought it would be fitting to leave civilized through the gate." Both men laughed. "I walked out the palace door right under King Amet's watch also. He didn't even recognize me and paid me a small gold piece as I left because he thought I was part of the performing troupe."

"Really?" Theo asked in amazement. "So when you finally decide to leave us, you'll just vanish?"

"That's how I work," Leila told the truth. There was no need to lie to these men. They weren't the ones holding her against her will.

"I hope you decide to stay," Theo added. "It's nice to have someone around that doesn't fear Nalick."

"I honestly didn't think there was a woman out there that could handle the man Nalick has turned into over the years," Macarius explained. "He has been king for quite a while now and yet showed no sign of wanting to take a bride, until you came along."

"Miss Lei..." began a young man who walked up beside her. She waved to him to stop before he used her real name. "I'm honored to be in your presence. I've heard many tales about you, but none can actually compare to meeting you." The young priest had a starry gaze in his eyes. Theo and Macarius stayed behind, and the man ushered Leila away into the priest's quarters.

"Will you help me and my friend escape?" she whispered, eager to be on her way.

"Escape? But I thought you were brought here so that I could teach you the rituals that need to be followed to marry our King?" the young, confused priest said.

"I do not wish to marry your king," Leila responded.

"But I thought it was your destiny to stay here." The young man was now truly confused.

"I've always chosen my own destiny," Leila explained, "and I don't plan to stay here any longer than necessary. If you're unwilling to help me, our conversation here is done. I'll find my own way out of this palace." Leila turned and started to walk back toward the hallway and waiting men.

The young priest was startled by the news that this woman didn't want to stay. Once he realized she was leaving, he ran to catch up with her.

"That's not required," an old man's voice said from behind Leila and the priest. "I don't think she will leave quite yet."

Leila stopped walking away and turned to face Gabor. "So, you won't be helping us?" she questioned the old man angrily.

"Have you ever thought that maybe I'm doing the best for you?" Gabor asked.

Leila glared at him. "You are just full of lies. I'm not staying. I'm going to get Kay out of here first, and then I'll be on my way, whether you want me to or not."

"What would it take to make you stay anywhere?" Gabor pondered, not moving any closer. "Would you stay if I told you that you'd be happy here?"

"How could I ever be happy being confined to a palace as a prisoner?" Leila turned to walk away. As she neared the door, Gabor made one last comment.

"Erich died wanting you to be happy. For once, child, stop worrying about the rest of the world and look in your own heart. Are you happy with your life?"

Leila pounded on the door until it opened. She didn't want to be told by some old man, who had his own priorities, what would make her happy. Angrily, she exited the priest's chamber and walked back to her room with Theo and Macarius in her wake. As all three approached Leila's room, she turned, took their keys, and opened the door herself.

"Thank you," she said. Theo stood in shock as she handed the keys back to him.

CHAPTER FOUR

How dare he talk about Erich? If it weren't for stupid kings trying to force me to marry them, he would still be here. Leila took some food off the table and stomped back to the bedroom. She climbed back up into her chair by the window, passing Kay on the way. It was past lunch time. Leila was hungry, but the chains around her wrists would not allow her to eat. Kay kept away, knowing that Leila needed time to think.

Leila tried to fight back tears. It had been two years since King Jahangir had imprisoned her in his jail when he made the same proposal that ended with the death of Erich, her partner and fiancé.

I'm happy, Erich, she lied to herself. *As happy as I can be without you.* Leila hadn't spent a day without thinking about her dead fiancé. She wanted to be happy, but without Erich, it wasn't possible. She stared out at the horizon. Just beyond her view were the mountains and the home Leila was raised in.

I need to get Kay out of this, she thought. *That's where she needs to be.* Leila heard the outside door open again, and she quickly wiped away her tears.

"Miss," a young servant girl asked, peering into the bedroom. "Could you please come with me?"

Finally, someone with manners, Leila thought. She climbed down from her chair. Kay stood in the middle room.

"You, too," the girl requested of Kay.

Kay and Leila followed the servant girl. Theo and

Macarius trailed them all.

"Please sit there," the servant asked, pointing to two chairs in the room. Theo and Macarius stopped and waited outside the room.

In one corner of the room was a lit fireplace. It seemed odd to Leila that a fire would be lit somewhere where the heat was hardly bearable, at least during the day anyway. Leila and Kay sat silently, waiting to see what was going to happen next. An older lady, with hair dyed bright red, and three male assistants entered. The lady walked over to Leila and pulled Leila's hair away from her face, examining her as Leila kept perfectly still. Then, the woman walked over and inspected Kay the same way.

The young girl returned, carrying a case that she sat on the table next to the chairs. The older woman opened her case and began to sort through the jewelry inside it. Every now and then, she would stop and hand an assistant something specific. Leila watched what was happening, but wasn't sure she remembered the tradition. In Lexia, women pierced their ears and wore ornate jewelry to announce their engagement. Nalick was marking his intentions. Leila stood up. All six people in the room looked at her.

"Kay, we're leaving." Leila turned to go out the door.

Before Kay had a chance to stand, one of the men placed both of his hands on her shoulders and forced her to stay in her seat. The two other men acted at the same time to hold Leila back down in her chair. Caught off guard, and with her hands tied to her waist, Leila was unable to fight back efficiently. She hadn't assumed the men were there to fight.

"The king has ordered you be prepared for your upcoming wedding," the red-haired woman explained.

"Then why are you holding Kay here as well?" Leila demanded.

"I was told that the king plans to marry both of you," the woman continued. Leila's heart sank. Was Nalick truly a man who would not only force one, but two women, to marry him? Leila struggled to try to free herself from the two men.

"I was told you were a fiery one. Everyone in the palace was told that they couldn't harm you for any reason, no matter how disrespectful you were, but the king never said anything about punishing her." The woman walked over and forced Kay's hands onto the table. The man holding Kay down placed her hands palm side up as the woman struck Kay's hands with the lash she had just pulled out of the bag. Leila continued to struggle as the two men held her in her chair.

"You will learn some manners," the older woman said to Leila. Kay closed her eyes but didn't make a sound as the woman whipped her hands five times. When she was done, the woman walked over to Leila. "You will learn that we all follow the king's orders, no matter who we are." Leila continued to struggle.

Kay opened her eyes. "Leila, please stop. It's okay. I'm fine," Kay lied to her friend to try to calm her down, although her hands were red with welts that were beginning to form.

"Let go of me," Leila said angrily to the men, still holding her in her chair. "I've never killed a person before, but there's a first time for everything." Both men immediately released her, somewhat shocked. Leila walked over to the door and opened it. Theo and Macarius were not outside the door, but a new guard was there.

"Where is Nalick?" Leila demanded of the startled guard.

"Um, at this time of the day, um..." The guard was beginning to get scared at the look on Leila's face. "He should be in his office, on the fourth floor of the royal wing," the young guard began to explain.

Leila knew where she was going. She took off down the hall as the young guard stood near the door wondering what he should do. There were two prisoners. Which one he should follow was the question, but before he could make the decision, Leila was out of his sight. On her way up the staircase, Leila came across Theo coming down the stairs. He was so startled to see Leila that he just stopped and let her pass by. After Theo realized Leila was alone, he hurried to catch up with her. Leila leapt up the stairs two at a time and was soon on the fourth floor. Theo followed close behind, but didn't try to stop her. From the look in her eyes, Theo had a good guess where Leila was heading, and he didn't want to bear the brunt of her anger. Leila took a sharp left at the fourth floor door and pushed past the guards that stood in the doorway. Nearing Nalick's office, she noticed a figure standing on the balcony at the end of the hall. It was him. She walked down the hall quickly.

"How dare you!" Leila yelled at him.

Nalick slowly turned around, unfazed by the angry Leila quickly approaching him.

"This is the best time of the day," Nalick said, turning back to look out the balcony over the city. "The city gets this deep red haze that fills the sky." He continued to ignore the anger in Leila's voice.

"She doesn't deserve to be punished for what I say." Leila wanted to slap Nalick, but with her hands chained down she was unable to. "You're truly the man I heard tales about, forcing two women to marry you unwillingly."

Nalick still didn't give into her anger. "As a child, I would sit here for hours, just waiting for the sun to set and the sky to turn blazing red."

Out of frustration, Leila turned around and walked away from Nalick. She walked halfway down the hall before she stopped and returned to him. "What do you want?"

"You already know." Nalick continued to stare out at the city. The sun was beginning to set and the sky was slowly turning a burnt red color. He paused and turned to face her. "I'm not a monster. You name it and it will be done. All I ask for in return is that you stay here with me."

"First, Kay will be set free," Leila began her demands as she continued to pace. "You will send no men to follow her. Kay will be allowed to return to our home alone. Second, I'll not be your prize. I do not want to be treated as an object that is placed in the palace as an ornament. I'll be free to come and go as I please." Leila paused to give Nalick time to object. He didn't, so she continued. "Third, you will take no other wives beside me. In my culture, we do not believe a man can marry more than one woman at a time. What you Lior nobles do is disrespectful. Fourth, there must be love. We do not marry unless we're in love where I come from. I won't marry a man I do not love, no matter what we agree now."

"Anything else you can think of at the moment?" he asked.

"You will free Kay right now." Leila checked his response to see if he would not follow through.

"Then it's settled." Nalick waved to Theo to come over to him. He took Theo's keys and unlocked the chains around her wrists and waist.

"I'll take you to your room where you can have supper." Nalick turned from the balcony and led Leila to the staircase.

Stunned, Leila followed him in silence. This time, instead of stopping on the fifth floor, they continued up one more flight of stairs. The doors to this floor were blocked by four men. They all stood and bowed as Nalick drew near. The doors opened to another hallway. Nalick led her to the left. At the end of the hallway, he opened the doors.

"These will be your quarters," he explained, as Leila walked past him into the room. "My room will be at the other end of the hall," he added, while Leila gazed around the room in awe.

Leila had thought the room downstairs was ornate, but that room was nothing compared to this one. This room was at least ten times the size of the room down below and the ceiling was over two floors high. The right side of the room opened to a balcony along the entire wall. In the middle of the room was a large bed with a sheer curtain attached to the ceiling, encasing the bed in a light blue haze. Nearby was a fireplace with a chimney that reached up into the ceiling sitting in the middle of the room. Directly to her left was a table with eight chairs sitting on the back side of the fireplace. The left wall had two doors in it. Windows surrounded all the walls. Several chairs and couches were placed around the room. Everything was made of the finest wood and fabric. As Leila looked around, there was nothing familiar or even similar to the home she grew up in. *Could this really feel like a home?* she wondered to herself.

"Can I say good-bye to Kay?" Leila asked.

"No. I will not take the chance of the two of you being together without you being locked up. For the time being, if you need anything, Theo lives in the first room on the right." Nalick pointed to the door just outside the one they just came through. "If that's all, I'll be back in an hour to finalize our deal."

Nalick shut the door behind him. Leila walked back into the room. She looked outside and saw that it was nighttime again. She walked to the balcony and sat down near the railing, resting her head on the rail. Across the city, indoor lights were on. From her viewpoint, not only was the sky covered with stars, but the ground appeared to be also. Leila gazed up into the sky and looked for the constellations she knew. Something about the twinkle of little lights in the sky made her feel better.

Am I making the right choice? she asked herself.

The stars had always been her guide in life. When Kay left, Leila would be all alone with only the stars as her friends. Leila glanced down at the north gate and could see it opening. Though she couldn't see well enough to tell who the people were, she was sure Kay was leaving. Leila sighed. *If this doesn't work, you can always leave,* she reassured herself. Tears began to trickle down her face. She sat on the balcony until there was a knock at her door again.

"Nalick asked us to ask you to please join him in his office," Theo said, smiling at the fact that Nalick asked, rather than ordered, Leila.

Following Theo down the hallway, Leila entered the office alone. Nalick was at a large desk that was covered with various papers. He smiled kindly as she entered. His smile made him even more handsome than he already was. Leila still was confused about how she felt about the man in front of her. He let Kay go, but was still holding her captive. Leila cautiously walked over to his desk and sat down across from him, not smiling back.

He handed her a piece of paper.

"Please read this over," Nalick asked. "I think I remembered everything I agreed to before. If you'd like to add anything, just go ahead." He handed her a pen. "You can always add more later, of course. All I ask in return is that you marry me. If, at any time, I break my end of the deal, you're free to walk out of here without any explanation and disappear to where ever you go to when you leave kings. I promise I'll not follow or hunt you down. Your friend has been freed and is on her way home." He smiled at her again. "Do we have a deal?"

"Yes," Leila replied, still not smiling back. Kay was safe, and that was all that mattered.

"Now, for your end of the deal..." Nalick paused, not wanting to do what he had to do next. Two men moved into the room and began to set up equipment on Nalick's desk. Nalick stayed out of their way and leaned against a window.

"Each noble family has a specific emblem. All family members of each family have this mark on their back. To be part of my family, this sign..." He pointed to the crest on the letter he had just handed Leila. "Will need to be etched into the skin on your back." Leila nodded her head even though he wasn't finished. "Also, to be a royal..." Nalick pulled up his sleeve to show the intricate design that started at the palm of his right hand and continued up his forearm.

"This is the custom that must take place before I'm presented to the priests?" Leila guessed.

"Yes," Nalick said, waiting to see if Leila would refuse. "If you'd like to wait a few days, that would be okay," he offered, not wanting to wait, but also trying to avoid getting on her bad side.

"No, we can do it now," Leila said, handing back the paper. She already knew that he would request that she get the permanent lines on her shoulder and arm. It was a well-known Lior tradition. Leila turned to the artists.

"The procedure can be very painful. We have two ways to deal with the pain. The first is a cream that numbs the area that's going to be worked on. The other method is to give you some pills to make you fall asleep. That way you only wake up with a sore arm, but you don't have to feel the pain," the younger of the two men explained.

"Neither," Leila replied. Drugs commonly used to make people fall asleep did not work on her, and she had experienced more than her share of pain over the years and was confident that she could deal with it.

"My Lord?" the young man questioned Nalick.

"Do as she wishes," Nalick ordered, though he, too, appeared worried.

"First, we need to match up your left arm with King Nalick's right arm," the old man said.

Nalick moved nearer to Leila. Instinctively she jumped back a little as he approached. Only Nalick noticed. He sat down beside her and laid his right arm on the desk. The old man took Leila's arm and placed it on top of Nalick's. Leila tried to ignore the warmth of the arm beneath hers. The man quickly sketched the same pattern on Leila's arm until it matched up exactly with Nalick's.

"Thank you," he said to Nalick, who quickly stood up and returned to the window sill.

What am I getting myself into? she thought, watching the man finish the pattern.

"Now, to the shoulder," the man pointed to her left shoulder.

Leila stood up and turned her chair around. She sat back down, straddling the chair carefully, and unbuttoned her dress slightly so that the back piece fell, exposing her shoulder. The skin on her shoulder was much more sensitive than on her arm, but Leila held her face completely still. The old man finished drawing and began setting out bottles of liquids in a variety of colors.

"Are you sure you don't want anything for the pain?" the old man asked kindly.

"No, thank you," Leila responded.

The old man and his apprentice began their work. The pain simultaneously shot through her arm and shoulder. Leila tried her best to not wince or to let the tears come out that she felt welling behind her eyes. She refused to let on that she could be hurt. Instead, Leila stared straight ahead at Nalick. Nalick didn't break his gaze with Leila. The two men continued to work for hours and Leila and Nalick continued to silently stare at each other. When it was over, the old man gently wrapped her hand in a cold cloth and then placed another rag over her shoulder, which was burning more than her hand, thus signaling the end of the procedure.

"Anything else?" Leila asked.

Nalick shook his head, *no*.

Leila walked back into her room, pushed the curtain aside that surrounded the bed, and lay down.

Three hours, she thought. *What did I just get myself committed to?* Leila sat up and stretched her hand beneath the cloth. With every little movement, she could feel each spot that had been pricked. Leila looked around the room but decided to not move. She lay down on her stomach, being sure not to move or touch her left arm or shoulder. It wasn't long before she fell asleep.

CHAPTER FIVE

Leila could hear the soft sound of footsteps as someone entered the room. Although she didn't open her eyes, she could see the faint light of the daytime. Leila wanted to just sleep and forget the past two days, but her hand was still throbbing from the night before. The person who entered didn't make any noise beyond quietly walking across the room toward the bed.

If I just keep my eyes shut, maybe they'll go away. Leila tried to not to move. The swish of the curtain told her that whoever it was was near. She felt them sit down on the edge of the bed. Leila waited but the person didn't leave. She slowly opened her eyes to unexpectedly find that it was Nalick, not a servant of his, sitting on the end of the bed.

"Did I wake you?" Nalick asked softly, the tone of his voice and the look in his eyes wasn't the same as those of the man she stood before two days earlier. Leila didn't answer, mesmerized by his deep brown eyes and kind smile. He was much more handsome when he wasn't angry at her.

"I brought you this," Nalick said as he held out a small jar as a peace offering. "It will help the swelling go down from last night."

Nalick cautiously moved closer. Leila didn't move but curiously watched him as he shifted closer and tenderly unwrapped the cloth from around her hand. He opened the jar and gently rubbed the cream over the black lines that crisscrossed her hand and arm. Immediately, the burning feeling was gone. While he was busy concentrating on her hand, Leila took the moment to study him. The young king was physically much larger than any of the other older kings she had met over the years. The tales Leila had heard of him leading his army into war were most likely not *just* tales. Today, though, Nalick appeared more real, not like the authority figure she met on her first night in the palace. His hair, which had been pulled back from his face before, fell loosely, almost to his shoulders. His concern for her was drawn all over his face. He turned her arm over carefully and began massaging the cream on the inside lines also. He was gentle with his calloused, warrior hands.

"If you put this on a couple of more times, the swelling and pain will be gone for good," Nalick explained, finally looking up at her. Leila dropped her eyes to her hand also.

"Would you like me to also put it on your shoulder?" he asked.

"Yes," she responded moving her hair. Nalick began rubbing the cream over the mark on her back. Leila involuntarily shivered as tingles went down her toes. It was surprising that a man so fierce could be so gentle.

"Excuse me," a woman's voice said from behind the bed.

Startled, Leila quickly turned around to see an old woman dressed in a dark purple dress with a crisp, white shirt underneath. Leila looked around the room curiously. She hadn't heard anyone enter from the heavy front doors that led into the room. Nalick offered Leila his hand to help her out of the bed. Once Leila stood, she realized the old lady was giving Nalick a stern gaze; Leila had to keep herself from laughing. That a tiny woman would be giving a man almost three times her size a strict look was amusing.

"Leila, this is Mauve," Nalick said, introducing the

lady. "She's responsible for taking care of you." Mauve still glared at Nalick but managed a quick curtsey to Leila.

"Nothing was happening," Nalick explained to Mauve. "I was just putting cream on her arm and back to ease the pain." Mauve still didn't look like she believed him. "Really, I wasn't trying to do anything but help her."

"It's improper for you to see your future bride before we've had time to dress her for the day." Mauve moved over and began pushing Nalick out of the room. "Now that you have woken her, we will get her ready." Nalick was pushed out the door.

"Sorry, dear," Mauve said to Leila. "I knew you had a rough night, and I was trying to let you get your rest. He snuck in when I just left the room for a moment. He was raised to have manners, and trust me, dear, he does, but sometimes I just need to remind him." Leila liked this woman.

"There's breakfast on the table," Mauve said, pointing to the table, which was filled with every breakfast food Leila had ever seen. "I didn't know what you preferred, so I had them make a little of everything."

After she ate, servants bathed Leila and returned her to Mauve for inspection. Leila had never been cleaner, so Mauve would have no complaints.

"Theo and Macarius should be here soon to escort you to the priests," Mauve said as Leila passed inspection. "I'm so glad you decided to stay, dear. You look absolutely beautiful. It's nice to finally have a woman back in Nalick's life." Mauve and the servants left the room.

Leila walked out onto the balcony to wait. She could feel the hot breeze blow on her, even though she was standing in the shadows. *Why would anyone purposely build a city in the middle of a hot desert?* she wondered. Leila grew up in a valley in between two of the largest mountains in the range. The days were typically warm, but there was always a cool breeze. A hot breeze wasn't much of a breeze at all. *Can I really get used to this?* she wondered, sitting down on the balcony rail. Leila gazed over the rail and could see the city below. People and carts moved around on the streets below. *Free.* She had lost her freedom to run, regardless of the open windows and balcony.

"My lady." Theo approached from inside the room. "Nalick is meeting with the priests right now. He requested that we kindly ask you to join him," Theo said with a smile as he offered her his hand.

"Does he still think I'm going to run?" Leila asked her two armed escorts while they led her out of the room.

"Are you?" asked Macarius. While Theo seemed to have a kind disposition toward Leila, Macarius seemed more cautious of accepting her.

"I don't know." Leila told the truth, but Macarius didn't seem to appreciate it.

Leila walked the rest of the way in silence. Nalick beamed as she approached. She was more beautiful than he could imagine. Dressed in a long green dress that complimented her red hair, Leila looked the part of a queen. Mauve, as always, had done an excellent job.

"You didn't know I cleaned up so well?" she joked. *He doesn't clean up too badly either*, she thought.

A priest stood in the doorway and coughed to get her attention. Nalick gave her one last look before she faded from his view into the private chambers of the priests.

The meeting was brief as Leila was grilled by the priest elders. They asked questions about everything from her parentage and background to her time and date of birth. Each priest had their own objective, but Leila couldn't figure out what they wanted to know.

After the priests left the room, Leila turned to Nalick. All the questioning by the priests made her think of her own questions for Nalick. "I still don't understand. You know very little about me, and yet, you want to marry me. Isn't every woman of marriageable age waiting for you? You must have over a hundred noble women to choose from. Why do you want me?"

"I was five or six when you were born." Nalick stood up and walked over to one of the windows. "You were special. You were seen as a prize when everyone else found you." Leila joined him by the window. Nalick chuckled to himself. "I guess you still are by most of those kings."

Nalick seemed to be caught in how to say the next part. "Lior has had its problems over the years. The nobles and their factions often feuded between each other. The poor fight with the nobles and the nobles fight amongst themselves. Twice while I've been king, neighboring countries have taken advantage of the turmoil within Lior to attack us. I was eighteen when I led my first army to defend our country. Before I even became king, the older priest, whom you just met, told my father how he could stop all this internal fighting." Leila waited for the answer she guessed was coming.

"It was you." Nalick took Leila's hand and walked her back near the bench. "Each spring, my father sent scouts up to the North Country to find you. It was years before the scouts came back with news about you. But it was too late. Roger of Whitmore Valley had already found you."

Leila sat back down on the bench with Nalick close beside her. Roger was the man that took her in and trained her to be a courier. He was the manager of the courier station at Whitmore Valley. It began to make sense to Leila now. She had always wondered why Roger allowed her to start training at the age of twelve, when everyone else had to wait until they were fourteen.

"I was king by the time the scouts actually found you again. By the time we finally figured out which courier you were, kidnapping wouldn't work. Why do you think the first thing Roger probably taught you was how to escape?" Leila could remember her harsh years of training to escape any situation.

"Since no one would be able to touch you while under his protection, we waited for you to start assignments. That wouldn't work either. You were always accompanied by Erich, who was just as good at protecting you as Roger was himself." Nalick wanted to reach over and touch her just to hold her hand, but she was far too scared of him still. "When Erich died, Roger couldn't protect you anymore. You began taking the hardest missions. So we made a deal with Roger. If he promised to send you on any assignment that would take you to Lexia, then we would make sure you could get out of any trouble you got into elsewhere." Nalick waited for her to respond.

"Roger agreed to a deal like that?" Leila asked in disbelief.

"He didn't have much of a choice. With every noble out there wanting to marry you, he found no other way to protect you. We were basically the only ally he had that didn't want to force you into marriage at the time. The priests here felt the best approach was to wait for you to come to us.

"I was completely happy waiting for you. I've never wanted to get married. I watched my mother in an unhappy marriage. But then everything changed. I was in Dria when I briefly saw you. You caught me off guard because you made no noise. I thought I was seeing a wood sprite."

Leila thought back to that day. She had stopped at a creek to fill her water flask when she noticed it led to a small pond. Leila spent over thirty minutes gazing over the edge of a rock at the large colorful fish swimming at the bottom of the pond when she noticed that she herself was being watched. As soon as she realized who it was, she quickly disappeared into the forest.

"Did you realize that Roger was no longer giving you assignments in Lexia? Somehow that man knew I was planning to keep you here, and he did his best to prevent you from coming." Nalick rose and walked back to the window, then he paused and came back to her. Tentatively, he took her hands in his, waiting for her to protest. "You may think I know nothing about you, but that's not true. I know you much better than you think. I know there will never be a better woman for me than you. If you give me a chance, I can make you happy," he promised her.

Leila didn't know what to think. His hands were warm against hers and she could slightly feel the pulsing of his heart. As she stared into the eyes of the man before her, she realized that he was the first man in a long time that saw her not for the symbol she was, but as the person she was.

Can I trust him? she asked herself.

"But why me?" Leila whispered to him.

"Ever since I was a child I asked the same question. What was so special about this girl everyone was searching for? You're not afraid of me. I deal with people all day and have never met a woman who was as bold as you were. The strength and intelligence you have in just your little finger is more than any noble woman in the country has in their whole body. You make me a better person. I'll try my best to match you and hope that I will never disappoint you, because I know how quickly you will be gone if I do." He chuckled.

Leila didn't have time to respond, as the three priests from earlier returned.

"We have decided," the elder priest said to Nalick. "If you'd please join us, everyone has been waiting."

Theo and Macarius stood on either side of a balcony,

holding open a curtain. Nalick walked through first with the priests. Through the small opening, Leila could see there was a crowd gathered below. Leila waited behind.

"What is happening now?" Leila whispered to Theo as Nalick stood beside the priests.

"It's customary to announce the engagement of the king to the people of the city," Theo explained. "When you step out, to your right will be about forty people seated on a lower balcony. They are the representatives from each of the noble families," he explained to her.

"Today is a glorious day," the elder priest began. "Our King Nalick has finally chosen to marry. We have consulted the stars and met with the future bride. With great pleasure I get to introduce our future queen, Queen Eia." There was a hushed silence over the crowd as Theo gestured to Leila to enter. Nalick offered his hand to Leila stepping up onto the balcony. Below hundreds of faces stared up at her.

"I thought part of our deal wasn't being made into an object," Leila whispered to Nalick.

"Sorry. This is all part of tradition," he replied.

The silent mass waited as the elder priest continued. "The wedding will take place three months from the day after tomorrow." The crowd erupted into applause and cheers while the nobles sat silently.

"You can't please everyone," Nalick whispered in her ear, waving to the people and then turning her back toward the room. "I need to stay here for a little bit." He stopped in the doorway. "Theo and Macarius will escort you back to your room. Just don't get lost on the way." He winked.

Leila waited in the doorway to her room until she heard both Macarius and Theo leave. She quietly walked back down the staircase. The guards at the entrance to the floor were startled to see her. She smiled as she passed them. Retracing her steps from the first day she was escorted through the palace, she looked for the garden. After several wrong turns, she found the garden door. No one was guarding it, so she quietly slipped in. She sat down on a small patch of grass. It had been two weeks since she came to Lexia with Kay. Though the city was familiar, and felt like a second home to her, in her mind nothing could compare to the forests that lined the mountains of the North Country. Leila was getting sick of all the sand, but yet here in the garden she could faintly be reminded of home. She leaned against the tree and closed her eyes. The breeze was still warm, not cool like she had hoped, but the grass between her fingers would have to be the best comfort she would get out of this place. Leila heard the click of a door and immediately hid herself behind the largest tree in the garden.

"But Momma," a girl complained to an older woman, "if he has chosen a bride, why can't I get married to someone else?"

"King Nalick is king and can take as many wives as he wants. Trust me, dear, Father will get him to take you on as his head wife," the older woman commented as she led the younger girl through the garden.

"But doesn't the head wife belong to the first wife?" The girl stopped thinking of questions and began to twirl her hair.

"Emma, don't dawdle. This girl he has chosen isn't of noble birth." The older lady grabbed her daughter's hand away from her hair and pulled her the rest of the way through the garden.

The nobles weren't as welcoming as the people had been, and now she knew why. They still had hopes to get their daughters on the throne.

CHAPTER SIX

Leila woke the next morning to complete silence. After the chaos of the day before, she was happy to not have anyone around. Though it was early in the morning, from the balcony Leila could see that the city was full of activity. Seeing the people run from place to place made Leila want to be free of the palace's cold, confining walls.

He did say I was free to come and go as I please, she thought to herself. *Maybe I should test what he said.*

"Awake already, dear?" Mauve yawned, rubbing her eyes. Leila had quietly entered her room to find her dressed but sleeping in a chair. "Can I get you anything?" Mauve asked.

"Is there anything else that I can wear? The clothes here are all beautiful," Leila assured Mauve. "I'd like to go down into the city, but don't want to give away who I am. I just want to go as a normal person."

"But, dear, why would you want to do that?" Mauve asked, setting aside the garment that she had fallen asleep sewing

"I just want to be able to be me again. This..." Leila indicated to everything around her. "Is not me. I'm much less complicated than all this." Mauve rummaged through a trunk and handed her a common dress without another comment.

"Thank you," Leila responded, leaving the room with the simple dress. Quickly, she dressed and disguised herself, adding gloves and a scarf to cover the lines on her arm and her bright red hair. She quietly walked over to the door to check if anyone was in the hallway. As expected, Theo was standing outside her door.

"I hope you weren't planning on sneaking away today. Nalick wasn't happy yesterday to find you had wandered off without telling anyone," Theo scolded Leila. "We need to go get Macarius to join us."

"Why?" Leila asked. "He doesn't seem to like me too much. It would be much more enjoyable for just the two of us to leave."

Theo shook his head *no*.

"Fine." She pouted as they walked down the flight of stairs to get Macarius.

"Macarius doesn't dislike you; it's just that he's a bit protective of Nalick," Theo tried to explain.

"Either way, he doesn't like me," Leila commented as they reached Macarius' door. Theo knocked loudly.

"What?" Macarius asked, answering the door. He stood for a minute looking from Theo to Leila, and then he realized it was Leila.

"Our charge would like to go to the market, and you know Nalick would have our heads if we lost her again," Theo explained.

"Does Nalick know where we're off to?" Macarius asked as they continued down the stairs, getting dressed along the way.

"No, but I'm sure Mauve will tell him soon; like she came and told me," Theo responded. As they walked through the palace, not a single person turned to look at them as they passed. Leila was happy. Her disguise would work well in town if the people of the palace didn't even recognize her.

Leila hadn't been in Lexia during the open market for a while. As they approached the city square, the crowd grew dense and the look on the two men's faces turned to worry. If Leila wanted to vanish, this would be the best place to do so. Theo and Macarius had no intention of disappointing Nalick, but Leila was an expert in disappearing. Leila, however, had no plans of leaving Lexia quite yet, so she turned and placed a hand through each man's arm, as not to lose them, and began to walk to the first shop.

"I'm not running off anywhere today," Leila tried to reassure them, but neither of them seemed completely convinced. Leila walked closer to the first booth. Around her were people trying to sell every type of item imaginable, from fresh vegetables to a cloth that could supposedly clean anything. The bright colors of the nearest fruit stand caught Leila's attention, so she stopped and let go of the men's arms. Macarius moved to the edge of the stand to keep watch while Theo followed closely behind Leila. She wandered through the rows of produce. She was amazed to see fruits that were not in season back home.

"Whatever you'd like, I'll pay for," Theo offered, as he saw Leila looking at the berries.

"Have you ever had these before?" she asked Theo.

"No, miss," Theo looked at the strange, blue-colored berries.

"They grow them back where I am from," Leila explained as the owner of the stand came up behind them.

"My husband and I grow those," the lady explained. The woman curiously looked Leila over. "It began as a hobby, but now it's our full time job. My husband helps with the harvest, but he has his own tent over there." The lady pointed across the market.

Leila continued walking from one booth to the next. At each stop she found something that reminded her of her home, and the owner of each would explain everything to her. One stand had a necklace made from the blue stones found in the mountains near Leila's home, and another had the style of baskets that her mother had tried in vain to teach her how to weave. Leila was comforted to know that even though she was far from home, there were still reminders right here at the market. And she was surrounded by good, nice people, unlike the nobles who already dismissed her.

"Want to show your alliance to a certain noble family?" the next tent owner asked.

"Too late," Leila commented under her breath. "I'm not from around here," she responded in a voice loud enough to be heard.

"In that case, would you sit a bit and keep an old man company? Maybe a pretty girl like you would bring me more business," the man asked.

"Anything to help," she replied, sitting beside him. It was nice to finally get back to the people of Lior. She always felt more comfortable around the normal working people than the nobles of any country.

"Business has been slow the last two trips into town. I guess I shouldn't complain. My son is apprenticing here. Less work for me means more work for him." Leila remembered back to the other night. After staring at the man a bit more, she could see the resemblance between the man and the apprentice that had made the lines on her arm and back. "Why are you here now? If you're looking for a husband, I'd not mind introducing you to my son."

"Sorry to disappoint you, but I've already agreed to marry someone," Leila replied.

"That's too bad; my son could use a nice, pretty wife like you." The man smiled. "I think your escorts are getting impatient." Leila looked to the two men and stood to join them.

"Would you like anything to drink or eat?" offered Theo, as they began walking again. Leila nodded and they ushered her to a nearby table.

"So tell me," she started, looking at Macarius. "Why do

you dislike me so much."

"Um...," Macarius stalled as he tried to think of how to respond. "I don't dislike you." He was a terrible liar. His face turned bright red.

"Don't worry. I don't actually care if you like me or not, I'm just curious as to why you'd dislike me, because as far as I know, I've not done anything yet to earn your dislike," Leila explained. Macarius tried to think of an answer but couldn't.

"I don't know," he responded honestly. Theo approached with drinks for everyone and they were silent.

Normal people, Leila thought, watching people move from tent to tent. A young boy dragged his father to a tent where they were selling toys, while the mother stopped at the nearest tent selling clothing. Over in the other direction, Leila watched as a young man tried his best to catch the attention of a girl nearby.

This is where I belong, not in a palace, she told herself. *Can I really be happy being locked away from all this?* Leila smiled at the chaos of people around her. She quietly sat and enjoyed her surroundings. Music started to play behind Leila. She turned to watch as the courtyard began to fill with people dancing. Young and old, the people happily danced around. Leila turned to the men with her.

"Anyone up for a dance?" Leila asked. A young boy nearby overheard this and readily came up to Leila.

Bowing deeply, he asked, "My Lady, may I have this dance?"

The boy was no more than twelve years old, but was trying his best to act older. He was tall for his age, but his youth was visible in his face. His dark hair barely covered his twinkling eyes as he waited for her response. He held out his hand for her.

"I'd love to," Leila replied, taking his arm as he led

them to the dance floor. The music changed and Leila turned to the boy. "I'm not from around here, so you will have to teach me this one."

The boy smiled and said, "No problem, even my little sister can dance to this one." He waved to an even younger, light-brown-haired, smiling boy and beautiful little girl sitting next to one of the tents.

When the song ended, the two children ran into the crowded dance area.

"'Lip 'Lip," the little girl called to him, and her short, light brown curls bounced as she ran. The younger boy was close behind.

"This is my sister, Ruth, and my brother, Tim. I'm Phillip," he said, extending his hand to shake Leila's with a formal introduction. "And now we must be on our way." He disappeared with his siblings into the crowd.

Knowing that the men escorting her were getting hungry, Leila made her way back to the south side of the market. Leila wandered into a book tent as Theo stopped by the fruit tent they had visited earlier. She paused near the wanted posters. Leila picked up the pile and paged through them. She had seen most of the sheets before, but it was always best to know what everyone else already knew about you. Behind Leila, a man quietly approached her. Leila didn't turn around as she addressed him.

"Done watching?" Leila asked Nalick. She had noticed him earlier when she was dancing with the young boy. Nalick was also wearing gloves and normal clothing to blend in. No one except her had any idea who he was.

"You left me no choice but to watch," he argued. "You didn't even invite me to come along," he teased.

"I didn't think mixing with the common people was on your list of things to do for the day," Leila responded, smiling at the bookseller as he returned.

"Interested in Mele? Here you go," the bookseller said,

handing Leila one book he had been searching for. "You can learn both Mele and Comamele from the same book. They are very similar."

"So you're not leaving us so soon?" Nalick wondered about her new interest in their religious and noble languages.

"Not until you mess up your end of the deal," Leila replied, nodding in thanks to the man as Theo appeared beside her and paid for the book.

"We were just going to head back," Leila explained as Theo and Macarius appeared, surprised to see who was with Leila.

"Let's just make one stop first," Nalick suggested as he offered Leila his arm. She cautiously took it as he led her through the crowd of people. Nalick seemed more relaxed and happier than normal. The person Leila was now walking with was not the king she imagined. Nalick wanted to be free from the palace as much as she did. He led them away from the market and down several streets to an inn. Theo ran ahead and opened the door to the restaurant in front of the inn. At the back of the restaurant was a bar that ran the length of the room. Nalick and Leila followed behind Theo, who was leading the way upstairs.

Inside was a modestly-furnished family room with a window that overlooked the street below. Near the window sat Theo's son, Dimas, playing by himself. Through the doorway to the left was a kitchen with a large table. An older woman was busy cooking while Theo's wife, Micaela, was setting the table.

"Oh my, what a sight. The three of you made your way here." Theo's mother beamed at Theo, Macarius, and Nalick. "And you must be the captive I've heard so much about." She took Leila by both hands and led her to a chair in the kitchen. "Please sit down and relax, dear." She then turned to Nalick. "Taking a pretty child captive isn't a nice thing to do," she scolded him. Leila watched as the old woman gave each boy a hug. "Better set the table for four more," she said to Micaela.

"It has been quite a while since you boys have all been over here," a large man with an older face of Theo commented as he opened the back door. He was about to continue talking, but stopped when he saw Leila. "My, you're more beautiful than they said you were." Theo's mother turned around and nodded in agreement. "Now, where did Nalick find such a girl as you?"

"Sitting outside the palace walls trying to get back in," Nalick replied. Theo's father started laughing and pulled up a chair beside Leila.

"Any good stories about these boys?" she asked, trying to get dirt on Nalick.

"Many." Theo's father started telling stories over lunch. "Let's start with when we first met the future king. He was only about eight years old when Theo met him at the market. I guess Nalick had been mad at his father and told him he was going to run away. So he packed a bag and left." Nalick shook his head in agreement, but Leila could also see a bit of embarrassment. "Once he got to the market he didn't know what to do. The poor child had never been outside the palace without an escort to show him his way home. He didn't know it at the time, but he did have an escort. Macarius there had seen Nalick leave and followed after him. Between the two of them, they didn't know how to find their way home and each was too afraid to tell anyone who Nalick really was."

"That's how I found them," Theo explained, interrupting him. "They were standing in front of that tent arguing." Theo took a large bite of his stew.

"We were hungry," Macarius defended his argument with Nalick.

"Yeah, they were hungry and had no money," Theo corrected, patting Macarius on the back.

"Well, I really didn't plan that far ahead," Nalick inserted into the story.

"I thought we should just tell a food shop owner who Nalick was and then they would feed us, but Nalick didn't want to tell anyone because he said they would make us go home." Macarius laughed. "The thing was; I wasn't running away. Nalick was the only cousin I had that was nice to me, so when he left, I kind of just followed. I didn't want to run away."

"Either way," Theo's father continued. "Theo brought you two back home with him and said you were hungry. I knew right away who Nalick was, so I sent word to the palace he was at my inn and safe. I didn't tell the boys, though." Both Nalick and Macarius shook their heads. "I offered them a room in exchange for helping with chores. After less than twenty-four hours of doing chores, they decided they didn't exactly like life outside the palace." He patted Nalick on the back, which caused the king to crack a smile. "So, they came to me to tell me who they were and that they wanted to go home. I pretended to be surprised and took them home myself. After that, though, every time palace life made Nalick upset, he would be on our doorstep asking to stay in return for doing chores."

Nalick smiled. "And every time I'd realize I had to go home and face whatever problem I was running away from. I wished I could just stay here and pretend I didn't have another life. Here we could be kids and run around the inn and to the market on market days."

"Oh, they used to terrorize the market," Theo's mom said with a smile. "They had some game that would always end with the biggest, meanest, tent owner dragging the three boys back here and scolding me to keep better track of them."

Macarius laughed. "Oh, you mean tent dodging." All three men laughed. Leila watched Nalick. He was carefree and laughing, something she never expected to see. He was actually starting to seem like a normal man.

"We would make up routes to run through the market between the tents and see who could run it the fastest," Theo explained to Leila. "Macarius always won because he was the shortest; Nalick and I would get caught easier."

"Hey, I won because I was the fastest." Macarius sulked.

"It's so nice to have you boys all here." Theo's mother changed the subject.

"You should be thanking Leila," Nalick said, winking at Leila. He had already finished his food and was intently watching her.

"Well, dear, hopefully you can bring him around more often. We do miss seeing them all together." Theo's mother stood to pick up the dirty dishes off the table. Leila offered to help, but Theo's mother wouldn't let her.

Leila found the place all three men actually called home. All four reluctantly prepared to return to the palace. After hugs and good-byes, they were on their way.

"I remember reading that you were quite young when you became king," Leila tried to start a conversation with Nalick.

"I was fourteen; the lowest legal age that the council would let me take the throne. From the very few civil conversations we had when I was growing up, my father told me that everything here reminded him of my mom, and he needed to get away from it. He was counting the days to my fourteenth birthday and I was counting the days until he would finally leave me," Nalick explained.

"Isn't fourteen a little young to be ruling a country?"

"I was eighteen when I first led an army into battle. Yes, fourteen is too young, but I didn't have much of a choice." Nalick smiled. Leila was actually talking to him and asking questions. Through their conversation, they had reached the palace gates. Nalick walked Leila to the stairway to the royal quarters.

"I'll have to leave you here. I need to finish preparations for tomorrow. We will be heading to Dria early tomorrow morning. My father has sent word, asking to meet you, and it's customary to get his approval before we wed. Not that it matters to me." Leila nodded and began walking up the stairs behind Theo and Macarius. She turned around and watched Nalick walk back the way they had come.

Maybe this won't be so bad after all, she thought.

CHAPTER SEVEN

The next morning, before the sun had risen, Nalick silently crept into Leila's room. Leila was sound asleep on the bed in the middle of the room and Nalick didn't wish to wake her. He gently scooped her up in his arms. She stirred a little and faintly opened her eyes, smiled at him, and then went back to sleep. Once aboard the boat, he laid her in the bed in the captain's quarters and covered her with a light blanket. He gently moved aside the locks of hair covering her face. She was completely defenseless and looked younger than he had ever seen her.

It was early morning, after the sun had already risen, when Leila awoke. She rubbed her eyes and looked around the room. Vaguely, Leila remembered being picked up by Nalick. Through the rose-colored tint of the light streaming through the window, Leila could see in the Nalick quietly watching her from the corner. She was lying in a large, swaying bed in a lavishly decorated room. From the slight rocking of the room from side to side she could tell she was on a boat. It was the most well-furnished boat she had ever been on.

"I didn't want to wake you," Nalick explained.

"How late is it?" Leila asked rubbing her eyes again.

"About mid-morning," he replied. "We're about halfway to Dria. Would you like some breakfast?"

She nodded while yawning. Nalick left the room and within five minutes two women from the palace were entering with trays of food.

Leila quickly ate and then moved to the right side

window of the cabin. Outside, she could see the shoreline of a city they were passing by. On the pier, a large crowd of people stood cheering. Leila moved to the back window. Behind their boat were three more boats serving as escorts. Leila had traveled much on her jobs but most of the time she traveled with the lowest classes of people on horseback or by herself. It was much easier to fit in and go unnoticed if you traveled in a group of peasants, but it wasn't the most comfortable way to travel.

So this is what it's like to travel as royalty, she thought.

Leila looked at the large container of water sitting in the corner that the servants had filled when they brought the food. It was just big enough to sit in. Leila had expected it to be cold, yet it was quite warm.

What a change, she thought about her life. Leila wondered if she would ever get used to the luxury of being part of a royal family.

After she was clean, she dried off and wrapped a robe around herself, then climbed back on the bed and lay down on the mountain of lush pillows. It was the first time in days that Leila had a moment to herself to reflect on everything. Am I making the right decision? Nothing will be easy, but am I ready to stay in one place?

As the maids began to dress her, Leila couldn't believe the ornate decorations on the dress and the amount of bare skin the dress displayed. The dress exposed her shoulders and arm so that all could clearly see the markings. Leila shivered and blushed at the same time from being so exposed. One dress could feed a family in the North Country for a month.

Leila stepped out of the cabin door into the sunlight. It warmed her exposed skin. She could feel the wind blow and was happy to finally feel a cool breeze. Across the deck at the front of the boat, Leila could see Nalick leaning against the rail, looking forward. She walked down the five stairs to the main deck and crossed over to him. As Leila passed the crew, each man stopped and bowed to her. Leila walked over near Nalick and leaned backward against the rail so that she could see his face.

"You know, this bowing stuff really needs to stop," Leila complained with a smile. "The people around here spend so much time bowing. You know, I bet if you add it all up it would amount to months of bowing that could be used more productively."

Nalick smiled at her, "You're so practical. Next time there's a council meeting I shall bring that up." He moved closer to her and she didn't move away. He was finally beginning to build her trust. Leaning down he whispered in her ear, "You look beautiful."

Shivering at the warm breath on her ear, Leila winked at him. "Well, I figured, since I'm meeting your father and all, I could at least behave for one day. Maybe."

Leila turned and looked over the horizon at the front of the ship to distract her from him. She could see a city up ahead. "Is that Dria?" she asked. Leila had never approached Dria from the river before. The boat swayed slightly and Nalick put his arm around her to grab the rail and steady the both of them.

"Yes," Nalick returned his gaze to the water but didn't remove his arm.

"How long has it been?" she asked, aware of his arm being so close.

"I've not seen him in five years. He refuses to travel to Lexia, and for the most part, I refuse to travel to him." Nalick was anxious about the trip. Leila reached over and touched his hand. Nalick's heart raced. It was the first affectionate gesture she had shown him.

"Your father is one of the few kings I haven't met. Trust me, he can't be as bad as some of those men," Leila tried to reassure him. "The palace is on the water, right?" she asked.

Nalick nodded.

From the shores of Dria, one could see the beaches of the North Country. Leila was eager to be so close to home.

"My King," said a sailor, approaching them from behind, "we should be there shortly. Your father will have horses waiting at the port for you and the queen. Would you like Master Theo or Macarius to accompany you to the palace?"

"No, that's fine," Nalick replied, as the man bowed and then left. Leila giggled.

"See," Leila replied, as Nalick also laughed.

"I saw the wanted posters yesterday," Nalick commented. "Are they all you?" he asked.

Leila smiled coyly, but didn't respond.

"We attribute anything to you if there are no witnesses or we can't tell who committed the crime," he added.

"Oh, I don't commit crimes," Leila smiled at him. "If it was a crime, then it wasn't done by *me*." Nalick nodded his head sarcastically. He was marrying a thief—and a good thief at that. "I merely right some previous wrongs," she explained. "And yes, they were all me. Though it's a bit disappointing," she paused.

"Being on a wanted poster is disappointing?" he asked.

"Well, I noticed that you're only actively looking for four of my previous identities. I've been to Lexia quite a few times, and yet you only want to find four versions of me," Leila said with a grin.

"The only version of you I want to find is standing right here in front of me," he responded, and he gazed back over the water, not wanting the boat to stop because he would have to move his arm.

Leila smiled as the boat pulled up to the port filled with people. Nalick protectively kept his arm on the rail around her. Below, the crowd cheered as they saw Leila. Nalick slipped his arm around her waist as she turned. Leila looked down at everyone. Nalick stood and waved to the people, who cheered louder.

"They are all here to see you," he whispered in her ear.

These people will be so disappointed if nothing changes, she thought.

Nalick escorted her off the boat and to the waiting carriages. It was a quick ride through the city filled with the smiling faces of those wanting to see the king and his future queen.

"Your majesty, your father is in his study," a man informed Nalick as they approached the palace.

Nalick took Leila's hand and led her through the palace. If he hadn't been so nervous, he would have been more appreciative of how easily Leila accepted his hand. Unlike their palace in Lexia, the Dria palace was all one level, and there were no stairs to climb. Nalick led Leila through many passages until they arrived at the back of the palace. Nalick opened the door for Leila. As she entered, Leila glanced around the room and saw books lining the back wall. Off to the right was a room with an open balcony looking over the water. Nalick led Leila to the room on the left. Lying on a couch, with a book over his face, was an old man. His hair was white from age and he had a long thin beard that appeared from beneath his book and stretched down to his chest. He didn't move as they entered.

"Lule, I'm taking a rest. My son should be here soon, and I want to be rested," the man complained.

"Hello, father," Nalick said coolly, startling the old man causing him to drop his book to the floor.

As the former king regained his composure, he sat up and smiled. Even though his hair and beard were white, he wasn't as old as Leila originally thought. "Welcome," the man said, jumping up and kissing her hand. "It's a pleasure to finally meet you." Nalick's father greedily eyed Leila.

Leila didn't know how to respond. From the look he was giving her, he was just like any other king she had ever encountered. Luckily, Nalick responded for her.

"Father, please behave yourself." Nalick gave the old man a disapproving glare. Leila was not the only one that noticed the former king's attitude. "Did you not just take a new bride last year? One even younger than Leila?" Nalick commented. The former king had several wives. "Remember father, this is my future wife here." Nalick continued to glare at his father while putting a protective arm around Leila.

"Leila, this is my father, Godfrith," Nalick introduced his father but continued to hold Leila near himself. Leila could feel the tension between them.

Godfrith understood his son and apologized, "I'm sorry if I offended you, miss. I had heard tales about you, but they just don't do you justice." The old man's attitude changed. He walked over and shook Nalick's hand.

"It is so good to see you son." Godfrith was sincere. "How long has it been?"

"A few years," Nalick replied. The strain in the air hadn't lifted. Not wanting to be between the two men, Leila drifted over to the window.

"After being on a boat all morning it would be good for me to go for a walk," Leila suggested. Nalick did not like the idea of her being alone, so she took Nalick's hand and squeezed it. "I'll be down by the shore. Would you like me to go get Theo or Macarius?" she asked. Nalick shook his head no.

Godfrith walked over and opened a hidden door. "This is the best way to get down there."

Leila gazed one last time at Nalick, but he didn't try to stop her as she walked down the stairs to the shore. At the end of the stairs, Leila removed her shoes and wandered out onto the sand. From her position on the beach she could see the shore of the North Country. She was so close to home, yet still very far away. Cautiously, Leila lifted her dress and wandered into the water to get her feet wet. The contrast of the cold the water compared to the hot sun that was beating down on the beach made Leila laugh to herself. Boats passed, going out to sea. The colorful sails billowed in the wind. Sailing off on an adventure was the kind of life Leila always expected to have, yet now she had agreed to be stuck in one place; Leila again began to doubt her decision. Leila didn't need to turn around to hear a single person walking down the staircase from the palace. *Theo or Macarius?* she wondered. Without turning to see who was watching over her, she continued her walk along the shore.

Nearing the farthest end of the former king's beach, she could hear the laughter of children. Looking up, she could see five children running through the gardens near the beach. All five were running full speed toward the area where Leila was standing. As the first child neared Leila, he stopped in his tracks.

"Mica, who is she?" a young girl dressed in a filthy blue dress asked the first child. The boy didn't respond but just stared at her.

"I'm Leila," she said to the girl in the blue dress.

"Where did you come from?" the boy with bright yellow hair standing next to the girl asked.

"Over there," Leila pointed at the staircase that Macarius was sitting on.

"She's the new queen," the first boy finally spoke. "Sorry for disturbing you," he said to Leila, and he began to usher the younger children back toward the garden.

"Why are you leaving?" Leila asked.

"My mother said you're a dangerous person," the boy replied.

Leila laughed. "Do I look dangerous?"

The children stopped and pleaded with the older boy. The little girl whispered loudly, "Is she really a queen?" The girl eyed Leila from head to toe.

"Can't we stay?" the younger boy asked.

"Yeah," the tall thin boy behind him begged.

The older boy began pushing his friends. "My mother said she robs and steals from people," he stated, matter-of-factly.

"Oh," the short fat boy shook his head in understanding. "You're a courier."

The tall boy joined his friend and gazed at Leila. She wasn't tall like he imagined couriers to be, or even strong. She was a normal girl not much older than themselves.

"They let girls be couriers?" the thin boy asked in amazement. "I thought you had to be strong."

"Girls can be anything," the little girl pushed her friend aside and curtsied. "Pleased to meet you my majesty," she said sweetly, before pulling Leila into their game.

CHAPTER EIGHT

Nalick watched out the window. He was trying his best to talk to his father, but it had been years since they had seen eye-to-eye on any issue. Watching Leila was much easier than listening to the old king. Nalick didn't hear the last statement his father made, and soon Godfrith was standing right next to him.

"She sure is a beauty," Godfrith said, looking out the window, alongside Nalick, at Leila. "So I heard you're forcing her to stay. You know you can't win a woman's heart by force."

Nalick walked away from his father to the doorway. "And you would know." He opened the door and walked out onto the top step. Below, in the sand, Leila was blindfolded as the children cheered. She tried to catch them as they ran away from her.

"Do you think she will really stay?" Macarius asked Nalick when he passed.

"I hope she does," Nalick replied.

Leila removed her blindfold after catching the last child and noticed Nalick sitting with Macarius, while above King Godfrith watched from his window. Godfrith loved his son, but just didn't know how to communicate with him.

"Hold on one second," Leila said to the children. She ran over to Nalick and grabbed his hand. "It's your turn, my king." She pulled him back to the children and tied the blindfold around his eyes.

Leila and Nalick played with the children until dinner

time. After washing and redressing for the meal, Leila followed Nalick to the dining room. Former King Godfrith greeted Leila at the dining room door.

"Leila and Nalick, this is my newest wife, Lule." Godfrith presented his young wife. Lule was short and a bit heavyset. Her round face smiled brightly as she was introduced. The girl was younger than Leila. Lule's hair, and other body parts, bounced a little as she did her best to curtsey for Leila and Nalick, but the young woman was quite uncoordinated and almost tripped over her own feet. "And here, dear, is where you will be sitting, to the right of your future husband," he added. Leila counted the four seats next to the former king. *Four wives*, she thought.

"The guests should be arriving soon. Lule, please go get the others." At Godfrith's order the girl quickly ran out the front door and down the hallway, stumbling along the way.

"Picking them quite young, now," Nalick commented to his father. Godfrith didn't respond.

Turning to Leila, Godfrith asked, "If you could stand here with me, I'd like to introduce you to the nobles as they arrive." Godfrith led Leila to the door on the right of the room. Nalick followed close behind. From the other door, four women entered, all elegantly dressed. Leila noticed Lule was the last in the row of women.

As each woman approached, she bowed to Nalick and then to Leila. Each woman was extravagantly decorated with jewels, and each was younger than the one in front of them. To Leila, they looked more like street performers than wives to a former king, but she kept her comments to herself. Godfrith waved his hand and the youngest three women walked over and seated themselves. The oldest wife stood to the right of Godfrith while Leila stood on his left. In pairs, the nobles of Dria arrived to the dinner. A lady stepped forward, followed by her equally ornately-decorated husband.

"She married the father so that she could be with the sons," Nalick whispered in Leila's ear. Leila watched as the two men behind the lady both purposely escorted their step-mother to their seats with their hands in places they should not have been, as their father stopped to talk to Godfrith. "They have been trying to get me to marry their daughter since she was eight and I was seventeen," Nalick said.

"King Nalick," the bushy-haired father called out. "It's so great to see you. Have you thought about my offer?" The overweight man asked.

"One wife is more than I can handle," Nalick replied, as the man was ushered into the dining hall by the next group that approached.

"They never give up," Nalick whispered to Leila.

Leila continued to meet people until the dining hall was filled. Nalick escorted her to her seat before sitting himself beside his father. Staff served the guests in a well-orchestrated manner so that everyone was fed at the same time. Leila was amused to watch waiters dipping and dancing around each other. Not a single plate of food or drink was spilled.

After dinner, a dancing troupe and band were brought in. As the music started to play, guests meandered through the hall, greeting old friends they hadn't seen in a while. Leila watched quietly. She studied each, intently trying to remember the names of the specific nobles. Leila had never done a job in Dria. Dria was just across the border from the North Country, and it was too difficult to do jobs so close to home. She scanned over the crowd. Suddenly, Leila stopped. Across the room, she recognized a face from their one and only encounter. He was a courier based in the country of Samael, directly to the west of Lior.

Leila leaned over near Nalick and asked, "Who is the

family over there?" She pointed in the direction of the man she recognized.

"Nobles from the western border," Nalick replied, studying the group and noticing the one that stood out.

"He's a courier from Samael. The last I heard about Seth was that he stopped working for his courier station and was working directly for King Jahangir." Nalick understood without Leila finishing.

"How good is he?" Nalick asked, a little worriedly.

"Not better than me, but that's not why I'm concerned." Leila continued to stare at Seth. Seth noticed and raised his glass to Leila before giving her a wicked smile. Leila stood up, and Nalick rose to follow her. She placed a hand on his shoulder.

"Wait here," she instructed. Leila passed the crowds of people and walked out onto the dining room's adjoining balcony. Theo and Macarius followed her from a distance. She stood looking over the city, waiting for Seth to join her. It wasn't long before he approached.

"The famed ghost courier. It is an honor to be in your presence," he said with a flamboyant bow. "And your own personal guard. I see you've moved up in the world."

Leila turned to look at the man who had been tracking her for years. "What do you want?" she asked, staring directly at him. Seth was a rather small man who barely stood the same height as Leila. He was not a personal threat, but his knowledge of her becoming the next queen of Lior would be a problem.

"I'm here to extend to you an invitation to join me on my way home to Samael." Seth smirked at Leila.

"Do you even need to ask?" she replied. "Haven't the last few years taught your king anything?"

"Oh, yes, to catch the legendary ghost courier, one needs to get the upper hand." He walked around to the other side of Leila. "Or so I've been told. How did he do it? Please do tell."

Seth flicked a finger toward Nalick who was watching the two of them intently. "From what I've been told, he's just like any other king; boorish and self-centered. Yet, somehow he convinced you to stay." Leila looked over at Nalick, who was now visually starting to get upset.

"Go back to your king, and tell him I'm not interested. I wasn't then, and I'm not now." Leila started to walk away. Seth grabbed her arm to stop her. Leila swung back around and slapped the man across the face. Nalick rose to join her as Macarius and Theo moved closer.

Seth chuckled, rubbing his cheek. "Feisty as ever." He let go of her arm. "I was offering you an invitation so that we can avoid what will come next if you don't join me. One way or another, King Jahangir won't stop until you are his queen."

Leila walked away as Nalick quickly came over to her. Seth disappeared into the crowd before Macarius or Theo could stop him.

"Are you okay?" Nalick was worried.

"You brought Anatolio with us," Leila said to Nalick. Nalick was shocked to find that Leila knew that the young tracker was with them. "Send him to follow Seth. I don't know what he's up to, but I doubt it will be anything good."

CHAPTER NINE

Before dawn, Leila woke to a gentle shake and a hand over her mouth. Opening her eyes, Leila found herself face-to-face with Anatolio. He put his finger to his lips to indicate that she should be silent and motioned for her to follow him. Leila passed Macarius and Theo, who were asleep on the two couches in the room. Neither man stirred when Leila and Anatolio walked past them. Leila could make out the faint hue of the sun coming near the horizon.

Not very good guards, Leila thought.

"Does Nalick know you're back?" Leila asked.

"Not yet. I was told to follow Seth on your orders, so I thought I should first report back to you." Anatolio continued, "I followed him across the border where he met up at a war camp. Just outside Lior, King Jahangir has an army ready to march here to take you back with them. I could only hear parts of the conversation, but I know they'll be here by midday."

Leila nodded her head. "I estimated about forty people on our ship and less than that on the other four that came with us. That's not enough to protect this city. So what are Nalick's options?" she asked, knowing that the boy had more information on their traveling companions than she did.

"Nalick traveled here with less than one hundred trained men, and there's a small force permanently here in the city. From what I saw, Jahangir has at least three times the amount of people as us. We do have enough to stay here in the palace and be protected until reinforcements arrive."

Leila sat down in the sand to ponder her options. Jahangir was an evil man and would stop at nothing until he had her, even if it meant killing innocent people. In fact, he would deliberately target the innocent to get to her. The easiest solution was to run north. Once Leila got across the sea, she would be in her own territory. If only she could just leave so easily. Leila had made a deal, and so far Nalick was holding up his end of it. If she left alone, she would not be able to just return like nothing had happened. Leila contemplated a third option.

How much do you trust him? she asked herself. *If I take him with me, my deal is still good, but can I trust him to know where I come from?*

"So we have until about midday?" she asked. The sun was beginning to rise in the east, and the water began to twinkle as the light bounced off the ripples in the water. Anatolio nodded his head.

Leila walked silently back into the room, but it wasn't necessary to be quiet. Theo and Macarius were sitting on the couches, staring at their feet, while Nalick was pacing around the room, looking worried. None of the men noticed as Leila and Anatolio entered.

How did they find out already? she wondered.

Anatolio coughed to get the three men's attention, and Leila could sense the mood change as they realized she was standing there. Nalick's concerned expression quickly changed to relief. Leila understood; they weren't worried about the situation, they thought she had already been taken.

"Not good news?" Nalick inquired, after he calmed down a little. Leila shook her head, *no*, as Anatolio repeated his findings to the three men.

"How could we not be prepared for this?" Nalick asked, starting to get upset. "How do you march an army of three-hundred people near the border without anyone noticing?" Nalick began to pace the room again.

"But it's not a problem. We can stay right here and wait for reinforcements," Macarius replied. His decision was easy; keep Nalick safe at all costs.

"No," Leila replied, interrupting the men. They all turned to her with shocked expressions. "I know what Jahangir will do, and no person in this city will be safe, even if we are. That's not an option I'm willing to choose." Theo smiled and shook his head in disappointment. She was right.

"Then do we try to get home?" Macarius asked, confused by her apparent unwillingness to stay safe.

"First of all, I've never run from a battle, and I'm not about to start. Second, he could easily cut us off. There isn't a safe route home," Nalick explained.

"Are you finished?" she asked, while standing up and going over to her belongings. At the bottom of the case that held her dresses for the trip was her courier travel bag. Leila never went anywhere without it. She brought it to the table between the men, sat down and opened it. The men watched her curiously.

"I've considered our options. First of all, I agree that taking the water route home isn't safe." Leila began unpacking her bag and neatly arranging the clothing she took out of the case. "Second, I refuse to sit here while the city is attacked. Jahangir won't be satisfied to just attack the palace. He will go after the people of the city, and the women and children will become the victims if we sit here in safety. I'll not stand by and watch that. So, I've made a decision. I will be going home for a short visit." The three men looked at her in shock.

"But what about the deal?" Theo asked. He actually seemed to like Lexia, and to Theo's own surprise, Leila was getting along with Nalick.

"I will not be traveling alone," Leila replied, beginning

to unlock the inner compartments. "You three will be coming with me." The men all stared at her, not knowing what to expect.

"We'll send one of your father's fastest ships with a decoy. Anatolio and one of my maids will dress in our clothing. Leave the rest of your army here to protect the city. Once Anatolio returns to Lexia, he will arrange the necessary force to escort us home safely. It should take about two days to get our forces here and set up."

Leila unpacked her wigs and chose a dark-colored one. She put the rest away as she continued to lay out her plan, "If Jahangir stops the boat, Anatolio will allow him to search the vessel. When he finds he has been tricked, he will leave. He's not a very bright man, but attacking an unarmed ship in another country is far too stupid even for him to do." Leila pulled out a case of makeup and hair dyes.

Leila continued to open hidden compartments in her case. "Theo and Macarius, find clothing to travel in that will allow you to fit in with the local people around here. You will need two complete outfits each. Nothing ornate." Anatolio, Theo, and Macarius all quickly left. Once everyone was gone, Leila turned to Nalick. "Please don't make me regret doing this."

"Are you really going to take us with you?" Nalick asked in disbelief. "This isn't just a way to lose us?"

"You were worried about me when you didn't find me here this morning," Leila said, changing the subject. "Why?"

"I thought something had happened to you," Nalick said, while getting up and turning away from her. "I know you said you wouldn't be taken by that man that was here last night, but even you have been caught numerous times."

Leila smiled. "Then this is an even better reason to take you back to my home. If I should ever go missing, you will know exactly where to find me. But, just for future reference, you don't need to worry until I'm gone for several days. Contrary to popular belief, I can take care of myself." Nalick returned and sat next to Leila as she opened some jars she had retrieved from her case. Inside each one was rubbery, peach-colored makeup. Taking Nalick's right arm, she began to put a thin coating of the makeup over the lines on it. "It should be dry in a few minutes." Leila then began covering the lines on her own arm.

Anatolio returned dressed in Nalick's clothing, accompanied by a very sleepy maid. Although he wasn't as broad across the chest as Nalick, Anatolio would easily pass as the king from a distance.

"We will be back in three days' time. Can you get an adequate force here in that amount of time?" Anatolio nodded his head. Grabbing Elena's arm, he escorted her out of the palace. Leila passed the waiting men and got ready herself. When she returned, the men finally understood how she could have just disappeared. Standing before them, in a blue peasant blouse, ruffled red skirt, and a short black wig, she didn't look anything like herself. She was a citizen of Dria now.

"Nalick, can you cover this for me?" she asked, lowering the neck of her shirt to expose the king's emblem on her shoulder. Nalick used the makeup paste and covered it. While she waited for it to dry, she explained to Theo and Nalick how they would leave.

Finally, she stood to make her last inspections. Leila tapped Nalick's neck while inspecting the men. Nalick removed his shirt. Leila gently touched the large emblem that spanned his back. She knew how painful it had been for the small, hand-sized, crest on her own shoulder, so she couldn't imagine one as large as Nalick's. Nalick sat with his shirt in his hands as he waited for the makeup she had applied to dry.

"Any questions?" Leila had to look away so she wouldn't blush in front of the men.

"So how do we get out?" Macarius asked, suspicious that Leila was going to leave the group behind.

"Much easier, at least in my opinion," she replied, without giving any details. Leila looked over the men in front of her. Nalick had no reservations with her plan, but the other two men were a bit skeptical.

"She's not leaving us," Nalick guaranteed the men, surprising them both with his confidence. "She's trying to protect the people of this city." Even with his markings gone, his hair now brown in color, and the peasant clothing he was wearing, Nalick would stand out. Leila smiled at the trusting man before her.

"You guys are ready to leave. Do your best not to draw suspicion to yourselves, the less people that follow you, the less we will have to get rid of over there." Both men nodded. Nalick and Theo rose to leave.

Leila followed behind the two men as they neared the door. She grabbed Nalick's hand lightly, and he slowed and turned. Pulling him closer, she spoke quietly so that only he could hear, "Be careful. No matter how we try to disguise you, you will be a target."

Nalick smiled at her concern, "I haven't survived this long just because I'm king. I do know a thing or two about defending myself." Lightly, he touched her face. Leila's heart fluttered a bit. "We will be waiting, but please don't take too long. I might get worried." Leila smiled as he left with Theo.

Leila turned to Macarius and she dug through her bag until she found two small gold rings. She put one ring on the smallest finger on her right hand and walked over to put the other on Macarius' hand.

"We will be leaving by the beach." Leila rose, and Macarius followed. Leila led them through the palace and into the garden by the beach. Macarius didn't understand where they could leave from, but he followed Leila as she walked down the beach, toward the stairway that led to Godfrith's study. Leila neared the stairs but didn't climb them. Instead, she walked to the front of the building next to the stairs. The water of the river was rippling against the building as waves came in. Carefully, she took one step. There was a ledge just beneath the water she would be able to cross to the other side of the palace. Macarius cautiously followed her. After they made it back onto land, Leila led Macarius to the outside wall of the palace. She scaled the wall in only a minute.

"I thought you said this would be easier," Macarius commented.

Although Leila appeared lithe and delicate, she was actually stronger than any person Macarius had ever met, man or woman. He had once heard that the ghost courier was an expert at everything: escaping, fighting, disguises, and languages. Now he was beginning to see that what he had been told in the past was actually the truth.

Leila silently led Macarius through the streets. Every now and then she would turn down a street and backtrack. Although Macarius wasn't trained in tracking, he noticed she was trying to lose someone. He moved quickly, trying to keep up with her. Before long, all of their jogging across the city led them to a boatyard. Leila counted as she walked down the pier.

"I hope you can swim," she said. Leila approached a man sitting on a boat. Macarius heard her speak to the man in another language. Looking at Leila's hand, and then at Macarius' as they walked on to the boat, the man nodded.

Macarius followed Leila down the stairs of the boat to the under cabin. Leila quickly walked down the hallway to the last room and opened the door, where they found the captain's quarters. She walked over to the wall and opened the hidden safe door. Once the safe door opened, Macarius followed Leila down a staircase that led into the water. She carefully waded to the opening. Holding onto the rungs of the wall, Leila pulled herself alongside the ship like a ghost. Macarius followed as she moved to the boat next to them.

Using the rungs on the side of the next boat, Leila proceeded to pull herself down to the next three ships. Macarius noticed a blue flag with a lion on it flying at the top of the main sail. Leila pushed a side panel of the boat and a door slid open, just big enough for them to slide in sideways. Once inside, they climbed up a staircase to the inside of the hull of the ship. Leila hurried over to the door and locked it. She put a small bag on the wall and pulled a lever. The bag rose to the ceiling and disappeared. Leila began unpacking her bag as the boat began moving.

"We need to change clothes and then we can go up on top." Leila explained, removing her shirt. Blushing, Macarius quickly turned away and began to change also. Once he was done, he turned to face Leila, but was yet again facing a woman he didn't recognize.

"I'll need this back," Leila said, removing her ring and taking the ring back from Macarius. Leila led Macarius through the ship and walked onto the ship's deck, where she proceeded directly to the captain. He greeted her with a hug.

"It's so good to see you, missy," the captain said. "How was your trip?"

"Same as normal," Leila replied, walking over and sitting down behind the captain. Macarius warily followed and sat next to her.

"Picked up another one?" the captain asked, nodding toward Macarius. Leila nodded. "Good sailing today. We should get in early."

Leila watched as the pier behind her began to

disappear. She was heading home. She closed her eyes and felt the cool wind whip through her fake hair.

"Will there be more?" Macarius worriedly asked.

"Probably," Leila responded without opening her eyes. "I counted thirty-two trackers on our ride to the palace yesterday. We lost over a dozen but there will be even more with Nalick."

Men went about their work all around them as Leila and Macarius sat on the bench.

"How old is she now?" Leila asked the man that was closest, after she finally opened her eyes.

"Fourteen," he replied. "She still speaks of you every day. We will never be able to repay you." The man bowed before Leila. "Thank you so much." He dropped off a basket of food for her.

"What?" Leila asked Macarius, as he sat studying her. "Here, eat. We may not get another meal before tonight." Macarius took the food but continued to gaze at Leila.

"These men," he began. "They seem to admire you." Leila looked around for admiring men and found none.

"Oh." Leila realized Macarius was talking about the men on the ship. "I travel a lot on this boat." Leila kept eating and waved to a man that approached. "And do favors for them from time to time." Leila stood and hugged the man. "Don't tell me Henry is in trouble again," she teased.

"Gosh, no," the man replied. "Not after the last time!" Leila and the man laughed. "I just wanted to check with you. Henry heard a rumor when he was in Dria two days ago. Are you really..." he began, but Leila stopped him by covering his mouth. "Does this mean you're retiring from runs?"

"Let's just say, for the time being, I'm taking a break from assignments, but only assignments. If anyone needs my help, I won't hesitate," Leila replied. "Besides, it's not like you guys won't know where to find me. Don't worry about me. I chose to stay. No one is forcing me." The man didn't really seem to believe her.

"He's a good man. Really." She patted the older man's hand.

The man smiled at Leila. "You really do seem happy." He hugged her again before leaving.

Leila returned to leaning against the rail with her eyes closed. Macarius watched her quietly and studied her. From her appearance, Leila was one of the most beautiful women he had ever met. Outwardly, she appeared to be a quiet, sweet girl, but he was there the first night she had been brought into the palace before Nalick. He knew better.

In the back of his mind, Macarius had always thought of Leila as a thief that was running as a courier to get money. To find that Leila had been doing just as many assignments without pay made him start to doubt the person he had always envisioned her to be. It wasn't long before they were approaching the shore. Leila stood up as the captain walked over to them.

"Tell your wife I said *hi*." Leila walked to the side of the boat as it slowly pulled up to the dock. Three men jumped off and tied the boat up, and two more placed a plank to connect the boat to the pier. Leila waved good-bye to the disappointed men as she walked down the wharf toward the dirt road leading to the city of Cath. Macarius followed Leila in silence, unsure how to even talk to her. She wasn't the person he imagined her to be.

"There are six people outside, and probably a few more inside." Leila pointed to the building as they neared. Quietly, they approached a window of a tea shop. Leila placed a small bag on the window ledge and then directed Macarius to follow her silently. They walked to another building, and Leila unlocked the door. Inside was a sparsely-furnished room, which only had windows at the top of the wall so that no one could see in. After five minutes, Macarius watched as a panel on the floor began to be lifted. Leila helped move it to the side. From beneath the floor, Theo and Nalick climbed into the room.

"That was so neat," Theo said excitedly. "Can we do it again?"

"We need to be quick. There are six men outside that will be searching for you soon. You both need to change, and then we'll head into town for supplies." From her bag, Leila removed another wig, lighter in color than her own hair, but shorter. "Here," she said to Nalick, placing it on his head and tucking his hair beneath it. Then she handed Theo a hat. Leila walked over to the wall across from the door and opened a secret half door. "This way," she said to the men. "Follow the path, and it should end in a barn. I'll be right behind."

Cath was a port city that attracted people from many countries, so it was easy to mix into the assorted crowd of people. Leila was all business, heading right into her plan and to her layover station. She led the men into a barn next to a clothing shop. Leila opened the door to the stall and pushed the men in. Inside, to their surprise, were a bed and several chairs. Clothing was strewn all over the room and the bed was not made.

"I'll be right back. Don't open the door for anyone. I'm the only person who has the key for the room, so once I leave, lock the door behind me." The three men nodded. They were now in her territory.

Leila left the room and the door locked behind her. She walked back to the main building, through the storage area, and into the shop in the front. The stop was empty. She quietly browsed the racks until the owner returned. "Melinda?" the woman asked. "I thought you were going to be gone much longer. Can you stay for a bit of tea?"

Leila smiled and hugged the woman. "I wish I could,

but I'm transporting people," Leila replied, following the woman through another door.

"Promise we will have tea and catch up the next time you stop through," the woman added.

"Of course," Leila replied as the woman left the room. Leila shut the door and quickly changed. They would be heading into the mountains, and the further in they got, the colder it would be, so Leila packed several layers of clothing for everyone.

Leila returned to the stall where her room was and cautiously opened the door. Inside, the men were anxiously waiting. She handed them each a stack of clothing. "Sorry about the mess," she said, referring to the room. "I was in a bit of a hurry to catch up with Kay, I didn't exactly pick up before I left." Leila noticed the men were surprised by the amount of clothing she had returned with. "Just choose a shirt and pants," she said. "The rest we'll bring with us." Theo held a big fluffy jacket in his hands.

"How cold?" Theo asked.

"It will be fairly cold tonight at Roger's, but tomorrow, by the time we reach my home, we should be in snow," Leila explained. "Trust me; you will want to keep that jacket with you." She smiled at the shocked reaction on Theo's face. "The restroom is right there," she said, pointing to the wall that was covered by a blanket. Nalick pushed the blanket aside to see the room next to it. He grabbed his clothing and walked inside. Leila began to pick up clothes around the room while she was looking for her boots.

"Where to now, boss?" Nalick asked Leila once they were all changed.

"To Roger's," she replied, before pausing to add, "Though, I don't think he will be too happy to meet you."

CHAPTER TEN

Leila found Kay outside the courier stop, leaning against a horse while she waited. Leila ran over and hugged her. "What are you doing here?" Leila asked.

"You said not to wait for you, but I thought I could wait a couple of days. I knew it wouldn't take much for you to get out of there." Kay was beaming at Leila, but her smile quickly faded as she saw the three men behind her. "I thought you'd have lost them by now," Kay said, disappointed.

"I brought them with me," Leila tried to explain, but Kay just glared at Nalick. Leila began to recalculate her plan. With an extra person, it would actually make getting the men out of Cath easier.

"So you didn't escape?" Kay was confused. Leila shook her head, *no*. "He forced you to stay, just like all the other kings. And it's my fault." Kay looked like she was about to cry.

"No, no, no." Leila hugged her friend. "It's not your fault. I chose to stay. Really." Leila indicated to the men to remain with the horses while she pulled Kay a little distance away. "Kay, I've had many opportunities to leave. I can leave at any time. Nalick isn't holding me prisoner. I'm staying with him because I want to. It's a chance for me to have a new life. One where I'm not reminded daily about Erich." Reluctantly, Kay nodded. "I know he seems just like any other king, but he's different. Trust me. Now, he was followed here. If you could escort Nalick and Theo to Roger's ahead of Macarius and me, I can see if anyone else is following him still."

Kay smiled. "Good plan. Then, I should lose them on the way?" Kay asked, wanting to help her best friend.

"No," Leila quickly replied. "I expect to see Nalick tonight." Kay looked disappointed. "Promise?"

"Fine, but all you have to do is ask," Kay replied. "I'd gladly lose them on the way." Kay was much better at her job in the familiar terrain of her home country.

Kay and Leila walked back to the men.

"Kay will take you and Theo by road to Roger's. It's the easiest way to find his place if you should have to do so in the future," Leila explained to Nalick. "Macarius and I will take a shorter and more direct route." Leila handed each man the reins to one of the horses. While handing Nalick the reins, she didn't let go of them. He moved closer to her.

"Kay doesn't trust you," Leila said quietly to him. "I made her promise to not lose you on the way, but I doubt that means she will go easy on you. Please talk to her. She probably thinks you're keeping me chained up in a room."

Nalick smiled. From the short time since they had met up, Nalick could see Macarius was acting different toward Leila. The least he could do was try to get Kay to understand him a bit. Nalick leaned over and kissed Leila's forehead.

"I'll do my best," Nalick said, before hopping up onto his horse. Leila mouthed the words *thank you* as the three of them headed out of the city with Kay in the lead and Nalick and Theo following.

Kay kept her promise, and after a three-hour ride, they arrived at Roger's inn. Following a short hike into the woods outside the inn, they stepped out from behind a set of trees to discover an entire camp. Macarius was sitting near a fire, slowly stirring a pot. Kay ushered him out of the way and began tasting the food. She then quickly ran to a door in the ground and walked down the steps. Nalick watched as Kay disappeared from view. He looked around carefully. Set to one side was a lean-to shelter built against some trees, and underneath the shelter were five mattresses and blankets. On the other side of the camp was the door Kay just went through. Nalick cautiously walked near the door as Theo pulled up a chair and sat beside Macarius near the fire. It was nearing sunset and the air was getting cooler. Nalick looked down the doorway in the ground.

"It leads to our camp supply room," Leila said, approaching from the woods. Dressed in her normal clothes and with her hair down, she looked like a new person before Nalick. "Would you like to see inside?"

Leila led the way day down the stairs. The room at the bottom was lit by several oil lamps and they found themselves completely underground inside a long, rectangular passageway. Along both sides were stocked shelves. To one side, he saw more mattresses like the ones that were outside. Further down, Nalick saw that the shelves were lined with food. Kay was at a bench adding spices to a bowl.

"Did you taste that stuff?" Kay asked. Leila shrugged. "Well, I'm going to fix it." Kay hurried back out the door with her bowl of spices.

"I'm not really into the whole cooking thing," Leila explained to Nalick. "So, this is the half-way point between my home and Cath. We will spend the night here to lose any stray trackers. If anything should happen tonight, that door there leads back to the inn." Leila pointed at a table.

"That table is a door?" Nalick asked.

"Behind the table," Leila replied.

Nalick moved closer to try to test his luck. Leila hadn't shied away from him since the first day they met. Leila stood still as Nalick slowly put his hands around her waist. She was so tiny, yet so powerful in everything she did. Nalick wished to be able to hold on to her forever. Leila kept her breathing steady as her heart raced. Just being alone near him was enough to make her heart race, but his hands resting on her hips, holding her close to him were pushing her heart into irregular flutters. Leila closed her eyes, leaning forward and resting her forehead on his chest. His heart was beating just as fast as hers. It had been so long since Leila had felt her heartbeat speed up from someone's touch.

The clanking above the doorway reminded Leila of reality. Sighing, she stepped back and led Nalick out of the room to join everyone around the fire. Kay was busy fixing the food, and Macarius and Theo were huddled near the fire.

"Did Roger say anything to you?" Kay asked.

"No," Leila replied. Kay stopped stirring and looked up at Leila with a worried expression on her face.

"Is he mad at you? Does he know you're going to stay in Lexia?" Kay started with more questions, not giving Leila time to respond. Leila was always Roger's favorite courier. Kay couldn't believe he would not come and greet her.

Leila shrugged. "I doubt he's mad. More than likely he's too ashamed to come and talk to me in person, since he made a deal with Nalick, and now I know about it. Either way, tomorrow morning I'll need to stop by and get the herbs from him."

"A deal?" Kay asked. Leila shrugged. Leila still didn't know how she felt about Roger's actions. He had always protected her over the years. Roger was like a second father to her.

"Would you like me to go and get bowls?" Leila asked Kay, trying to change the subject.

"I'll help you," Kay replied, handing the spoon to Theo. "Keep stirring it."

After they were alone, Kay stopped Leila. "Nalick gave me this," Kay said, opening her hand to reveal the ring to Leila. Her assignment had been to retrieve the ring. They always thought it was with the noble Andres, and he had been their target in Nalick's palace. "I guess he had it all along."

Leila chuckled. She had been so unaware of the situation that, the whole time they were running their assignment, she didn't even know where the ring was. *I should have known*, she thought. "I'm not surprised," Leila replied, handing Kay five bowls.

"Nalick loves you," Kay said to her friend. Leila stopped reaching for the spoons. Shivers tingled at her back even though she wasn't cold. It was strange to hear the words said aloud.

"I know." Leila didn't turn around to respond to her friend. "I can see it in his face." Leila felt a mix of emotions for Nalick.

Kay patted Leila's shoulder as she reached for the spoons. "You know, it's acceptable for you to fall in love again; it has been two years already."

Leila nodded without turning around. "I'll be up in a minute," Leila told Kay, who left her alone. Leila wiped the tears that were forming in her eyes. It had been two years since Roger's oldest son, Erich, died. The loss had been devastating. Erich wasn't just Leila's partner; he had been her future husband.

Leila walked over to the table in the dimly-lit room and sat down upon it. She rested against the shelves and looked at the opening in the ceiling across the room above the stairs. Leila could hear the voices of her friends outside laughing. *Can I really fall in love again?* There was no one else in the world that was as perfect for her as Erich had been. He understood her and her need to run free. He never tried to stop her, and instead just followed and helped her accomplish anything she tried. He had been her support over the years and had never wavered. Leila admired every quality of his and could never imagine a world without him. When Erich died, her world had been shattered. She felt that she could never depend on another person, and would eventually have to grow strong enough to support herself.

"Are you going to join us any time soon?" Kay asked through the opening.

Leila quietly stood and walked back to the staircase. She looked around the room. Nothing had changed over the years.

Can I really change? she asked herself.

Leila took the bowl and sat outside near the men around the fire. Nalick nodded his head but his eyes looked at her questioningly.

"Can it get any colder?" Theo asked, while he grabbed his jacket and put it on.

"You sleep outside in this weather?" Macarius asked Leila. She laughed, nodding.

"Well, don't get used to this," Leila watched as they both looked relieved. "It's even colder where I'm taking you tomorrow." Both men were disappointed. Everyone moved to go to bed, but Leila didn't join them. "I'm going to make a check of the area, just to be safe," she said. Kay understood. Though she was in the company of three men that would lay down their lives to protect her, Leila still didn't feel safe enough to truly rest.

Leila didn't object when Nalick followed her to the entrance of the camp. He carefully walked behind her in her exact steps. Every now and then, Leila would stop and check traps that were set. She seemed satisfied, but instead of turning and going into the camp, she continued walking. Nalick trailed in silence. He was surprised to discover that he had followed her to a lake. Near the edge was not sand, as most shores are, but large boulders. Evergreen trees surrounded the lake, and in the distance were the mountains that Leila called home. In the moonlight, Nalick could see that the tips of the mountains were covered with snow. Leila carefully climbed from one rock to the next until she stopped and sat down. Nalick joined her. Together, they sat ten feet from the shoreline. They were surrounded by the water and the wind gently blew against the rocks. From their seats they could see the mountains and the stars that lined the sky. Leila lay down and looked up into the sky.

"You know, even though it's warmer in Lexia, the stars still look the same," she said to him. Nalick shivered at the coolness of the rock beneath him. His life had been very busy, and he couldn't remember the last time he just sat and just looked at the sky.

"I told Kay that if you want to stay here, you can," Nalick said, but Leila didn't respond. "I really do mean it. I know you made a deal with me, but if you're happier to stay here, then I'd be willing to break the deal." Leila still didn't respond.

"If I asked whether you missed your home when you're far away, how would you reply?" she asked him.

Nalick thought for a moment. "Do I miss the people that live where I call home, or the place itself?" he asked for clarification.

Leila laughed quietly. *So he did understand the question*, she thought. *Exactly how I'd reply*. Leila thought for a moment before sitting up and taking his hand into her own.

"I'll be returning to Lexia with you. See, I will always miss the people at home, like my mother and father, but not so much the place. It stopped being home when I started my runs as a courier. I discovered the world. In fact, this is more like home to me, outside in the fresh air where you can feel the breeze in your face." Nalick was relieved. In his heart, he didn't really want to let her go. Suddenly, Leila stopped talking and looked around the lake. Nalick was startled, and he tried to look around the lake in the dim light. Leila sighed. "Wait here, I'll be right back."

Carefully, Leila climbed back between the rocks until she was on the land around the lake. Not wanting to leave Nalick's view, she waited for the approaching man to come to her. Nalick watched intently as Leila waited. Slowly, the man approached and stopped within feet of Leila.

"It's good to see you're okay," Roger said to Leila, unsure if she was mad at him or not.

Leila walked over and gave him a hug. "Did you have any doubts? I've been in far worse situations before. Look," she said, spinning in a circle. "No cuts for you to fix up." The older man chuckled and hugged the much younger girl again.

"So that's him?" Roger asked, nodding his head toward Nalick.

"Yes," Leila replied.

"And you will be staying in Lexia for the time being?" Roger asked

"Yes," she responded again. Roger probably knew of her agreement with Nalick only moments after she said yes.

"He has told you about the deal," Roger guessed. Leila nodded her head.

Leila walked over to the nearest boulder and leaned against it. "Why didn't you tell me?"

"First, I was afraid you wouldn't come back if you felt I had betrayed Erich, and then after you started to take all the hard missions, I felt that if I told you, you'd go and do something stupid." Roger shook his head. "I should have told you, but I just didn't know how. All I wanted to do was protect you."

Leila nodded.

"I brought you supplies," Roger said, handing Leila a

bag. "Everything that you will need for now should be in there. I have runners near, or in, Lexia weekly, so if you need anything else, just contact one of them."

Leila took the bag. "How long have you known he was looking for me?" she asked him.

Roger smiled. Leila was the best courier he had ever trained, and he had known from the day he met her that she wasn't meant to stay in the North Country. As they stood in the darkness, the moonlight on her face showed Roger she still had the same all-knowing eyes as the first time they met, wise beyond her years. She was smart and resourceful. Oftentimes, her stubbornness and quick tongue got her into trouble, but her dedication to excel at everything made her worth the extra effort that was needed to keep an eye on her. It was hard for Roger to look at the woman before him and not think of her as the young girl she once was.

Roger sat beside Leila, "I got a report after your last trip from Dria that he had changed his mind on the deal we had. After you got hurt the last time, I was actually relieved that I could take you off assignments altogether, that way I wouldn't have to explain to you why you couldn't go to Lior. But, as always, I couldn't keep you from doing what you wanted to do."

Leila patted Roger on the shoulder. Roger had always cared for her like she was his daughter. When she was hurt, he always was there to fix her up. When she wanted to learn a new technique, he would spend hours watching over her until she got it correct. When his oldest son asked her to marry him, Roger was just as happy as Erich that she said yes.

"But I thought my stubbornness was my best trait," Leila joked.

Roger laughed. "I don't know about the best, but strongest trait I'd agree."

"Would you like to meet him?" she asked, nodding her

head toward Nalick, who was waiting patiently.

"Not tonight. I just wanted to stop by and drop off your pack so that you could check it over before you left in the morning, in case I forgot anything." Roger stood and hugged her again. "You will make a great queen," he said, and he slowly made his way back into the woods.

Leila climbed back onto the rocks that Nalick was sitting on. She was relieved that Roger wasn't mad at her for her decision to stay in Lexia. Nalick stood as she neared him. As Leila was about to climb up on the boulder that Nalick was standing on, he easily picked her up and sat her beside him on the stone. Again, her heart raced at his touch, and she tried to keep her tone casual.

"It was just Roger," Leila said, sitting back down on the edge of the rock. Her feet dangled several feet above the water. "He wanted to drop off my pack." She patted the bag hanging from her shoulder. Nalick looked worried. "It's full of medicines and herbs," she explained. "I kind of got myself in a little trouble the last assignment."

"What kind of trouble?" Nalick wondered.

"The kind you don't exactly heal overnight from." Leila shook her head. "It was a stupid mistake. Actually, just a little miscalculation. I'm sure Roger will want to check it over before I leave tomorrow to make sure everything is healing correctly."

Leila shivered. It was a cool night, and she could see her breath as she blew out. Nalick sat down next to her and pulled his arm out of the right side of his coat. Gently, he draped his coat so that it covered both himself and Leila. He strategically placed his arm around her to share his warmth. She smiled at him in thanks. "So, have you been to the mountains before?" she asked.

"I still don't understand how you could miss this cold weather." Leila grinned. He wrapped his arm that was under his jacket around her waist to pull her closer.

"I think the cold breeze is just what you need to remind you that you're still alive. Besides, it's not just the cold I like, but what you will see tomorrow," Leila explained.

Nalick raised his eyes brows in question. "Snow?" he guessed.

"Have you ever seen snow before?" she asked.

"Well, if I squint a bit, I'd guess over on that mountaintop is snow—so that would be a yes," Nalick replied, while Leila shook her head no and gave him a friendly pat on his stomach. "Oh, you mean up close. No, I have not. I grew up in Lexia and only traveled a little over the years."

Nalick and Leila sat in silence. Leila's hand rested on Nalick's leg as she huddled close to him to keep warm. In the cool North Country air, it seemed they both found something they didn't want to move away from.

CHAPTER ELEVEN

As Leila had predicted, it wasn't yet light out, and Kay was already making breakfast in the hope of waking everyone up. Kay checked her pocket again. Inside was the ring Nalick had given her the day before. Kay was very excited to give it to Roger. She held it close to her face and moved it around.

Leila joined Kay by the fire. *How could such a little thing cause so many problems?* Leila thought.

Sitting down, Kay mouthed the words *"we're going home"* and then grinned, ear-to-ear. Kay continued to make breakfast as Leila opened the bag Roger had given her the previous night. Inside the bag were several smaller pouches. Each had a different herb or medicine inside. Roger had given her double the usual supply of everything.

What does he think is going to happen to me? she wondered.

The men woke to find it just as cold outside as it had been the night before.

"You know, I don't think you should be outside if you can see your breath," Theo commented.

Macarius nodded his head in agreement.

"How long before it's done?" Leila asked Kay.

"Fifteen minutes or so," Kay replied, adding more spices.

"Then I'll be back in fifteen minutes." Leila stood and turned to Nalick. "Would you like to finally meet Roger?" Leila asked him.

A short trip through the woods led them back to the inn. Leila proceeded to the stables attached to the main house. Instead of going in the front door on the main level, Leila climbed the stairs that were between the stables and the house. Without knocking, she let herself into the home. Nalick followed and was surprised to find that the room they entered was not a normal room, but seemed to be more of a medical room. In the center of the room were two long tables with clean white sheets on them. Along the inside wall of the room were a changing screen and two chairs. A number of various plants blocked the south wall window. As they crossed the room, Nalick could see that the drawer of one of the tables was partially opened. He could see the slight glint of metal tools inside the drawer.

Leila continued through the room and into the next one. It was a kitchen of sorts. The cupboards weren't stocked with food, but rather, with herbs and plants. Leila continued to the next door, which led to another staircase. She quickly bounced up the stairs two at a time. Nearing the top step, Leila slowed down. She gently tapped on the door twice.

"It's open," a muffled voiced yelled from inside.

Leila opened the door and walked into a greenhouse. Nalick hadn't noticed that on the top of the main house of the inn was a large hothouse. The greenhouse was in the ideal location. At the top of the third floor, it allowed the best access to the sunlight in the forest. Several tables were lined up in rows and various plants were on each table. The warm, humid air of the greenhouse was a stark contrast to the cool breeze outside. Leila quickly removed her coat and hung it on the railing of the staircase. Nalick did the same. Leila then walked through the rows, stopping every now and then to check a plant.

"Your *pulegium regium* doesn't look as good as normal," Leila commented, "and your elderberry doesn't look like it will flower on time this year yet again."

Roger appeared from beneath one of the tables.

"Right as always. What am I to do without you around to point out the plants that aren't doing as well as the others? She never compliments me on the plants that are doing well," Roger said to Nalick. "Roger," he said, introducing himself before wiping his hands on his apron and extending his right to shake Nalick's.

"Now that you have met, back to business," Leila said, interrupting the two men. "Kay is making breakfast, and you know how she is about food. So, we only have ten more minutes before we must be back."

Roger shook his head as he removed the apron around his waist. Roger led the way as he talked to Leila. "Which route are you planning to take home?" he asked, as they went down the stairs.

"I'd prefer the upper trail," Leila responded, following Roger through the kitchen into the first room. "But you know that Kay will want to take the evergreen trail."

"Yes, but I got word that it snowed just a few days ago. You could get blocked up on the evergreen trail if too much has fallen. I agree with the upper trail." Roger began washing his hands. Leila removed her sweater and sat down on one of the tables in the room. Nalick stood in the doorway and watched.

"What about the valley trail?" Roger asked putting on his glasses. "It should get you home at least a bit quicker than the upper trail."

"The upper trail would get me home the fastest, but by bringing Kay, it will go pretty slow. I'll try to suggest the valley trail," Leila replied as Roger handed her a pillow. Leila laid face down on the table and Roger lifted the back of her shirt.

"How's your hand?" he asked.

"Still feels fine. The strength is completely back," Leila replied, as Roger adjusted the light above Leila.

"The upper portion here looks like it's completely healed, but it looked fine before you left. No sign of infection," Roger commented. Nalick watched as Roger's fingers traced the trail across her back that had been slashed open on her previous assignment before her trip to Lexia. Leila turned a little onto her right side as Roger continued to inspect the line.

"So did the stitches come out okay?" Roger asked, as he neared the end of the line on her hip. Leila pushed the waistband of her pants down a little, exposing the harsh red line that was the end of the cut.

Nalick silently moved closer to see. The last three inches had taken longer to heal than the rest of it.

"The stitches? They came out fine. I took them out during our first night in Lexia," Leila replied. Roger stared at Leila over the rims of his glasses. Nalick was shocked.

"I told you to have Kay remove them," Roger scolded Leila.

"You know how she gets. Trust me, I did a much better job myself than she would have done," Leila complained. "But it looks fine, right?" she asked, with slight concern in her voice.

"Yes, it's fine. But if you'd have stayed here, like I asked you to, I could have removed the stitches and then there would have been no scarring. Now I'm afraid you will have a slight scar here by your hip." Roger had tried, in vain, to keep Leila away from Lexia. Roger gently pulled her shirt back down and Leila sat up again, with her feet dangling over the side of the table.

"How has your strength been?" he asked.

Leila shrugged. "Normal." Roger put his hands on both her shoulders.

"Turn," he instructed. Leila turned her upper body to the left. "Now, the other way. You still seem a bit weak on that side, but it's much closer to normal now than it was before you left." Leila hopped off the table and grabbed her sweater. "And it hasn't affected your left leg?" he asked, and Leila shook her head *no*.

"We should start to make our way back," Leila said to Nalick.

Roger gently patted her head. "I don't need Kay to be mad at me." Leila smiled and hurried back into the other room to put her coat on. Nalick turned to leave, but Roger quickly caught his arm.

"I may look like an old man, but if I hear anything has happened to her because of you, I'll be to Lexia in the blink of an eye," Roger whispered so that Leila couldn't hear.

"I will protect her with my life," Nalick replied sincerely.

In the last few years, Roger had grown used to Leila showing up at a moment's notice. She always came back with more tales of her adventures that made him laugh and envy her youth and energy. The shy and determined girl that she was when she first arrived was gone, replaced by a confident, stubborn woman. Roger loved her as if she was his own child. He had also assumed that, over time, Leila's heart would mend from the loss of Erich, but he was wrong. It pained him to see her fade away from the chance of ever finding love again. Roger sniffled a bit and shuffled back up to his greenhouse. He was no longer sad for Leila, as he could see in her eyes that she was finally happy again.

"She's going to be fine," Roger said out loud to the empty room, "just like you wanted, Erich."

CHAPTER TWELVE

The ride home took longer than expected. There was fresh snow covering part of the valley's path, and it was slow going at parts. They had been riding all day, and everyone was eager to get off the horses and relax a bit. As they turned the last corner, Kay hurried her horse ahead of the rest. Leila let her friend run ahead so that the men could take in the sights around her home.

Leila's home was in the valley between two of the biggest mountain ranges on the south end of the North Country. The city, which they lived near, was situated on a lake in the valley. Her parents' land extended from the northeast shore of the lake up the mountain side. The path they were walking on took them around the outskirts of the town and to the backside of her parents' land. Any open view gave a picturesque view of the lake and surrounding mountains. Of all the places Leila had traveled over the years, her parents' home was one of the most beautiful.

As they approached Leila's home, the men couldn't see the house hidden behind the evergreen trees. Leila hopped off her horse as all three men stared at her. On the way to her home, they had to walk through the thickest parts of the trail, and they didn't wish to do so again. All three men were thoroughly frozen to the core.

"Well, do you guys want to get inside, or have you grown accustomed to the cold and wish to stay out here?" The men looked confused. As Leila walked ahead, she pulled back the branches to expose her home.

"If you want to stay outside that's fine, but can I at

least put the horses in the barn?" she asked.

Nalick, Theo, and Macarius instantly jumped off their mounts and followed Leila and the horses into the barn. After they were finished with the animals, she cautiously took Nalick's hand. She was feeling nervous, and he could tell. He squeezed her hand and smiled down at her. Macarius and Theo could feel the anxiety as well. Bringing home a king and two noble soldiers wasn't the nicest greeting for someone often kidnapped.

"We could wait here, if you'd like," Theo suggested, trying to ease the tension.

"No, the more people, the less likely anyone can get mad at me. It should be near dinner time, so everyone should be busy. Hopefully I can introduce you to a few at a time," she replied.

Nalick raised his eyebrows, "How many people will we be meeting tonight?"

"There are normally fourteen, including me, as long as my brothers don't have any friends over or any other family is visiting," Leila explained quickly. Leila led the men out of the barn and around to the front door of the home. She paused at the entrance, trying to build up the courage to enter.

Now or never. She pushed open the door.

Leila led the men into a small room before the main house. She removed her coat and shoes before opening the door and took a deep breath before entering the house. Once inside, the three men followed Leila into a large kitchen. Along the entire left side were cupboards and a large sink and oven. Standing at the counter, cutting vegetables, was a woman. She didn't turn around at the opening of the door. With eight adults and six children running around, the woman was accustomed to the door being opened and shut often. Leila stood just inside the doorway not saying anything.

"Hi, Momma," Leila said, quietly hoping that maybe

her mother would not hear her. The lady turned around and dropped what she was doing to give her daughter a hug.

"Welcome back, sweetie," Leila's mom said while sticking out her hand to shake the hands of the men with Leila. "I'm Anselma," she said to the men. "Everyone calls me Selma or just Ma around here." In turn each man shook her hand and introduced themselves. Shaking Nalick's hand, Selma stopped and looked closely at him. Moving back near Leila she asked, "So is this the man Kay said something about?"

"Depends on what she said," Leila replied quickly.

"Just that you were traveling with three men and one plans to marry you," Selma replied.

Leila blushed and nodded her head. It had been so much easier to tell her parents that she was going to marry Erich. Erich had started out as her partner for courier runs, and he would make sure she was safe by traveling home with her. Her parents appreciated that Erich watched over her. Erich would frequently stop by for meals or just to visit even when they didn't have an assignment. Her parents had two years to get to know him before he ever asked her to marry him. Things would be different this time around. Nalick was a stranger from another country, a king with much power and wealth: two qualities that would not endear him to her parents. Leila was sure her parents would automatically distrust him.

"Is Dad around?" Leila asked, wanting to get both introductions done with.

"He's visiting your grandfather and probably won't be back until after supper." Selma returned to her cooking. "Kay was going to get washed up. She said she would start warming the water for you guys also."

Selma would be in a questioning mood. Leila did not want to stick around to answer any questions; so she hurriedly grabbed her bag and shoes and led Nalick through the kitchen into the family room. Leila quickly put on her boots, and Nalick followed her out the back door before they met anyone else in the house. Outside, Leila led the way to another building that wasn't attached to the main house.

"This is our bath house." Leila made a sweeping gesture toward the building. "You do know how to bathe yourself?" she asked teasingly. "Wait, maybe you don't. Do you have several women bathe you at the palace?"

Nalick chuckled at the thought. "Well, that's a secret," he replied with a wink before they entered the building to get cleaned up.

After spending over an hour getting bathed and dressed, Nalick and Leila had to return to the house and the many people that would be waiting to question them. Leila loved her family, but she was not ready to admit her feelings for Nalick.

"Could we just run away and pretend we got lost on our way to the bath house?" Leila asked, dreading going back inside and facing her mother's relentless questioning.

"I suppose we could, but then there's the problem of Theo and Macarius," Nalick replied. "Maybe they have answered all your mother's questions, and she won't have any left for us."

"We can only hope," Leila pulled her coat on and put her hood over her wet hair before leading the way back to the house. Once inside, she could hear laughter coming from the kitchen. She cautiously approached to find Theo, Macarius, and her mother all seated around the table, playing a card game while Kay was cooking. Leila saw her mother's expression change back to a serious one once Leila and Nalick entered the room.

"How long before supper is done?" Leila asked Kay, trying to ease the tension.

"About thirty minutes," Kay replied, while expertly handling four different pots on the stove at once.

"The baths are all ready for you guys," Leila said to Theo and Macarius. "I'll show you where it is." Leila offered to leave the house before her mother could ask any questions, but to her surprise, her mother was just watching her and not talking. Leila couldn't make out the expression on her mother's face. Selma wasn't happy, but she wasn't mad either.

"Could you get Nael for supper?" Selma asked Leila, turning to leave. Leila nodded before quickly grabbing Nalick's arm to drag him with her. Leila didn't want to face her mother, but the thought of leaving Nalick alone with her wasn't comforting either.

"Do you want to stay here when we go back?" Nalick asked cautiously as they left Macarius and Theo at the bath. He was prepared for her response and just held his breath, waiting for her to say *yes*.

"Not really," Leila replied. It wasn't the response he had expected, nor was it one of complete reassurance either.

"I mean, yes, a part of me will always want to be here. I grew up here. To wake up in the morning and see the sun rise over the mountains and shine on the lake, it truly is awe inspiring. But..." Leila paused and stopped in her tracks, thinking. "It's just not the place for me. It's a little too quiet and sometimes quite boring." Leila looked up at Nalick to see if he understood.

"Maybe someday in my life this is what I will want, but right now I just want to be somewhere a bit more exciting. I was never one of those little girls that dreams about how they'll marry a guy from their home village and then move in right next door to her parents, and he would take over the family business."

"Is Lexia exciting enough for you?" Nalick asked cautiously.

Leila smiled. "It will do for now," she replied coyly.

Nalick followed Leila, who was leading him by rows of dormant grape vines. "This is my family's business." Nalick could see that she was leading them to a small stone structure toward the middle of the vineyard. As they drew near, he could see it was a building built into a hill. Leila walked around to the side door and led Nalick through several rows of barrels until they were near the back of the building. Sitting in a room next to a well-lit fire was a dark-haired man reading papers, Leila's oldest brother Nael. As Nael looked up, his face turned from serious to having a big smile. He quickly jumped up and lifted Leila and tipped her upside down as he hugged her.

"Welcome home, squirt," Nael said, putting her down not too gracefully.

"Thanks," Leila replied. As she stood back up, her brother's expression changed again at the sight of Nalick.

"What the heck did you get yourself into?" Nael asked, pulling up the sleeve on her left arm. Though her brother ran the family winery, he was the most educated person in their family. In his free time, he loved to read, and would pick up a book about anything. Nael knew what the lines on her arm meant. Part of Leila was disappointed in his seriousness. She had been hoping that Nael would be her one ally in the house when she explained to her parents why she would be staying in Lexia. Nael finally acknowledged the man standing in the doorway.

"Is this his fault?" Nael asked Leila, pointing behind her accusingly.

"No," Leila quickly replied. "It's my fault. I made the choice." Nael looked like he didn't believe his little sister. Though Nael had been told Leila was the best courier Roger had ever trained, it was hard to believe that his little sister was any good at it when she was constantly coming home hurt. Nael knew all about the troubles she had gotten herself into over the years and the many people who had offered bounties on her head to try to force her into marriage.

"Does Roger know about this?" Nael asked.

"Yes," Leila said, not backing down from her angry brother. Nalick was amazed that the quiet, shy girl she had been just moments before, when she was with her mother, was gone, and the spirited, headstrong woman he had seen before was back.

Nael proceeded over to Nalick and extended his hand. "I'm Leila's brother, Nael."

Nalick shook his hand, but before he could say anything Nael added, "I know who you are, King Nalick." Leila held her breath. While they were nearly the same size, Nael standing eye-to-eye with Nalick, Nalick was more muscular and in better shape physically. Leila waited to see if her brother would be foolish enough to pick a fight with a man she doubted he could beat. Nael briskly turned and walked back to his seat to go back to his work.

"Nael," Leila complained. "You have more manners than that."

Nael looked at his sister. "When is the wedding?" he asked. "Or, rather, should I ask when your priests have decided when the wedding should be?" Nael asked Nalick sarcastically.

"In three months," Nalick replied kindly, not taking the bait for an argument.

"Three months?" Nael repeated, assuming he heard incorrectly.

"Why do you think so many kings wanted to marry her?" Nalick replied. "Your sister is very special." Leila smiled up at Nalick. She had heard numerous people tell her over the years how special she was, but it meant something else coming from Nalick. Nael caught the smile on his sister's face. It had been four long years since Erich died. It had been just as long since he last saw her truly smile, as she had just now done at Nalick. Nael sat and stared at his little sister. Though it was subtle, something about her seemed to have changed.

"He has offered several times to just let me stay here," Leila explained to her brother, "but I'm going back with him to Lexia, no matter what you or anyone else says to me. I was only hoping I could introduce Nalick to everyone, but we seem to keep getting the same reaction."

"Oh, so you talked to mom first?" Nael laughed as he put down his papers. "Sorry about that," he said as he walked over and patted Nalick on the shoulder. Now they were allies.

Nalick was surprised Nael's attitude changed so quickly. "I could have told you not to meet her quite yet. She just needs some time to adjust to new people after meeting them. Ah, the first time I brought Gisela home... I didn't think my mother would ever like her, but now they're best friends. Our mom is just naturally cautious with people. Trust me; it will be much easier meeting our father." Leila was relieved to see the change in her brother. "Just give our mom a little time. If Leila has decided you're safe enough to bring home, then you can't be all that bad." Leila smiled, as Nael had never said he trusted her judgment before.

"We better get going home. Mom actually sent us to get you for supper. Kay is cooking," Leila replied, happy that this meeting was over.

As they returned to the house, the commotion in the kitchen could be heard outside the door to the house. Leila walked in, following her brother. In the middle of the room, four young children were standing in front of Selma having their hands inspected. As Selma approved each child, she patted them on the head and sent them to the table. Theo and Macarius were already seated. Both men slightly bowed their head at Nalick's entrance.

Leila commented under her breath. "Doesn't that ever get old?"

Once the children noticed Leila was standing in the room, all four jumped up to greet her with hugs.

"Auntie Leila," all four called at once, rushing to her. "What did you bring us back?" one asked.

Leila picked up each child, hugging them. As she picked up the last child, the young boy asked, by whispering in Leila's ear, "Who's that?" Pointing at Nalick.

"That's Nalick," Leila said before setting him back down on the ground.

A woman carrying a small girl walked in from the doorway to the right of the kitchen table. Smiling, she also greeted Leila with a hug.

"This is my sister-in-law, Sabine," Leila said, introducing the woman hugging her. "Sabine, this is Nalick. And Theo and Macarius," Leila said, indicating to the men sitting at the table. Sabine sat down at the table and joined in with the conversation the men were having.

"That one right there." Leila pointed at a young girl with golden ponytails. "Is Sabine's oldest, Gabi, and the child with Sabine is Karin. The young boy there is Luca. He's Kay's son. And the two older children are Dierk and Cara. They are Nael's oldest children."

Leila seated herself next to her niece, Gabi, and Nalick sat between Theo and Macarius. After everyone was settled, Kay brought the food to the table. Nalick noticed an empty seat and tried to figure out who was missing. Nalick quickly found out, as a younger, and very loud man entered the house.

"Where have you been, Leon?" Sabine scolded the man. "You're late again."

Leon grinned as he ignored his wife and noticed his sister was home. "Sis," he called as he bent and hugged her around the neck. "Long time, no see."

"Yes," Leila replied, prying his arms off her neck so that she could breathe. Leon continued to ignore his wife, who was giving him a stern stare.

"And you brought friends," Leon added, as he walked to the other side of the table. "Let me introduce myself. I'm Leon, Leila's favorite brother." Nalick stood to shake Leon's extended hand and was surprised to find himself a whole head shorter than the young man.

Dinner was louder than Nalick was used to, but very entertaining. Through all the conversations, he learned more about Leila than he did from all his notes. After dinner had finished, Selma insisted that Leila's group head to bed. Leila tried to help out with the chores, but no one would let her. She finally gave up and took the men upstairs to the bedrooms. Leila showed Theo and Macarius each to their own accommodations.

"You guys are really going to need to stop that," she complained at Theo and Macarius as they bowed to her before going into their rooms. Leila walked Nalick to the next room. As they entered, Nalick could tell it belonged to Leila. The room was small, but cozy. The bed was pushed against the wall and two chairs sat next to the three windows on the wall across from the door. Leila quickly picked up the clothes that were lying on the floor.

"You can have my room," Leila said to him. "Just don't go snooping through my stuff."

"But where will you sleep, then?" Nalick asked.

"I'll be downstairs on the couch," she replied, turning back to the door. Nalick gently grabbed her hand and pulled her close.

"I don't want to take your room away from you. I'll sleep downstairs," he said, going to the door himself.

"No," she said. "You are a guest in our house. I won't let a king sleep on our couch."

Nalick could see she wasn't about to let him have his

way. He continued to hold her hand and pulled her closer to him. "Well, if I don't want you to sleep on the couch and you don't want me to sleep on the couch, how can we find a compromise?" Leila shook her head no to a compromise. "How much trouble would you get in with your mother if we both slept here?" Nalick indicated to her bed. Leila's mind began to rush through several questions, *what does this mean, what is he asking me to do, is he actually serious?* "I mean no disrespect to your mother and father and have no plans to compromise your integrity, I promise, but since neither of us wants the other to sleep on the couch..." Nalick trailed off. His hand found its way around her waist as he talked.

"I suppose," Leila began, but stopped, as she couldn't believe she was actually considering his compromise. Nalick waited for her to finish. "We're going to be married in a few months, so my parents won't take it as a sign of disrespect, but..." She didn't find the words to argue with Nalick. Nalick gently leaned over and kissed her forehead.

"Good. Then it's settled. Goodnight," he said as he walked over to the opposite side of the bed, removed his shirt, and climbed under the covers. Leila was too tired to argue, and too shocked to respond with normal banter, so she also climbed into the bed. She shivered and pulled the covers around her body. Nalick moved slightly so that his body was close enough to keep her warm. Leila's shiver wasn't just from the cold. She felt her eyes get heavy and thankfully sleep came before her heart had a chance to begin beating uncontrollably.

CHAPTER THIRTEEN

"**G**ood morning," Leila said, as Nalick entered the kitchen, the last to wake for the morning. She stood and offered him her chair. "Would you like coffee or tea?" Leila had woken up early in the morning, as usual, and lay in bed for over an hour watching Nalick sleep. She was surer about her feelings toward him, but still she was confused. He was still a puzzle to her. The gentle, kind man she saw when they were alone was a stark contrast to the king he was.

"Does this mean the Nalick stories will have to stop now?" Kay asked, disappointed.

"Tea," Nalick said to Leila. "What sort of stories?"

Theo turned away as he answered, "Oh, nothing much. We were just answering their questions."

Nalick looked to Leila to see if she would give him any clues to what they had been saying, but her lips were also sealed. Leila brought over his tea along with the basket of muffins. "I have to get my chores done," she said to the men. "Kay will keep you company."

While dreading time alone with Selma, after chores with her mother, and getting questioned about Nalick, Leila was relieved. She felt like she had passed the first test of getting her mother to trust her in her decision. Next, Leila would need to work on gaining her father's trust. She finished hanging up all the clothes she had washed and followed her mother back into the house. Once inside, Leila could hear more people in the kitchen talking. To her surprise, she found Nalick sitting with not just Theo and Macarius, but also her brothers Nael and Leon, and her father, Dirk.

"That's my girl," she heard her father say as she entered.

"What did I do now?" Leila asked. All five of the men turned to look at her. Everyone was smiling and getting along, which surprised Leila.

"Oh, we were just telling your brothers and father about how you escaped the jail and then asked to be put back in," Theo explained.

"You know your guards are not very efficient," Leila said to Nalick, casually putting a hand on his shoulder. "I did have to wait over an hour to be let back in." The men all laughed.

"Hello, Papa." She greeted her father with a hug and a kiss.

"So how was your trip?" Dirk asked, while hugging her back. "Besides finding a husband." He winked at her. Leila quickly turned to Nalick, who just smiled.

"It was fine. I ran into a bit of trouble with Kay, but it all got sorted out. She was able to finish the assignment," Leila said, while sitting between her father and Nalick.

"So, when will you be heading back to Lexia?" Dirk asked.

"I figure we better head back tomorrow. I don't want to worry everyone if they find out their king is gone," Leila explained.

"Well then, you better get busy and show this man around," her father suggested. "There are still some daylight hours left."

"But you just got home," she complained, wanting to stay and visit with her father.

"I'm not going anywhere. We can catch up after it gets dark out," Dirk said. He pushed her to stand back up.

"Fine, but you better not go off anywhere. This way," she said, standing up and directing the three guys, but

Theo and Macarius remained seated.

"We'll stay here," Theo offered.

Leila and Nalick bundled up in fur-lined coats and boots. For hours, Leila walked around their village, hand-in-hand, with Nalick. He listened intently as she talked about various buildings, homes, and people. As their tour finished and they returned to her parents' home, Leila grew quiet again.

"Could we sit out here for a bit?" he asked. Leila was happy he had asked because she thought it would sound silly if she had asked to stay outside rather than visit with her family.

Leila led Nalick over to a bench beside the house and wiped the snow off the seat before sitting down. Their backs were protected from the cold wind. The snow had stopped falling and the yard and trees were covered. As the sun had already started to set, the world outside her home looked magical as everything was coated white while sparkling. As a child, she had always waited for the moments when she could pretend she was in another world. In a way, her dream was coming true, Lexia indeed felt like another world.

"I'm having a hard time understanding you. You seem to be happy here, so part of me wants to just let you stay, but then you say you want to return to Lexia. If you only want to return because of our deal..." Nalick picked up her mitten-clad hands and stared straight into her eyes. "I'll leave with Theo and Macarius, and you can stay here."

Without breaking his gaze Leila asked, "Do you love me?"

Nalick tried to turn his head away before responding, but Leila slipped off her gloves and quickly caught the side of his face to hold it facing her. "Yes," Nalick replied, looking down quickly after answering.

Leila smiled at him kindly. "Then I'll return with you

to Lexia."

"What was Erich like? You don't mention him and seem to cringe anytime someone else does," Nalick asked about the one man who had once won her heart.

Leila leaned back against the house and closed her eyes. "I was fifteen when he asked me to marry him, and at that point, I didn't think life could get any better. I fell in love with him years after I met him, but he always told me he loved me the moment I followed him home. Within months of telling everyone we were going to get married, I messed up an assignment in Samael. I panicked, and I signaled to Erich. Erich got me out, but he was cut by a poisoned blade in the process. I brought him back to Roger, but there was nothing he could do. Instead, we both sat with Erich and watched him die. He was the first and only man I ever truly loved, and yet, there was nothing I could do to help him." Leila involuntarily reached up and felt the ring that was hanging on the necklace beneath her shirt.

She opened her eyes and looked at Nalick, who was watching her. "Erich was a good man, and his life was cut short because of me. I've spent the last years training and taking on every hard assignment so that I could get better at my job. I never want to be the cause of someone getting hurt again. Part of me died that day with him."

"Did you love him?" Nalick asked.

"Yes, very much so," Leila replied. "Will you still want to marry me, even if I don't love you back?" she wondered. "I just don't know if I can ever love again."

"I'm willing to wait. I truly believe you will love me some day. If we don't get married in three months, then so be it," Nalick tried to reassure her. "When I looked into your eyes that day we met in the woods, I saw what I always have felt: loneliness. I no longer feel it." Nalick removed his gloves and gently took her hands in his. "I'm willing to do anything for you, even if it means somehow explaining to the priests that you aren't ready to marry." Nalick thought for a moment. "Do you at least not hate me?"

Leila laughed. "I don't think I ever hated you."

"But you were quite mad with me the day that you agreed to stay," Nalick responded.

"Only because I felt like I was failing to protect Kay. I had tried so hard to get better and the one time I was put to the test to see if I was better; I was failing," Leila tried to explain. It was freezing out, but she didn't want to take her hands out of his.

"Hopefully you will let me lighten your load a bit and help you protect everyone." Nalick causally put his arm around Leila. She rested her head on his shoulder and smiled. It had been a long time since she trusted someone. Nalick was wearing down the barrier she kept around herself. They sat together in silence. By the time they both realized they were quite cold, they had to sneak back in the house, as almost everyone had gone to bed. Nalick and Leila stopped briefly to talk to her parents.

With night settling in, everyone remaining rose to go to bed. Leila and Nalick returned to her room and she lay down quickly and closed her eyes. Quietly, Nalick joined her. Leila wasn't asleep, but because she was not opening her eyes, he played along. Nalick took his time getting into bed while studying her face.

He could vaguely see the crease in her right cheek where she got a dimple when she smiled. Her light skin was periodically speckled with freckles. Leila was the most beautiful woman he had ever met, and she was by far the most unique. With her red hair and eyebrows, she was much different than the dark-haired women of Lior. Even her odd green eyes captivated him. Her eyes told a story, and revealed her mood. He had caught himself wondering what thoughts were going on behind those eyes many times over the past few days. As she lay with her eyes shut, Nalick still wondered about her.

Nalick gently leaned forward and kissed her forehead. He whispered quietly, "Thank you for bringing me to see your home."

Leila didn't respond. She was still awake, but didn't know what to say to him. In the quiet of the room, if Leila opened her eyes she would not be able to hide the way she felt.

CHAPTER FOURTEEN

After brief good-bye, Leila escorted the three men back to the port of Cath. Once on Nalick's ship with the army escort, it took two days to make it home to Lexia. By the time they reached the palace, Leila had spent three straight days traveling. She was very tired and couldn't wait to just relax a bit and catch up on her sleep. Being royalty did have a few benefits. Nalick, however, didn't have time to sleep and relax. Nalick had been away from Lexia for almost a week, and out of Lior for several days. His country needed his guidance.

Late in the evening, after being back in Lexia for two days, Nalick finally found time to talk to Leila alone. He quietly entered her room and could see she was on the balcony where he had been told she spent most of her time. Time spent either on the balcony of her room or in the garden below helped remind Leila that she wasn't trapped in the palace. Nalick approached her cautiously. It had been several days. Though he felt they had been moving forward with their relationship in the North Country, everything was halted back in Lior now that he was gone all the time. Leila heard the footsteps behind her but didn't turn around.

"Finally got away from your work?" Leila asked.

"I've been trying for days to get away, but there's always something to get done." Nalick walked around the bench Leila was sitting on. She moved to make room for him, and he sat down beside her. "It seems Lior's ally, King Endika, wants to make a formal visit to congratulate me on my upcoming wedding." Nalick watched Leila's expression as she laughed a bit to herself.

How nice, she thought sarcastically, but held her tongue from saying it.

"That, or he just wants to see if the rumors are true," Leila replied, when he took her hand in his.

"So you have met him before," Nalick guessed, gazing over the city with her.

"If you're referring to the diminutive man that couldn't actually even beat a girl in any sort of competition, then *yes.* I've met him before. Personally, I wondered how he could really be king, but I didn't wonder why he wasn't married," Leila responded as Nalick laughed. They agreed on most things, including King Endika.

"Since he's an ally, we've been trying our best to arrange everything. He will be here tomorrow, and there will be a feast in his honor. He has requested lunch with us and a few of the noble families for the next day," Nalick explained, waiting for her to pull away. Instead she leaned into the arm that he had snuck around her shoulder.

"Since he's an ally, does that mean I have to be nice to him?" Leila questioned. Nalick smiled and nodded his head. Leila gave Nalick a disappointed expression.

"And the nobles, too?" Leila pushed her luck. Nalick nodded again.

"Is it wise to be having foreign kings visiting?" Leila asked, changing the subject. "Will he not be traveling with a substantial army?"

Nalick nodded, "*Yes,* but it's also not wise to rebuke a foreign king who wishes to visit, especially since he's an ally. Besides, the main force of our army is here in Lexia and will be in any city you're at from now on."

"I doubt that will do any good for Jahangir." Leila cringed at the thought of that man. Nalick pulled her closer, hoping to emphasize that he would always keep her safe. Leila felt the security in his arms, but was still horrified at the thought of the man.

"My reports so far have indicated that he's back in his castle, sulking at being deceived by you again. Our spies in all the other countries also say so far there's no threat to you," Nalick tried to reassure Leila.

"Do they know about Jahangir's newest plans?" Leila asked. Nalick raised his eyebrows. Roger would keep Leila informed, but Nalick didn't know that she had already met one of her courier contacts since they had been back.

"My report was that he has sent his best spies and couriers into Lexia to look for an opportunity to get his hands on me." Nalick looked a bit alarmed at her statement. "Don't worry. Seth would need to bring more men with him than he currently has to get anywhere near the palace. Anatolio has done a good job securing the palace." Nalick seemed to be a bit more relieved. "So what time tomorrow will the dinner be?"

"Just past sunset," Nalick replied. Leila leaned against Nalick as she relaxed and looked into the sky. Feeling his skin touch hers made her heart race, but also comforted her at the same time. Though she had two days of leisure, it had been a bit lonely without Nalick to tease. "Do you regret coming back?" Nalick asked, more somberly.

"Not at all," Leila replied, scanning the sky for familiar constellations.

Nalick was relived.

"It has been a bit lonely, but Macarius, Theo, and Anatolio all try their best to keep me company." Leila didn't look to Nalick to see his response. He was just as unhappy as she was about his job taking so much time. Most of her assignments over the year had been alone, so she was used to it by now. It was just after she had been home at her parents', where there was always commotion; it was a bit lonesome to then be by herself. The quietness that followed her around the palace made her feel a bit isolated.

"I know," Nalick said, stroking her hair. Leila tried to hide her heavy breathing as her head tingled every place he touched. "I really wish I could spend more time with you. After I get everything back in order, it should be better," he reassured her.

Leila continued to rest her head on his shoulder. "Can you at least stay a little bit now?"

"Of course. Anything for my queen," Nalick replied. Leila closed her eyes. Though she had been resting for several days, she was still a bit tired from everything. She had been on assignment for two weeks in Lexia before the whirlwind of motion from agreeing to marry Nalick had begun. She never slept well in new places, but sitting in Nalick's arms made her feel safe while she slowly drifted off to sleep.

The next morning, Leila awoke alone in her bed. It was early enough that Mauve hadn't yet woken. She quickly dressed and hurried to leave before Mauve found her. Leila didn't enjoy the demands placed on her, making her get ready for the formal meals that were planned for the upcoming evening. Leila quickly grabbed a letter from the table and hurried silently out the door of her room. As she passed the surprised guards at the bottom of the stairwell, she found Anatolio waiting for her. He smiled as he yawned to greet her.

"Up a little earlier than normal," Anatolio commented.

"I was hoping to escape. If Mauve found me, I'd have been stuck all day in that room." Leila led the way to the palace garden. As they neared, Anatolio signaled to several guards to better watch the passageways around the open aired room. They were in the middle of the palace, which wasn't an easy place for intruders to enter, but Anatolio worried anyways. Once in the garden, Anatolio climbed his normal tree as Leila walked over to the largest patch of grass and sat down. She opened the letter from Nalick and smiled as she read it.

As Leila read, another person entered the garden. As she had done each of the previous days, the young woman would enter and sit on the opposite side of the foliage. Each day the woman moved closer and closer. Leila could tell she wanted to approach her, but the young woman was a bit hesitant. This day she was much closer. Leila stopped reading and looked up at her. The girl quickly looked away. Slowly, Leila was winning over the shy girl. The girl hadn't said more than a couple words to Leila, but each day she was closer.

Suddenly one of the doors opened. Anatolio quickly jumped down from the tree, startling the shy young girl Emma, who didn't know he was nearby. Mauve walked in with two of the maids following her.

"Miss Leila, you're a difficult person to find," Mauve scolded. Anatolio relaxed as she approached. "You weren't supposed to wander off this morning. We need all day to get you ready for tonight."

Leila's freedom was short-lived and she spent the rest of the day in her room being prepped for the dinner that night. Everything was tedious and silly. Leila didn't understand why she had to be so presentable to a bunch of people who hated her anyways. Mauve, on the other hand, felt it was even more important to make Leila look her best for the nobles because they all disliked her. Mauve fussed for hours over every little detail; by the time she was finally satisfied, Leila was ready to call it a night. Nalick waited for her to finish since Leila needed to make, at least, an appearance. Leila took Nalick's outstretched hand, and walked with him to the entertainment hall. Nalick was happy to see Leila, but part of him worried about King Endika meeting her.

"Could we just possibly get lost and make a wrong turn?" Leila asked, as Nalick shook his head *no*. He stopped before they entered.

"This is the one part of the job I also dislike," he told her. She smiled to know that he didn't like meeting with foreign kings either. "I know the nobles aren't happy about the situation, but they'll just have to get over it. And Endika will just be Endika, an ally we appease to keep our borders safe." Leila liked his resolve.

Nalick raised his right arm, and Leila placed her left arm on top of his as he led her into the room. The room was filled with people. Leila recognized many of the faces as nobles who lived in the palace. Other faces she remembered from the day she was presented by the priests. Leila tried not to giggle as everyone bowed and greeted them; some found it more painful than others to bow to her. Leila scanned the crowd to see if Endika was there. Seated at the head table was the man she remembered. Nalick led Leila reluctantly to Endika and introduced her, though it was not necessary.

"King Endika," Nalick said, while shaking the smaller man's hand. Leila tried to cover her laugh with a cough. Endika was literally half the man Nalick was in every way. Next to Nalick, Endika looked like a child, an older-looking, bearded, child. He was half Nalick's height, and shorter than Leila. He had a full beard to try to make himself look older, but she always felt he looked like a small child playing dress-up. "This is my future bride, Queen Eia," Nalick introduced Leila as the diminutive man took her hand and kissed it.

"My, you seem so familiar, as if I've met you before," Endika added, while ogling her, trying to get a response. Leila quickly took back her hand. Endika made her feel disgusted.

"I get that a lot," Leila replied.

Endika continued to stare at her. He was just the same as all the other kings Leila had met over the years. His stares made her feel like a prize that someone could win at the faire. She was glad to have Nalick seated between her and the creepy man. She was trying her best to not say what she was really thinking. Nalick quietly tried to thank her, but Leila would not let him. Nalick turned to his guest, and they began to talk. After the meal, the entertainment started and Leila used it as an opportunity to go onto the balcony. As she stood, Nalick turned to her. She leaned down next to him, balancing herself with her hands on his shoulders.

"I'm just going onto the balcony for fresh air," Leila explained, as Endika continued to eye her up and down. Nalick nodded, and Anatolio, who was standing behind Leila, followed her out onto the balcony.

"Is everything all right?" Anatolio asked.

"That man just gets to me with all his staring, not that these dresses leave much to the imagination," Leila explained, gesturing to her dress. Anatolio gazed back across the room and stared at the other king. Anatolio gently moved Leila to the left of the balcony and undid one of the curtains.

"Is that better?" Anatolio asked.

Leila turned to see that she was out of view of Endika while still being in sight of Nalick. She smiled at the young man standing with her.

"Yes." She leaned on the rail of the balcony. She was sure Anatolio wasn't a noble and she had watched the glares he often received from everyone in the past few days. "Do these people ever get to you?"

"No. It has been like this my whole life. I'm used to it," Anatolio explained, keeping a distance between them.

"I've not read about you," she said to him.

"But I have about you," the young man replied, leaning against the rail next to her.

"Why did you take this job?" she asked. "If they have always treated you like they treat me, why would you purposely want to work in the palace?"

"I was offered this, and I really couldn't come up with

any reason to turn down being able to work so close to a legend. I hoped that maybe by being so close to you, something might rub off and make me a better tracker," Anatolio replied. Leila smiled at the young man, who was finally opening up a bit.

"I don't think I'll let you learn all my secrets," Leila teased. The young man chuckled while tossing his blond hair out of his face.

"Just a few will be better than none," Anatolio replied. "Let's not worry Nalick any longer." Anatolio escorted Leila back to Nalick's side, and she sat down next to him. Endika had left his seat to mingle with the nobles.

"Is your wonderful friend already tired? It must be past his bedtime by now," Leila said, referring to Endika.

"I thought you promised to be nice?" Nalick replied, putting his arm on the back of her chair.

"I'll be nice, if he returns. Little Endiki must be tired, being up so late," Leila responded, and Nalick had to suppress a laugh. "Besides, it's very hard to be nice to such a creep." She was doing her best not to tell the other king how she felt.

Leila watched as the nobles huddled in groups. She could tell which families were allied, and which were not. On the dance floor, Leila watched Endika dancing with Lady Maclen, mother of her soon-to-be new friend Emma. In the corner of the room, Leila could see the sad face of Emma. Glancing to the area where Emma was looking, Leila could see a young man with his parents. Leila was wondering who the man was, but her gaze returned to Endika. Something about him being so familiar with Lady Maclen made Leila's stomach churn. After the song finished, Endika approached the head table in front of Leila.

"I was wondering if you'd be so kind as to dance with me," Endika asked Leila.

Leila smiled politely. "I'm sorry, but I'm so exhausted

from our recent trip to meet my family. With Nalick's permission, I was just going to head to bed." *I would not touch you with a ten-foot stick,* she thought. Asking her to dance with King Endika was stretching the amount of nice she had already shown, so Nalick nodded as she stood to leave.

"Will you be up later?" she asked Nalick.

"Of course," Nalick replied. He had checked in on her before he went to bed each night. He assumed she had been asleep, but as always, she seemed to know more than she ever let on. Leila was only now making it obvious to irritate their guest. Leila smiled at the hint of jealousy that crossed Endika's face. To add to it, Leila leaned over and kissed Nalick's cheek.

"Good night, my king," Leila said before leaving. Nalick grinned as he watched her leave. The sparkle in her eyes made him want to follow, but he needed to stay with his guest. Trying to hide his grin from her blatant actions to make Endika jealous, Nalick resumed his conversation while watching Leila move across the room and out the doors.

Leila returned to her room. Anatolio, as he always did, checked the room thoroughly before he bid her goodnight. After shutting the door, she carefully removed the jewelry around her neck and arms. Underneath her dress, she felt the necklace she refused to remove. On it was the ring Erich had given her the day he had proposed. Leila sat down on the edge of her bed and started to remove her hair clips, thinking of him. *What would Erich look like now if he was still alive? Where would we be living? Would we still be running assignments for Roger, or would we have started a family by now?* Dozens of unanswered questions ran through her head. Leila was unsure how to feel; she was beginning to have feelings for Nalick, but part of her felt she was betraying Erich's memory.

After Leila removed all the hair clips and jewelry, she could let her hair down. What took hours to do was undone in a matter of minutes. Leila closed her eyes, though she wasn't ready to go to sleep. As she tried to stop her racing thoughts, she pictured Erich. Erich was taller than her, and much less muscular than Nalick. He had scraggly, dark blond hair that was always getting in his eyes. Though Leila's job required her to blend in and be similar to the people around her, Erich always told her that her greatest asset was that she was different in looks and mind than everyone. Her ability to befriend and build the trust of people around her made her a better person than anyone he had ever met. Erich convinced the young, scared Leila that she could make her life into anything she desired; she just needed to decide what she wanted. Leila tried to remember Erich's smile, but the image that came to her head was the painful smile; the one of the man she loved, who asked her to promise him, as he lay dying, that she would never give up on love. Erich had known all along that one day she would meet Nalick, and if she were to give him a chance, she could learn to love him. Leila had Erich's blessing all along to marry Nalick.

Leila opened her eyes and stared at the ceiling. If Leila threw herself into assignments and didn't slow down, she didn't have to admit that he was really dead. Now, she had time for leisure and could actually think about it. It just hurt to finally admit to herself that Erich wasn't coming back. As Leila lay on her bed, it hit her. Erich really was gone and never coming back. Carefully, she wiped her tears and sat up. She needed to get her mind off of Erich, so she walked out to the balcony and sat down. The stars normally calmed her heart, but not tonight. Leila found no comfort in the familiar stars. She returned to the bed and lay down. Leila wasn't tired, but sleeping was the only way she figured she would feel better.

Later that night, Nalick returned to say goodnight to Leila after everyone had left. She was already tucked into her bed. When she had left the dinner, Leila had been her normal, challenging self. He gently smoothed her hair away from her face. The chain around her neck was outside her shirt. He could now see the ring. As Nalick studied her ring, Leila opened her eyes. "Everything is done for tonight?" Leila asked, sleepily rubbing her eyes.

"Sorry, did I wake you?" Nalick asked back, looking up from the ring.

"I tried to wait up for you, but I must have fallen asleep." Leila sat up and noticed she was under the covers. "What time is it?"

"Late," Nalick replied. "I think Endika was trying his best to keep me there so that I couldn't come up here to you. You did quite a good job of rubbing it in his face that you're staying here with me." Nalick smiled as Leila feigned an innocent look.

"Did I really do that? He must have just misunderstood." Leila chuckled.

"Are you okay?" Nalick asked, changing the subject. Leila didn't understand, and he gently rubbed the dried tearstains on her face. Leila blushed.

"Oh, that was nothing. I was just a little sad," Leila replied, finally noticing that Nalick was sitting very close to her. Her heart, for once, wasn't racing like mad while he studied her. It somehow felt different, somewhat comforting, to have him so close while she felt so sad. She looked up into his eyes and could tell that her crying wasn't "nothing" to him. "Really," she said, trying to convince him. Nalick picked up her hand and held it next to his face. He gently kissed the palm. Leila shivered as the faint touching of his lips to her hand sent goose bumps down her arms.

"I'll do anything for you to be happy," Nalick said.

Gently he touched her cheek. His hand drifted down and touched her necklace. "It's from Erich," he guessed. Leila nodded without looking into Nalick's eyes. Nalick gently raised her face to look at him. "I'd never try to replace him. I want you to know that." Nalick understood why she had been crying, and he wasn't jealous or angry. He leaned closer and gently kissed her forehead as he had done each night since they returned. "Goodnight, my queen."

Nalick stood to leave, but Leila grabbed his arm, startling him. The sadness she felt was quickly returning the farther away he got from her. Leila didn't want to be alone. The moment she was alone again, she would begin crying. Nalick was surprised that she stopped him from leaving.

"Please stay," Leila begged softly, her self-assurance gone. Nalick sat back down. "Not just until I fall back asleep." She was asking him to stay the night. "I know Mauve will be upset, but I just don't want to be alone. Besides, she'll only be upset with you," Leila joked, but Nalick knew it was true. He hesitated, but the look in Leila's eyes told him she needed him to stay there with her.

Slowly dropping his shirt and shoes on the ground, Nalick moved around to the opposite side of the bed and lay down next to her. She turned to face him and smiled.

"Thank you," she said.

Nalick tenderly stroked her hair as she laid and stared at him. Her expression of sadness changed. As she looked into his eyes, Leila didn't feel like crying anymore. Nalick had never been in love before, but he knew that what he felt inside was just that. He repositioned himself to lie on his back and Leila moved closer to lay her head on his chest. Nalick smiled and kissed her head. Leila felt safe with his arms around her; slowly, she drifted back off to sleep.

CHAPTER FIFTEEN

In the morning, Leila woke to find she was still sleeping on Nalick's chest. Without opening her eyes, Leila felt the muscular man beneath her hands. She wasn't dreaming. Nalick had stayed the night. She rubbed her hands down to the thick arm that was now her pillow. He was a warrior king, and it showed through his well-defined muscles. Rubbing her hands back across his bare chest, she couldn't help but smile. He was actually hers. She slowly lifted her head. Nalick was already awake. She smiled at him. He was happy. Cautiously, she looked around the room for Mauve.

"Don't worry," Nalick replied. "She's already stopped by this morning. I'm in for a good scolding. Yes, you're not getting in trouble. Just me."

Leila grinned. Getting a king into trouble was a funny thought.

Leila moved so that her face was just inches from his. It was now Nalick's turn to feel his heartbeat race in her presence.

"Thank you for staying," Leila said quietly. "I just was a bit sad last night, but somehow you make me feel better. Thank you."

Nalick cautiously moved closer and pressed his mouth to hers. Leila felt his soft lips graze hers and then move more passionately. Leila didn't back away, as he thought she would, but instead returned the kiss. More than ever, Leila wanted to be close to him. She had spent days denying the feelings she had for him, but now she was too exposed to keep lying to herself, or to Nalick. Her head was spinning, and she felt like she would tip over, but she remained leaning halfway on top of him. Inside his chest, Nalick's heart raced at an unbelievable pace. Casually as possible, Nalick's hand moved down her back and traced the outline of her thin figure. Nalick's hands had made it down to the scar on her hip and paused. Both wanted to savor the moment of their first real kiss.

"Young man, come this way," Mauve ordered, ending the moment. Though Nalick didn't want to let go of Leila, he reluctantly followed Mauve. Leila smiled and watched across the room, where Mauve was scolding Nalick. After Mauve was done yelling at him, she pushed him out the door and returned to Leila. Leila watched Nalick unwillingly leave the room. "We need to get you ready for your lunch today," Mauve said cheerily, with a completely changed attitude.

"Mauve," Leila said hesitantly. "Why did you yell at Nalick? Is this not his palace?"

"Yes, but he should have better manners. He was raised to be a good kid," Mauve explained.

"He's a good man," Leila replied. "I asked him to stay."

Mauve seemed shocked.

"I was lonely last night, and didn't want to be alone," Leila continued.

"Oh child." Mauve tried to comfort Leila. "I know you're far from home."

"Then why can't Nalick stay here with me?" Leila wondered.

"He has promised the priests he won't let anything happen that will tarnish your honor before your wedding, and he's a hot-blooded boy, so...," Mauve wouldn't say directly what she meant, but Leila understood.

"That wasn't what was happening," Leila quickly replied, trying to stop the blush from forming. "He was just keeping me company."

Mauve wasn't completely convinced because of the kiss she saw shared between the two of them. She continued to dress Leila in silence as two of the girls were fixing her hair. Leila wasn't excited to again be seeing Endika, but at least she was happy he would be leaving soon.

Nalick waited outside her room as Theo came in to fetch her.

"Are we back to this now? Doesn't he want me to join him?" she asked Theo.

"Yes, he would like you to join him, but Mauve has told him that he's not allowed in this room unless you two are supervised," Theo explained, while giving her a questioning look. "And I guess I don't count."

Leila rolled her eyes. "It was only a kiss," she complained, and she followed Theo out to the hall to meet with Nalick. Leila laughed when he really waited in the hallway. Mauve seemed to be the one person that could order the king around. "So, here is the bad boy," she teased, leaning against him to mock Mauve pulling on his ear. Nalick replied by scooping her into his arms.

"Thanks for not helping me," Nalick grumbled. Leila playfully protested being picked up.

"No problem. It's fun to watch her yell at you," Leila said. Nalick set her down and she took his hand.

"So does that mean you won't be staying with me again tonight?" Leila smiled as she teased him. Nalick was surprised that she would even offer. He searched her face, afraid that she might still be sad, but he could see no signs from the night before.

Leila entered the hall she had been in the night before, and noticed immediately that the room had been rearranged. There was now one, single, long table in the room. Several couples were already seated there. Endika sat across from two empty seats at the one end of the table. Leila was happy to see that she would not be sitting next to Endika, and thought it would be easier to eat, but then she realized she was to be seated directly across from him. Leila cringed, and Nalick could see the reason why. He leaned over and whispered in her ear.

"I'm willing to bear the wrath of Mauve if you can find it in your heart to behave just one more day, and then he will be on his way home," Nalick said quietly.

"He saw what he wanted to see, so why can't he leave right now? I'm even willing to help boot his butt out of the palace," Leila replied.

"Please be nice," he whispered.

"So are you willing to break Mauve's new rules?" Leila asked.

Nalick nodded in response. Leila felt she was getting the better end of the deal, so she nicely greeted Endika and sat across from him.

Next to Leila sat Lord and Lady Maclen. Neither of them acknowledged Leila but both bowed their heads toward Nalick. Nalick controlled his anger toward his nobles as well as Leila controlled her disgust with Endika. Leila studied her drink and listened to the conversations around her since the nobility assumed she didn't speak their language. The Maclens were very amoral people who seemed to be very upset that Nalick would not marry a local girl. Others were just disgusted that a common person was sharing their table.

The food was served, and the conversations died down a bit. Leila recognized the slightly bitter taste in her drink at her first sip. It was poison. She decided to play along, since it wouldn't affect her, and she carefully scanned the people eating with her as she took another sip. Lady and Lord Maclen were doing their best not to watch her, but they both kept checking her.

"Don't change the expression on your face," Leila whispered, and Nalick nodded his head. "I'm going to get up and leave and just tell everyone I'm feeling tired. Tell

Anatolio to follow me, but stay out of view." Nalick didn't understand what Leila was doing. Suspiciously, Nalick eyed the guests as his table.

Leila slowly walked down the hallway leading back to the royal chambers. Along the way, two young men greeted her. Pretending that she was getting tired, she yawned as she greeted them back.

"Would you like us to walk you to your room, my queen?" one offered.

"That would be so nice," Leila said, taking the arm the one boy offered her. As Leila walked, she pretended to be falling asleep. When she began keeping her eyes closed for longer periods of time, the two men began to lead her away from her room. The men were leading her to the stables. When they thought she was asleep they put a plain dress over the top of the one she was wearing, and covered her hair with a scarf.

"Hurry up. They'll soon notice she's gone, and then we won't get her out of here," one complained. Leila felt them lift her on to a cart and place a blanket around her.

"Come on," the other said. "Once we make the trade, we can come back, and no one will notice."

Leila felt the horses move, and knew she was being pulled on a cart. She opened her eyes just a slit to observe the situation. They were pulling the cart to one of the gates. As they stopped, Leila closed her eyes quickly.

"Hi Mica. Hi Nell," a guard spoke. "What are you two up to today?"

"One of our maids got sick and we're taking her home," the first said. Leila heard the guard walk around to look into the cart before he let the boys leave. The cart moved on into the city. Leila calculated where they were in the city in her mental map. They stopped at another gate. This time, though, no one checked the cart, and just let the two boys pass. Finally, the cart came to a stop outside the city, and she could hear Mica and Nell arguing.

"We need to take a left here," one said.

"No, I think we missed it. We should have taken a left back there," the other replied.

Leila slowly got out of the cart. As she approached the front of the wagon, Leila could see the two young men were both standing on the ground, holding onto a map. They seemed to be lost and arguing over the directions. Leila looked around to see if Anatolio was near, but she couldn't see him. *Oh well*, she thought, *I'll just do this myself.* She quickly approached and disarmed the larger of the two boys and knocked him unconscious before turning to the other boy. He quickly surrendered. Leila then tied up the two boys and placed them on the ground in back of the the cart together.

"Who were you going to meet with?" Leila asked, but the boy seemed too scared to answer. "Then, let's try an easier question. What is your name?"

"Mica," the boy barely whispered.

"Then this must be Nell. What family do you belong to?" Leila asked.

The boy seemed scared to answer again. Leila walked over and pulled the back of his shirt to see the emblem on his back. It was the Maclen family. She then checked the unconscious boy, who had the same emblem. Leila walked back to the boy who was still awake.

"Who were you going to give me to?" Leila asked again.

"I don't know," Mica quickly answered. "Nell had the plans; I was just helping him. What are you going to do with us?" He was going to cry soon.

"For now, we're going to sit here until I get all the answers I want," Leila replied, walking back to Nell. She slapped his face a few times to wake him up. Groggily he opened his eyes. After he focused on Leila, he quickly tried to move, but he was tied up. The   n she saw the terror in his eyes as he realized he was caught.

"But you shouldn't be awake," Nell said.

"There are a lot of things I shouldn't be," Leila replied. "So the question for you is: who were you going to meet?" Leila repeated her question for the older boy.

She wasn't someone he wanted to lie to; he hesitantly answered, "His name is Marx. He offered us a lot of money if we transported you to him." Leila smiled. It had been almost a year since she had seen Marx. She was tempted to ask about the meeting point, but by now Nalick would be worried.

"Who drugged me back in the palace?" she asked, though she already knew her answer.

Both boys shook their heads. "If we tell you, then we will be killed by them," Nell explained.

"And what do you think Nalick will do with you?" Leila asked as the color drained from both the young men's faces. "Here's the deal, I will ask Nalick to spare your lives if you tell me who drugged my drink."

The boys looked at one another. "Our uncle came to us about everything, Lord Maclen. I think it was our Aunt, Lady Maclen, that was actually going to put the drug in your drink," Mica told her.

Leila smiled. Her assumption was correct. In the distance, Anatolio approached. Leila waved to him as she sat on the edge of the cart. "About time," she called to him. "I figured I was going to have to wait all day for you to join us." Anatolio began to protest, but the smile on Leila's face made him stop.

"So these two boys figured they could kidnap you?" Anatolio questioned.

"Yep, but, as you can see, we didn't get too far before they got lost." Leila smiled as she replied. "We better get back. I didn't have time to explain anything to Nalick, and I am sure he's worried by now."

"Or furious," Anatolio suggested, looking at the terrified faces on the two boys.

Anatolio helped Leila into the cart before hoisting up the two boys like sacks of potatoes. Leila and Anatolio quickly took the cart back to the city. Leila immediately went to Nalick's office, sure she would find a worried king waiting for her there. As soon as Leila entered, Nalick quickly hugged her and checked her over for damage.

"What is going on?" Nalick asked worriedly. "You said you were going back to your room, but when I checked, you hadn't made it there. Anatolio left a message at the gate saying he was leaving the palace."

"I've had a nice ride through the country today, due to Lady and Lord Maclen," Leila explained, seeing the anger building in Nalick's eyes. "I asked the two boys, and they said they were to meet a man named Marx. I was tempted to go meet him, but I came back instead. I've not seen Marx in a long time. The last I heard he was working for Endika. Marx is an old courier friend."

"So they were trying to take you to Endika?" Nalick asked.

"Probably, though Marx wouldn't have followed through with it," Leila replied, watching Nalick continue to pace around the room. She quietly sat on the top of his desk and just watched him. The anger continued to grow within him. Suddenly he stopped and turned to Leila. His expression completely changed as he stared at her.

"Why are you okay?" Nalick asked, finally realizing that Leila had been drugged. "You don't seem to be affected by the poison, nor are you mad for being poisoned."

"Courier, remember? I knew immediately what drug it was. There's only one drug out there that will put me to sleep, and Roger is the only person that has it. Also, these boys weren't a threat. They really are quite harmless. I didn't even break a sweat tying up both of them. My problem is that you have people in your own court that were willing to do such a thing," Leila explained. "How am I supposed to stay safe if your own court is willing to sell me out?"

Nalick moved closer to Leila and wrapped his arms around her. "Please, next time tell me what's going on. I was so worried." Nalick took a deep breath before kissing the top of her head.

Leila smiled up at him. "There was no need to worry. I had it all under control." Nalick understood Leila was capable of protecting herself, but he still wanted to be the one to shield her. Gently, he kissed her forehead again. Leila reached up to his face to continue what they had started in the morning, but they were interrupted once again.

There was a soft knock on the door and Theo stuck his head in the room. "Nalick, everyone is assembled in the judgment hall."

"Is Anatolio still out there?" Nalick asked, reluctantly moving to the door.

"Yes," Theo replied.

"How will you punish them?" Leila asked, knowing that Nalick wasn't kind when it came to handing out punishments.

Nalick wanted to explain, but Leila didn't want to hear how they would actually be punished. Her heart was too pure to deal with the reality of running a kingdom.

"Please give both boys a break, and their daughter, Emma, too. I know she wasn't involved," Leila asked. Nalick gazed into her eyes and wasn't able to refuse her.

Nalick put his arm around Leila as he escorted her out the door. "As you wish," he replied. As they approached the door to the judgment chamber, Nalick stopped. "This isn't something I want you involved in, ever. I don't want this to weigh on you, so please stay here with Anatolio."

She understood. She also didn't really want to know what would happen to everyone.

"I want to first talk to the court, and then I might need for you to come in for a minute. But that will be it," he explained.

Leila watched as the doors were opened before Nalick. The room where she had first met him was now packed full of people. The court all stood and bowed to the entering king. The doors shut, and Leila was left to wait. She couldn't make out the words, but from the tone, Nalick wasn't in a good mood. He was now the man everyone feared. Down the hallway next to the room, Theo appeared from a side doorway. Theo motioned for Leila to come over to him.

"Nalick will need you to join him for one minute." Theo escorted Leila to the side door. Anatolio waited outside the door for Leila to enter behind Theo. Theo led her past the first row of people, and everyone sat motionless as she entered. The steely stare Nalick gave the room changed when he saw Leila. Leila walked over and took Nalick's outstretched hand. Again, like the first day she was presented to the nobles, Leila could feel their cold stares as she stood before them.

"May I?" Nalick asked, lightly tugging her sleeve. Leila stretched out her left arm for him as he gently rolled her sleeve back. Leila could hear a gasp that started from the front row and the whispers proceeded to the back of the room. Nalick gently placed her arm on his and turned to the crowd. "We predicted that we might encounter problems with other kingdoms wanting Queen Eia. So, the priests decided that she would join the royal family not as a princess, but as queen." Leila did not understand, but it wasn't the time to ask. "Thank you," he said to Leila, softly kissing her cheek before Theo returned to her side to escort her back out of the room. Leila turned one last time before she left the room to see the hardened stare of Nalick as he stood opposite of the Maclens.

Once outside the room, Leila walked back to Anatolio. "What did Nalick mean that I'm already queen?"

Anatolio nodded his head and replied, "Oh, so you finally found out?" Leila stared at him, waiting for him to explain. Anatolio tried to usher her back to her room, but she stood waiting with her hands on her hips.

"Nalick was worried when you said yes to marry him that other countries might try to claim you in the time before the wedding. Lior has many peace treaties that are very unstable and rest on the exchange of noble family members. Nalick thought that if you were given the title of princess, other countries might rightfully ask for your hand in marriage. So, he asked the priests to make you the queen."

"But how did everyone in the room not know that until now?" Leila asked.

"See, when a royal son comes of age, about age twelve to fourteen, they get a marking on their hand; the same marking as the one you have. The same goes when the bride is chosen for a royal son. The difference is that when one becomes king or queen, the lines are extended. When you're just a prince or princess the lines end at the wrist. Because your lines continue up your arm, you are not a princess, but a queen." Anatolio looked to see if she understood. He laughed to see her shocked expression. Since he met her, nothing had seemed to shock her. Leila was the most experienced courier he had ever met, and yet she was only a few years older than him. Leila quickly pushed his right shoulder and tipped him off balance. Anatolio hadn't noticed he was leaning only on the edge on the wall behind him. Leila then laughed with him. Anatolio stared at Leila with admiration. Though she didn't understand the court customs, there was so much he hoped he could learn from her.

CHAPTER SIXTEEN

By the time everything had been settled and the paperwork signed, Nalick had returned to find Leila already asleep for the night. Leila awoke the next morning to find Nalick sneaking out of the bed next to her. He didn't want to face the wrath of Mauve, but he didn't know that Leila had already told Mauve that she had asked him to stay with her at nighttime. As soon as Nalick noticed that he woke her, he sat down next to her.

"Busy day starting already?" Leila asked while yawning. Nalick bent down and kissed her forehead.

"It hasn't slowed down since we returned, why should today be any different? A king's job is never done," Nalick replied. "I need to oversee advancement day for the military, and I need to pick two more personal guards for you when you leave the palace walls. It seems there's a high price on your head in many countries, and they now know where to find you."

"You know that's just being a bit excessive. I really can handle myself," Leila replied.

Nalick knew she could. From all the reports he had read about her, she was probably better than most of the men in his army; since she was a woman, most men would not take her seriously before it was too late. Anatolio had told Nalick how she handled the two young men the day before without even breaking a sweat.

"What will you be up to today?" Nalick asked.

Leila thought for a moment. "I don't know, since we finally got rid of Endika."

"Would you like to come with me?" he quickly asked.

Leila shrugged. "Sure," she replied. *Beats sitting around here*, she thought. Nalick was nervous, but happy to be spending more time with her.

Nalick escorted Leila to the training courtyard. It was already filled with men of various ages. Leila watched as a line of men were getting numbers painted onto their shoulders. Leila and Nalick stood together on a balcony that looped around three sides of the courtyard, giving them a view of the whole courtyard.

"I'll choose the top eight to spar with me tomorrow so that I can truly gauge how good they are," Nalick explained as Leila eyed him over. A normal king would never put himself in such danger of getting hurt. "Once I get everything going, I'll come back up here with you to watch."

Leila waved across the way on the balcony to Anatolio, who stood in the shadows. Catching her wave, Anatolio bowed his head to her. Leila sat on the edge of the balcony with her legs dangling over the side. She was happy to be outside and away from her room. The crowd of men broke up into smaller groups as they started to put on protective clothing. She smiled down at Nalick as he made his way through the crowd and back to the staircase. Leila remembered one of these events from a previous courier assignment.

Leila rested her chin on her arms that were draped across the railing. She had already scanned each group and had determined the winners of each matchup. To her left was a group of men with red numbers. One looked very familiar. When Leila gazed back across the way she could tell Anatolio was also carefully watching the same man fight. After everyone had fought once, Leila turned to Nalick, who was studying her as much as he was the soldiers below.

"Red fourteen, red twenty-six, and blue sixty-two are

the best," Leila said. "Though I doubt blue sixty-two will make it to lunch today." Nalick scanned the crowds below and found the man she was talking about. He watched as he was easily beat time and time again. As Nalick looked for the other numbers, he recognized the faces. They were already officers in the army, but they had entered anyway because Nalick was looking for more personal guards. Everyone in high-ranking positions was looking for a way to gain closer access to him in hopes of becoming an aide to the king.

"Why blue sixty-two?" Nalick asked.

"He's thinking too much. When he finally figures out how to just react rather than think, he will be better than most of the people that are down below," Leila explained. Her analysis was exactly correct.

"So what about you," Nalick said; she turned to him, giving him a questioning look. "Where would you fit down there?" Nalick was curious about all the combat reports on the ghost courier. Leila smiled coyly.

Nalick gazed down at all the men still fighting. "Which could you beat?"

"The list would be much shorter if I could name the ones that I might not be able to beat," Leila responded while turning to gauge each man again. Nalick grinned. He figured that much, but wanted to see how modest she would be. Leila caught his smile and asked, "So when you do this, you personally fight each of the top men? Have you ever been beaten?" She tried to turn the tables on him.

"Once or twice," he responded nonchalantly.

"Tomorrow should be interesting then," she replied. Watching the men below, her gaze stopped on number fourteen, the man who looked like Anatolio. His style was quite similar to Erich's, and Leila doubted she would be able to beat him, but the rest were less impressive.

Somewhere in the crowd below, a whistle was blown

to indicate it was lunchtime. Reluctantly, the soldiers quit fighting. Leila joined Nalick back in their room.

"What about the guy that I saw that looks like Anatolio?" Leila asked.

"That's his oldest half-brother, Nikias. He actually commands quite a large portion of the army already. I've a feeling he's here because he wants to have the additional post of watching over you. I'm sure that's why Pallas, another half-brother, is here also," Nalick explained.

"Nikias is very good," Leila said. "Anatolio acts like he has no family. He always seems to be following me, day or night."

"He has just his mother, who refuses to leave her job as a maid to one of the cities' nobles. So I gave him an apartment in the palace when I asked Anatolio to come work for me. His father's family, which includes his half-brothers, doesn't acknowledge him as being part of their family at all. Basically, he's an illegitimate child, and won't inherit any title or money from his father. That will all go to his half-brothers," Nalick explained.

After they were finished eating, Nalick asked, "So I was wondering..." He paused and stopped talking, trying to formulate his thoughts. Leila watched him search for words. She knew what he wanted to ask, but was finding it fun to watch him unable to talk.

"I didn't think you ever got tongue-tied," Leila said to him, leaning in to distract him with a kiss. Pulling away she caught a slight blush in Nalick's cheeks. "So you want to know if the rumors about me are true? No, I can't sail a ship on my own, nor can I fly like a bird. Also, I can't disappear into thin air." Leila watched him smile as she named off myths she had heard about herself over the years. "Can I really fight?" Nalick nodded his head. As he had watched her over the days, he began to doubt how true it was. She had such a kind heart that he couldn't imagine her actually hurting another person.

"It's just that..." he paused again.

"I don't need to actually harm someone to win. Erich didn't take *no* for an answer. He wanted me to be able to protect myself, and in the last few years it has really come in handy. Trust me, I don't periodically get sewn up by Roger because I think it's fun to get stitches in me." She chuckled. A knock at the door interrupted them to go to the next round of trials for the guard posts.

Nalick walked with Leila to a different wing of the palace. Instead of the wide-open courtyard, they went to a room that had a stage down in the front of it. The seats that they passed were on an angle, sloped down toward the stage, so that everyone seated would have a good view of the event. On the stage to the right were empty seats at a table. Nalick led the way past all the seated men and took Leila to the front of the room.

"I'd like to hear your opinion on each of the match-ups after they're done," he said to her quietly before walking down to the front of the stage to confer with the judges.

Anatolio stood silently behind Leila. Leila motioned for him to come near. Anatolio approached Leila and kneeled beside her.

"Have you ever fought Nalick before?" Leila asked curiously.

"Once," Anatolio replied, not elaborating as Leila wished, because Nalick returned to the stage. The men in the room all quieted down.

"This afternoon we will have twenty-eight match-ups," Nalick began. "We matched everyone based on their skill, rank, and the position they are trying for. As many of you suspected, there will be an additional round tomorrow." A murmur spread through the crowd. "I'll be choosing the top eight from today to continue tomorrow with the chance for posts as personal guards." Leila watched as the men who were not fighting seemed to be disappointed they didn't do better earlier.

"Then let's begin with the first match," Nalick said. Two people rose and walked onto the stage as Nalick returned to Leila's side. "Pull up a chair," Nalick said to Anatolio, who shook his head *no* and returned to his spot behind Leila. Nalick turned to Leila. "Tomorrow's top eight is your choice."

"I have to choose from the men fighting?" she asked.

"Any of the people here," Nalick replied.

"You really are going to let me choose?" Leila asked again.

"Yes. They are going to be your guards, so it's your choice," he replied.

"Then do I also get to test their strength tomorrow?" She smiled sweetly, trying to get her way.

"Prove to me tonight you should test them, then sure." Nalick smiled back at her.

Not a problem, Leila thought, before settling in to watch the men fight.

"Who do you think was the best today?" Leila asked Anatolio after all the matches were finished as they waited for Nalick to finish with the judges.

"Nikias," Anatolio replied. "But I didn't expect it to be any other way."

"Do you know your brother well?" Leila asked.

"He's a good man and an excellent fighter. I heard a rumor once that in practice he actually beat Nalick. I just wish I could have been there to see it." Anatolio realized Leila was watching him intently as he talked. "So you know who he is?"

"Yes, but I didn't need Nalick to tell me. You look very much like him," she replied.

"So I've been told by those that don't fear his family." Anatolio watched his older brother walk away. "He's the only decent one in the group."

"How many other half siblings do you have?" Leila

wondered.

"Six, but I was raised by my mother as an only child," Anatolio explained.

Nalick returned to Leila and Anatolio. "So do you still want to show me that you should be the one testing them tomorrow?"

"Of course," Leila replied.

"Then follow me." Nalick led Leila to the vacant courtyard. As it was now late afternoon, the sun was casting shadows over most of the yard. They would be all alone, as everyone had returned to their homes. Underneath one of the balconies, Nalick opened a door to a storage room. He rummaged through a stack of clothing on one of the shelves and found some that would fit not only himself, but also Leila.

"If you put this on, it should protect you from getting any cuts from the weapons. The blades are dulled, but it still can hurt," Nalick explained, as Leila fingered the fabric. Leila raised her eyebrows at the thought. "I'm afraid we don't have any shoes small enough for you, though."

"I prefer to be barefoot," she replied.

"You can change in here," Nalick told her while picking up a box of weapons. He then left the small room.

Leila quickly changed. The clothing fit her, but it wasn't as light as she was used to. She walked back out to the courtyard to find Nalick had also changed and was sitting on the ground stretching. She sat down beside him and began to quickly braid her hair to keep it out of the way. Nalick watched in awe as she began to stretch to the left and right. He had never met someone quite as flexible. She stood and easily put her elbows on the ground in front of her; she reversed the motion, stretching backward until her hands were on the ground behind her. She easily kicked her legs up until she was standing on her hands. *A little stiff*, she thought, shifting her weight from hand to hand. It had been many days since she had last trained. Normally, by now, she would have been on another assignment and trained for two straight days to be prepared. After she was done, Leila walked over to the box to see the kinds of weapons she had to choose from. Nalick joined her.

"Practice blades," he explained.

"What? Are your people not skilled enough to practice without actually hitting the other person?" Leila teased.

"Some are not, but in our case, I don't need to get in any more trouble with Mauve," Nalick said. Leila chuckled, picturing an angry Mauve yelling at Nalick for a tiny scratch.

"Fine," she replied while sulking. She looked though the weapons, but none would work for her. Most were too heavy or bulky. She had focused her training without weapons since a courier didn't routinely carry one on assignments. Her strength came from her maneuverability, and as such, she would need to choose a weapon that would still allow her to be nimble. After looking through everything, she settled on a set of four daggers. Three of the daggers were normal size and the fourth was a little larger. Nalick watched her choice. Daggers were a choice for someone that was quick, not for someone who was powerful. Nalick chose a single, double-sided blade that was almost the length of his arm. Leila quickly strapped daggers to her ankle, thigh, and upper arm. Nalick looked at the arrangement and was confused.

Leila smiled at his confusion. "I don't really have a preference for left or right hand," she explained. Nalick nodded. She was trained better than he had expected. "Shall we begin?"

For over an hour Anatolio watched as Nalick and Leila fought, evenly dancing from side to side of the courtyard. In the beginning Leila tested Nalick to get his reactions.

She even gave him openings to win, but he was smart enough not to take them. As the fight progressed, Anatolio could tell she was very well trained. Even though Nalick was stronger and better with his weapon, Leila's stamina and analytical skills compensated for the difference between them.

After a while, though, Leila could feel the muscle in her hip start to get sore. Leila had told Roger she was fine, but she hadn't put herself to such a harsh physical test since she had been hurt. Her hand, however, was holding up better than she had expected. After analyzing each move, Leila found a pattern to Nalick and possibly a way to compensate. Since her hip was getting worse, she decided to try it. Moving into position, she began her attack. Before Leila could finish the move, she was flat on the ground and Nalick's sword was at her neck. She chuckled as he dropped his sword and lay down next to her. Winded, he heaved deep breaths while Leila lay quietly, analyzing what went wrong. Nalick was amazed Leila was not tired.

"You could have won if you didn't try to end it so soon. I'm beat," Nalick said. He was impressed. She was much better than anyone had ever said.

"I figured you'd be too stubborn to give up, even if you were tired," Leila replied.

"You finished this for me?" he asked. "You are really amazing."

"And weapons aren't even my specialty," Leila said back. Nalick rolled over and stared at her.

"Once I catch my breath, I'd like to see how well you fight without them, then," he said, taking in gulps of air.

"So did I earn the right to test the men tomorrow?" she asked.

"Yes, that's for sure," Nalick said, smiling at her and slowly standing for a second round.

"Really?" Leila asked. He was still out of breath but

wouldn't quit. "I'll make this quick, then." Leila stood in front of Nalick. "Ready?" Reluctantly, he nodded his head, unsure if he should back out while he still could. Leila tested, and Nalick was an easy read without weapons to hide behind. Within two minutes she had Nalick pinned to the ground with her bare foot on his neck. Leila bent over to offer him a hand to stand up, and Nalick instead pulled her down on top of him.

"I don't ever remember being taken down so quickly, and certainly not by someone even half my weight," he said in awe, finally catching his breath.

"I told you it was my specialty," she said. Leila felt her heart begin to beat faster as she lay on top of Nalick. Beneath her, she could feel that his heart was also beating fast, but she didn't know if it was from the previous match, or for the same reason that hers beat so fast. Nalick didn't let go of her waist, keeping her pinned to him.

"I'd like to try again sometime when I'm not as tired," Nalick said while gently tugging her braid. Leila bent down so that her face was only a breath away from his. She stared into his eyes, contemplating making the first move. Nalick's eyes were warm and inviting, so she gently pressed her lips to his. Nalick responded by also gently kissing her in return. His hands rested peacefully on her hips and he felt that he was finally winning her over completely.

"The result will be the same," she said with a grin. Nalick wanted to reply back, but it was probably true. Reluctantly she stood. Lying in the sand in the middle of the practice was not the place to continue playing.

Nalick waited for Leila to change. Anatolio was still keeping guard and had watched the whole match. Nalick walked over next to him and sat on the staircase beside the younger man.

"So, what do you think?" Nalick asked Anatolio.

"She truly is amazing," Anatolio replied.

"Better than me?" Nalick asked.

Leila exited the storeroom to find the two men sitting on the staircase to the upper balcony. They both beamed as she approached. The men escorted Leila back to her room where she could barely contain the excitement from the afternoon. Her practice with Nalick was the first time since Erich died that she fought someone that she couldn't beat easily. After Leila's long bath, Nalick was sitting on the balcony where he normally found her. Leila sat down next to him.

"So, was I everything your scouts told you I was?" Leila asked.

"Much, much more," Nalick replied while wrapping the blanket that was around him around her, also. "You must have trained for years." Leila moved close to him so that his arm was draped gently around her shoulders. She wouldn't object to continuing their play from earlier.

"I trained almost daily. The couriers at Roger's aren't especially good at fighting, so we train more than normal. If they were, I guess they wouldn't be couriers." She laughed. "Now do you believe me that I don't need more guards?"

"I always knew that, but I'd feel better if you had more men watching out for you," Nalick said.

"Why are you so worried?" Leila asked. She searched his face, trying to predict his response.

"I got a letter from Roger yesterday. He said that Jahangir has a plan to take you, but Roger didn't know the details. All he knows is Jahangir has men in the city, and they are all working to find a successful way to kidnap you." Nalick truly feared losing the woman sitting next to him.

"I'll be fine," she replied. Leila also feared being taken from Nalick by Jahangir. Though she was afraid to tell Nalick, she loved him, and did not want her love life to repeat itself. Trying her best to hide her own fears, Leila stood. "I better get some rest for tomorrow," she said cheerily. Nalick could see the hesitation in her eyes at the mention of Jahangir, but as easily as she worried, she was fine again. Nalick couldn't be as easily calmed. He stood and followed her to bed.

Leila was still sore from their practice and couldn't fall instantly to sleep like Nalick. She quietly rolled over and watched him sleeping next to her. She gently touched his face and he didn't wake. His tan, olive-toned skin was a stark contrast to the man she once loved. Everything about Nalick was different from Erich, and yet she was attracted to him. Leila softly traced Nalick's features. He looked so peaceful while asleep. Cautiously, she picked up his right arm and looked at the lines. She slowly turned his palm over and looked at the words. From her studying, she could make out many of the letters.

Why me? she wondered. *Of everyone in the world, Nalick chose me.* As she studied his hand, she failed to notice he had woken. He, in turn, just watched as she was intently tracing the lines on his arm. Following the lines, she finally noticed him watching her.

"Sorry," she whispered. "I didn't mean to wake you." Nalick didn't mind being woken up by such a beautiful smile.

Nalick reached over and pulled Leila halfway on top of him. Out of the corner of his eye, he caught movement. He quickly turned to see Mauve sitting in the corner of the room. He couldn't tell if she was awake or asleep.

"She has been there every night," Leila explained. "Since I told her I wanted you to stay, she decided we needed to be watched so that we behave." Nalick smiled and pulled the covers over their heads so that they were out of Mauve's view. He quickly kissed Leila as he could hear Mauve standing. Mauve was awake.

"Nalick," she said sternly. Nalick pulled the covers back down and looked innocently at Mauve before settling down to go back to sleep.

CHAPTER SEVENTEEN

Two days later it was market day, and Leila rose early. She was eager to visit with the children she had met there. She was surprised that Nalick was already gone before she woke. He had left a note promising to join her as soon as he was finished with his work for the day. Nearing the door, she could hear Anatolio and Macarius talking.

"It was great," she heard Anatolio say. "She let Pallas come to the stage to fight her, and within moments he was lying on the ground looking up at her. You should have seen the expression on his face."

"Oh, knowing Pallas, I'm sure he wasn't taking it well," Macarius replied. "He's the hothead of the group. I can't believe you're actually related to him."

"Not if you ask him," Anatolio replied.

"Don't you ever sleep?" Leila asked Anatolio. Every time she tried to go somewhere, Anatolio followed. Anatolio became quiet again around her while they were in the presence of another person. Leila shrugged when she got no response and greeted Macarius instead. "So is it just you today?"

"We've been knocking on Theo's door for the last five minutes, but he hasn't answered," Macarius explained. "Micaela was going to take Dimas to Theo's parents, but he must have gone with them. I don't think he expected you to be up this early, as you were quite busy yesterday beating up all the guards."

"That was nothing," Leila replied. "Just a little

entertainment." Macarius wished he had been there. "Since he knows where we're going, can we leave without him?" she asked, though she had a feeling what the answer would be.

"Nalick doesn't want you going anywhere outside the palace without at least four guards," Macarius explained. "So, we will have to wait for Theo." Leila added it up in her head. The two new men from yesterday, Anatolio, and Macarius made four. Macarius could see her confusion. "Sorry, Anatolio doesn't count." Leila looked to Anatolio for an explanation, but he just shrugged his shoulders in reply.

Leila looked at both men, but neither seemed to budge on the issue. "So I won't be let out of the palace if I try to leave?" Macarius shook his head, *no*.

He promised that I'd be free to come and go as I please, Leila thought, getting upset.

Anatolio could see her anger building and quickly suggested, "Why don't we wait in the garden? Macarius can come and find us as soon as Theo returns." Anatolio understood her better than she thought. Leila nodded her head and followed Anatolio to the palace garden.

Once inside the garden walls, Leila sat at her normal spot. Anatolio joined her rather than climbing into the nearest tree. In her disguise, if anyone passed them, they wouldn't know he was talking to the queen. Leila understood and moved over to make room beside her.

"The arrogant man yesterday..." she began, but he interrupted her.

"Is also my half-brother," Anatolio said, ending her sentence. "Four older brothers, one older sister, and one younger brother, but they mean nothing to me. My father did nothing except get my mother pregnant, and he has done nothing since. The only person in that family that acknowledges I exist is Nikias."

Leila thought back to the previous day, and wondered

about the stoic-faced man she met. "You look like him, and even act like him." She observed, running her fingers through the cool grass.

"He was the only man close to a father figure in my life. In front of everyone, he would treat me the same as anyone he met, but on the other side, he was always there for me. If I needed advice or training, he would help me. He's a good man," Anatolio said, staring into the clouds above.

"And Pallas?" Leila asked.

"Is just your typical, rude noble," Anatolio easily replied.

"So how did they handle you getting to work directly with Nalick?" Leila wondered, looking over at Anatolio while he stared up at the sky.

"Though they wouldn't show it publicly, I knew most of them hated it. Nikias was happy for me, but Pallas was furious. I always thought that if I accomplished much, they would finally accept me, but I know that's not true. I'm working directly under the king, and they still don't accept me," he explained, still staring up, as it was easier than to looking into her knowing eyes. Leila never missed anything.

"Things are just so much more complicated here," Leila commented, going back to the grass on her hands.

"It's not like this back where you're from?" he asked, looking down at her.

"There are no kings and queens, or noble families. Some people have more, and some less, but no one acts as if they are better just because of their name," Leila explained. "Maybe it's the heat. It makes everyone in Lior a bit crazy."

"I wouldn't doubt it. My mother isn't from Lior either, and she always complained about the heat." Anatolio casually observed the walls around the garden. "Are you afraid of being caught by Jahangir or Aiolos?" They were currently safe, but Leila's safety would always be an issue.

"I don't fear being caught by anyone. There's always a way out if you try hard enough. Most of the time, you just need to be patient. Maybe it helps knowing that they all want me alive. If they wanted me dead or alive, then I might worry some," Leila explained, and Anatolio chuckled. He understood her reasoning, but couldn't help but admire how courageous she was.

"Would you teach me?" Anatolio asked quickly before he could stop himself.

"What do you want to learn?" Leila asked, puzzled by the question.

"Everything. You're great at everything a courier needs to be good at," he said.

"Sure, what should we start with?" Both of their heads quickly turned to the door opening to their left. Theo looked around the garden. Leila stood, realizing he couldn't see them behind the flowers.

"Sorry, Miss Leila," Theo apologized. "I just walked Micaela and Dimas to my parents. I caught Nalick this morning, and he said you were still asleep."

"Not a problem," Leila said, trying to reassure him, and stop him from continuously apologizing. "So, where do we pick up the new guards?" she asked, leaving the garden. As she turned, she noticed Anatolio had backed away, and was going to follow in the distance as always.

"They are both waiting at the gate," Macarius explained, joining Leila and Theo.

Though it took a little time to convince both of the new guards that Leila was the person in the disguise, all four men finally accompanied her to the market. Nikias and Javed both kept two steps behind her, and quietly searched the surrounding people for any sign of something being out of place. Leila ignored the two new men and proceeded to walk from tent to tent, dragging

Theo and Macarius along.

Once near the square, Leila found Phillip standing over his two siblings as they clapped along with the music and watched the people dance. As she neared, the small boy, Tim, noticed her first. He quickly jumped up before Phillip could catch the edge of his shirt and dodged the people as he ran over to her. Leila picked him up.

"Found her," Tim cried, calling to Phillip.

"Hello, Phillip," Leila said, carrying Tim back over to his brother.

"I was just going to go sit down and get some drinks. Would you guys like to join me?" she asked. Phillip picked up Ruth and followed Leila through the crowd to the tables. Tim remained on her lap and started to tell her stories about his week. After he finished his first story, Leila reached for one of her bags. "Which bag would you like to look in first?" she asked Tim.

He quickly grabbed the toy bag. Inside, he found a toy cart and doll. He handed the doll to Ruth and he began to race the cart around the table.

"So what do you do for work?" Leila asked Phillip.

"I work for a meat cutter here near the market. I don't make much, but it's enough," Phillip explained.

"And you make enough to take care of all three of you?" Leila wondered.

"So far," Phillip replied. "Our mother died, and there was no place for us to go. If we went to an orphanage, they would split us up and make even Tim work. I do better to take care of us. Besides, I'm almost old enough to get a real job," Phillip tried his best to convince Leila they were doing fine.

"Bag please," Ruth asked for the unopened bag. Leila handed it to Ruth, who squealed when she saw the sweets.

"There are several sweets in there," Leila said, when

Tim stopped circling the table as soon as he heard his sister squeal. "If you have one now, Phillip can then hold on to the rest and then you can have some later." Ruth nodded and picked out one piece. Tim walked over to his brother and held out his hands for one, also.

"Thank you," Phillip said to Leila as Tim hopped back on her lap. Sweets were a treat he couldn't afford to buy his siblings.

"Why is that man watching us?" Phillip asked, pointing behind Leila. Leila turned to see Nalick standing only feet away, but not approaching them.

"That's the man I'm going to marry in a few months," Leila explained. "He's a bit shy."

"Oh," Phillip said, nodding his head. Phillip recognized the man from the countless images of the king he had seen over the years. Without Nalick wearing a crown, Phillip couldn't be sure, but he suspected.

"Are you a noble?" Phillip asked Leila bluntly.

"Gosh, no," Leila replied. "I'm from a place where they don't have nobles." Phillip seemed more relaxed.

"Is he?" Phillip asked about Nalick.

"Yes," Leila told him truthfully. "I didn't like him too much at first, either, but then I found out he really is a good man." Theo and Macarius were sitting on the other side of the table listening to the conversation. Leila actually admitted to liking Nalick. "Would you like to meet him?"

"He really is a good person?" Phillip asked. "Around here, they don't talk nicely about most of the nobles. The only person they seem to like is the new queen."

"I promise he's a good guy," Leila said, motioning for Nalick to come over and join them. Nalick sat down next to Leila, and Tim huddled closer to her. "It's okay, Timmy. This is my friend." Tim relaxed as Phillip eyed Nalick suspiciously. "These are Phillip, Ruth, and Tim," Leila said, introducing the children to Nalick.

"Pleased to meet you," Timmy said while shaking Nalick's hand. Nalick smiled as the young boy tried to greet him like a grown up.

"Pleased to meet you, also," Nalick replied. Nalick shook Phillip's hand, also. Ruth just smiled and offered him part of her treat. Nalick watched Leila play with the children while talking to Phillip. The children seemed to like her the instant they met her, two weeks before, and now they acted like they were all old friends. Leila sparkled while talking to the children. The lunch bell rang to interrupt their meeting. Phillip rose, collected his siblings, and left.

"Phillip reminds me of someone," Nalick observed.

"Someone?" Leila asked.

"I think I knew his father. He taught me how to ride horses and fight, and he died eight years ago protecting me while we fought in a war."

"A noble?" Leila asked. Nalick nodded. "Then, you'd know his grandparents. Could they take care of them?"

"They don't know anything about Phillip. Andor did everything he could to take care of his family. Before we left for the war, he tried to tell his parents about their mother, but they wouldn't listen. I heard that their mother refused to marry anyone else because she hoped Andor would return. He never did," Nalick explained.

Leila shook her head. "How can you just turn your back on your family?"

"I don't know," Nalick replied. "I've never understood it either."

As they walked through the gates, Nalick nodded as Nikias and Javed bowed before leaving. Nalick walked Leila to the staircase. He paused to gently caress her head, hugging her to his chest.

"Not joining me again?" Leila asked.

"Too many plans to be made." He sighed.

"Do you need any help?" Leila asked.

"You will have your part, too. Enjoy them not bugging you yet about everything," Nalick referred to the priests. "I have a feeling your freedom will be short-lived." Leila raised her eyebrows. She was curious about what else she would have to do to please the priests.

CHAPTER EIGHTEEN

"Could we work in the garden?" Leila asked the nervous young priest. The boy nodded, relieved that, this time, his orders had been correct.

For the first time, Anatolio wasn't close behind her, but Leila continued on to the garden without him. *He must be running late*, she thought. As she sat down next to the priest, something seemed out of place. Carefully, Leila scanned the walls. The priest seemed to not notice the difference. *I must be overanalyzing it*, she thought. But again, Leila felt something was not right.

"How about we continue this later," Leila suggested to the priest, too distracted to listen to him.

"As you wish," the priest said, while gathering up his papers.

Leila continued to scan the garden. Anatolio had never been this far behind before. *Something is wrong.* Leila watched the priest stand to leave. He bowed to her and turned to walk to the door on the left side of the garden. Leila stayed where she was and watched him. He casually pushed on the door to open it, but found resistance when it didn't move. Leila quickly jumped to her feet. Something *was* wrong. Leila dashed over to the priest when several men appeared from within the garden. Several more scaled down the walls. One of them lunged to stab the priest, but Leila quickly disarmed the man and picked up his weapon.

"Stay right behind me," she told the priest.

Behind one of the trees emerged a man, clapping. "I expect nothing less from the famed ghost." The man gave her an extravagant bow. "You are outnumbered twenty to one. I'm sure you wouldn't have a problem fighting all these men alone, but can you protect the priest behind you the whole time?"

Leila glared at the man. He was correct. She could easily fight twenty to one if she only had to worry about herself. Being a live target meant they would never do anything to harm her. The priest was not needed, however, and thus expendable in their eyes.

"Don't worry about my life," the priest said to her. "I live to serve my God and my king. If it's my time to die, then, so be it." The young man shook visibly.

"What a brave priest," the man across from Leila said. "Come with us, and we will spare the man behind you."

"And how do I know that as soon as I lay down this sword you will actually spare him?" Leila questioned. "Jahangir isn't the kind to spare people so easily."

"So, you knew we were coming?" He kept his distance, though eager to approach her.

"Seth has never been good at keeping his mouth shut when he's excited about something," Leila replied, angling the priest behind her to protect him.

The man held up a key. "This key will open the door behind you. I'll give it to you, if you come with us." There was no way for her to protect the priest and herself at the same time, and it could be hours before anyone would check on the garden. She checked one last time and knew she was trapped.

"Fine," Leila said. "Give us the key, and I'll stay."

The man didn't hesitate. Leila was good for her word. He threw her the key. The priest bent down and picked it up.

"Leave now," she said to the confused priest.

"Come with me," the priest whispered, ready to bolt and pull her along. Leila was the best fighter anyone knew, but she was still his queen.

"I can't. I said I'll stay, so I will stay." Leila waited to hear him unlock the door. The priest hesitated. "As your queen, I'm ordering you to leave. Find Nalick and Anatolio. Tell them I have been taken." The priest couldn't disobey her command. He opened the door. "Lock the door behind you." The priest removed the key and placed it in the door on the other side. As he started to slip through, he paused. Leila handed him the sword she was holding. "Protect yourself and make it to Nalick alive," Leila told him, and he shut the door. Leila remained where she was until she heard the lock turn and his footsteps race away. She calmly walked over to the man she had negotiated with. "What now?" she asked, standing toe-to-toe with the man.

"You truly are as amazing as everyone says you are." The uninvited guest motioned and several men tied her arms behind her. "I'm Argon," he introduced himself. "It's unfortunate that I agreed to work with Seth; otherwise, I think I'd be taking you home for myself."

Leila glared at him as one of the men wrapped a blindfold around her eyes and gagged her to prevent her from screaming, which wasn't exactly her style anyway. She was walked near the wall and a man grabbed her tightly around the waist. They carried Leila away and out of the palace. Leila tried her best to keep track of the time during the long trip, but the blindfold didn't let her see the sunlight. Suddenly, the cart they were traveling in stopped. She felt someone pick her up and move her outside it. Leila still couldn't see, but she felt something pierce the skin on her back below the royal emblem on her shoulder. Someone gently placed her back inside. The ride continued. When the cart finally stopped, it was nighttime. Someone pulled her gently from it and chained her to the wheels. Then someone carefully removed her blindfold and gag. She stared at Argon.

"Such a pretty girl," Argon said as he stroked her face. "A waste to give you to Jahangir." He moved his face closer to Leila.

Leila was working on removing her hands from the chains as he spoke, but, reacting to his comment, Leila spit in his face. It disgusted her to have a man such as Argon touching her. As he raised his hand to slap her, someone stopped him.

"No one is allowed to touch her," the man said from behind Argon.

Leila felt sick to her stomach. She knew who the man was before she even saw him. Behind the flickering firelight, Seth appeared alongside the angry Argon.

"Long time, no see," Seth said to Leila. Leila gave Seth a defiant stare in response. She was still standing within inches of Argon, and she carefully tested the length of the chain on her legs. Leila would not be able to kick him; so instead, she stomped on his foot with her full force.

Argon yelped in pain and glared at her furiously. Leila laughed and waited for his reaction. Seth would not be able to stop Argon as he was twice Seth's size, and Argon was very mad. Three men jumped up from behind to restrain him.

"Employing a hothead now?" Leila asked the other courier.

"Feisty as ever, I see," Seth replied, moving closer, but staying out of her range.

"So what's in this for you?" Leila asked. "Did he finally agree to let you have his daughter?"

Seth was surprised that Leila knew, but tried not to show it on his face. "Do you think I need anything other than an offer to catch the famous ghost?" Seth had spent the last four years working in her shadow. Every time he tried to compete with her on an assignment, she was always victorious.

"So you're doing this purely for your own enjoyment?" she asked. The three men holding Argon down continued to struggle with the large man.

"That girl needs to learn some manners," Argon complained, straining to stand.

"And you don't?" Leila retorted, spitting in his direction, but missing. Argon growled, but he couldn't break free of the men holding him down. More men approached Seth from behind. Confident that he had Leila restrained, Seth didn't move away as they talked.

"We have three couriers following us and Lior is mobilizing their army," the first man replied.

"Which couriers?" Seth asked.

"Two are from Roger's company, and one from Canor," the second man reported. Leila smiled. She hadn't seen Marx in a while. Marx wouldn't pass up the opportunity to help her, especially if it meant beating Seth. Seth returned to the group of men sitting around the fire.

"Argon, keep your men here and distract anyone that comes this way. My men will keep moving with our prize. The sooner we get to Jahangir, the safer we will be," Seth said to his men. Half the camp quickly began to pack up. Seth returned to Leila.

"It seems Marx has plans to rescue you," Seth said, as five men restrained Leila and began weaving the chains around her so that she couldn't move.

She did not reply.

"Put her back inside," Seth commanded as they tied the blindfold back around her eyes. She was gently lifted and laid down on the pillows inside the cart she had been riding in.

Leila sat in the dark and silence for the remainder of the trip. She had tried to loosen her arms, but her left shoulder was throbbing from whatever had pierced her skin earlier. She could feel that it wasn't making her sleepy like she suspected, but instead it was making the whole left side of her body weak. Leila could still move, but it took more effort than normal. It would be a waste of her energy if she continued to struggle. She didn't like sitting in a place without seeing it. Leila wiggled until the blindfold was off. Then she propped herself up against the pillows and wall and waited. *Mobilizing his army, I wonder how Nalick is taking this*, she thought.

Leila was in complete darkness. Softly she drifted off into a light sleep. Leila would need all her energy to get away from the castle of Jahangir for the third time, since each time she returned he had made adjustments to better hold her.

After what Leila guessed had been almost two days, with only brief stops along the way, she could hear noises outside her ride. She could hear people faintly talking now outside her cart. As the days had progressed, Leila was getting weaker and weaker. As the ride came to another halt, Seth conversed with the guards to the palace. The guards wanted to see her, but Seth wouldn't let them. After the cart passed the gates, Leila followed the route in her mind leading them to the castle stables. The cart stopped, and the door opened. Leila adjusted her eyes. Going from sitting in complete darkness for days to the soft glow of the sun setting, the stables had a fuzzy glow. Two men gently picked her up and placed her on her feet. Leila felt a bit unstable and noticed her balance had also been affected by the weakness she was feeling in her left side of her body.

"It took longer than I expected, but to see the great ghost not as strong as normal is quite a treat," Seth teased. Leila adjusted for the difference in strength, and stood eye-to-eye with Seth.

"I don't know what you did, but it still won't be enough to stop me." She glared at him.

Seth chuckled, waving his hands in the air to dismiss her comment. "Trust me. This stuff can stop anyone. Even you, my dear." Seth motioned and several men held her arms and legs as Seth checked to make sure she was tightly secured. Leila just stood still. He was being extra cautious, but he would eventually let his guard down, and then she would find her opportunity to leave. Seth wrapped the blindfold around her again, but little did he know that she didn't need her sight to navigate this castle. Leila felt someone pick her up because she was wrapped so tightly there was no way she could walk. After the person weaved through various passageways of the castle, he finally stopped. The man carrying her then set her down in the middle of a room. The locks on metal doors clanked shut. Someone's hand removed her blindfold.

Leila opened her eyes to find she was in a large cage within an ornately-decorated room. She turned her head to face Seth. He was grinning ear-to-ear.

"I really would like to see the famed Leila get out of this one, but I have better things to do with my time. Here," he said, while throwing clothes inside the cage. "Once I unlock you, change into these. We want you to be presentable when I take you before the king to get my reward."

"So, if I leave before you present me, then you won't get your reward?" she asked.

"Trust me; you won't be leaving so soon." Seth smiled.

"What if I don't feel like changing?" Leila asked haughtily.

"If you're not dressed by the time I return, I'll do it myself," Seth replied. "Now be a good girl and just change." Leila glared at him. She would dress herself as the thought of him touching her disgusted her as much as meeting with Jahangir.

"I can't change if you don't unlock me," Leila said as he turned to leave.

"I almost forgot. Too bad, though, I was looking forward to changing you." He smiled and unlocked all the locks, but made no effort to remove the chains.

CHAPTER NINETEEN

Seth left the room, but the guard that had carried Leila in remained. She quickly unwound the chains, freeing herself. Leila tested her strength as she stretched and found her left side was still weaker than normal. Glancing around the room, the window was the best way to leave, if she could actually scale the walls; Leila was three to four floors above the ground. She looked at the clothing before her and changed into the thin dress. They purposely gave her a dress that would be too cold for the weather outside. It was the end of winter, and though they didn't have snow in Samael, the nights were bitterly cold until summertime started. As Leila turned back around, the guard was sitting and grinning ear-to-ear from the peep show.

"Can you come here a moment?" Leila asked him sweetly. The man moved closer. When he was within arm's reach, Leila grabbed his head and banged it against the bars. The man slid to the floor, and she removed his keys. He had several identical keys, each of which would unlock the cage. She removed a key and placed the keychain back around his waist. She quickly hid the freed key in the closest pillow. She then gently walked back to the man and slapped his face a few times. He woke with a start.

"You tripped and hit your head," Leila told the man. *Men always believe sweet, innocent stories.* He seemed confused, but didn't disagree with her. "I was going to see if you could get me something to drink," she said sweetly.

The man nodded.

The guard stood and walked out of the room, which provided Leila an opportunity to quickly unlock her cage. She walked to the window and looked down. Under normal circumstances, it would be easy to scale down, but with the numbness on her left side, she doubted it would be that simple. Before she could make her decision, the door opened. Seth walked in the room.

"Having second thoughts?" Seth asked. If Leila was feeling fine, she would have already been out the window and down a few floors. "Now that you're dressed, would you care to join me?"

Leila wasn't going to be able to leave quite yet, so she walked back to Seth. She held out her arms to be locked back up. She would need to think of another plan, but it would be easier after everyone went to bed. They had to sleep sometime. Leila had rested for two days, which meant she wasn't tired enough to need sleep. Seth locked her hands together, followed by her feet. She couldn't walk very easily, but there was enough chain to allow her to shuffle. Seth continued to grin like a conquering hero.

"Well, let's go get you your reward, though from what I hear, she will be very disappointed." Jahangir's oldest, and unwilling, daughter was the prize Seth wanted. Leila figured of anyone in the castle, she would be the best bet to help Leila escape. Leila walked behind Seth and two men held her arms as she walked. Seth didn't want to take any chances of losing her while transporting her. Once Leila was inside the royal chambers, Seth posted two guards at each door and window. Seth then chained her feet to a rod in the middle of the room, unchaining the rest of her.

"Please try to be presentable," Seth whispered in her ear as the main door opened.

Jahangir was an old man, fat and balding from age. He already had three wives and over a dozen children, some of whom were as old as Leila. Using the country's taxes, he had spent many resources in the past ten years, attempting to track her down to keep her in his castle. Leila figured that with all the chasing he didn't have much time for anything else, and she believed the rumors that claimed many of "his" children were not his own blood. Leila gave the man a disgusted look as he approached her. She stood up tall and proud as he circled her. As he stopped behind her, she could hear Seth approach him. Together, they whispered amongst themselves. Jahangir moved back around and faced her. Jahangir smiled as if he won a contest; Leila just glared back at him.

"Welcome back, dear child," Jahangir said. "I hope they weren't too rough in getting you here." Leila didn't respond. Talking to him wasn't worth her time.

Jahangir moved closer and picked up her arm. Leila tried to contain her disgust from being touched by him. "Such a barbaric custom. I bet it hurt a lot. I'm sure my doctors will find some way to remove it." Leila still didn't reply. Leila knew enough from her previous encounters with Jahangir that he had a short temper. As weak as she already felt, Leila didn't wish to test him.

"I'm surprised you're not thanking me," Jahangir said smugly. "I thought I was doing you a favor by rescuing you from Nalick. I hear he's such an appalling king even his own people fear him." He was trying to bait her to respond, yet she kept quiet. Jahangir moved close enough for her to feel his breath on her face.

"We've been making preparations since we knew where to find you. The wedding will be in two days," Jahangir said as he looked down the front of her dress. "And I can't wait." Leila was ready to gag, but kept her thoughts to herself. Nalick wouldn't wait two days to rescue her, but she also didn't want to start a war. Jahangir walked away, as he wasn't satisfied by the quiet

Leila that stood before him. With a wave of his hand, men surrounded her and locked her back up to take her back to the cage.

"Until she figures out that there's nowhere for her to run to, keep her locked in that cage," Jahangir ordered. Jahangir knew, as well as Seth, that Leila probably already had a plan to run away. "Also, don't unlock her."

Outside Jahangir's room, Leila commented to Seth, "No prize yet?" Seth was upset.

"That's none of your business," Seth replied.

Once she was locked back in her cage, Leila sat down to evaluate the situation. She was still locked in more chains than she wanted to deal with, but chains were never the problem. The problem was the weakness in her left side that was slowly spreading to the right. As the guards changed, Leila noticed that something seemed different. In the dim light of the room, she couldn't see the face of the guard, but he seemed familiar. Seth checked on her one last time before he headed to his own quarters for the night.

"Do not go near her, for any reason," Seth ordered the guard; the guard nodded. Once Seth left the room, the guard sat down opposite of Leila and stared at her.

Leila knew the eyes of the guard, but she couldn't remember where she had met him before. She continued to stare at him as she began to work her hands free. The man stared back knowing full well what Leila was doing, and he made no move to stop her. Leila looked to the window and could see most of the castle had gone to bed. The guard noticed, also. Slowly, the guard stood, blocked the door with his chair, and approached her.

"How've you been, kitten?" the man asked, as he unlocked her door. The familiar voice made Leila immediately stop worrying.

Leila smiled and leapt to her feet to try to hug the man. "Marx," she said. "It has been so long." With her free hand, she playfully batted the fake nose he had on. The man hugged her back. It had been a long time since he had last saw her, but in his eyes, she never changed. Leila was still as beautiful as the day he first met her.

"Let me undo these for you," Marx said, turning her around and unlocking the chains. "We will need to wait here a little longer. The guard change outside won't be for an hour or so." Leila nodded and quickly searched the room for her old clothing.

"Have you seen anything of mine?" Leila asked.

"I got here too late. They already took everything away, hoping that it would discourage you from going out in the cold. Little do they know that you like the cold." Marx strategically moved more of the furniture to block the door. "We shouldn't be disturbed tonight, but if so, I'd rather not have to draw my sword."

Marx had always been a pacifist. Leila often wondered how he stayed in the job for so many years. What she didn't know was that he stayed just so that he could run into her from time to time.

"Here." He offered her some food.

"What about the other guards and Seth?" she asked.

"The guards all looked a little sick earlier. I think they need me to fill in all night long. I assured them I was feeling fine and up for the job. And, well, I don't think Seth will be awake any time soon." Marx smiled.

"You didn't," Leila said. Marx winked. Marx was the only other person Roger trusted with the medication that would put Leila to sleep. Even after Roger used it on Leila, he would always brew a special tea to wake her back up. Even the smallest dose could keep a grown man asleep for days. Seth wouldn't be waking any time soon. It was the pacifist in Marx coming out again, always avoiding a fight.

Leila sat next to him, their backs on the door. "So the whole Endika kidnapping thing was your idea?"

Marx nodded. "I was quite far into the North Country when I got the news a courier had been caught by Nalick. When I heard the woman escaped and then walked to the gate and asked to be let back in, I knew it was you. Why'd you go back if you already escaped?"

"Kay was inside. I thought I got her out, but then she got caught again as I was on my way out," Leila explained, while eating the bread he had given her.

"You're the only courier I know that has enough guts to actually tell someone you escaped and want to be let back in. By the time I made it down to the palace in Lexia you had already headed north to visit King Godfrith. I lost track of you for a few days, and before I could pick your trail back up, you were back in Lexia." Marx had spent the last four years trying his best to follow her trail. She was always gone in a flash, and he knew this time would be no different. While they were friends, they worked for different governments, and would always be kept apart. Marx used the little time with her to put to memory every one of her movements, since it would be awhile before he would see her again. King Endika would not be happy when he was late again on an assignment because he had been diverted to help Leila. "So, once the opportunity came to get you out of there, I tried. I agreed to work with Endika, but there was no way I was really going to give you to him."

"I figured that much. I was almost tempted to meet you, but Nalick would have been worried," Leila explained, finishing the bread.

"When I heard you went back on your own, I knew you didn't need my help, so I finished out my own assignment and headed home. I was in Dria when I heard the news Jahangir and Seth were going to take you from Nalick. I sent a scout to follow Seth and then came directly here. You know, you could take a little bit of time off between being caught. It would make my life easier."

Marx had been in love with Leila for many years, and would do anything to help her. Leila playfully punched him.

"Is he a good man?" Marx asked seriously.

"Yes," Leila replied without looking into his eyes. She had always felt the love Marx had for her, and didn't want to hurt his feelings.

"Does he love you?" Marx asked, gently forcing her to look in his eyes.

"Yes." Leila wanted to look away, but she couldn't. In Marx's eyes she saw happiness, not pain as she expected.

"Do you love him?" he asked, letting go of her face. Even Marx didn't want to really know the answer.

"Yes," she said, barely loud enough to be audible.

"Then, I guess I should get you back to him," Marx said, standing and looking over the windowsill. "It is almost time." Leila stood behind him. Marx turned around to Leila beside him. His heart raced. It had been years since he had been so close to her. "All I've ever wanted was for you to be happy," he explained as he gently touched her face, wanting to give her one last heroic kiss.

Leila looked into his crystal-blue eyes. He was telling her the truth. "I know. I just didn't want to hurt you again," she said quietly. She turned from his gaze. Leila looked over the edge of the window. She still didn't know if she had enough strength. Marx could see the worry in her eyes.

"You can't hurt me by being happy." Worry was still etched on her face. "Is something wrong?" he asked. He had never seen Leila hesitate before.

"My left side seems weaker than normal. Seth put something in my back on the left side, and it has been getting weaker ever since," Leila explained. Since Marx was also risking his life to save her, she was not about to lie to him. Marx turned Leila around and looked at her back.

"There's something here, right under the skin," Marx said, moving his hand over the spot. "Roger will have to take it out, but first we need to get you out of here."

Marx gave Leila his hand. "Squeeze my hands," he directed. Leila in turn squeezed both of his hands. The look in his face confirmed what she thought. Leila wasn't just weak on her left side; she was slowly losing muscle control.

"I don't know what he did to you, but the quicker we leave, the better. Would you be able to hold on to me?" Marx asked.

"Maybe," Leila replied, amazed that he wanted to scale the wall with her on his back.

"Then let's go," he said, climbing out the window. Leila followed. Once outside the room, Marx moved closer to Leila. "Climb on." She obeyed. "Now just don't let go."

Marx moved down the wall as quickly as he could with her on his back. As couriers, they trained extensively with weights, and her size wasn't a problem, but more of a balance issue. Leila used all the strength she could muster to hang on, since Marx wasn't only scaling the wall, but worrying about her at the same time. Her shoulder ached and the numbness was spreading. Leila closed her eyes and pressed her face into his back. Marx tried to hurry, as he could tell this was straining her. At the halfway point, Leila could feel her strength completely failing.

"I'm going to slip soon," Leila said to Marx. She looked down in the darkness and could just make out the faint outline of the ground. "We're almost close enough that I shouldn't get hurt," she said, judging the distance. She didn't want to let go, but it was becoming apparent that she wouldn't have a choice at this point. Marx began to move faster, which only jarred her grip and made her use more strength to hold on.

"Just hold on a little longer," Marx begged, feeling her grip loosening. Leila tried, but it was no use.

"Sorry," she said as her hands slipped. Leila adjusted herself during the fall, landing on her right side in an attempt to compensate for her weak left side, but as she hit the ground Leila realized that was a mistake. She heard a cracking sound coming from her lower leg while stumbling forward. In the darkness, something ripped across her upper right thigh before she hit the ground; she felt warm liquid trickling down her leg. It was too dark to see the damage. Marx quickly was at her side.

"Are you all right?" he asked, trying to help her stand up.

"I think I broke my leg," Leila said, not even attempting to stand on it, but trying to stop the excessive bleeding.

Marx scooped her up into his arms. Even though excruciating pain rushed through her body, Leila remained silent. He quietly moved from shadow to shadow until he was near the castle wall. Marx set Leila gently on the ground so that he could find the entrance. Marx ran his hand across the wall, tapping every now and then. Finally, he found the spot he was looking for. He moved a few pieces of the wall, opening a hole in the base. Leila watched as a part of the ground moved to expose a staircase. Marx picked Leila back up and continued down the stairway. Once they were at the bottom, Marx set her down and closed the opening. Leila looked around her. She hadn't known about the underground passageways. It wasn't much brighter below than it was above, but Marx seemed to know his way around.

Marx found a torch and lit it. He brought it near and handed it to Leila. Leila looked around at the stone-lined walls. They were just as old as the castle. *How could Jahangir not know about this?* Leila wondered. Leila looked back at Marx, who was now kneeling to examine her. He moved her blood-soaked dress to expose her leg. It was bleeding much more than either of them expected. Leila watched his face to get clues to as to how bad it was. Marx kept his face passive and Leila knew that meant he was hiding something. Marx removed his jacket and wrapped it around her. She hadn't noticed her body shivering from the cold.

"Thank you," she said quietly.

Marx then took the knife out of his bag and quickly ripped a piece off the bottom of her dress. He wrapped it tightly around her thigh. "This should help stop the bleeding for now, but we need to get you to Roger." Marx picked her back up and continued through the passageways. Even though she was eager to see where they ended up, she simply couldn't keep her eyes open any longer.

Less than an hour later, Leila awoke and found herself leaning up against Anatolio. Leila didn't know when she had fallen asleep, but now Matthew and Ian, fellow couriers for Roger, were busy trying to stop the bleeding in her leg. Leila looked around the makeshift camp as far as her weary eyes could see, but she didn't know where she was.

"How are you feeling?" Leila asked Anatolio, remembering that he hadn't been there to protect her, and thus must have been drugged. She couldn't see the couriers working, but she could see Anatolio.

Anatolio smiled to see she was awake. "I'm much better than you." He repositioned her body to let her better supervise what was going on.

"First time being drugged?" Leila asked. Anatolio nodded. Matthew and Ian returned and examined the wound again.

"Leila, this isn't good. We can't get it to stop bleeding," Matthew said to her.

Leila looked down and could see the blood seep through the bandages. She hadn't noticed, until then, that Nalick was standing only feet away. She smiled up at him and faked strength she didn't feel. "Is Marx here?" Leila asked Nalick.

"I'm right here, kitten," Marx said, as he stood next to Nalick.

"Do you have a way to get across the river?" she asked, though she couldn't see him.

"Yes, a boat is waiting. Once we get you fixed up enough to travel, Matthew and Ian can take you to Roger," Marx said. He watched as she shut her eyes again. She was losing too much blood.

"Good," she replied, and nodded her head slightly. "Then we better get going now." She felt her leg being lifted. Even though it was quite painful, she didn't have enough energy to protest. Marx carefully set her leg with the boards Theo brought.

"Nalick," Leila said, still with her eyes close. Nalick moved closer and held her hand. "Send Anatolio with Marx to divert anyone who may be following me. Then Matthew and Ian can get me to Roger's quickly without having to worry about losing anyone." Nalick nodded while gently touching her face. "Take the army you have with and retreat to Dria. Wait there for me, and I'll return as soon as Roger can fix me up." Leila opened her eyes to see the worried expression on his face. Straining, she lifted her hand and touched his lips. "Don't worry. Roger hasn't failed me yet." Nalick took her hand and gently kissed it.

"I'm going with you," Nalick said to the men standing with her. "Anatolio will go with Marx. Theo and Macarius will take my army back to Dria, and I'll go with Matthew and Ian."

Leila slowly was losing consciousness again. The five men carried Leila to the boat Marx had waiting. As soon as they were across the shore, Theo and Macarius quietly marched the army back to Dria. After they were in the North Country, Marx stayed behind first. Anatolio continued with the group until he noticed they were still being followed. Anatolio led the trackers astray as Nalick and the two men took off full speed to Roger's. Using several short cuts, the group was able to get Leila to Roger by noon the next day. Leila had awoken once during the trip in Nalick's arms.

Roger saw them coming and rushed to meet them. "What's wrong?"

"Her leg is broken, there's a deep gash on her thigh that has continued to bleed, and Marx said something is in her shoulder that's making her weaker," Nalick replied, carrying Leila up to Roger's medical room. As he laid her on the cold table, she opened her eyes.

"Hi, Roger," Leila said with a faint smile.

"You couldn't just hurt one thing," Roger scolded.

"You know me," she said. Roger began mixing a white powder in a small vial to drink. He handed it to Leila as Nalick helped her balance while sitting. She drank the mixture and smiled at Nalick. "See you in a while." She closed her eyes.

"Did Marx say what this was?" Roger asked, looking at her back.

"No, it was injected before Marx found her at the castle," Nalick explained. "Will you be able to save her?"

"She's a fighter," Roger replied as he began to work with his son at his side. "She will be fine."

CHAPTER TWENTY

"**W**e can wake her now if you'd like," Roger said to Nalick. Roger left and returned with a cup of tea. Gently, Roger propped Leila up into a sitting position and asked her to drink the tea. After the small glass of tea was gone, Roger laid her back down. "She should be a bit groggy, and maybe a bit angry after that, since I didn't wake her last night, but then she should be fine. Please try to keep her from moving too much." Roger left the room.

Nalick held Leila's hand, waiting for her to wake. He hadn't slept much through the night. Everyone could reassure him she would be all right, but until he heard it from her, he was finding it hard to believe. Leila had lost a lot of blood. Nalick closed his eyes and pressed her hand to his mouth as he waited.

"Did Roger not feed you?" Leila asked quietly. A startled Nalick opened his eyes and smiled. "So, how much damage?" She rubbed her eyes.

"Just like you said. A cut in your leg, some sort of poison stones in your back, and the broken leg," Nalick replied. Leila didn't exactly remember telling him about anything.

"What time it is?" Leila asked, finally noticing that it was light outside.

"The morning," Nalick replied, not sure himself.

Roger appeared in the doorway. "Just keeping an old man on his toes?"

"I thought you could use some practice," she replied. "Why didn't you wake me?" Roger shook his head. As

Roger expected, she wasn't happy with the extra sleep.

"Well then do I at least get to head home?" she asked.

Roger sighed, "Can't you sit still for even a moment?" Leila waited for an answer. "As long as you're still feeling fine by lunch time, I'll take you back to town myself. Now, get some rest, and I'll check back later. You, too," he said to Nalick. Both Leila and Nalick nodded their heads like young children being put to bed. Roger left the room. Nalick stood to follow, but Leila grabbed his hand.

"Stay a little longer," she begged. Nalick sat back down. It hurt him to see her lying in the bed almost helpless. "I really will be fine. This cast will limit how much I'll be able to run around the next few weeks, but I'll be fine. Maybe I'll even stay in the castle now." Nalick didn't laugh at her joke. "Sorry I worried you," she said, apologizing for not returning to him quicker.

"There's nothing for you to be sorry about. The priest ran immediately to my office and told me what happened. We followed as quickly as we could. We can talk later," he said while gently stroking her face. "Now, get some rest so we can go home."

For the first time in her life, Leila had a place she could truly call home. Nalick noticed her smile and gently kissed her forehead. *Thank you*, she thought, falling back asleep. Nalick left her alone and went into the kitchen where Roger was eating his breakfast.

"So this tracker, Anatolio," Roger began to ask, as he stared at Nalick over his spectacles. "Is he the one?"

"Yes," Nalick replied.

"And she doesn't know yet, does she?" Roger replied. Nalick stared at the middle-aged man sitting in front of him. It was expected, but Nalick wondered, nonetheless, how Roger knew so much.

"Not yet. I'll tell her when the time is right," Nalick said, as the old man went back to studying the stone.

"I love her like my own child," Roger explained, in

response to the unsure stare he received from Nalick. "I make sure to know everything that can and will happen to that child." Roger set the stone down. "One day you will have to tell her. Now off to bed." Roger watched Nalick walk away.

Leila hobbled to the kitchen as soon as Nalick was asleep.

"Silly child," Roger complained. "I told you to rest. You just can't take an old man's advice." He was actually surprised that she stayed in her room as long as she did.

"Broth is not dinner," Leila complained, as Roger heated the broth. Leila picked up one of the stones. "So this is what was causing me so much trouble?" Roger nodded.

Roger returned to the table and gave her a cup of broth. Leila wrinkled her nose, but accepted it anyway. "So who is this young man who is watching over you?" Roger asked. "He doesn't seem to be keeping you out of any more trouble than normal."

"Trouble? I just had a little misunderstanding with Jahangir. See, he seems to think I'm a prized horse, not a fully-capable woman." Leila sipped her broth while Roger chuckled. "Why are you interested in Anatolio?" She had never known Roger to ask about something without wanting direct information.

"Well, he isn't too good, if he lost you while inside the guarded palace," Roger commented, looking at the stones more.

"It wasn't his fault. He was drugged," Leila defended Anatolio. "And besides, he's only a boy. He can't be much older than sixteen, which would give him at most three to four years' experience. He's not trained to keep up with me." Roger nodded. He was pleased to see she had some sort of relationship with the young man. "Are Ian and Matthew still here?" Leila asked, changing the subject.

"No, they both left after dropping you off. They were

going to check on Anatolio and Marx. I figured Anatolio could stay at Lou's until you return. So, Marx came to the rescue yet again?" Roger tried to analyze Leila's response, but all she did was nod. "I'm sure I'll be able to give him my thanks in person when I drop you off in Cath. He did a good job with your leg so that no further damage could occur on the ride here." Leila nodded and continued to sip her broth as she waited to finally go back home to Lexia.

After Roger and Nalick had lunch, they loaded Leila onto Roger's cart. Nalick and Roger sat together in the driver's seat and Leila leaned against it. Leila could hear their conversation slightly, but she didn't take much interest.

"Who is Marx?" Nalick asked Roger. "Besides a courier from Canor."

"You really want to know?" Roger asked. Nalick nodded. "Marx was the first person to ever propose to Leila." Roger chuckled as he watched Nalick's expression.

"So she was going to marry him?" Nalick asked, with a tone of jealousy.

"No, no," Roger replied; Nalick gave a sigh of relief. "She has had over a dozen marriage proposals over the years. His was simply the start of it. But, if you ask me, he was quite foolish. First, you don't ask a fourteen-year-old girl to marry you, especially when you're eight years older than her, and second, you should ask a girl that's actually interested in boys. At fourteen, Leila was still running wild. She wanted to be riding in the wind more than chasing after boys."

"She seems to know him quite well," Nalick commented.

"She should. He has been doing the same job as her for as many years. After Erich died, I taught him a little bit of first aid since he was always the one bringing her home when she couldn't make it on her own. And on the times she came back on her own, he would stop by and check to make sure she made it," Roger explained.

Leila listened to the men continue to talk about Marx. *Where would I be right now if I had said "yes,"* she wondered. *Would I have a family? Would I still be working?* Then she paused, as small tears formed in the corner of her eyes. *Would Erich still be alive now?* Leila didn't like questions she couldn't answer.

Leila closed her eyes and listened to a bird singing in the trees. Roger drove the cart directly to Lou's and tied the horses up. Leila watched as people bustled through the city. As people passed by, she recognized a number of faces from Lexia. *So the army came here to wait*, she thought. Leila turned to look at Nalick, who was busy helping Roger. As Leila turned back to watch the people passing, someone hopped into the cart with her.

"You know they all stand out like a sore thumb," Marx complained as he sat next to Leila. "Feeling better, kitten?"

"Yes. I truly believe Roger can fix anything," Leila commented.

"One, two, three." Marx pointed to the men he was counting and was correct. "I think you might need to teach lessons while you're locked up in the palace."

"Ugh, don't remind me of my new sentence. Have you ever tried to teach a soldier how to fit in?" Leila asked. "There's a reason why these men joined the army, and it wasn't to fade into the background."

Leila stopped joking and looked at Marx. Marx was his normal happy-go-lucky self. Even after she had told him she didn't want to marry him, she noticed he wasn't saddened or even mad. He just smiled and said, "One day you'll regret it." Leila wished every man she had turned down was so easy to deal with. Marx noticed her quietness. Leila grabbed his hand and stopped his counting.

"Thank you," Leila said to him. "I might not have made it out of there alive this time."

Marx gently patted her head. "You would have been fine. I know it. You're stronger than you think. I wish I could stay and keep you company, but I'm sure to get an earful when I get home late. You're not the best excuse to tell the wife." Leila laughed. "Now, please, give it a rest and stay in Lexia. If I have to run out to rescue you again, I'll have to sleep outside for weeks, not just for a night."

"Don't you already sleep outside?" Leila asked. Marx's wife was not a fan of their friendship.

"I mean it. For once in your life, just relax and get better," Marx begged. "Let that man you love, over there, take care of you." Nalick was trying to discreetly hide his obvious interest in her and Marx.

"Will you stop by and visit if you're in Lexia?" Leila asked, as Marx stepped off the cart.

"Have you ever known me to pass up a chance to see you?" Marx leaned over the cart and kissed her forehead. "Till then, kitten." He disappeared into the crowd. Leila smiled as she watched him walk away. Nalick moved back to her side.

Leila turned to Nalick to see a mixture of anger and jealousy. "There's nothing to worry about," she tried to reassure him. "He's married and devoted to his wife."

"He may be, but he also is quite devoted to you," Nalick replied as he searched the crowd, though he could no longer see Marx.

Leila reached over the seat and took Nalick's hand to pull him closer. "We're just friends. That's all we've ever been, or will be." Nalick stared at her. She was telling him the truth, but he couldn't help but be jealous. "I've known him since I was fourteen. I told him *no* then and would again if he asked me to marry him. I am marrying you. I'm in love with you." Leila kissed the back of his hand, which she was holding.

Across the street, Anatolio sat on the stairs to a shop. Anatolio was intently watching Leila with Marx first and then with Nalick; he had been so focused on her that he didn't see Roger approaching. As soon as he noticed Roger, Anatolio stood up. He had never met Roger in person before, but from the man's walk and stare, Anatolio knew who he was.

"No need to stand," Roger replied, sitting down next to Anatolio. "I've heard much about you from my sources and a bit from Leila and Nalick." Anatolio didn't reply, as he didn't know what to say to Roger. "How long have you been assigned to follow Leila?"

"Just over two years," Anatolio replied, continuing to watch Leila. Every movement she made was locked into his memory. He was always amazed. Everything she did was calculated and direct. She was trained better than Anatolio had ever imagined a person could be.

"She's the most beautiful woman I've ever met, inside and out," Roger said, staring over at her, also. "Here." Roger handed the young man a small package that fit in the palm of his hand.

Anatolio took the package and began to question Roger about it, but he was interrupted. "There are directions inside, and if you don't understand them, talk to Leila about it. I'll be in Lexia in two weeks' time to check up on her. Until then, please don't let her walk around and keep all sharp objects, such as scissors, away from her. As soon as she's sick of the stitches, she tends to remove them herself." Anatolio nodded. "She can be a pain when it comes to recovering. If you need to, chain her up," he seriously suggested. Anatolio didn't know how to respond, not knowing if the man was kidding or serious. "When I return, you will get to see firsthand how I fix her up. It's probably something you should learn because I won't be able to help her when she's so far away." Leila relied heavily on Roger any time she was hurt, and Anatolio was honored that Roger was willing to teach him to be the person she could rely upon.

Both men sat and watched as Leila talked to Nalick.

"How long?" Roger asked Anatolio.

"Ten years," Anatolio replied, rolling the stones in his fingers. They were very small and looked like normal stones, but they had such an effect on Leila.

"And you're willing to wait?" Roger asked, staring at the young man next to him.

"Wouldn't you?" Anatolio replied, and Roger laughed. Roger agreed. If he were young and unwed, he would be willing to wait ten years to have someone such as Leila for his wife.

"Who gets to tell her?" Roger asked, looking back over at Leila laughing with Nalick.

"Nalick. I'm not to tell anyone, and have not," Anatolio replied, handing the stones back to Roger. "How do you go about telling someone as strong willed as her that fate has not dealt her the best of hands?" Roger shook his head in agreement. In the past four years, Roger had only seen Leila let Marx into her heart as a friend, but Roger assumed much of that had to do with Marx's personality.

"Do you have arrangements made to get back home?" Roger asked, changing the subject.

"Marx was quite helpful and everything is ready. There's a ship willing to sail us back to Lior and all the way to Lexia if we want," Anatolio explained. "It seems there are quite a few ships with complete crews that are loyal to her." Leila would never tell Roger how, but she had friends in many places that helped make her jobs easier.

"That's one of ours," Anatolio said, standing alongside Roger as another man approached Leila and Nalick. Roger studied the man's face.

"A relation?" Roger asked Anatolio.

"Kind of," Anatolio replied as he and Roger walked

over to join Leila, Nalick, and Nikias.

Leila smiled as they approached. "Long time no see." She had spotted him the moment they arrived in Cath. Leila searched his eyes for a response. As normal, with others around he made no reply, but he was relieved to see her.

"Arrangements are ready to take you back home," Nikias said to Leila and Nalick. "There is a ship waiting in the port for you."

"Well, you had better get going," Roger said, approaching the group and startling Nikias. "It would be best to get you back in Lior by sunset."

"Our ships are waiting on the Lior side of the waters. If anyone tries to make a move, you will be safe," Nikias tried to reassure his king.

"I'll take you to the port, and then help you get Leila on board," Roger said, hopping back up on the cart and driving them to the waiting ship at the port.

"Roger," the captain called in a booming voice as he extended his hand to the crew members as they arrived. "Marx said your courier and a few men needed a lift, but I didn't expect to see you." The captain noticed Leila was not moving. "Injured?" he asked, and Leila shrugged.

"A minor setback," she replied, and the man laughed.

"Minor indeed," he said, noticing her leg. "Load her up then."

"Just remember, I'm not a package," Leila said to the large captain, who grinned at her.

Once Roger was fully convinced Leila was safe, he stopped one last time to talk to her.

"Promise me you will follow my orders for once," Roger begged. "Leave the stitches in and stay off your bad leg. Two weeks is all I'm asking." Leila nodded. "I'll be there in two weeks, I promise."

Roger bent and hugged Leila. "Please rest and heal."

"Okay, boss," she said, hugging him back.

As Roger left he stopped by Nalick, Anatolio, and Nikias. "Please keep an eye on her. She isn't very good at resting." The men nodded their heads. As Roger stood on the shore, watching the boat sail away, he hoped that for once in her life Leila would follow his directions. She had always been impatient in the past. Twice, Roger caught her sneaking off on an assignment before she had fully healed. He could understand that her youth made her impatient, and her quick healing actually made it acceptable for her to do what she did, but Roger had worried that a time like this would occur where she would actually need the rest to get better.

After the ship was loaded and had begun to sail, everyone took their positions for the short ride to their own ship across the sea. Leila sat alone while everyone wandered around the deck on their own tasks.

"You can't even spare a moment to see how I'm doing?" Leila asked sarcastically, as Anatolio walked by. He stopped and turned to face her. He wanted to lie to her, but it would never work. It was his job to protect her, and he didn't.

"I'm sorry," Anatolio said without looking her in her eyes.

"There's nothing for you to be sorry about. You couldn't help it," Leila replied, trying to make him understand that she didn't blame him. Anatolio moved closer and stared at her to see if she was really telling the truth.

"It won't happen again."

"That's why I asked Roger to give you the pack he gave you earlier," she said. Anatolio was surprised. He didn't think she was watching him while he was watching her. "It's what we use to build up our endurance to the various drugs out on the market." Roger wasn't the best at assignments when he was a courier, but he was excellent at analyzing substances.

Anatolio kneeled to be face-to-face with Leila.

"Are you really fine?" Anatolio asked with tenderness in his voice. He kept his hands to himself, but he wanted to reach out and touch her to make sure.

"Yes. I can't say I've done worse before, but I'm fine now," she replied. "So I guess training you to fight will have to wait for now." Anatolio nodded. He had forgotten about their deal.

"I'm still sorry," Anatolio said before standing and leaving.

CHAPTER TWENTY-ONE

Two weeks passed quickly for everyone but Leila, who had nothing to do but to sit around. The day before Roger was to return, Leila sat on the balcony and sulked. She wanted to be down at the market, and as she watched the people walking toward the center of the town, she couldn't help but be disappointed.

"It's not fair," she complained to Nalick, who was sitting outside with her, reading his papers.

"I know," he replied, without looking up from his work. Nalick was as eager for Roger to come as she was.

"I don't understand why I can't be down there," she added.

"Because it would be obvious to everyone who you are," Nalick replied, setting down his papers. "Theo promised to bring you back treats from the market." Nalick stood and moved over next to her. "Roger will be here soon, hopefully. Tomorrow isn't that far away."

"I found him at the market," Theo said, while walking out on to the balcony with someone behind him. Leila strained to turn to see Roger standing with Theo.

"You're early," Leila cried out, trying to stand to greet him, momentarily forgetting about her leg. Nalick quickly stopped her.

"I figured Nalick would need some relief from dealing with you," Roger replied. Theo stood behind Leila, vigorously nodding his head. "Do you have a hospital wing in your palace?" Roger asked Nalick, knowing the answer. "Is Anatolio around?"

"I'll go get him," Theo replied, quickly hurrying out of the room.

"Have you been behaving?" Roger asked Leila.

"As much as I can," she answered. "Though I'm not happy to have to sit in one place all day."

"It's good for you," Roger said. "It should help teach you patience."

"I have patience," Leila responded. "I just don't like to overuse it." Roger smiled and patted her hand. He missed her quick wit and was finding it quite lonely in the north knowing she wasn't coming back.

"You can get your first lesson. How to remove stitches," Roger said to Anatolio, who was entering the room.

Anatolio brought Leila to the hospital ward of the palace, and Nalick finally was left to get his work done. With Leila around, Nalick's unfinished workload seemed to only increase day after day. Nalick finally understood why his father always had extra men to help him.

The hospital staff quickly cleared several rooms for Roger to use. Leila sat alone as Roger and Anatolio cleaned his tools in the nearby room. She was bored with waiting, but they hadn't left any sharp tools in the room for her to do it herself. Roger returned along with Anatolio.

"So I hear you haven't tried to remove the stitches in your leg?" Roger asked.

"No, I could find anything sharp enough," Leila said truthfully. Had she found anything that would cut, she would have removed them a week ago.

Roger smiled and patted Anatolio on the back. "Then I guess, for once, I get to do the honors."

Leila carefully pulled the edge of her skirt up to her thigh to reveal the stitches. Anatolio was shocked to see how many there were. Roger moved closer and studied the area.

"Did you take all the medicine I gave you?" Roger asked.

"Yes, all of it," Leila said, also looking at her leg.

Roger probed the healing wound a bit more began to worry that it was not completely healed. He explained the procedure thoroughly to Anatolio and then began cutting the stitches, pulling slightly to remove them. When there were only a few left, Roger offered his small scissors and tweezers to Anatolio and asked him to try. Leila watched as the young man meticulously copied the movements Roger had made. Roger stood beside Leila while he observed. Roger moved next to her broken leg. He examined it.

"It has healed enough for you to put a little pressure on it." Roger examined her leg with the cast removed. "Now, I'm not saying you can walk on it, but you can use it to balance your weight when standing. You can use crutches to get around now, but I'll need to check back in a few weeks to make sure it's still healing. It seems your leg was further away from the poison and not as affected, which is fortunate for you," Roger explained to her as he reached over and took her hand. Quickly, he pricked the tip of her finger.

"Thanks for the warning," she said sarcastically. Roger put a drop of her blood on a tin plate. Leila watched as the blood turned from a red color to yellow. "What's that mean?"

"You still have some of that poison in your blood. It should have been out of your system by now," Roger explained. "There must be more left in you. I need to take a look at your back." Roger rummaged through his bag. "I tested the stones' reactions and found something that will indicate where the leftover piece is—even through skin."

Leila sat on the table and began unhooking the straps of her dress. Anatolio quickly looked away and began to blush when he realized she was undressing in front of him. Leila laughed, moving her top to her waist as she laid down on the table with her back exposed for Roger. Leila wasn't shy around Roger.

"Roger, I think your new apprentice has never seen a naked woman before," Leila teased.

"Leila, be nice," Roger scolded. "He's just a young one." Roger began to remove the stitches in her back.

Leila laughed again. Anatolio's reaction amused her.

"I guess the best way to lose you when you follow me is to just undress." Leila cringed, feeling Roger spread a cold cream on her back. "You could at least warm it up first," she complained to Roger.

"And you could at least be a bit nicer to this boy. He will be around for quite a long time," Roger replied. He also found it amusing that Anatolio was embarrassed to see Leila's body, but Roger needed to defend the young man.

"This isn't good," Roger commented.

Leila picked up her head to view Roger's reaction. Over the years she had learned to read his facial expressions, even through his attempts to cover up the truth. Roger was obviously not happy, and a bit worried.

"Leila, how have you been feeling?" Roger asked, as he began removing more of his tools from his bag, setting them aside on another table in the room.

"More tired than normal," Leila replied, giving a yawn to prove her point. Leila had known since the day she left him in Cath something didn't seem right, but she assumed it was from being poisoned.

"I count six more pieces in your back," Roger said.

"Good thing Roger came to visit," Leila said to Nalick as he entered the room. She lowered her upper body slightly to keep herself covered. Anatolio noticed and chuckled to himself. She was modest with Nalick, but did not seem to be with Roger.

Roger put Leila back to sleep and then removed the extra pieces of poison he had missed. Anatolio watched as Roger delicately cut the skin on Leila's back. Afterward, he carefully sewed the incision closed and checked again. Anatolio was amazed by the quickness and accuracy with which Roger was able to remove the stones. After Roger was finished, Anatolio went to get Nalick.

"All finished," Roger explained, showing Nalick the small pieces he had removed. "She should heal much quicker now." He placed the stones in a small container. Roger gently pulled her dress top back on and rebuttoned it. "You can take her upstairs. If you could get me some hot water, we will join you shortly to wake her back up."

Nalick tenderly scooped Leila into his arms, leaving Roger and Anatolio to clean the surgical instruments.

"So do you have the stomach to do this?" Roger asked Anatolio, who had just seen his first surgery ever.

"Yes," Anatolio replied, continuing to help clean everything. "Who trained you?"

"No one," Roger replied. "In all honesty, I'm never quite sure what I'm doing, but she depends on me to figure it out. Someday, it will need to be you that she looks to." Roger watched the young man clean each tool. Anatolio was perfect for the job. "You will have a lot to learn, but between me teaching, and Leila getting hurt often, I think we'll be able to do it."

"So, you've never seen a naked woman before?" Roger asked, changing the subject and causing Anatolio to blush again. "Well, I'll tell you, she pretty much ruins seeing any other woman." Anatolio was surprised. "I may be old, but I still know who is beautiful. She's probably the most perfect woman you will ever see—clothed or not." Roger chuckled as he continued to place each instrument in its correct designated location in his bag.

Anatolio and Roger returned to Leila's room to find Nalick sitting on the bed, watching her. Neither man wanted to interrupt him as they stood in the doorway and watched him tenderly touch her face. The love Nalick felt for Leila was obvious.

"The water is in the pot on the table," Nalick said, finally noticing. Roger quickly brewed the tea and brought it over to Nalick, who gently sat Leila up and helped her drink the tea. After he handed the cup back to Roger, Nalick again laid her down on the bed. A few minutes later, Leila slowly opened her eyes.

"It better be the same day," she warned Roger, who laughed.

"See," Roger said to Anatolio, who still stood in the doorway. "Good as normal." Roger was on his way back home, and Leila was left to spend two more weeks recovering.

Since Roger had given Leila his approval to move around carefully, she spent every morning working with Anatolio and Theo the following two weeks while waiting for Roger's return; she tried her best to teach Anatolio how to fight better without physically showing him how to do anything. She was quite surprised to see how quickly he progressed, and had no doubts as to why Nalick had chosen him. Each day, they worked on a new move, and by lunch time he had mastered it. With Leila able to move more, Nalick could go back to his work full time, but Nalick was even more distracted without her around. The day before Roger was to return for the second time, Nalick left his office before lunch to check on Leila. She was in the training courtyard. Nalick was surprised to find that she was not just there with Anatolio and Theo anymore.

"Why are so many people here?" Nalick asked the nearest man.

"I heard Nikias agreed to fight Anatolio," the young

man said eagerly.

Down below, Nalick watched as several people helped Leila sit back down. She didn't see him in the crowd; she didn't seem to see the crowd at all. Nalick stood with the men and watched as Nikias approached Anatolio. The matchup was unfair; Nikias had many more years of experience, but Anatolio didn't seem to mind. Nikias made the first move, and Anatolio quickly evaded it. Nalick watched Leila study the two men's movements. The match lasted longer than Nalick had expected, though Anatolio lost in the end. After they were finished, Leila made Nikias repeat his last move as she walked Anatolio through how he should counter it and use it to his advantage. When the men standing around saw how Leila could have easily won the match, they cheered. Leila smiled up at the men watching her and finally noticed Nalick was standing in the crowd.

"You are not supposed to be walking," Nalick said, scooping her into his arms.

"Roger will be here tomorrow, and he will give me permission to walk gently on it. I'm just getting a head start," Leila explained, though did not ask to be set down. Being in his arms was comfortable.

"So what do you think?" she asked, referring to the two men who were sitting and resting after their long match.

"I'm honestly amazed." Nalick didn't set Leila down. "But, for your last day before Roger returns, I'm going to insist you spend the rest of the day relaxing. Roger will scold me if you hurt yourself right before he gets here." Nalick turned to carry her away.

"Thanks, Nikias," Leila called, and waved to the two men as Nalick carried her from the courtyard. Anatolio bowed his head to her as she left.

Nalick took her straight to her room and set her down gently on the balcony. He began to pace, wondering how to tell her his thoughts. "I thought I'd get so much more work done now that you can do whatever you want, but..." He paused.

"You missed me," she guessed, grinning.

"Yes," he said, sitting down next to her and moving her to his lap. Leila casually put her arms around his neck. It was warm and inviting to sit so close to him. Her heart began to race, and she needed to concentrate to hear to him talking.

"I've decided I'm going to choose a few men to work right below me to help get all this work done. It was fine to fill the entire day working before you came along, but now I just don't find it entertaining." Leila was happy he wanted to spend time with her. "Life's too short to spend behind a desk."

Leila nodded. "I figured that out when I was five years old. Glad to see you've finally caught up."

"Hey," Nalick said, and he tickled her ribs. The knock at the door interrupted their conversation. Nalick rose and opened the door.

"Early again?" Leila asked, turning to view Roger as he walked out onto the balcony behind Nalick.

"Would you rather I was late? I can go back to the inn at which I plan to stay and return in a couple of days," Roger suggested, pretending to turn and leave.

"No, no," Leila cried, grasping into the air because she couldn't throw herself at him to stop him. "I'm glad you're early."

"So, I can guess by the smile on your face you are doing much better this time around," Roger said, sitting down next to Leila. He picked up her injured leg and slowly unwrapped the support around it. "It looks good. Have you been following my advice and not walking on it?"

"Do you think anyone around here would let me get away with walking on it?" she responded, nodding her head toward Nalick.

"I knew he would be good for something," Roger joked before giving her the okay to walk on it.

Leila rose the next morning, excited that she could finally return to the market. Roger had given her consent to walk again with a cane. She was awake before everyone and happily humming to herself while getting ready. Nalick was surprised when he finally woke to find she was already to go. He hurried to not keep her waiting. Leila, though, didn't mind waiting for everyone. After one month she would finally get to leave the palace. She felt cramped and caged. The one comfort she had in the palace was the garden, but she no longer felt safe sitting alone there. Only Anatolio had noticed.

Leila led Roger along with her escorts to the market. Roger hadn't been to the Lexia market in years, and was surprised to find Leila excited to go to it. She wished to hurry along with the crowd, but it was slow walking with the cane, and her leg wasn't yet healed enough to walk without it. Nearing the first stand, Leila searched the crowd for the young children that met her there when she first went to the market. She didn't see them and continued on to her favorite fruit stand. Leila introduced Roger to the people she passed on the way.

"How many people know who you are?" Roger whispered to Leila under his breath.

"Just a few." Leila shrugged. Part of her charm and ability to win over people's loyalty came from her honesty and openness to trust them.

As the day proceeded and there was still no sign of the children, Leila began to wonder where they were. *Did Phillip recognize me?* she wondered. She had seen him in the crowd on their way back into the city after being kidnapped, but she wasn't sure he saw her. Leila joined the men sitting at a table enjoying snacks and drinks as she continued to search the crowd.

"Is something wrong?" Roger asked her.

"Normally I meet three children here: an older boy and his younger brother and sister. I haven't seen any of them yet today." Leila looked at the clock and could see it was getting close to the time Phillip would normally leave for work.

"Could they just be late?" Roger asked. Roger remembered that she had mentioned the children to him before.

"The oldest works and always made them leave at the midday bell." Leila pointed to the clock above the market. "I hope they're okay."

After everyone was finished with their drinks and snacks, they stood to return to the palace. Leila continued to search as she followed but could see no sign of the children. Nalick put his arm around her as he could see she was worried. As they neared the last stand, Leila noticed Tim standing by himself. As soon as Tim saw Leila he ran to her and smiled. Balancing against Nalick, Leila carefully picked him up.

"Where's Phillip?" Leila asked, looking around.

"With Ruth," Tim replied. "Ruth is sick, and Phillip stayed with her to make her better."

"How long has she been sick?" Leila asked.

"I dunno," Tim replied. "Phillip told me to come and tell you we can't see you today."

"Could you take me to them?" Leila asked. "My friend here is a doctor, and maybe he can help Ruth." Leila set Tim back down on the ground.

Tim stared up at all the people standing with Leila. "I'm not supposed to take grown-ups to our home," Tim said. Leila looked at the men around her.

"Can Roger and Nalick come with?" she asked.

"Nikias, Javed, Theo, and Macarius, go on back to the palace. We will stay with Leila," Nalick said. The men followed their orders and walked back toward the palace.

"Is this better?" Leila asked. Tim smiled and began to walk between two of the nearest buildings. Leila followed close behind him as quickly as she could. The young boy had failed to notice that she was limping, but he slowed when she wasn't walking close to him. Soon, they arrived at a broken-down, three-story building. Inside, Leila could see several children hurriedly hiding. Roger quickly stopped Leila from following the young boy into the building.

"Leila, you're not completely healthy yet. You should stay out here, just in case it's something contagious," Roger warned as he and Nalick began to follow Tim.

"Anatolio is nearby, so you should be safe," Nalick said, carefully entering through the broken half door. Leila watched as the remaining children ran from Roger and Nalick. They all feared adults.

Once inside, Tim led the two men to the back of the building. In a corner near a window, Phillip was sitting with Ruth. Phillip was desperately trying to get Ruth to drink the small glass of water in his hand. When he saw Tim return, Phillip was relieved, but then became startled to see the adults with him.

"Tim, who are they?" Phillip asked as Roger approached in front of Nalick. "Is Leila with you?" Leila was the only adult that the children could trust.

"She's outside. She has been sick, and I didn't want her to get any worse. She sent me in to look at Ruth," Roger tried to explain to the young man who was eyeing him anxiously.

"This is the man who trained Leila and always fixes her when she gets hurt," Nalick explained, and Phillip relaxed a bit. Roger moved near Ruth and carefully began to examine the young child.

"How long has she been like this?" Roger asked Phillip, reaching down to feel Ruth's face.

"About two days. She hasn't been eating much, and anything she has eaten came back up," Phillip explained, backing up to give Roger room to move. "I tried to get her to at least drink some water, but she stopped doing that this morning."

Roger felt the child's forehead again before he began to prod around her body. "Has she been this warm the entire time she has been sick?"

"No. Sometimes she's warm and other times she isn't," Phillip said.

"Can we bring her back with us?" Roger asked Nalick. "I can do a better job back in the medical ward. Who knows what diseases they are passing around here."

"Of course," Nalick said, moving to pick Ruth up. A scared Phillip stood by and watched.

"Can you make her better?" Phillip asked the two men.

"I'll do the best I can," Roger said.

"Can we come with you?" Phillip asked, not wanting to let the two men leave with Ruth.

"Of course," Nalick replied. "We will hurry ahead with Ruth, but Leila is waiting outside. She will bring you back with her." Phillip and Tim followed the two men out of the building. Once outside, Leila neared the men, but Roger quickly pushed her back.

"We're heading back to the palace. Leila, you need to stay away for now. I don't need you to get sick again," Roger said to her. "She has some sort of infection. Until I find the source, you need to stay back. "

"Is Anatolio here?" Nalick asked, keeping her at a distance.

"Yes." Leila waved to the shadows and the young man appeared.

"Please walk Leila and these young boys back to the palace. We're going to hurry ahead," Nalick explained. Anatolio nodded with a bow.

"Once you get her back to her room, please join me,"

Roger asked, and again Anatolio nodded. Roger and Nalick hurried down the street with the young girl in their arms.

"Phillip, this is Anatolio. Anatolio, this is Phillip, and this is Tim," Leila said about the young boy pulling on her dress. Leila smiled down at Tim. "Sorry, I can't carry you today." Phillip stared at Leila. He watched as she began to slowly walk using the cane in the same direction as the men had hurried.

"You're her, aren't you?" Phillip asked, picking up his younger brother and beginning to walk alongside Leila.

"I thought I saw you on our way home," she said to him, not answering his question.

"I heard you got really hurt bad when someone tried to kidnap you," Phillip said, checking her for some major new scar.

"I was hurt, but that man who left with Ruth fixed me. I'm almost back to normal," Leila explained, continuing to walk in her slow pace.

"Leila, if you need to stop, we can," Anatolio said to her. Phillip looked at Anatolio.

"Is he your guard?" Phillip asked. "He doesn't look much older than me."

Most people would underestimate Anatolio due to his age for the rest of his life. Leila turned back to Anatolio. "I'm fine, really," she said, but did not convince him. "Exercise is good for me. I need to build my strength back up." Leila was stubborn, and any protest would fall on deaf ears. Without objection, Anatolio wound his arm around her waist to balance her as she continued to walk.

"So that man really is a doctor?" Phillip asked.

"Where I come from, he is," Leila said. She patted the young man on his back. "Don't worry. Roger has never failed to fix me up and I get hurt all the time."

They continued to walk in silence. Leila kept walking

at a steady pace, but as they neared the palace she began to slow. Macarius and Theo quickly hurried over to her as she approached.

"Nalick said to help you," Macarius explained as he scooped Leila into his arms. She was too tired to protest, and Macarius carried her back to her room. The two young boys followed and were soon amazed as they walked into her spacious, richly-furnished room.

CHAPTER TWENTY-TWO

"Tim, do you like to draw?" Leila asked. The young boy turned to her with a grin and nodded vigorously. Leila grabbed paper and pencils from Nalick's desk and set them on the table. Tim climbed into the chair and began to draw. It was the first time she had seen him be quiet for more than a minute. She returned to Phillip, who had fallen asleep. Leila walked back to her bed and sat down. Her leg was getting tired, and she decided to rest a bit also. After a while, Tim was bored with drawing and soon joined Leila. She watched as he hopped on to the bed next to her and then wiggled until he was within inches of her.

"Is it nap time?" Tim asked, pointing to his brother.

"Sure," Leila replied. Tim lay down and grabbed the nearest blanket. Within moments, Tim was also asleep.

Nalick returned not long after both boys fell asleep. Leila stood and slowly walked to the door to join him.

"Ruth had something stuck in her foot. It wasn't treated and caused an infection. Roger was able to get it out, but he had to put in stitches. It will need to be tended to for a while. Right now she's asleep," Nalick explained. "Anatolio will bring her up when Roger is finished." Leila nodded and returned to the room. Slowly she made her way to the balcony and sat down outside in the fresh air. Nalick followed her.

"He's so young to be having to raise his siblings on his own," Leila said to Nalick.

"How old were you when you began to train for your

job?" Nalick asked, knowing the answer was that she was younger than Phillip was now.

"I know. But I was never responsible for anyone else except myself. It's a whole different story when you have to take care of someone else," she said. Nalick understood. His life was far less complicated when he was alone, but he had no desire for things to be the way they used to be.

"Will she be all right?" Leila asked about Ruth.

"Roger seems to think that she'll be fine, but she will need to be watched closely for the next few days," Nalick explained.

Leila and Nalick failed to hear the soft footsteps approaching them from behind. Tim had woken from his nap and was hungry. Following her voice, Tim found Leila and Nalick sitting outside. He gently tapped Leila's shoulder. Startled, Leila turned to find Tim standing, still holding the blanket from the bed and rubbing his eyes.

"Is Phillip still asleep?" Leila asked, picking up Tim and sitting him on her lap. Tim nodded his head without talking and stared at Nalick.

"Tim, you remember Nalick," Leila said, trying to ease the small child's hesitation. Tim continued to look at Nalick, and then, as though he finally remembered, he grinned ear to ear. He eagerly slid from Leila's lap to Nalick's as he began to tell Nalick the same story he told Phillip earlier. Leila watched as Nalick listened intently to the small child's ramblings. Leila was used to children when living at home, since she had many nieces and nephews that were always running around. She wasn't sure how Nalick would handle the small child at first, but he seemed to be a natural.

Phillip woke up to the sound of Roger and Anatolio bringing Ruth back. Leila quickly stood and hurried as best she could to the men to see how the child was doing. Anatolio carried the small, sleeping child and laid her down in Leila's bed.

"She will probably be asleep through the night," Roger explained. "She was fussing so much that I couldn't get the object out of her foot, and I wanted to drug her, but I've never given sleeping drugs to such a small child before. It's a good thing Anatolio was there to help hold her down to let me get whatever it was out of her foot. I couldn't tell if it was metal or a piece of wood, but it was stuck quite well." Phillip stood and looked at his sister before turning to Roger.

"How much do I need to pay you?" Phillip asked.

"Nothing," Roger replied. "She was much easier to fix than Leila, and I've never charged Leila." Phillip didn't seem to know how to respond. "She will need to drink this medicine with each meal," Roger explained, handing Phillip a small jar. "Just add ten drops to a drink. She will also need to be cleaned twice a day and have her foot bandaged until it heals. Anatolio knows how to do it, so just ask him." Phillip nodded. He would do anything to make his sister better.

"Is it time for food now?" Tim asked, finding the first opportunity to interrupt the grownups.

Leila smiled. "Sure. Roger and Anatolio, do you want to stay for dinner?"

Roger shook his head no. "I've had my fill of kids for the day. I'm going to take Anatolio up on his offer for a nice, quiet dinner at his place." Leila smiled. Roger didn't have very much tolerance for screaming children. "I'll be back in the morning to check on her. Now, you get some rest, also. You're not completely healed yourself, so don't overdo it," Roger ordered.

Leila sat down to dinner with Nalick and the two boys. Since she had been living at the palace she had found it strange to be so isolated. Her days were spent in silence, and meals were only her and Nalick. Now, with the two boys at the table, things felt more normal to her. The palace was beginning to feel more like a home than the isolated, cold environment it felt like her first night there. Tim was a great source of entertainment. He continued to talk through the whole meal, and let his older brother say very little. When Tim got too excited, his brother had to calm him down before he woke Ruth, who slept through the meal.

As bedtime neared, Nalick offered to take the boys and stay in the guest room down the hall, but Leila saw that Phillip didn't want to leave his sister. Phillip offered to stay on the couch, if he could just stay near her, so all five people ended up sleeping in Leila's room. Nalick and Leila lay on the edges of the bed with Ruth and Tim nestled between them. Leila was amazed by how quiet the room had become. She drifted off to only the sounds of people lightly breathing.

Before dawn, Leila slowly opened her eyes and found herself face-to-face with a smiling Ruth. The little girl grinned and continued to touch Leila's face.

"Lei," the little girl whispered, "pretty." Ruth picked up a piece of Leila's hair.

Leila mimicked the small child and touched Ruth's face. "Pretty," Leila said, and the child giggled.

"'Ere's 'lip?" Ruth asked. Leila pointed to the couch across the room where Phillip was still asleep. "Tim?" Leila pointed behind the child. Ruth turned and giggled more. "Tim's sleepy," she said, turning back to face Leila. Leila marveled at the small child. The day before, Leila had watched Nalick carry off the sick child, and today Ruth smiled and giggled as if nothing were wrong. Leila watched as the small girl's forehead wrinkled in thought of her next question. "Is Ruth better?" she asked Leila. Ruth pulled her foot to her face and tried to remove the bandage.

"No," Leila said, stopping her. "That will make you all better if you leave it on." The servant door clicked as it opened. The shy, but curious, Ruth climbed slightly onto Leila to get a better view of Mauve walking in the room.

"For us?" Ruth asked about the food, and a startled Mauve turned to find Ruth and Leila awake. Mauve's face melted into a smile upon seeing Ruth. Leila sat up carefully and put Ruth on her lap.

"This is Mauve," Leila whispered, introducing her, and Mauve cautiously moved toward Leila and Ruth.

"I brought some muffins and juice for those that woke up before the rest," Mauve explained. "The girls were going to bring the rest of your breakfast later."

"That's good," Leila said. "I'm going to get this little girl cleaned before we eat." Leila cautiously stood while holding the young child and was relieved to find that she was small enough for Leila to carry. "Do you like water?" Ruth continued to smile as her dark curls bounced up and down with her head. "Good." Mauve hurried ahead to start the bath water.

"I'll send someone in to help," Mauve said, leaving the bath room.

Leila sat on the edge of the bath and began to unwrap Ruth's bandaged foot. Ruth watched intently to see if her foot was still beneath the cloth and cheered upon seeing it.

Leila lifted Ruth into the water. The small child stared around the room, amazed by the size of the bath, and she began to ask about everything she saw. In no time, a maid was sent to help Leila and Ruth bathe. By the time they were done, the boys were all awake and waiting for breakfast. Leila returned with Ruth wrapped in a towel. Nalick stood quickly as they entered and offered to help, but Ruth shied away from him.

"I'll go get Anatolio," Nalick said, leaving the room instead.

Once Nalick was gone, Leila sat down at the table with Ruth on her lap. Phillip and Tim were both excited to see that their sister was feeling better.

"Is he really the king?" Phillip asked Leila, as he sat down next to her.

"Yes," Leila said, interested in Phillip's questioning without Nalick present.

"Would he know my father? My mom said he was a noble, and since Nalick is king...," Phillip trailed off.

"You should ask him about it, not me," Leila said, knowing the young man was not completely comfortable around Nalick. Nalick returned with Anatolio, and Phillip became quiet once again. Anatolio quickly put medicine on the cut on Ruth's foot and wrapped it back up in a new, clean cloth. Leila was surprised to see that Ruth wasn't afraid of Anatolio. After he was finished, Anatolio bowed his head to Leila and then to Nalick and left without a word.

"Is Roger still here?" Leila asked Nalick.

"Yes, I think so. Anatolio said Roger went out this morning but would be back to say good-bye to you before he left for Cath," Nalick explained, sitting across from Leila at the table. Tim hurried over and sat next to Nalick. It hadn't taken the small boy very long to figure out where he could get something to eat. Several of Leila's dressing women returned with food. The children's eyes all grew larger as the saw the feast placed before them. None of the children moved; they just sat and stared at the pile of food.

"What would you like?" Leila asked Ruth. Ruth pointed at several items, and Leila put each on the plate before her. Everyone else quickly followed.

After their large meal, Nalick insisted the two older children take baths, also. Tim complained, but Phillip dragged him to the bathroom with him. Nalick followed after the two boys to show them where everything was while Leila took Ruth out onto the balcony.

"What's that?" Ruth asked, pointing to the city

beneath them.

"That's Lexia," Leila explained, and she sat down with the small girl. Cautiously, Ruth slid from the chair and tried to see how much her bandaged foot hurt. Ruth was very happy to find she could walk on it and slowly wandered around the balcony asking about everything she saw. Leila smiled at the young girl's curiosity. Nalick returned and sat down next to Leila.

"She seems to be doing fine," he commented.

"I don't think she even knows how bad she was hurt," Leila replied. "So what do we do with them?" Leila asked. Leila didn't want to return them to the broken-down warehouse they were currently living in.

"I figured I could take them down to meet Gabor, and maybe he would know what they are supposed to do in their lives," Nalick replied. He didn't want to return them to where they found the children the day before either. Nalick quickly bent over while Ruth was distracted, and kissed Leila.

After the three children were washed and dressed, Leila and Nalick left them with Gabor and walked to the palace gardens. Leila hadn't returned to them since she had been abducted from it. As they entered, several of Nalick's guards patrolled the inside and around the courtyard and Anatolio was in his usual tree, overseeing everything. Nalick wanted Leila to be comfortable in the garden, but with all the company, Leila didn't find it the same.

"So, any plans for what to do with them?" Leila asked, sitting on a bench beneath a tree.

"Why don't we keep them here with us in the palace?" Nalick suggested. Leila was stunned. She wanted to keep the children herself, but doubted Nalick would choose to do that.

"You really want to have three children running around?" she asked, and he nodded.

Leila and Nalick stopped their conversation as Tim ran into the garden, leading his brother, who was carrying Ruth. All three children were laughing with Gabor and following behind Phillip. Tim ran to the closest tree and tried to grab the nearest branches. Anatolio quickly slid down and helped the young boy climb onto the branch. Phillip joined Leila as they stood to greet Gabor. Gabor and Nalick walked to a point in the garden where Leila and the children couldn't overhear them.

"He's a seer, right?" Phillip asked Leila, sitting Ruth on the grass next to the bench. Ruth began to entertain herself by pulling at the flowers next to her.

"Yes," Leila replied, shocked that Phillip knew who Gabor was.

"Leila?" Phillip asked in a serious tone. "What will happen to us?" By not showing up to work the past two days, Phillip had lost his job, and had no way to feed his brother and sister.

"I don't know," she replied honestly. "If it were up to me I'd like to keep you here, but it's not up to me." Phillip intently watched as Nalick finished his conversation with Gabor and returned to Leila and the children. Nalick led the way back to their room with Tim on his back. Phillip tentatively followed.

"I need to talk to Mauve first, and then you three," Nalick said to the children. Leila could tell from his tone he had made a decision and the process was starting. The twinkle in his eyes told her what he had decided. Nalick went to Mauve and then returned. Leila sat on a couch, playing a game with Ruth when Nalick returned. Phillip quickly hurried over to him.

"I know you've decided what to do with us," Phillip quickly sputtered out. "I know we're just peasants and shouldn't even be allowed in this wing of the palace. I'm ready to leave, but please keep Tim and Ruth. They are really good kids. You can provide so much more for them than I can. Please just keep my brother and sister," the twelve-year-old begged.

"How about we keep all three of you instead?" Nalick suggested, picking up Ruth, who finally warmed to him, and joining Leila, who was sitting on the couch. Phillip began to argue as he didn't listen carefully to what Nalick had said, but once Phillip realized, he stopped.

"But we...," Phillip began, not understanding.

"I don't know if you noticed, but I'm not too worried about what class you're from," Nalick said. "Leila isn't a noble, and she's a queen." Leila nodded. Phillip stared at Leila, and Nalick continued to play with Ruth as if nothing unusual happened. "You see, the good thing about being king is that I get to make up the rules." Phillip continued to stare at Nalick. Phillip had imagined the king to be just like the rest of the nobles and was shocked to find he was so different.

"So we can stay here?" Phillip looked around the room, wondering if he heard correct.

"We would like it very much if you'd stay," Leila said. "But that's your choice."

Tim stopped running around the room as he heard part of the conversation. "We don't have to go back to our home with the other kids?"

"Not if you don't want to," Leila replied.

"Hooray!" the small child yelled and jumped up and down.

Ruth looked at Leila. "Lei my new mommy?" she asked Phillip. Phillip was too stunned to reply, and the small child pondered her own question.

"There are some laws I cannot change as easily," Nalick explained to Phillip. "You and Tim will be given the title prince and Ruth princess, but none of you will be able to become king or queen. I hope that doesn't disappoint you too much," Nalick added, smiling at the shocked expression on Phillip's face.

"I'll be a prince?" Phillip repeated in disbelief.

"Yes," Nalick replied. Nalick stood to leave. "I need to get everything in order for tomorrow." He bent down and kissed Leila's forehead. "There will be some men coming here with Theo and Macarius to open up the extra rooms." Leila didn't understand, but nodded anyways. Nalick would be busy again, as everything he did required paperwork. Leila had no doubt where his heart was.

"What is tomorrow?" Phillip asked before Nalick left the room.

"I'll present the three of you to the nobles and court of Lior as our children," Nalick said before leaving the room.

Phillip sat stunned beside Leila. Tim again began to run around the room with his paper bird, oblivious to what was to become of their lives. Ruth continued to stare from Phillip to Leila, waiting for an answer to her question. The knock at the door interrupted Phillip's thoughts, and Leila stood to open it. She held the door open as Theo quickly grabbed it and was followed in by Macarius and several men.

"Nalick asked us to open up the extra rooms," Theo explained.

"That's nice," Leila said, as the men entered the room and each bowed to her. "What extra rooms?"

"Some courier you are," Macarius said, joining them. "This is the royal wing of the palace. Nalick was raised here as a child. After he became king he didn't need all the extra space and had the rooms closed. Now that you need more room, we're here to open all the extra rooms, of which you didn't notice," he pointed out.

"If you could just move the kids to the balcony, we can do this quicker and then Mauve can have all the rooms cleaned," Theo explained.

"Phillip, Tim," Leila said to the two boys, who were still running around as Tim's bird chased Phillip. "Can you run onto the balcony?" Phillip changed his direction and ran to the balcony. Leila quickly scooped Ruth up and took her there.

"Miss," the maid, Elena, said quietly, approaching the balcony and blushing as soon as she saw Anatolio standing there, also. Anatolio bowed his head to Leila and quickly retreated back into the shadows of the room. "Mauve has told me that she wants me to help you with the two younger children," she explained. "I brought some toys." Elena offered the basket of toys to Ruth and Tim who each quickly found a toy and began to play.

"This is Tim, Ruth, and Phillip," Leila introduced the children. "This is Elena," Leila said. Phillip shook her hand, and Tim mimicked him.

"Lena," Ruth repeated Leila.

With Elena watching the children, Leila snuck back into the room to see what the men were doing. Leila first noticed that Macarius was removing many of the tapestries that covered the walls. Behind each she could see a doorframe that had been filled by a flimsy wall. She was surprised when the men removed two large tapestries and the walls behind them on the west wall farthest from the entrance, because beyond them was another large room. She slowly walked past the men into the large, empty room. Windows surrounded the room on three sides.

"This will now be your bedroom," Theo explained, coming up behind her. Quickly, several of the women, along with Mauve, entered the room and began to clean it. Leila backed out of the room as they worked. "We'll move your bed in here after it is clean."

Leila returned to the main room to find that near the door to the bathroom, four new doors had been opened. She peeked her head in to find that they were all additional bathing rooms, all about half the size of the larger one. She continued around the main room and was shocked as the men removed the largest tapestry and wall to the left of the doorway. Behind it was a staircase that led to a second floor that extended over the hallway and Theo's home.

"There are all the extra bedrooms," Theo explained. Leila hadn't thought much about where she was living, but it seemed to make sense. If this was the royal wing where Nalick was raised, it must have been more of a home than just a large room like it was when she moved in to it.

Leila walked through the door behind Nalick's desk. In the new room was a large kitchen with enough space for a table. Everything was covered in dust, and it hadn't been used in years. Through the kitchen was yet another room. She cautiously walked through the dusty room. Several paintings were sitting against the wall. She carefully looked through them. Each was a painting of the same woman.

"That was his mother," Theo explained. Leila looked at the beautiful, dark-haired woman and could see the resemblance to Nalick. Each painting seemed to capture the sadness in her eyes. "King Godfrith couldn't bear to take these pictures with him after she died."

"She looks *so* young," Leila said, still staring at the pictures.

"She was," Theo replied. "She was fourteen when she married King Godfrith, and sixteen when she had Nalick. She didn't love the king, but King Godfrith hoped that someday she would. I don't know if that ever happened. She really was a great mother to Nalick, and he was crushed when she died."

Leila wandered back into the main room as several of the men were moving her bed into the new room. "I'd take you upstairs, but Nalick told me he wanted to show you something up there." Leila nodded and looked curiously up the stairs. She would have to wait, since

Theo would never go against an order from Nalick.

Nalick returned in time for dinner. All the rooms had been opened and cleaned. After dinner, Nalick took the children and Leila upstairs. Leila noticed the hallway that extended to the right immediately at the top of the stairs, but followed Nalick as he led her down the main hallway. Leila was surprised by how much was hidden upstairs.

"The first room to the left here is where Anatolio is going to stay," Nalick explained. "It's easier to watch over Leila if he's living here, now that we have more room. The first room to the right will be for Elena. She has volunteered to be the nanny for the younger children. That way, if either of you get scared during the night, she will be right here, and you won't have to go all the way downstairs by yourself," Nalick said to Tim and Ruth. "The second room to the right will be for Ruth." Nalick opened the door to the room and Phillip set Ruth down. Carefully, she walked around the room, feeling the pillows and blankets on the bed. "See." Nalick opened the door on the left side of the room. Ruth peeked her head into the next room. "Elena will be right there." He pointed to the empty bed. Ruth nodded.

Nalick led the way back into the hallway, and Ruth grabbed the doll off her bed and brought it with her. "The second room on the left will be for Phillip," Nalick said as he opened the door to the room. This room also had an additional door, which Phillip opened to the next room.

"That leads to Tim's room," Nalick said as Tim walked in and eyed the stack of toys in the corner of the room. Ruth sat down next to her brother and began to look through the toys, also.

"I'll stay here with them until they get bored," Phillip suggested, as Leila and Nalick left the room, going back into the hallway.

"And the other five rooms?" Leila asked.

"Empty for now," Nalick replied. Leila raised her

eyebrows and Nalick chuckled. "When I was growing up, they were all empty except for my room. My father didn't have any more children until after I became king."

"So where does this hallway go?" Leila asked as they neared the stairs.

"I wanted to surprise you with it. Go ahead," Nalick suggested.

Leila walked down the hallway and opened the door. She followed the walkway as it turned left and went up a few more stairs. At the top of the staircase Leila finally realized that there was a garden on the roof of the palace.

"I know you like to spend time downstairs in the palace garden, but you haven't been back there except for this morning. I thought that maybe this would make you feel safer, and you still could sit in a garden," Nalick explained. Leila turned around and smiled at Nalick. She quickly ran over and hugged him.

"Thank you," she whispered in his ear, sending tingles down his spine.

As evening approached, Nalick helped Leila get the children off to bed. Ruth was unsure about sleeping in her own room, but once Elena showed her that she was in the room next door, Ruth settled down to sleep. Tim, on the other hand, refused to sleep alone. Phillip didn't mind, and easily shared his bed with his brother. Quietly, amidst all the commotion, Anatolio had moved his few belongings into the room next to Phillip without anyone except Leila noticing. Once the downstairs room was quiet again, Leila made herself a cup of tea and sat outside on the balcony. Her life had continued to change drastically in the past two months. She was beginning to forget how alone she felt now that she was surrounded by many people who loved her. Nalick joined her outside and looked at the stars.

"You really should get to bed," Nalick commented. "Tomorrow should be even more hectic than today as I'm sure Mauve won't let a single one of us leave this room without meeting her expectations." Nalick rested his arm around Leila. She figured the day would be hectic but did not want to reach the next day any sooner than needed.

"I'd rather just stay here for a bit," Leila replied, laying her head on his shoulder and moving closer to him. Nalick nestled his face in her hair before sighing and looking into the sky. As she watched him gaze at the sky, she knew something was on his mind, but he wasn't comfortable talking about it. Leila rested her head back on his shoulder and didn't ask.

CHAPTER TWENTY-THREE

Leila woke the next morning before everyone else. It was strange to be alone with Nalick in a new room. Though Leila pondered staying in bed and watching Nalick sleep, she would end up waking him up if she did. Instead, she quietly stood and walked into the main room. She could hear the bustling of the women in Mauve's room, but it was just the calm before the storm. Leila quickly filled the bath water before anyone could ask to help her. She then sat and enjoyed the silence, but was beginning to realize that she might not get much more silence with three children running around.

"So, you gave up your nice quiet apartment in the palace to come babysit us here?" Leila asked, exiting the bath to catch Anatolio watching over the busy room.

Anatolio smiled. "I like the commotion. I was an only child and always wished I had tons of siblings to play with. Besides, being here will make it much easier to follow you around. I won't have to sleep out in the hallway anymore."

"Doesn't that get boring?" she asked.

"Never," Anatolio said, before bowing and quickly leaving as Nalick approached.

"So, has the chaos begun?" Nalick asked, as he sat down next to Leila at the table. Nalick's hand automatically drifted to Leila, wanting to pull her closer to him. He settled with holding her hand.

"I haven't seen Mauve yet, but I'm sure she's already driving everyone mad," Leila commented, while grabbing a muffin off the stack in front of her. As if on cue, Mauve entered the room.

"Good morning miss," Mauve said to Leila. "Nalick, your clothes are arranged for you after you bathe." Nalick nodded. "I have everything picked out for the children, but I figured it would be best to dress them after they eat."

"Do I get to eat first, also?" Leila asked, biting into her muffin. Nalick chuckled as Mauve seemed to not understand that she was joking.

"Are the children awake yet?" Mauve asked, trying to hurry everyone.

"Yes," Leila replied.

Mauve nodded, mentally checking off items on her list, and then went upstairs to collect them.

"Do you think if I hide under the covers she might just forget about me and leave me alone?" Leila asked Nalick.

"You mean you don't like being treated like a doll and dressed up?" he replied, using the terminology she had used before to describe it to him.

Leila finished her muffin and hurried back to her bedroom, hoping to be forgotten in all the confusion and bustle that was beginning in the palace.

"I might as well try it and see if it works," Leila suggested. Nalick joined her.

"For some reason, I think she might know you're there," he said, as Leila pulled the covers over her head. Leila pulled the covers back down and looked at Nalick.

"I wish I could freeze time and just keep things at a standstill. Not having to get dressed up or meet people who basically hate me for no reason," Leila complained.

"Nobody hates you," Nalick said, sitting down next to her. "They all just need a little time to adjust to you."

"You make it sound like I am a bad-tasting vegetable or something." She laughed, pulling her feet from beneath the covers and throwing them across his lap. He picked up her feet and wiggled her toes.

"No. I mean they just don't remember how to deal with real people. They're all so caught up in this fake world of nobility that they forget they're just like everyone else. You just happen to remind them of this, and I don't think this makes them too happy. In time, they'll adjust. I promise." Nalick rubbed her feet.

"Nalick." Leila was watching him. "You're not telling me something." Nalick didn't look at her face. "I can tell."

"Don't worry about it. We can talk about it later," he said, still not looking at her. Nalick was keeping a secret from her. It was becoming harder to do so, but he didn't feel ready to tell her.

Leila sat up and turned his face toward her. "Promise?"

"Promise," Nalick replied, leaning forward to steal a kiss before they would inevitably be interrupted again.

Leila could hear Tim yelling as he ran down the stairs, and she watched through the doorway as the young boy made his way to the table. Tim was happily singing about food as he looked everything over and decided what he wanted to eat. Elena had brought Ruth to the table, and Phillip joined them. All three children sat together and ate.

"So we really are going to keep them?" Leila asked Nalick. "Do you think we're ready to be parents?"

"I don't know if we will ever be ready, but I know as long as I have you by my side, I feel like I can do anything." Nalick pulled Leila close to him to make his point. She nodded. Leila felt the same way. Nalick stood, but Leila quickly grabbed his hand.

"Don't leave yet," she begged, pulling him back to the bed beside her. Nalick sat down and gently pushed her semi-wet hair from the side of her face. Nalick wanted to tell her his secret, but he couldn't stand the thought of making her sad. Leila could see the struggle behind his eyes, but didn't question him further. She was happy to just have him sit near and hold on to her.

"What did we get ourselves into?" Leila asked. Tim decided he would run a lap around the table after each bite of food.

"You can't change your fate," Nalick said somberly, standing again.

Leila watched him walk away and tried to analyze his last sentence. *You can't change your fate*, she thought. *What does he mean by that?* Leila searched her mind, trying to remember anything Gabor had said to her about her fate, but could not remember. She had done her best not to be told her own fate. Across the room, Leila could see Mauve trying to hurry the children so that they could get ready. Leila used the diversion of the children to escape upstairs. She silently made her way along the stairs, unnoticed by Mauve, and quickly she ran out into the rooftop garden.

"Too bad there are no trees for you here," Leila said to Anatolio, approaching him from behind. She sat on one of the benches while Anatolio sat on the ground with his back to a large planter, which was filled with tall grasses. The position was strategically chosen so he could sit and talk to her, but still be unseen to anyone who approached from below.

"I guess it's just a little too much noise for the morning, after all," Anatolio added. "It might take some getting used to."

Leila shrugged. "I can't say it's bad, since it made a great diversion to get away from them."

Palace life wasn't for Leila. She wasn't the kind of girl that enjoyed being fussed over and pampered. "But isn't playing dress-up so much fun?" he teased.

"It is when you're six," she replied. "I don't know how any grown woman could enjoy being dressed so fancy with so many decorations and so little fabric. I understand it's hot here, but give me a break." Anatolio laughed again.

Leila looked over at the young man. He tossed his blond hair aside as he laughed. When they were alone everything was comfortable. There was an air about Anatolio that changed when others were around. Somehow she understood that this was the real man behind the boy.

"Do you know what Nalick isn't telling me?" she asked, changing the subject.

The twinkle left his eyes, and he gave her a one word reply: "Yes."

"And I suppose you aren't going to tell me?" she asked, raising her eyebrows. She already knew the answer, but somehow hoped he would give in anyway.

"I was told he would tell you when he was ready," Anatolio replied, still looking her in the eyes. Leila could read his reaction, and he, as much as Nalick, did not want to tell her what Nalick was hiding.

"I don't get it," she said, closing her eyes and leaning her head back. She wasn't going to get even a clue from him. "What could he be so scared to tell me? It's not like I haven't dealt with enough in my life to be able to handle something new. I'm not made of glass."

"He knows that. I guess, maybe, he's just as afraid to tell you because he doesn't want you to get hurt, or, he doesn't want to admit the truth to himself either," Anatolio explained. "Sometimes life just doesn't turn out the way you want it to." Leila opened her eyes and looked at the young man in front of her. She couldn't tell if he was talking about Nalick or himself.

"So, when do we get to start training again?" he asked, changing the subject on her. She was analyzing him, and he didn't want the conversation to continue. Anatolio wanted to keep his promise to Nalick.

"As soon as you want," Leila said with a smile. "In fact,

in a week or so I'll be able to show you how to do things myself, and we won't have to use Macarius or Theo." Anatolio was happily waiting to be taught directly from her.

"I'm looking forward to the opportunity to test everything I've learned from you," Anatolio replied. He began to say something else, but stopped when he heard footsteps coming up the side staircase.

"Oh, thank goodness." Elena approached. She didn't know Anatolio was behind the plant as she continued to talk as normally, and if she had seen him, she would have turned several shades of red and run off to hide. Most of the maids were shy around Anatolio. "Mauve sent me to find you. She wants to get you and Ruth dressed first while the boys are both bathing."

Leila reluctantly stood and followed Elena back down the stairs. Anatolio chuckled at the disappointed face she made as she left the garden. He, on the other hand, was happy for it to be quiet again. Anatolio had almost told her too much. If he lied, she would know, but he also didn't have a way to keep her from asking.

It took Mauve over two hours to get everyone dressed to her satisfaction. Leila tried her best to set a good example for the children, but it was hard. She waited as her hair was fixed for a second time, and Mauve checked everyone over. As they left to follow Nalick to the meeting room, Leila removed several of the bracelets around her wrist and handed them to Elena. Nalick went inside the meeting first. Leila and the children sat outside the room as Nalick began the meeting without them. Macarius stood and watched over the four of them.

Phillip paced the hallway as he waited. He was anxious, but Leila didn't know how to calm the boy. Every now and then, Phillip would stop by the door and try to hear what was going on inside. Macarius stopped Phillip's pacing by placing his hands on the boy's shoulders.

"There is nothing to worry about. Everything is already done. Nalick just wants to introduce you three to everyone. Nobody will stop it from happening." Macarius could relate to the young man. Phillip stopped pacing and sat down beside Leila and Ruth.

"Why do Macarius or Theo follow you everywhere you go?" Phillip asked, trying to get his mind off what was going to happen.

"Nalick wants them to watch over and protect me," Leila replied. "Anatolio is also always here." Leila nodded her head to the shadow nearby but Phillip didn't see him. Anatolio briefly stepped out of the shadow so that Phillip could see he was standing there, and then he returned to his hidden spot.

"How did you know he was there?" Phillip was amazed that Leila knew Anatolio was there, as Phillip couldn't see him at all.

"He's always close, so it's easy for me to spot him. Besides, he doesn't hide from me, just everyone else," Leila explained. "Out of the three men, he truly is my personal guard. Theo and Macarius just keep me company. Anatolio is always watching over me."

"But, he can't be much older than me," Phillip said, trying to find Anatolio again in the dark corner.

"He isn't," Leila explained. "But don't be fooled. He's much stronger and better trained than most men twice his age." Anatolio could hear the conversation and tried to suppress the smile forming.

"How long have you trained?" Phillip asked, moving back to Leila as the subject of conversation.

"Eight years," she replied. Ruth tried to slide off her lap, but Leila kept a firm hold on the little girl so that she would not tumble to the ground.

"So that would make you only eighteen," Phillip said in awe as he counted on his fingers. "You're not much older than me either." Leila smiled at the young man. She was only a few years older than him, but she had lived enough to fill several lifetimes in the last four years alone.

Soon, the side door opened and Theo came out. Leila stood and picked up Ruth. Phillip followed her, tightly holding onto Tim's hand. Leila heard him whisper before they entered the room.

"Tim, please behave. Remember, you promised," Phillip told his younger brother.

Phillip was surprised as they entered the room to see how many people were there. He followed as Leila led them all to the stage that Nalick was sitting at. Nalick stood and took Ruth from Leila as she carefully climbed the stairs. Phillip's grandparents knew who Phillip was immediately. Nalick offered Leila his seat, and she gladly sat down. Nalick went to hand her Ruth, but the small child held onto him tightly. He smiled as Phillip stood next to Leila, and Tim energetically hopped on her lap instead.

"For the last point of today's meeting, I wanted to use the opportunity to introduce everyone here to our new children," Nalick said. "I'd like to introduce Prince Phillip." Nalick pointed to Phillip. "Prince Tim." Leila lifted Tim's hand, and he waved to everyone. "And Princess Ruth." Nalick tried to get Ruth to look at the people seated in front of him, but she just nuzzled her face into his shirt while her curls bounced. The crowd just chuckled at the small child's shyness. While icy stares greeted the boys, no one could resist the little girl. "That's it for today's meeting. There will be no meetings next month since the wedding celebrations will already have begun."

Nalick nodded his head and the people all slowly began to leave. Some people stopped along the way to greet old friends, and others hurried to the door. Leila watched the back of the room, where Emma was trying to make her way up to the stage. Emma bowed to both Nalick and Leila.

"I'm so happy to see you can walk again, Queen Eia," Emma said. "Thank you so much for knowing it wasn't me that wanted you gone. I'm so sorry my parents put you through that. Thanks to you, I got to get married finally. I wanted you to meet Dareios, but I couldn't get him to come up here with me." Leila smiled as Emma waved at a man who was waiting in the back of the room. "I can't thank you enough." Emma noticed Nalick approaching and quickly stood and bowed again to him before hurrying away.

"Here, Leila," Nalick said, handing Ruth to her. "I need to take Phillip with me for a second." Ruth sat on one knee and Tim on the other, while Nalick whisked Phillip away. He stood close enough for Leila to overhear the conversation.

"Lady and Lord Pillas, I wanted you to meet my son, Phillip," Nalick said, and Phillip shook each of their hands. Phillip was amazed by how happy it made him feel to have Nalick call him his son. He had never really known his own father, as he died when he was quite young, and Tim and Ruth's father never acknowledged that Phillip even existed.

"Lord Pillas trains horses," Nalick explained to Phillip. "He even taught me how to ride when I was a little younger than you are now. I was hoping he would be able to teach you how to ride, also." Phillip grinned ear to ear. Everything was becoming more real to him as Nalick talked about teaching him how to be a prince. "Of course, it will have to be after your classes and all, if Lord Pillas could fit you into his schedule."

"For you, my king, anything," Lord Pillas replied.

"Did you hear that?" Phillip yelled, running back onto the stage and missing the next question.

"Is he?" Lady Pillas asked. Nalick didn't need to answer, as all three knew the truth. Lady Pillas wiped away the tears forming in the corners of her eyes.

"Thank you," she said quietly, before her husband comforted her as they walked away.

"Leila, I get to learn how to ride a horse," Phillip said, running up to Leila, who was still holding the two children that were reaching their limit of behaving and sitting on her lap. Tim wiggled more and more.

Leila sat him on the ground while still holding Ruth. "Go tell Nalick your new story," she told the young boy, who was more than happy to run over to Nalick, who was talking to someone else. Nalick lifted him into the air, and Tim cheered.

"I wonder what else I get to learn...," Phillip added while picking up Ruth, who had quit wiggling and fallen asleep on Leila's lap.

"Trust me, I'm not the person to ask," Leila replied, standing next to Phillip. "Let's go back upstairs. Maybe you can talk to Theo or Macarius about lessons."

Once upstairs, Leila took Ruth from Phillip and laid her in Leila's bed. Tim occupied himself with the toys lying around the room and Phillip and Nalick talked about what Phillip would be doing for his training. Leila drifted off to sleep watching the men sit and talk at the table.

Nalick and Phillip let Leila and Ruth sleep until dinner time. Tim had joined them while they were asleep. Nalick didn't want to wake them since all three were cuddled in the bed together so peacefully. He gently picked up Ruth and rocked her in his arms as he softly called her name. With a yawn, she opened her eyes and giggled. Nalick set her back down on the bed and softly shook Tim's foot. Tim sat up and both children began to tug on Leila. Leila smiled and kept her eyes shut.

"Lei, wake up." Tim patted her face.

"Lei," Ruth said, also tugging on her hand. Reluctantly, Leila got up for yet another formal dinner.

Nalick brought his entire new family to their first formal dinner. He had expected them to sit still for only a minute and then begin to run, but they stayed in their seats the entire time. The three children sat between Nalick and Leila at the head table and were quite amused by the amount of people that came to the feast. Following the dinner, Leila took the two younger children back to their quarters and put them to bed. After all the excitement, even with their naps, the children went right to sleep.

On her way back to the meeting room, Leila took a detour outside to the training courtyard. For the first time since she brought the children home, she was truly alone, and she could clear her mind and think. If she returned to the party, she would not be alone. Leila walked to the center of the empty courtyard and looked into the sky. Everything in her life at the moment seemed to be working out for the best. Leila stared at the stars. Her life was never that easy, and she felt unsure of what was truly bothering her. *What does Nalick know about the future he's too afraid to tell me?* It was hard to believe in fate. Leila wanted to be in control of her own life. Anatolio watched from the shadows. Leila was cold. As he approached, Leila didn't move, and he gently wrapped his outer shirt around her shoulders, pressing his body close to hers to warm her.

"It's a little too cold to be standing out here," he said to her. "Besides, you're not dressed to be standing outside. I think those dresses are made for daytime or indoors."

"I suppose I'm not dressed to train you right now," she replied, and he laughed.

"You really should get back inside before Nalick becomes concerned that you're gone," Anatolio suggested.

"I know," Leila replied, but didn't move. "Do you believe in fate?"

"Yes," he replied quietly.

"So you don't think we have control over our own lives?" she wondered. "Doesn't it scare you to have no control over how your life turns out?"

"You know how you don't fear being kidnapped?" Anatolio explained. "I don't fear that I can't control the way my life turns out." Leila wished she could just sit by and let her life make its own decisions, but she just couldn't let go of the chance to make the decisions herself. "What's meant to be is meant to be."

Turning her head sideways and up to look over her shoulder, Leila stared at the young man with her. She couldn't understand how he could be so calm with not being in control of his life.

"I've never had much say," he continued to explain. "Maybe if I was as free as you are, I'd not like the concept of fate, but since I've never had control, it makes no difference to me now."

"Let's get you back to the dinner," Anatolio said, putting his arm around her and directing her back inside. "You can't sit and worry about losing control of something you have never had control of to begin with." Leila smiled, realizing that the young man's words actually comforted her. As they neared the door to the meeting hall, Anatolio let go of her and faded into the background.

He might even be smarter than his years, also.

Inside the hall, the music had already started playing. Leila made her way back to the table and found Nalick was walking around the room introducing Phillip to everyone. She could see how proud both Phillip and Nalick were, and happily sat and watched them. As the music changed, Phillip ducked away from Nalick and ran over to Leila, dodging people and tables as he ran.

"Leila." Phillip panted from his run across the room. "Can I have this dance?" Phillip caught his breath. Leila recognized the music and accepted his outstretched hand.

Leila and Phillip danced two songs before Nalick cut in. "Do I get a chance to dance with her this time?" he asked. Phillip nodded and ran back to the head table.

As the night wore on, Leila excused herself and Phillip from the party before she took him back up to their rooms.

"So, do you think this is an okay life?" she asked him on their walk through the empty hallways.

Phillip grinned ear to ear even though he was exhausted. "It's great." Leila walked upstairs with him and checked on Ruth and Tim, who were sound asleep in Ruth's bed. Phillip went to his room. As she approached the top of the stairs to go back down, Phillip came back out of his room and ran over to her. He quickly hugged her.

"Thanks, Mom," he said, before running back into his room and turning the light off. Leila walked back down to her own room. It was strange to be called mom. Her life hadn't turned out as she had imagined, yet it was so much better than she could have ever guessed. *Could this be my fate?*

CHAPTER TWENTY-FOUR

The next week, Leila started a new schedule. She began training Anatolio again in the afternoons after she put Ruth down for her midday nap. What had started as a training session with just Anatolio had escalated, until by the end of the week she had fourteen men working with her. As the days progressed, more men started to show up to watch, as they had done before. Those that arrived early were brave enough asked to join in.

After the last training session of the week, Leila was finally ready to test her leg to see what she was still able to do, but she didn't want to do it in front of an audience. While Ruth and Tim were busy playing with Elena, Leila changed and snuck off to the garden on the roof.

Leila started by slowly stretching, and there was some limitation to her recovering leg. It would not be a problem, but she needed to stretch every day for the following few weeks to get it back to the strength of her other leg. Leila took the time alone to plan out the following weeks. It was still three weeks until the wedding, but her family would be arriving in less than a week. Roger had sent her a note telling her the day he planned to be there, and to again warn her to be careful. Leila was excited to see her family, but also worried that they wouldn't like it in Lexia. She remembered her first run into the city, and how she asked Erich why someone would purposely live there. Leila chuckled at how ironic her question had been. Over the years, she had gotten used to Lexia, but she doubted that on their first trip to the city her family would find it too inviting.

Leila slowly moved her leg, rolling her foot from side to side. She couldn't feel a difference, but she wouldn't know until she tested it more. She began to make a mental list of what needed to get done before her parents arrived. She stood and stretched her leg more. She was being overcautious, but she was like this every time she recovered from a major injury. Leila stood on her uninjured leg and pulled the other to her chest. She could feel the tightness in it. Cautiously, she reversed her legs and stood on her bad one while pulling her other up past her head. She slowly began to run through her set of exercises. Except for two moves, everything seemed to be normal. In the shadows near the wall she could tell Anatolio was watching her. He didn't interrupt her as she continued to run through the exercises again.

"I think after the weekend I'll try it out down on the training grounds," Leila said to him. Anatolio had been waiting for her to get healthy to learn more. She was the most amazing courier he had ever met, and wanted to learn as much as he could from her. Anatolio stayed in the shadows as Phillip came running up the stairs.

"Mom, Mom," he called. "Dad said I can get my own horse."

Leila quickly diverted the excited boy as he came close to tripping on the last step to the patio she was standing on. "So, you have gotten the hang of riding?" she asked, sitting down.

"It's so much fun," Phillip said, sitting down on the bench beside her. "Dad said that since I only go two days a week for lessons, I should practice here at the palace. So, at the end of next week, I get to pick one out."

"That's great," she said. Phillip was given the chance to be a child again.

"Will you come with me?" Phillip asked. "Dad said you'd know more about horses than he does." Leila doubted she knew more than Nalick, but he always wanted her to be included in everything.

"Of course," she said.

Nalick arrived and sent Phillip downstairs to study.

"Roger is worried about you," Nalick said, as soon as Phillip was out of hearing distance.

"Roger has never stopped worrying about me. Why do you think he made a deal with you?" Leila replied. She wasn't worried.

"You don't exactly always put yourself in the best situations," Nalick commented.

"Well, I don't think you regret that quality about me." She smirked. He couldn't argue with her on that point.

"We will need to find more guards," he said, changing the subject. "Now that Nikias is working with me, and there are the children to also watch over. I doubt Theo, Macarius, and Javed will be enough."

"Actually, I think Anatolio will be enough," Leila said. "And I wouldn't let anything happen to the kids."

"I'm more worried about things happening to you." Nalick brushed the hair from her face. "Until I get more guards for you, can you please stay within the palace unless I am with you?" he begged. Leila nodded. She didn't want to worry him any more than he already was. He picked her up and placed her on his lap so that he could hold her close, if only for a moment. "Besides," he continued, "the week after the wedding, we're going to head up to the North Country, so you only have to stay inside for a few weeks."

Leila stared at him. She hadn't heard any plans of going north from anyone. "What do you mean?"

"Roger sent me a note from your parents last week asking if we could go up north after the wedding, and get married in your hometown. They said they have a surprise for us. I just sent back a reply yesterday that we will gladly visit as long as they don't mind three extra kids running around." Nalick laughed at Leila's surprised expression. She hadn't heard from her parents in over a week, and assumed that was because they were coming to visit soon. "You forgot to write them about the kids, didn't you?" Nalick said.

"So, we're going to actually have a wedding there, also?" she asked, contemplating a change in plans.

"Yes, if it's all right with you," he said.

"But what about your priests? I can't believe they would be all right with you getting married in another religion," she said.

"Well," Nalick paused. "It was actually their idea. It seems that they feel that we would upset your God if we didn't get married there also, and it would bring bad luck upon our family." Leila shook her head. She couldn't understand how the priests would actually support it, bad luck or not. "They asked your hometown priest to talk to your parents about officially getting married there."

Leila didn't understand what he meant.

"So the wedding here won't be official?" she asked confused.

Nalick couldn't help but laugh at the concern in her innocent eyes. He hadn't meant to confuse her. "The wedding here is official. Trust me. Not that it matters, as in the eyes of Lior law, as you're already the queen. What I meant was that my priests asked me not to consummate the marriage before we're also married by your priests."

Leila blushed. His touch made her heart race enough; she hadn't even considered what it really meant to be getting married. Nalick smiled as she turned several shades of red. The one quality that he loved more than anything about her was her innocence. She was experienced beyond her years in so much, but not in love. Leila tried to stand so that he would not see her embarrassment, but he held onto her tightly. She hadn't thought very far ahead about what saying yes to marriage meant and, with the whirlwind that ensued, she hadn't had time to ponder it. Tim came running into the garden and Leila was thankful for the interruption.

"Dad, Dad," Tim called, forcing Nalick to let Leila stand. Nalick had been trying to find the courage to talk to her, but he had once again lost his nerve as Tim approached. Nalick didn't like keeping a secret from her, but he couldn't find words to start the conversation he needed to have with her.

"I need to talk to you, alone, sometime," Nalick said, the running boy leapt onto his lap and began to talk. Leila nodded before slipping away. She had been through enough embarrassment for one day, and she was ready to quickly run away and hide.

Leila returned to the full courtyard with Anatolio to train, and the men that were lounging around, waiting for her, cheered as she entered. The men could see she was dressed to train with them, and they were all excited to see her work. As usual, beyond the men she was training a crowd had formed to watch. She noticed Nalick sitting near the back of the crowd, but she didn't see Theo with Phillip. Phillip watched wide-eyed as his new mother easily taught the men below how to fight. Leila was a courier and told him she could take care of herself, but he never imagined she was so good. Phillip watched as she finished up her session with the men for the day.

"Now, most of you are quite young," Leila said to the fourteen men. Judging from their faces, she guessed they were all her age or younger. "For the next few years, you will mostly go against people larger in size. In my case, it's almost all the time." They laughed. "So, I figure the move you should work on next is a way to counter the fact that someone is twice your size. Since I've done enough beating up on Anatolio for the day, I figure my future husband, who is hiding at the back of the crowd, could help." The crowd, watching her, heard, and all of them turned to the back and saw their king.

Nalick moved through the bowing crowd and stood face-to-face with Leila. She demonstrated the move she had just described to them in slow motion, and Nalick immediately recognized it as the way she easily beat him when he tried to fight her. The smile on his face told her he remembered the move. Each man studied it again as she showed them, and then she was finished for the day. As the crowd departed, and Leila was left standing with Nalick and Anatolio, Nalick finally realized that Phillip and Theo were also in the crowd.

"Did you know?" Nalick asked Leila.

"After you started to walk up here I saw him," Leila replied, as Theo and Phillip began walking toward them.

Phillip stared at Leila and didn't know what to say. Leila chuckled, realizing he was tongue-tied. "Now do you believe me?" she asked Phillip. He nodded. "The reason I could go on all my runs, and not worry, was because I can take care of myself." Nalick nodded also. She could take care of herself, but he just worried to what extent people would try to get a hold of her.

CHAPTER TWENTY-FIVE

Leila rode her horse out of the city between the temporary guard. She was going to get Phillip and his new horse, and Anatolio followed at a distance, as normal. She had sent Javed and Macarius along with Phillip, and had to make due with several unknown men. As the group approached Lady and Lord Pillas' manor, something wasn't right. Leila entered the courtyard, and no one greeted them. Leila cautiously got off her horse and was quickly surrounded by the men who had come with her. Annoyed, she gave a whistle, and Anatolio quickly joined them and threw a small weapon to her. The men nearest her moved as she walked to the house.

Carefully, Anatolio opened the door, and Leila followed him in. The front room was in complete disarray. Leila scanned the room and found no one inside. Nikias indicated to Nalick's guards that they should go in opposite directions while he, Theo, and Anatolio stayed at Leila's side. She first walked to the kitchen. *Where would their wine cellar be?* Anatolio thought the same thing, and immediately he led her to the right side of the kitchen. Leila saw a pantry door that had been blocked from the outside. Leila put her ear to the door and could hear voices inside. Nikias and Anatolio broke the door so that they could open it, and below, Leila could see Lady and Lord Pillas, along with their staff, sitting at the bottom of the stairs. Phillip, Javed, and Macarius were not with them.

Lady and Lord Pillas were grateful to see Leila, but

confused at the same time. Once Leila and the men helped Lady and Lord Pillas out of the cellar along with their staff, Leila waited for the guards to return from their search of the house. All three men shook their heads *no* as they entered the kitchen. Leila began to worry about Phillip. There was nothing beyond the front room in disarray that indicated why or who attacked the manor.

"Did Phillip make it here this morning?" Leila asked Lord Pillas.

"I don't know. We've all been down there since last night. Did you check the guardhouse as you entered?" Lord Pillas asked. The men with her all shook their heads *no*.

"There was no one in them," Anatolio replied. The first sign to him that something was wrong was the missing guards.

"We were taken from our beds, along with the staff, by armed men in the middle of the night. Once they put us in the cellar, we didn't hear anything of what went on afterward. We don't have much of value in the house," Lady Pillas explained. "Did Phillip come alone?" She was worried.

"No, Macarius and Javed were with him. How many people entered your home?" Leila asked.

"I'm not sure," Lord Pillas replied. "I'd guess over ten or fifteen. I didn't have time to count, and it was dark."

"They were speaking a language I had never heard before," Lady Pillas said, starting to fret.

"They were from Enea," a young girl, who was standing behind Lady Pillas, said. Leila wasn't happy to hear the response. Anatolio had left but was finally returning. She cautiously moved away from the group of scared residents and talked quietly to him.

"How does it look?" she asked him, and Nikias and Theo moved nearer to hear the answer.

"There are horse tracks that head away from town. Lots of them. From what I can tell, Phillip, Javed, and Macarius came near, but didn't enter. For some reason they headed further south, but I couldn't see beyond a hill nearby," Anatolio explained part of what he saw.

"What is the current political situation with King Aiolos?" Leila asked Nikias. Anatolio had more to say, but didn't want to say it to his older brother.

"We're on fine standings with him for the time being. The last war with them was over ten years ago. King Nalick has never had a problem with him, but we are not allies either. We have, by far, the better military, so I don't understand why he would come into our country and do something like this," Nikias explained.

"Nalick's guards, stay near the front of the house," Leila ordered, and the three men stood. "If you see anything at all, come back here immediately." All three moved to the front room and posted themselves by the windows.

"Nikias and Theo, help get Lady and Lord Pillas some food and blankets, and then escort them back to the cellar." Lady and Lord Pillas looked shocked.

"It's the safest place for you," Leila explained. "If they return and find you wandering the house, you could end up dead. We will send word to Nalick and have a proper military force come to help you out, but until then, stay there." Once Nikias and Theo were busy, Anatolio took her away from them, out of hearing distance.

"There are at least ten people outside in the woods watching the manor. If we leave and head back out the front gate, we will be easily ambushed. There's a back route to Lexia from here, and if we send a guard, he can bring help, but I don't think they'll wait that long," Anatolio pulled Leila closer. "There was blood near the top of the hill I couldn't see over. Something happened there."

Leila stared at him as her heart began to pump wildly. Phillip was gone, and there was blood. Anatolio reached out an arm to brace her, thinking she would tip over. Leila caught her breath and her resolve. "We need to see whose blood it is," she said, beginning to pace the room. The attack was staged to seem as a random break in, but now Leila doubted it was random. Leila walked back to Lord Pillas.

"Lord Pillas, is there any other way to exit your manor?" she asked.

"The wall is built around the whole compound. We have an entrance at the front, and then one at the back, but the back entrance is always locked. We haven't used it in years," he explained.

"Can we have the key to the back entrance?" she asked, and he quickly ran to the nearby room and rustled through a desk.

"Take any of the horses you can use," he offered.

Leila returned to the men in the kitchen. Lord Pillas was the last to go back into the cellar, and he shut the door behind them. Leila looked out the back window, over the pasture and grazing horses. She needed to get to the other side of the hill quickly if anyone was hurt. Rationally, Leila thought, *Phillip would not be harmed to get to me, but I'm not so sure the same would not go for Macarius and Javed.* Leila walked around the house, trying to come up with her plan and Anatolio followed. Theo and Nikias waited for her return.

"We should head straight back to Lexia," Nikias said.

"No," Leila said while returning to the room. "There are several people waiting in the woods, ready to attack us on our way back. Since we don't know how many are there, we won't directly approach them. We're going to use the back gate to send two of the guards back to Lexia as quick as possible, with each taking a different route. We can then follow the wall around the compound to find out if Phillip is further down the road." Nikias tried to object, but Anatolio stopped him.

"We do what she says," Anatolio said. "She's the queen." Theo nodded. Leila was far better to assess the situation and make a plan than any of the three men were.

"One guard will be left here to throw off the people watching the manor, which will make them assume we're still here," she finished. One man volunteered to stay.

Leila led the remaining men out the back door, and to the nearest barn. Finding several horses unsaddled, she quickly put their reins on them. She handed each guard a horse and cautiously led them between buildings until she reached the back of the manor. The door was covered in vines and barely visible, so Anatolio ripped them off the door. The lock hadn't been opened in years. Once it was unlocked, Leila directed the two guards to take different routes back to Nalick with specific instructions. Nikias and Theo followed Leila, who was beginning to circle back around the compound outside the wall toward the front of the manor. Anatolio fell behind and kept watch over the group. As they neared the road that passed in close proximity, Leila slowed down. She handed her reins to Theo and checked for anyone following them.

The group that was waiting in the woods hadn't moved, and they were free to continue down the road. They were on the other side of the hill that Anatolio couldn't see over. Leila tried not to stare at the blood. Gazing down the road, she noticed several men lying face down. Quickly, Leila hurried over to them and the men followed. One by one she checked each man. They were all dead, and all foreigners. As she neared the last two bodies, she knew who they were. Leila kneeled beside Javed and rolled him over. She checked for a pulse and could not find one. Javed was slowly dying, but she could see that he was still breathing shallowly. He had been cut many times, and his shirt was soaked through with blood. Tears welled in her eyes. Nikias also checked over his comrade, and tried to see how he could help him. Leila looked up to see Theo running over to the last man.

Leila ran to the last man, also. Macarius was injured but still alive and able to talk, just not move. Theo sat his best friend up, and he opened his eyes to see Leila.

"Leila," Macarius choked out. "I'm sorry... I couldn't stop them."

"Theo, take them back to Lexia right away. Stop at the Shilling tavern on your way into town, and tell the bartender that Meg needs some assistance. Hopefully, Roger is close and can make it back," she said. "Nikias, please go with him."

"No, I'm staying beside you," Nikias said. His job was to watch over Leila no matter the circumstances, and Nikias was not going to fail his king. Leila gave a motion with one hand, and Anatolio moved near his older brother.

"Sorry," Anatolio said, as he hit a spot in the back of his neck.

Nikias crumpled to the ground, and Anatolio ran back to the wall and got a small cart to wheel over to the men. Anatolio put the two injured men in the cart as Theo attached it to the horses. Leila tried to help, but the two men took care of everything while she plotted her plan. When they were finished they turned to her and she explained.

"The reality is that Javed was the better fighter between him and Nikias. When he wakes, tell him I was sorry to do that. I'll go alone to Phillip. They won't hurt me, but that doesn't mean they won't hurt Phillip. I don't have time to waste waiting for Nalick, and please explain that to him. Anatolio is going to follow me, and if I need any help, he will be there. Anatolio will also look out for

Nalick." Theo nodded as Leila opened the back gate. "Take care of Macarius, please." Theo reluctantly headed back to the town with the men in the cart.

Leila went back inside the house. Anatolio followed her silently. She cautiously looked into the front room, the guard was gone, confirming what she suspected. He had been showing signs of nervousness ever since they had left the city, and his jittery attitude made Leila suspect his involvement. She was relieved to find the one bad seed of the group was the one that knew the least.

"I'm heading out that way now," she said. Anatolio nodded.

"Stay behind and follow at a good distance. I'm sure there must be a courier with them, so don't get caught. As soon as I get inside their camp and find Phillip, I'll send word to you. Stay to the east side of their camp." Leila walked to the door. Anatolio grabbed her arm.

"Be careful, please," Anatolio said to her, and she smiled.

"I always am," she replied, and he hid as she opened the door. She calmly walked out the front door and toward the front of the manor. She took the reins of her horse that was still sitting by the front gate, and she stared walking back in the direction of Lexia. Anatolio was surprised to see her so calm. It didn't faze her that she was going to meet unknown enemies. From behind, he couldn't see the determination in her eyes. Leila had trained hard for the last two years for this moment. This time, she wasn't going to fail to protect someone she loved.

As she neared the front gate of the manor, she could see the people hidden in the woods. She tied her horse to the gate and left it for Anatolio. From behind a tree stepped a fairly large man. His bushy, light-colored beard told her immediately he was from Enea. Leila estimated that he was as large as Nalick, but should be as easy to take down if she chose.

"Where's my son?" Leila asked, as more men appeared from the woods onto the pathway.

"Back at camp, safe for the moment," the first man said. As he walked closer she recognized the man. He was the head of Aiolos's personal guard: Mitchell. Leila never forgot a face.

"So, will you come willingly?" Mitchell asked, extending his hand.

Leila accepted his hand and stood still as a man approached and checked her for weapons. Mitchell took both her hands and tied them together.

"Do you really think I'm stupid enough to do anything before I see Phillip?" Leila asked sarcastically.

"Just a precaution," Mitchell replied, pulling the rope around her arms and leading her into the woods. "Is she alone?" he asked someone still hidden in the woods.

"It looks like it," the man said, stepping out from the shadows. "It's so nice to finally meet you," the man said, as he bowed deeply to her.

CHAPTER TWENTY-SIX

"**Q**ueen Eia. Hm. I don't think that name suits you." His small, beady eyes, with dark hair and pale complexion, told Leila who the person was. Leila had never met the man before, but he was Argo. He had been a courier with Marx for many years, but recently changed to work for Aiolos because he wanted more freedom to be able to kill people. Couriers in most countries worked on an oath to not kill people, and thus were not seen as criminals by their own government. Argo walked around Leila, viewing her from every angle.

"You're as stunning as Marx always described you. Why he never made a move on you is unknown to me." Argo licked his lips as he made the complete circle. Leila held her head high and did not reply.

She patiently waited for them to begin moving as Argo continued to eye her over. Leila followed Mitchell walking in the woods. Mitchell had several horses waiting for them as they neared the edge of the woods. They had one less horse than they had riders, so Leila would have to ride with one of the men. She took her chances with Mitchell over Argo, and followed him to his horse. With her arms still tied, she hopped onto the horse ahead of him. Leila was even agile with her arms restricted, and Mitchell saw the ties were unnecessary. Mitchell wrapped his arms around her as they rode. He enjoyed the distain from Argo as she had chosen to ride with him over the other courier. Mitchell didn't blame her.

Even though Mitchell was completely loyal to King Aiolos, he didn't approve of his choice to hire Argo. The man seemed to have a short fuse and was quick to kill anything that got in his way. Leila didn't pay attention to the men that stared at her as she rode; she was too focused on the path they were taking. She hoped Anatolio would stay far enough behind to follow and not get caught by Argo. She had heard from Marx that Argo wasn't very good at his job, but he was effective in killing any opponent that got in his way. Marx was more than happy when Argo quit his post to join Aiolos.

After several hours of riding they neared a city. Leila didn't know the town, but she knew they were still in Lior. The town was empty as they rode through it. Every now and then, she caught the sight of a person or two hiding in fear through the panes of the windows. Aiolos was as harsh and uncaring as Jahangir, the only difference being that Aiolos had the stature and ability to support his ruthlessness. As they neared the opposite edge of the town, a large tent city was well hidden, if not accessed through the town. She estimated Aiolos had half his army with him because they were taking over the whole area. Leila imprinted a map of the city in her mind as they passed by many tents on their way to the center. The ornate and much larger one they were approaching made it obvious Aiolos was there to personally greet her. Slowly, they walked through the tents, and past the people sitting outside each. As the neared the center, they passed priests who began chanting in their holy language.

As the group drew near the main tent, Leila hopped down from her horse before anyone could move to help her. She was stopped before she could enter the tent, and several more ropes were tied around her arms and legs. Leila laughed to herself when six men were ordered to not let go of her. Leila had seen so many easy opportunities to come and go in the camp as she pleased. Six men wouldn't be a problem if she chose. With the help of the priests, who offered their assistance on her way in, Phillip would easily be safe. No matter what they did, Leila was leaving as soon as she was alone with Phillip.

"So, Phillip must be inside," Leila guessed, waiting outside the tent, but Mitchell didn't respond. From the look in his eyes, she had guessed correctly.

"I was wondering," Leila said to Argo, waiting for everyone to be sure she was secured. "Will you end up like Seth if you fail, also?"

"Marx won't be coming to save you this time," Argo replied. Leila's expression didn't change. Word spread quickly through the courier community, and Marx would know soon enough. She just hoped she wouldn't need his help this time. There was unquestionably bad blood between Marx and Argo.

"I wasn't expecting him to," Leila responded confidently. Quickly, Argo began barking orders to the men standing around the tent. Everyone ran away swiftly, trying their best to secure the area. Even with their increased efforts, they would not be able to keep her locked away. Mitchell pulled on the rope around her arms, and she followed him into the tent in front of her. Leila stopped just past the front door as a lady approached her and removed her shoes. The floors and the walls were lined with expensive fabrics.

Though Leila found the palace in Lexia ornate, it was nothing compared to the lavishly-decorated tent she was in. Continuing further inside, she observed, to her disgust, several half-dressed women lounging on beds that they were chained to. Aiolos' love of power over women was evident. Mitchell continued to pull her forward as two men opened the second set of curtains in front of her. Leila quickly scanned the room. Toward the middle of the room, seated on a couch, and facing away from her, was Phillip.

"Phillip," Leila said, and the boy turned around.

"Mom," Phillip responded, trying to stand, but the two men next to him held him down. "You shouldn't have come here. This was a trap to get you."

Leila nodded her head.

"She already knew that," a voice said from behind another curtain. Leila didn't need to see his face to know who was speaking.

"It's been a while," Aiolos said, confidently moving the curtain as she was dragged to the center of the room. The men holding her backed away, but they continued to hold on to their ropes. Leila didn't acknowledge the man speaking to her, but stared at Phillip. He was covered in blood, and she couldn't tell if he had been hurt.

Aiolos walked over to Phillip and pulled the boy with him.

"I can't believe you actually care about this kid," Aiolos continued. "He isn't even your own child, and yet you came running without any backup."

"Phillip is my son," Leila replied, staring at Aiolos. Aiolos could see the fire behind her eyes, and smiled.

"Are you okay?" her tone changed as she looked to Phillip. He nodded his head meekly.

"Nalick was a foolish man to let you out of his palace alone," Aiolos commented. "But he did teach the rest of us how best to catch you. Just kidnap and hold someone dear to you and you will come running. I didn't know if this brat would be enough, but it looks like I finally won the prize."

Leila laughed, upsetting Aiolos. "What's so funny?" he demanded.

"You think I'm actually staying with Nalick because he took someone close to me? Come on now, think a little. My friend left the palace the day after I entered. What is the longest stay I've had in your palace? Either Nalick has some sort of super jail cell, or I'm staying of my own free will," she replied. Aiolos raised his eyebrows. It hadn't occurred to him that she was staying on her own free will.

"He might have taken my friend by mistake, but she has been home now for months. I can come and go as I please in Lior. Nalick wouldn't be foolish enough to try to keep me there by force, but it seems you are." Phillip was surprised by how easily Leila mocked the man that was holding her captive.

Aiolos pushed Philip onto the nearest couch and approached Leila. He walked around her, viewing her from every angle.

"It seems that you clean up pretty well. Being queen suits you. Too bad about this." He pointed to her arm. "Such a worthless custom."

"And shaving a woman's head before marriage isn't?" she replied, mentioning the one custom that other countries made fun of Enea for. Leila could see she was upsetting Aiolos, and she smiled. He moved closer and grabbed her, and her smile quickly faded. He was near enough that she could feel his breath on her face. He would be much harder to fight off when she was chained like this.

"Still a lot of spirit left in you, I see," Aiolos said, moving his hand to touch her. In response, she kneed his groin before her guards could tighten the ropes. Aiolos tried to conceal his pain as he backed away from her and sat down next to Phillip. Mitchell barked at the men to hold on to her tighter

"Where I come from, men don't go around touching women without their permission," Leila replied with a smile. "And they certainly don't make advances toward a soon-to-be-married woman." She couldn't help but rub in the fact that she had chosen to marry Nalick.

"Why would you want to marry a coward?" Aiolos asked, composing himself.

"My dad's not a coward," Phillip yelled, getting angry. He had been sitting with Aiolos for several hours and all Aiolos did was try to tell Phillip what a bad person Nalick was.

Aiolos smiled. "Seems the child does know how to talk."

"Phillip, be quiet," Leila scolded, and Phillip shut his mouth.

"No, no. I want to hear more. Why isn't Nalick a coward?" Aiolos asked, but Phillip didn't reply. "See, the child probably doesn't know about how you ran away when Jahangir's army was approaching Dria."

Leila tilted her head as though she didn't understand. "I don't recall running away from anyone. The last time we were in Dria, we were visiting Nalick's father, and I thought it was be great to take Nalick to visit my home and meet my parents at the same time," Leila said. Aiolos' eyes grew large. He was unsure if he could trust that she was telling him the truth, but he was still surprised that she would even suggest it. The one secret every courier kept was where their family lived. Leila stared at the man, challenging him to doubt what she said.

"You'd never take him home to your family," Aiolos finally said.

"Why not? I am marrying him in a few weeks. He would have to meet them sometime," Leila replied honestly. Aiolos stared at her. The rumors he heard were true. She was going to willingly marry his rival, King Nalick. Leila could see his anger beginning to boil as he comprehended the truth. She quickly looked at Phillip and began to worry. She should not have upset him so badly with Phillip around. Aiolos stood and walked to her. As he neared, she felt the ropes tighten that were holding her.

"Too bad the wedding will have to be cancelled." Aiolos moved near her and began to touch her face. It may have been a loving gesture for Aiolos, but it made her skin crawl. "It seems I've made other arrangements for you." Leila replied by spitting in his face.

"I wouldn't marry you if you were the last person left alive," Leila said, her anger matching his.

Rather than the upset reaction she expected, Aiolos began to laugh. "You will do what I say. And you know why? Because if you don't, I will hurt this kid that means so much to you. I won't kill him, but instead I'll hand him over to the interrogation squad, and let them find ways to make you do what I want." Two guards seized Phillip.

"Let's see," Aiolos said, picking up a knife from a nearby table.

"Which hand is it that's so important to a Lior prince?" Each guard flattened his hands on the table and Phillip stared at his own hands. Aiolos looked at Leila.

"Your left would mean his right." Aiolos walked over to Phillip, and Leila began to struggle with the ropes holding her.

"Don't you dare hurt him," Leila yelled at Aiolos. Aiolos smiled, pleased to be able to upset her. Leila glared at him.

"You don't think I'd actually worry about you or the code you follow," Aiolos replied.

"I wouldn't just worry about me," Leila said, pulling against her ropes. "It's not just me that lives by that code, but every courier out there. I think any one of them would want to repay you for hurting an innocent person."

"Well, I'll have to wait and see," Aiolos replied, taking the knife and stabbing it into Phillip's right hand. Leila struggled to get free, but there were too many people holding onto her. Phillip didn't make a sound as the blade pierced his hand and then was removed. Leila could see the tears forming in his eyes, but he didn't say a word, just stared at Leila. She had told him to be quiet, and he was following her orders.

"Take them both away," Aiolos said with a fling of his hands. "That was just a practice. Next time he might lose a finger or two. That should give you something to think about next time you feel like disrespecting me."

The men pulled her out of the tent before she could respond, and threw her into a tent cage with Phillip. Leila was happy to see they were thrown in the same tent together. Once they were sure she was secure and couldn't escape, the men finally let go of their ropes. Phillip hurried to untie his mother, but soon saw he would not be needed. Leila picked up his bleeding hand. She quickly ripped the bottom of her dress and wrapped it around his hand.

"Mom, you shouldn't have come. They were just using me to get you," Phillip complained.

Leila hugged the child. "Who knows what they might have done to you if I hadn't come. I'm just happy to find you in one piece. I'm so sorry about your hand. I promise I'll have Roger look at it once we get home."

"I'll have you out of here before morning, hopefully even by this afternoon," Leila said confidently. Phillip continued to stare at her. "Remember all the stories you've heard about the ghost courier? Well, you will get to add one more story, but make sure not to tell the details."

"We will really be out of here by morning?" Phillip asked, doubting that anyone could escape from the middle of a camp full of warriors so easily.

"I wouldn't want to worry your dad, so we better leave by morning at the latest," she explained.

Phillip didn't have the chance to ask her how they were going to leave because they were interrupted by two priests entering the room. Both men were thin and young. Leila smiled and greeted the two men in a language Phillip had never heard before.

"We want to get you out of here as soon as possible," the younger priest told Leila. "Tomorrow they plan to pack up and head back to Enea."

"I'm not leaving until my son is safe getting out of here first," she replied, and they nodded. One of the priests studied Phillip intently as they continued to talk.

"Is there someone who will meet you?" the priest asked.

"Yes, there is a young man that should be directly outside the east gate." Leila removed the ring around her neck. "He doesn't know how I get out of situations like this. You won't be trusted. Give him this when you go to tell him your plan, and he will believe you." The priest accepted the ring and nodded, exchanging it for a jar in his hand.

"We will return after sundown to get your son free. Will you need us to get you out of here, also?" the other priest asked.

"No. There are holes all over the camp. It should be easy to get out on my own," Leila replied. The priests stood and left. Leila returned to Phillip and unwound the bandage on his hand. She opened the container the priests gave her and rubbed the sticky yellow substance on his hand before rewrapping it.

"So, are they part of the story I leave out?" Phillip asked. Leila nodded.

It was hours past sundown by the time the priests returned. Two men quietly entered: a small one and a large, heavyset man. Leila thought the faces looked familiar from before, and once he was close enough, she could see it was the same man.

"We need to take the child now," the taller one said. Leila gently shook Phillip, and he opened his eyes and stared at the large man.

"It should take us fifteen minutes to have him outside the gate, and another ten to reach your friend." Leila nodded. The larger priest turned so his back was toward the entrance to tent. He pulled his arms within his brown robe and struggled a bit. With a quiet thud something fell to the ground and the second priest quickly moved it to the bed next to Leila. Leila could see it was a young child about the age of Phillip.

"What's wrong with him?" Phillip asked.

"The guards beat him until he was almost dead," the priest explained to Leila in their language. "The child is from the neighboring village and heard Queen Eia was captive here. He wanted to free his queen and came here looking for you. We couldn't save him… the guards got to him first. His last dying wish was to help save his queen."

Leila stopped Phillip from touching the child.

"He's dead," she told him.

Phillip stared at the boy who was about his own age.

"The guards killed him, and they'll do the same with you if we don't get you out of here."

Phillip looked at his mom. The kind, gentle eyes she normally had were gone, replaced by eyes that were steady and focused. "Climb under the priest's robes and climb up on him. He will get you situated, and once he starts to move, don't let go until you hear Anatolio's voice. They are going to bring you to him." Phillip nodded and quickly went under the robe. Soon, the priest looked the same as before, and he turned to waddle out of the room. The second priest handed Leila a long-haired wig that was the same color as her hair.

"I know you said you don't need help, but it should give you more time," the man said, and he turned and followed the first priest. None of the kings ever expected that their own holy men were the ones to help Leila out of their jails.

Leila tucked the dead child under the covers and

turned his face away from the front of the tent. She was sad to see such a small child get hurt trying to save her. She looked at the dark head of hair and could picture the same happening to any of her three kids. *He's just a child*, she thought. Leila felt bad that her own adopted children were now being dragged into the game of catching her. She had not meant to place them in danger, but now she could see that they were. The changing guards looked in on her, and she pretended to be going to bed. Leila waited to be sure Phillip was safe and easily left her makeshift jail, proceeding to the east gate. Scanning the woods while moving, she followed the nearest trail. She quietly crept into the woods to view the people she could hear talking. Anatolio was checking the wound in Phillip's hand while Nalick watched over and talked to the priests quickly.

Anatolio noticed Leila first as she quietly approached the group.

"That didn't take too long," Anatolio said, and everyone turned the direction he was talking. Nalick ran over to her and picked her up as he hugged her. His grasp was tight, like he had lost her for years.

"Please don't ever run off, chasing people like that again. I was so worried. I don't know what I'd do if you got hurt again," Nalick said quietly, so that only she could hear. He refused to let go of her.

"Are you okay?" Nalick asked, finally releasing his grip a little.

Leila kissed him and then responded, "I'm fine. Did everyone make it back to Lexia? How are Macarius and Javed?"

"Javed died before I left the palace, and Macarius was going to have surgery. We hoped Roger would make it in time to help out. One of Roger's couriers stopped by to say he would be in Lexia by the afternoon, but we left before he came," Nalick explained, finally setting her back on the ground. She held tight to his hand, which was wrapped around her waist.

"What are you planning now?" Nalick asked, seeing the wheels working in her mind.

"I need to borrow Anatolio for an hour, and then you may do whatever you please to Aiolos and his men," Leila explained as they neared Nalick's makeshift camp.

As they entered the camp, Nikias quickly ran over to them and bowed. "Surveillance says that we outnumber them two to one. We are easily set at the six points, and are awaiting your command to enter." Nalick had a much larger army amassed. He easily had the upper hand.

"We will wait an hour," Nalick said, and Leila squeezed his hand.

CHAPTER TWENTY-SEVEN

"**W**ill you fill us in on what you're planning?" Nalick asked.

"Just a little payback," Leila replied, sitting down and beginning to lace her boots up. "How is Phillip?"

"He's fine," Nalick replied, obviously trying to control his anger at Aiolos for Phillip's hand.

"His hand is my fault," she said, without looking Nalick in the eyes. Leila continued to rummage through her bag. "I should have kept my mouth shut, and I suppose I shouldn't have spat on Aiolos. If I hadn't riled him up, he would not have tried to use Phillip to make a point."

"It's not your fault," Nalick replied, proud of the fight in her. "Aiolos is the one who took Phillip, and this is something we will have to deal with the rest of our lives. There are many people out there that are desperate to get you, and the children are the easiest way."

"I hope to change that. All I need is one hour, and I'm ready to go," Leila said while standing. Nalick stood with her and grabbed both her arms, forcing her to look him in the eyes.

"Come back unharmed, please," Nalick said, trying to read her expression.

Leila was calm and unafraid. Determination filled her eyes.

"This isn't your fault." He gently kissed her forehead.

Leila slipped her knives into each strap around her ankles and carefully put four vials in her pocket. Anatolio followed behind her, entering into the forest.

"Be very careful with these," Leila emphasized. "We need to change the color of your hair since it's the obvious give away as to who you are. I don't need you to be a target on top of me already being one. Sit here." Anatolio kneeled before Leila, and she quickly rubbed the dark color into his blond hair.

"Was he mad?" she asked about Nikias.

"Oh, yeah, when Nikias woke up and realized what we did. Lucky for us, he was with Theo and couldn't get mad at him. Once he calmed down, Theo explained what you had said, and he understood. You gave him a way out, possibly saved his life, and at the same time made it so that Nalick couldn't get mad at him for not being with you," Anatolio explained. "Though I think he might still be a little mad at me."

"Well, he shouldn't be mad at you. Nikias should be mad at me. I'm the one that told you to do it," Leila said, finishing his hair. Anatolio stood beside her. With dark hair, Anatolio looked like he could be Nalick's younger brother.

"You can say that, but really, can he actually get mad at his queen? It's much easier for him to take out his last frustrations on his half-brother," Anatolio added.

Leila and Anatolio slipped back into the camp easily. Leila quietly walked through the back of the tent, and Anatolio followed. Aiolos lay in the bed in the last area curtained off from the various women, who were also asleep. Leila held herself from laughing out loud, thinking of how Anatolio would react if he saw the topless women. Thankfully, the lights had been blown out, and they were in complete darkness. Leila placed one vial between her gloves and easily broke it. Anatolio held Aiolos' arms down as Leila placed the wet glove across his face. His eyes opened briefly but then they closed again.

Anatolio helped her carry the king to a nearby tent.

Anatolio promptly used the same liquid to make the man inside also fall asleep. Leila quickly began tying Argo up, and Anatolio double-checked each knot to make sure he couldn't escape. Then, Leila tied Aiolos up, but instead of tying his hands together, she tied them to the base of the bed in the room. Anatolio gagged both the Argo and the king. Leila looked at the half naked king in disgust. Slipping the knife out of her ankle strap she quickly stabbed it through his right hand. Taking a second knife, she stabbed it through his left hand. Anatolio was surprised she could actually follow through with what she told him she was going to do. Leila kneeled before the king and slapped his face waking him up. Aiolos groggily looked at Leila as his vision returned.

"My children are not to be touched," Leila said and stood. Aiolos gazed at her and didn't understand the meaning until he realized he was tied down. Aiolos carefully looked to his right hand, and he finally understood. Aiolos tried to reply, but he couldn't speak. Leila turned one last time and stared at him. He could see the hatred in her eyes, and was surprised. Through all the years of dealing with her, there was anger, but never hatred.

"If you ever touch any of my children again, there will be no next time. Just be happy I was in a good mood and decided not to make a point by removing body parts." Leila walked out the front of the tent and back to the woods with Anatolio close behind. They found their way back to camp easily.

"We need to make a statement to all other countries that think they can march in here and just take the queen," Nikias said, and the second general nodded his head. "She obviously doesn't want to stay with them, so why do they keep coming for her?"

"I wouldn't have given up so easily if she turned me down," Nalick said, understanding the attempts of his fellow kings in winning over Leila by any means possible. Leila walked silently behind him and wrapped her arms around his neck.

"But I did turn you down," Leila spoke from behind him, and he quickly stood and hugged her. "Your forces outnumber them three to one," Leila added. "There are weak spots in their perimeter." Leila drew a map on the ground and marked the gates. She indicated several spots. "Here, here, and here. Teams of five or less can easily infiltrate and take out the guards at each entrance." Leila sat down on Nalick's lap, and he held onto her tightly. Gabor had promised him that if he was able to hang onto her long enough for them to get married, he wouldn't have to worry for the rest of his life. It was getting harder the closer they got to the wedding.

"And Aiolos?" the general asked. "He's there with them, and he won't surrender without a fight. He's one of the best they have."

"That's why I'll lead the men in," Nalick replied. Leila shook her head and smiled.

"He won't be a problem," Anatolio said from behind. Nikias stared at his newly dark-haired younger brother and could finally see the resemblance between Anatolio and his father.

"How can you be so certain?" Nikias asked suspiciously.

"Even if you find him, I don't think he will be in fighting form," Leila said. "You might want to check the tents around the king's tent when you finally search through the camp. There should be a man with him that's the one who actually orchestrated the whole kidnapping." She didn't explain any more. "Be careful as you attack. There are people from the town here being put to work for them. The women, children, and priests won't fight back. Do not harm them. Some of the men are also from the village, and I'm sure they won't fight back.

Please be careful." All three men nodded their heads. They didn't want to hurt their own countrymen either.

"My lord," Nikias said to Nalick. "We should get going as soon as possible to still be able to use the night darkness to cover our men."

"I'll be right back," he said to his men. Nalick stood and scooped Leila up in his arms, walking away with her. Nalick tried to savor one last moment of having her in his arms before he set her down beside a covered cart.

"Anatolio will stay here with you and Phillip," Nalick said, motioning to a cart that held Phillip as he slept.

"I'd rather you stay here," she replied. "No offense, Anatolio," she said to the young man who was standing near.

"I'll be back as soon as I can," Nalick said. "Please stay right here and don't run off." Leila nodded and pulled him close. Leila didn't like the feeling of him running off to fight a battle when she couldn't be beside him.

"Be careful, and don't do anything stupid," Leila said before kissing him. She finally understood the feeling he felt when she was kidnapped.

Nalick wrapped his arms around her. "I promise I will be back soon, and in one piece." Leila nodded and didn't want him to let go. The whistle behind him made Leila turn.

"It's time for me to go," Nalick said quietly, and she let go of him. Aiolos' camp would be easy to take over, but people would get hurt, and some even killed. She sat and silently watched Nalick strap on armor that Theo handed him as he walked away. He transformed into the king people feared. Viewing the faces of the men passing, she knew that, for most of them, it was the first time they had gone into a real battle. Leila regretted getting so many people involved, but there was nothing she could do to stop it. Beyond kidnapping the queen of another country, Aiolos had gone into Lior and set up a war camp. Nalick couldn't ignore this fact, and had to respond.

Leila began to scoot back in the cart to be next to Phillip after the last of the men passed, but Anatolio stopped her.

"I almost forgot," Anatolio said, digging in his pocket. "Here." He held up her necklace with her ring from Erich. Anatolio opened the clasp, and she turned and lifted her hair as he put it back on her. "I didn't know you ever took it off." Leila shivered as his fingertips brushed the back of her neck. Anatolio's movements were always gentle with her.

Leila moved back, lying down beside Phillip and watched him slowly breathe. He was deep asleep. Leila was amazed he could sleep so well after his eventful day. In the calm, she could hear the men talking around the fire, but she couldn't make out their words. Nalick was fighting in the distance, but there was nothing she could do to help. Leila felt her eyes get heavy, and she started to drift off to sleep.

Leila rose at the sound of men returning. From the looks on their faces, everything turned out good for Lior. She cautiously watched each man pass. The men who had been left behind with her seemed disappointed that it was over so quickly, and they didn't get to participate. Man after man passed, but she saw no sign of Nalick.

"He won't be back for a while," Anatolio said, standing near the cart. "The terms of the surrender need to be agreed upon before he will come back. I'll wake you if he returns."

Leila shook her head. She wasn't about to get much more sleep than she already had, at least not until Nalick came back. Leila watched as more men returned. Soon Theo returned, and she was happy to see him. Her happiness faded a bit when she saw Nalick was not with him.

"Oh," Theo replied. "I wasn't the one you wanted to

see. Nalick is fine. I guess he found Aiolos pinned to a bed with daggers in each of his hands. Seems Aiolos isn't saying how that happened." Theo winked at her, and she played innocent. "The area is secured, and prisoners have been apprehended. If you want to join Nalick, he's at King Aiolos' tent." Leila stood, but then looked back at her sleeping son.

"I can stay with him," Theo offered.

Leila slowly walked through the woods to the tents. She noticed the distinct change in the air. The eager brutes that had been waiting for a battle got what they wanted, and were strewn dead across the way. Leila did her best not to look at the bodies she passed and headed straight to Aiolos' tent. As she approached, Anatolio moved to open the door to the tent, and she cautiously walked inside. There were no longer women on the couches, but several men chained together. Inside the inner room of the tent, Nalick sat with his back to the door that Leila had entered. Nikias quickly rose and bowed to her, and Nalick turned around and smiled. Leila walked over and quickly hugged him before sitting beside him across the table from Aiolos. She quickly checked Nalick over. There wasn't even a scratch on him. Leila was relieved and held onto his arm as he continued to talk. Nikias continued to write and then handed the paper to Aiolos.

Aiolos seemed to be unharmed by the daggers Leila had put through his hands. She had purposely missed any major veins, as it would not make the statement that she wanted him to spread to his fellow kings if he were dead. Aiolos watched in envy as Leila sat holding on to Nalick. Leila was willingly staying with Nalick. Aiolos took the paper from Nikias. He agreed to give Nalick half the men he had brought with him, including any officers that were not killed during the battle, which left him only with a quarter of his force to return home with.

Removing the officers would have a lasting effect and keep the border between Lior and Enea safe for years to come.

"So you turned down all of this?" Nalick asked, gesturing to the lavish tent as Leila and Nalick left together.

"You know me, just a simple girl. I always kind of felt that this much decoration is trying to make up for a lack of something else," Leila replied, and he laughed and hugged her. The warrior king was completely gone.

"It's going to take a few days to clean this all up," Nalick said, maneuvering Leila away from the dead bodies. "I really should stay here, but you and Phillip can go home. Tim and Ruth are waiting," Nalick reminded her.

"Besides, you should have some guests arriving soon." Leila's family was coming to visit for her wedding. The arrival of her family was making the whole wedding seem more and more real.

"Are you sure you can't come back?" Leila asked with a sad face. Nalick scooped her into his arms and kissed up and down her neck while she squirmed.

"Why do you have to make this so difficult for me?" he asked, carrying her back to their camp. Leila wrapped her arm around Nalick's neck and rested her head on his chest as he walked. His job was to take care of his country, and because of her, there was quite a mess to clean up.

"I promise to return as soon as I can," Nalick vowed. Leila reached up and pulled him close to her. She kissed him gently and the soldiers walking by cheered. Leila blushed, letting go of him. He set her down in the cart.

Several men accompanied her cart back to Lexia. As the cart started moving, she climbed back next to Phillip and closed her eyes. She hadn't slept much the night before, worrying about Nalick and the fighting that was going on, but she was more relaxed now that she knew everything was fine. Just before they reached the walls of Lexia, Phillip tapped Leila until she woke up.

"Mom," he asked. "Where's Dad?"

"He stayed behind to help get everything cleaned up and organized. He will come back as soon as he can, but it might be a few days," she replied without opening her eyes.

"So, I guess that means I don't get my horse, then," Phillip said. Leila opened her eyes and stared at him. Phillip seemed to be unfazed by what had happened to him. After he refused to talk, she was afraid that he was stunned by the events that had taken place, but now she had the same old Phillip in front of her.

"I promise nothing like that will ever happen again," Leila said.

"You were amazing, Mom," he replied back as she hugged him.

CHAPTER TWENTY-EIGHT

Leila was surprised, but happy to find her mother and best friend sitting in her home waiting for her to return. They had arrived with Roger, and brought Kay's son, Luca, with them. Leila hadn't noticed he was on the balcony playing with Ruth and Tim. When both children saw Leila return, they ran to her as she hugged her own mother.

"Mommy!" Ruth called.

"Where were you?" Tim asked, as Leila picked up both children.

"'lip," Ruth sung out upon seeing her brother sneaking up the stairs to his room. Leila set Ruth down, and she chased Phillip.

"Where's Dad?" Tim asked.

"He's out with his army. He will probably not be back until tomorrow," Leila told Tim. Tim contemplated what she said and responded.

"Next time, he should take me with him. I'd make a good soldier," Tim said, hopping down and continuing to play with Luca, who waved to Leila. Leila was still standing in the traveling clothing she had changed into the night before. Selma recognized her clothing as the things she would have worn if Leila had gone on a run for Roger.

"Go clean up," Selma said to her daughter. "We're not going anywhere."

"If you see the older one, tell him he should take a bath also," Leila said, making her way over to the main bath. Elena quickly rushed in the room ahead of her and started the bath water. Leila bathed and returned to the main room to visit her mother and friend.

"What's so funny?" Leila asked, as Kay began to laugh when Leila walked near.

"Where did my best friend Leila go? What did you do with her?" Kay asked, jumping up and tugging at Leila's dress. Leila looked down and laughed with her. Growing up, Leila refused to wear dresses and only did so when she was in disguise. Kay had never seen her best friend in a dress if she didn't have a wig on to go with the ensemble.

"Does it look bad?" Leila asked, getting self-conscious.

"No, actually, you look great," Kay replied, and Selma nodded. "So you have a family now?"

"Sorry about not writing about the children. Everything has been quite hectic the last two weeks, and with yesterday it just didn't slow down," Leila explained as both of her guests nodded. Leila never lived a slow life. They weren't surprised in the least.

"Are you two hungry?" Leila asked her guests.

"Sure," Kay said. Kay had been very impressed with their late breakfast and was eager to see what dinner would be.

"Elena, if you could have the cook send up an early dinner, we would appreciate it. And if Phillip asks, he doesn't get dinner until he takes a bath," Leila said, as Elena quickly hurried away out the door to Mauve's room. As soon as Elena passed through the door, Mauve emerged.

"My dear, how are you?" Mauve asked, hurrying over to check Leila over for herself. "We were all so worried when we heard you had been taken again." Selma raised her eyebrows and only Leila caught her mother's reaction.

"I'm fine, and so is Phillip. Nalick is still there, cleaning everything up and hopefully will be back tomorrow," Leila said, seeing Mauve look around the room. "Mauve, did you meet my mother and best friend?"

"I can see where you get your good looks from," Mauve said, before she turned to leave.

"So that makes just about everyone," Leila said, trying to remember if she needed to introduce her mother and friend to anyone else. "Mauve takes care of basically everything, and fusses like you'd not believe over making sure I'm presentable to the court. Elena lives here with us to watch over the younger children and basically does the same things that Mauve does. Oh, yes, the last person is trying to sneak in the room right now without us noticing," Leila said, noticing Anatolio quietly walking to the stairway. "Anatolio, I'd like you to meet my mother, Selma, and best friend, Kay." Anatolio stopped and walked over to them. Gently he shook both Selma's and Kay's hands.

"The extra boy on the balcony is Kay's." Leila explained, as Anatolio quickly took an inventory of the room.

"Will you be joining us for dinner?" Leila asked, but Anatolio shook his head.

"I already told Roger I'd join him," Anatolio replied quietly.

"Is Phillip in his room?" Anatolio asked, and Leila nodded. "Roger wants to see his hand." Leila nodded again, and Anatolio quickly bowed and continued up the stairway.

"And what does he do?" Kay asked, eyeing the young man over as he hurried away. Kay had thought most of the men in Lexia weren't her type, but the young blond man was definitely cuter than any she had seen so far.

"Besides shy away from groups of people?" Leila replied sarcastically.

Anatolio had to have caught the comment, but he

didn't show it.

"He's basically my new shadow. He follows me everywhere I go and sometimes knows where I'm going before I even do. Nalick hired him to protect me."

"I could use some protecting," Kay teased, and Leila laughed. "You can send him my way if you'd like." Leila playfully punched her best friend's arm.

"When Nalick said you'd be bringing children when you come to visit, I didn't know what to expect," Selma said. "You do seem to always do things quickly, but deciding to get married and raise children in the span of a few months is a bit shocking. And then to find out that it's three children, and the oldest is only years younger than you. Phew."

"It just sort of happened," Leila said, watching Ruth desperately trying to play with the boys. Phillip returned down the stairs with Anatolio and didn't say anything as he left. Phillip was caught up in his own little world.

"Kind of like when you brought home that nest of baby rabbits?" Selma asked.

"Well, yes." Leila innocently shrugged.

"Had you two even talked about having children?" Selma asked.

"No, we're just trying to make it to our wedding day," Leila said. "At this rate, I may miss my own wedding."

Selma shook her head. "With all the resources available to Nalick, he can't protect you any better than Roger?"

"If it were up to just Nalick, I'd be safely locked away in this room forever. This wing of the castle is probably the most heavily-guarded place in the world. Mom, you know I'll never be safe. The only place I'm truly safe and free is at home in the mountains, where no one knows where to find me," Leila explained. Phillip returned and tried to sneak back upstairs. "Phillip," Leila called to him. "Please take a bath before dinner gets here." Phillip reluctantly took a quick bath.

"Can I eat downstairs? Lord Pillas said he would bring Nighttime by tonight, and it's going to be dark soon, and..." Phillip tried to convince Leila, who finally relented with a nod.

"Just make sure to take someone with you. I don't want you sitting there alone, okay?" Leila replied, and Phillip smiled and quickly filled a plate with food. Phillip hurried to leave, but stopped in front of the door.

"Oh, yeah," Phillip said, returning to the table. "It was nice to meet you," he said to Selma and Kay before he hurried off.

"What is that all about?" Kay asked as they continued their meal.

"The whole reason we went to the Pillas manor yesterday was because they gave Phillip his own horse. They said they would bring it by tonight, and hopefully they will, otherwise he will be very disappointed," Leila explained.

After they finished their meal, Leila gave her mother and friend a tour of the palace. Leila made a detour to the medical wing as she walked around. Roger put more stitches into Macarius than she had ever had in her life, yet he seemed to be breathing and alive. Bandages were wrapped everywhere around him, including his head. Leila was relieved he was alive. Turning to leave, she noticed Anatolio was in the room, also.

"Will he be fine?" Leila asked him.

"Roger said he did everything he could, and he should be fine. But we just have to wait and see for sure. Roger had to put in over a hundred stitches and remove three fingers that were too far gone to save. Roger thinks he was able to save his eye, but we will have to wait until he wakes up," Anatolio explained.

Leila slowly walked near to Macarius and looked at him closely. She couldn't help but feel like it was her fault he was hurt. If she hadn't come along into Nalick's life, Macarius would have never fought his heart out to save Phillip.

"It's not your fault," Anatolio told her, but could see she wasn't convinced. "You have to remember, the good you do by being here far outweighs the consequences. Just think, if you didn't meet Phillip, Ruth probably would have died weeks ago." Leila nodded and was happy Anatolio saw the good in her being in the palace.

"Thank you," Leila said, softly touching his hand before she exited the room. Anatolio's heart raced. For once, he was the one cheering her up. Anatolio had seen how easily Nalick could make her face light up into a bright smile, but he had never done that before. Anatolio watched her rejoin her mother and friend and continued walking down the corridor.

All three returned to the royal wing of the palace for the night. Leila bid her friend and mother goodnight, as she was ready for bed. They both could see how exhausted she was. As Leila entered her room quietly, Phillip had fallen asleep on the couch. She gently tapped his shoulder and called his name. He groggily opened his eyes and realized it was her.

"Mom, the horse is great," Phillip said. She helped him to stand and began to walk him to the stairs. "Tell Dad thanks." He started to climb the stairs, but his eyes were drifting closed again. Leila steadied him and walked him to his bed. Once in bed, Phillip opened his eyes again. "Thanks for taking care of everything," he said as he closed his eyes again. Leila smiled and pulled the blanket around him.

She shut the door quietly and walked across to Ruth's room. Ruth and Tim cuddled together in Ruth's bed. Leila smiled and sat down next to the two children. Part of her had feared that someone might try to take the younger children to get to her. Leila hoped she had made enough of a statement for everyone to leave the children alone. Ruth opened her eyes and smiled.

"Can Ruth sleep with Mommy?" Ruth asked.

"Of course," Leila replied. With Nalick gone for the night, she had plenty of room for the child to join her. Leila stood to pick up the small girl, but Ruth stopped her.

"Bring Timmy, too," Ruth added. Leila picked up the sleeping Tim and held onto Ruth's hand while walking them to their bedroom. Ruth quickly climbed into the bed and chose where she wanted to sleep as Leila laid Tim down in Nalick's spot. Leila lay down beside Ruth and watched the little girl go back to sleep. Her mother was right. Everything was happening so quickly, but Leila didn't want to change a single thing.

CHAPTER TWENTY-NINE

"**D**o you eat like this every morning?" Kay asked, joining Leila at the table.

"Mauve likes to overdo it from time to time," Leila explained. "Most of the time she does this to get me in a good mood before she's going to tell me something I don't want to hear." Leila was right. After the meal, Mauve brought her the schedule of events leading up to, and following, the wedding. Selma and Kay enjoyed watching Leila's expressions as the list was read to her. Most of the list was events she didn't want to do. Mauve didn't notice her disappointment, and was thrilled to show Leila off to all the guests that were coming.

Nalick returned in the afternoon. Leila heard the door open to their quarters, but she didn't check to see who it was as it was still early afternoon. Leila wasn't expecting Nalick to return until nighttime. She was surprised to see the younger children running by the doorway and then realized who had entered the room. Leila left her mother and friend and also hurried to the guest neither of them saw. Selma moved to the doorway and watched her daughter greet her future husband. Nalick picked up both the young children, one in each arm, and began to walk back to the balcony, but he stopped as he suddenly saw Leila's mother.

"I thought..." Nalick said, but stopped as he looked from Selma to Leila.

"We came early, but the men stayed home," Selma explained, preventing her future son-in-law from telling the secret of why.

"Well, welcome to Lior," Nalick said, still carrying the two small children. "Has Leila shown you around?"

"Just the palace," Leila answered for her.

"Give Roger a few more days, and then you can take them into town, also," Nalick replied. He set Tim down, who ran back to his toys, but he continued to hold Ruth, who wouldn't let go of him. Roger had brought her mother and friend to Lexia, but Leila hadn't seen him since she returned. It was odd since he was always there to greet her when he could, and she now realized that he was busy with something. "I saw that Phillip got his horse," Nalick added.

"Mauve gave me the schedule for next week. Do we really need to have a formal dinner each night leading up to the wedding?" Leila asked. She didn't enjoy the dinners, but they had many guests they needed to greet before the marriage.

"Sorry, but I thought by having several smaller dinners, it wouldn't be as bad," he explained, but Nalick could see any formal dinner, to her, was going to be bad.

The week passed quickly, and Leila was so happy to have her family visiting that she forgot about the conversation she needed to have with Nalick. By the end of the week, Leila's father, brothers, and their families arrived with the help of Roger's sons, Henry and Lars. Leila returned to her own room to gather up her children to meet the rest of her family. Leila returned to the guest quarters holding Ruth, who immediately hid her face upon seeing all the people in the room. Phillip and Nalick followed behind her, carrying Tim, who was trying his best to get down and run around the new room.

"Everyone, I'd like you to meet our children," Leila said to her family.

"This is Phillip." Nalick pushed the older boy ahead of himself, introducing him.

"Nalick has Tim." Everyone laughed as Nalick tried to hold on to the rambunctious four-year-old.

"And this one here is the youngest, Ruth. Can you say hi to everyone, Ruth?" Leila asked the child whose face was still hidden in her chest.

Nalick sat Tim down, who proceeded to run around and shake everyone's hand while telling them his name. Then, Leila introduced everyone, for Phillip's sake, and to remind Nalick, who could recognize the faces but not all the names.

"My brothers are there, Nael and Leon, and their wives Gisela and Sabine. My nieces and nephews—now your cousins, are Dierk, Cara, Carl, Gabi, and Karin. The last person is my father, Dirk." Phillip nodded, trying his best to remember everyone's name, but the light-haired people standing around easily confused him. Tim grabbed all the cousins near his age and began to pull them to the door.

"Can we go play with the toys?" Tim asked, once he had Luca, Carl, Gabi, and Cara grouped at the door.

"Sure," Leila said, and he pushed open the door and ran back to their room of the palace while the other children followed.

There had been times since Erich died that everyone in her family doubted Leila could be happy again. But they could see that Leila glowed any time she took care of the children, and any time she was in the presence of Nalick.

After visiting for hours, Leila and Nalick returned to their room to find that Gabi and Carl had fallen asleep. Leila and Nalick returned her nieces and nephews to her brothers before returning to their room to find Ruth and Tim already in their beds waiting to be tucked in. Phillip was leaving Ruth's room as they arrived.

"Mom, you sure have a big family," Phillip said, as he closed Ruth's door. Leila followed Phillip to his room as

Nalick went into Ruth's room.

"That was fun," Phillip said, as he closed his eyes.

"Goodnight Timmy, goodnight Phillip," Leila said, before leaving and crossing to Ruth's room. Ruth was already fast asleep, and Leila didn't want to wake her. Nalick said goodnight to the boys before he returned downstairs with Leila, who had climbed into bed herself. Nalick tried to build up the courage to talk to her, but he could see she was almost asleep. Leila reached up and tugged his arm.

"Come to bed," she said. "We can talk in the morning." Nalick nodded before joining her. The closer it got to the wedding, the harder it was getting to talk to her. Reluctantly, Nalick fell asleep.

Surprisingly, Leila woke the next morning to find everyone still asleep. She quietly crept out of the bed and dressed into practice clothes. She had a lot of nervous energy built up since her hectic wedding schedule was about to begin that night, with a formal dinner, meaning she would have to greet more people she had never met. Leila quickly wrote a note and left it on the table. She laughed quietly to herself and observed that, for once, Anatolio didn't see she was leaving. Easily she slipped out the door and shut it soundlessly behind her. As she walked down the hallway, the door to Roger's room opened, and the older man stared at her with an all-knowing expression.

"Running off without taking Anatolio with you?" Roger asked, as he, too, noticed the young man was not following Leila.

"I'm not going anywhere outside the palace. I'm just heading to the training grounds to practice a little and burn off some energy so that I can sit peacefully through tonight's boring dinner," Leila explained like a child that had been caught sneaking a cookie before dinner.

"Would you mind if I join you?" Roger asked.

"Not at all," she replied, taking the arm he offered her.

"So, are you really ready to get married?" Roger asked as they weaved between corridors, making their way to the courtyard.

"Ready as I'll ever be," she replied with a grin, but noticed he didn't laugh.

"Yes," she said more seriously.

"You're willing to take the good and the bad that comes with getting married?" Roger asked, testing to see if Nalick had finally talked to her.

"Of course, but I can't imagine anything getting worse than it is now," Leila was referring to being kidnapped. "They already know where I am, so it doesn't matter if I get married."

Nalick hadn't told her yet, Roger realized.

As they walked into the empty courtyard, Leila let go of Roger's arm and walked to the center. The courtyard was empty and Leila and he were alone. She closed her eyes, feeling the rays of the sun peeking over the walls. Leila stood still, and Roger watched her. She would never lose her free spirit. Roger cared for Leila like a daughter. Roger was eager for Nalick to tell her his secret, but there was no way he could force him. Somehow, even part of Roger didn't want her to know. He couldn't blame Nalick for not wanting to make her sad. Leila smiled, finally opening her eyes to find Roger staring at her.

"So, you're going to be my sparring partner?" she asked, playfully pretending to punch him.

Roger chuckled and backed away. "If I was only twenty years younger, gladly."

Leila sat down and began to stretch as Roger moved onto the balcony to watch her. She was magnificent in her ability to move. Erich had made sure she was well-trained in the years before he died, knowing she would always need to protect herself. As she crisscrossed the courtyard, practicing the same moves she had done for years, Roger could see the influence of Erich in her movements. It had been two years since he lost his son, at the same age Leila was now. As she matured, she reminded him more and more of his late son. It was hard to believe that Erich still had so much influence over her. Roger understood why she had such a hard time letting people into her life, since she clung so desperately to Erich's memory. Though Leila detested the idea of fate and predetermined outcomes, Roger strictly believed that events in life happen for a reason. Roger never regretted Leila's influence on his son and his son's life. He truly felt Leila was there to make his son happy for the brief time they spent together. Roger continued to watch her move around the courtyard as if she were dancing.

"Maybe the boy should tell her," Roger said to Nalick as he approached with Anatolio.

Anatolio quickly shook his head *no*. Anatolio didn't want to be the one to tell her.

Roger chuckled. No one wanted to tell her, but someone had to. "You can't escape fate. She will find out sooner or later," Roger assessed.

Nalick nodded as Leila stood and walked to the men. As she neared, all three men smiled and stopped talking.

CHAPTER THIRTY

Leila wasn't happy to be returning to her room in the palace. She tried to sneak into the room so that she could find a hiding place, but unfortunately the children were there to happily greet her. Nalick laughed, knowing she was trying to get out of getting ready for dinner.

"I asked Mauve to wait until after lunch," Nalick said. "Since you now have to do this for four days in a row, she promised to not take as long each time."

Leila was relieved and smiled gratefully at Nalick. "What were you three talking about?" she asked, picking up Ruth.

Nalick wasn't going to answer honestly.

"Is it what you need to talk to me about?" she asked, sitting down on the balcony with Ruth on her lap.

Nalick nodded. Leila wondered what Anatolio and Roger could know that Nalick was afraid to tell her.

"Dad, I...," Phillip said, running onto the balcony and noticing Leila. He stopped suddenly, and got flustered. Phillip didn't know what to say when he noticed Leila on the balcony also.

Leila was beginning to feel like everything was being kept from her, and she was a bit upset. Ruth slid off Leila's lap to join her brother, who was playing with his toys. Leila quietly stood and walked to the bathroom to find makeup to cover her arm. Silently, she dipped her arm into the light-colored makeup and covered the lines on her arm. If Mauve wasn't going to be looking for her until after lunch, Leila was going to use the opportunity to sneak into the city. Leila quickly changed into street clothes. While walking back into the main room, she saw that Elena was sitting, watching the children.

"I'll be back for lunch," Leila told her. Leila hurried out of the room and down the hall before Anatolio noticed. She quickly poked her head into the guest quarters and found Kay. "Want to go for a walk?" Kay quickly stood to join her.

Kay followed behind her friend, who weaved between corridors before exiting the palace through the servant's quarters. Kay had trouble keeping up with Leila, who continued to dodge people, weaving between streets. She had tried to see who was following them, but to keep up with Leila she needed to concentrate. Once Kay finally caught a glance of who was following them, she stopped Leila.

"There's only one person following us," Kay said to her friend.

"I know," Leila replied without looking back.

"And isn't it his job to follow you?" Kay asked about Anatolio.

"Well, I never asked him to," Leila replied quickly, catching her friend's arm and ducking between two buildings.

Leila stepped into a vacant room, and Kay followed her upstairs. Leila went to a door and it opened into a fully-furnished apartment. Leila quickly opened a secret door and pushed Kay ahead before following her. As the exited the building, Leila slowed down to a walk and Kay was finally able to walk beside her.

"Are you sure he won't get in trouble for losing track of you?" Kay asked.

Leila stared at her friend. "I think I can take care of myself. Besides, he'll find us again, eventually. He seems to be good at that." Leila thought of the various times she had seen him following her in the city before she even knew his name. He was getting better at keeping up with her, but she could still lose him if she wanted.

Leila made her way to the town square and was surprised when she got there to find men setting up tables to fill the space. Around the outside, the normal vendor tents were gone, and inside tables also lined the outside of the square.

"To the left," a man called from behind, and Leila grabbed Kay and moved her to her right.

"What's going on?" Kay asked.

"I don't know," Leila replied. She searched the faces of the men and quickly approached the youngest one. "What's going on here?" she asked the young man, who blushed to be addressed so casually.

"The king is finally getting married," the boy said. "So to celebrate, we're having a large feast here the night before the wedding. We have a couple of days to get set up, so I'm helping while they're short on men. Today, everyone that's older is busy at the town meeting. There's some guy from the North Country here talking about how to make the city safer. We want to protect our queen."

"Where would the meeting be at?" Leila asked.

"Gothreith Hall," the boy replied as Leila quickly hurried away.

Leila quickly navigated to Gothreith Hall. Kay followed, also wondering who the person was, as both women had a pretty good guess. People milled outside the building when Leila arrived, and she easily pushed her way into the back of the room. From the back, she could remain hidden while she viewed the stage. The man sitting in front was exactly who she expected... Roger. Roger had already given the audience a lecture and was now answering questions. Kay was as surprised as Leila, and she didn't notice that her friend had already left the room. Once Kay finally noticed, she quickly made her way back outside. Leila was waiting on the steps across from the hall. Kay approached and could see the sadness in her eyes. Leila was always the sort of person who would talk only when she wanted to. Kay sat down next to her best friend and patted her knee.

"Nalick's keeping a secret from me," Leila said to her best friend. "He won't tell me, even when I ask, but he has told Roger and Anatolio." Leila was the most honest and open person Kay had ever met. She rarely lied to people, even when on assignment, and never lied to her friends. Leila expected the same, and was hurt by Nalick.

"Why do men tell each other secrets they can't even tell their soon-to-be wife?" Leila asked Kay.

"Maybe he doesn't know how to tell you," Kay suggested, trying not to sound like she agreed with Nalick.

"But he can tell me anything," Leila replied, trying to hold back tears.

"Sometimes it's easier to talk to the same gender," Kay suggested, reaching over to adjust Leila's wig in a motherly fashion.

"Even so, what could be so hard to say?" Leila asked.

"Why don't you ask Anatolio?" Kay suggested, looking in the shadows for the young man.

"I tried, and he won't tell me," Leila said, not looking up.

"But could he tell you who *would* tell you, besides Nalick?" Kay asked. Leila smiled at her friend's ingenuity at getting around Nalick's inability to tell her.

"It's worth a try." Leila waved to Anatolio, who approached cautiously. "Since you won't tell me what Nalick is hiding, would you be able to tell me the name of someone who would?" Leila asked, and he stood and thought for a moment. "I'm not going back to the palace until I find something out."

"I don't think anyone that knows will tell you. It's

Nalick's secret to tell," Anatolio replied. Leila was not satisfied with his answer. "If you really want to know what your life holds, just talk to Gabor." Leila hadn't considered the seer.

"Good idea," she said while standing. Anatolio wasn't sure if it was a good idea or not, but he needed to get her back to the palace by lunch to keep Nalick happy.

Kay and Anatolio followed Leila back to the palace. As Leila reached the gate, the guard stopped her. Leila forgot the makeup was covering her arm. She was going to comment, but Anatolio stepped forward and the guard let them pass without knowing who they were. Leila stopped in front of the door to the priest chambers. She wasn't sure she really wanted to know what life had in store for her. She hadn't had the best of luck in the first eighteen years; she didn't know if the next eighteen would improve.

Anatolio escorted Leila to Gabor. Anatolio tapped on Gabor's door and there was a soft reply from inside the room. Anatolio opened the door and stood in the doorway, waiting for Leila. Hesitantly, she walked by Anatolio into the sparsely-decorated room. Gabor was sitting across the room, next to the one window, reading. He smiled as she entered. His smile widened as he realized the man behind her wasn't Nalick, but Anatolio. Gabor had seen the future of both of them and was happy to see them together.

"What a surprise," Gabor said to Leila. "Come, take a seat." He moved to clean the seat next to him. Leila helped, sitting down next to him. Anatolio quickly bowed and left the room to wait alongside Kay. Anatolio didn't want to be around for her initial reaction.

"So, what brings you here?" Gabor asked. "And in disguise."

Leila quickly removed her wig and untied her hair. "I was in the city," she explained her disguise. "Nalick is keeping something from me," she said, explaining her reason for her visit. "I figured you probably know what is going on." The old man smiled and nodded. Gabor wasn't going to give a verbal reply.

"But you're not going to tell me," Leila added disappointedly.

"It's not my place to tell you what he knows, or why he does what he does. That's for him to tell you, when he finds the courage to do so." Gabor removed his glasses. Leila stood to leave the room.

"You're quick to leave. Perhaps if you ask the right question, you might find the answers you seek." Leila sat back down beside him and stared at his questioning eyes.

"So you won't tell me what he's hiding, but you will answer other questions?" Leila asked, and Gabor nodded.

"I don't make it a habit of telling people the fate of others, but if you want to know about your own future, then that's an entirely different case. Ask anything about yourself, and I'll answer the best I can," Gabor explained.

"What do you see for my life with Nalick, or rather my marriage to Nalick?" Leila held out her hand and the old man took it. He closed his eyes and smiled as if he were watching an entertaining show.

He let go and smiled at her more. "You will have ten very happy years together with five more children beyond the three you have now. I'm not saying you won't have your ups and downs, like any marriage, but you will always be happy. Together, your union will produce the best king our country will ever have."

"Ten years?" Leila asked. "Will something happen to me in ten years?"

"No. In ten years' time you will be pregnant with your sixth biological child," Gabor explained, smiling as he closed his eyes. He could see the bright future waiting for his country because this one girl chose to stay.

"Does something happen to Nalick?" she asked, but

Gabor shook his head. Leila wanted to jump up and shake the man to get her answer.

"That I can't say, for that is his future. He wants to be the one to tell you," he replied.

"What about after ten years?" she asked, not truly wanting to know the full details.

"You will be happy. After fifteen years in Lior, you will head home to the North Country. You will grow old and see your grandchildren grow into adults. But there's no need to worry, as you won't be alone," Gabor said to the shocked woman sitting next to him.

"Phillip will take to heart the idea of being a prince, and learn as much as he can from Nalick. He will never be king, but it won't bother him. Instead, Phillip will find that he can serve his country and his family by teaching your first-born son how to do both.

"Tim will grow into your right hand man and learn your trade as well as if he were your own biological child. He will never leave your side, and do everything he can to make sure you're happy. That child will know as much about being a courier as you do, and will be just as good at it.

"Ruth will teach everyone how to love and compromise. While you're doing your best to make their lives better, they'll actually make your lives better than they were ever meant to be." She was still confused by the first statement he had made.

"Will I be happy?" Leila whispered, standing to try to avoid her fate.

"Yes, Nalick has made sure of it," Gabor replied.

Leila walked to the door quietly. All she could understand was that her marriage to Nalick would only last ten years, yet she wasn't going to move back to the North Country for fifteen years. All she could assume was that something was going to happen to Nalick. *What is your fate, Nalick?* she thought. Leila met outside the room with Kay and Anatolio.

"Did you get your answer?" Kay asked.

"Kind of," Leila replied. "I guess I just need to wait to hear Nalick explain it to me, as I'm a bit confused." *How could I be happy if he's dead?* she wondered.

"If you don't understand what it is, do you at least know why he isn't telling you?" Kay asked.

"I think, but I'm just not sure," Leila replied, leading the way back to the royal quarters. Anatolio studied her to see what Gabor might have told her. It didn't include him, and he was relieved. He didn't want the relationship between them to change, and he was actually happy Nalick hadn't told her yet.

They made it back in time for lunch, and she didn't say anything to Nalick. Before the lunch was even done, Mauve took Leila away to get her ready. Leila complied without a fuss. After she was dressed, Leila sat down on the couch and watched as Mauve fussed over Nalick. Leila barely noticed as Tim climbed up next to her and wiggled until he was almost sitting on her lap.

"Mommy, you look pretty," Tim said, as he cautiously touched the jewelry around her neck. Leila smiled at her middle child. He was trying to cheer her up. Leila picked him up and placed him on her lap.

"Thanks, Timmy," Leila said, snuggling him.

Nalick watched from across the room as Mauve was still fussing over him. Anatolio approached Nalick quietly.

"She wouldn't come back until I, or someone, told her what you have not," Anatolio explained, and Nalick nodded his head slightly. "So I sent her to Gabor." Anatolio waited for him to get angry.

"Thanks," Nalick said. "She had to find out sooner rather than later. Do you know what he told her?"

"No, I left her alone with him," Anatolio reported, while also watching Leila.

"She deserves the truth. The poor girl has been through enough in her life. The sooner she knows and accepts her fate, the better it will be for all three of you," Mauve said, butting into the conversation.

After taking Timmy and Ruth to visit their cousins for the night, Leila silently followed Nalick through the corridors to the main hall, where it was lavishly decorated. There wasn't enough time to explain everything to her on their walk to the hall, so Nalick didn't interrupt her silence. Leila happily greeted their guests as Nalick introduced her to everyone. She was upset with him, but nothing showed to the people who were visiting.

After dinner, Leila and Nalick again walked silently to their room. Once they arrived back, Leila checked on each of the children, who were tucked into their beds asleep. She was trying her best to avoid Nalick, as he would tell her what she didn't want to hear.

Assured everyone was asleep, Leila walked out into her garden and lit a torch near one of the benches. She thought briefly, when she first fell in love with Nalick, that everything was going to be perfect. Leila had finally found a man that didn't just love her for her appearance, but for the person she was. She was surprised, as more and more they got along great and were similar in so many ways. Leila had thought that since Nalick was a king, he would be just like every other king she had met. He was not. Theo and Macarius liked her because they thought Nalick had finally met his match, but what they didn't know was that Leila had also met her match in a man that could stand beside her in every way possible in love, in life, and in happiness. And now that would be limited to ten years.

CHAPTER THIRTY-ONE

Leila sat and watched the shadows cast by the torchlight flickering over the plants around her. It was dark outside, as the moon and stars were covered by clouds. As the clouds drifted by she could tell where the moon was, but they never completely moved so that she could view it. Leila felt utterly alone as she sat gazing into the sky and the absent moon was no comfort. *Is this what my life will be like?* she asked herself. Leila had not felt this feeling of loneliness since she had decided to stay with Nalick. She shivered, even though the breeze that blew by was warm.

Nalick checked on the children, but took his time. He wasn't sure yet how to tell Leila the truth. Nalick watched her walk to the balcony and knew she was waiting for him. He quietly walked out and approached her. She didn't turn to face him as he neared, but she kept looking for the moon in the sky. Nalick sat down beside her, and from the faint light of the torch he could see the dried tear streaks that lined her face. Nalick gently picked up her hand, and Leila turned to face him. He could see the change in her eyes as loneliness stared back at him.

"I've had this conversation with you a hundred times in my head," he said, as she held on tightly to him. "But I still don't know any way to say this that won't hurt you."

"Do you know why Anatolio is your personal guard?" Nalick asked, opening the subject he feared to discuss.

"Because of his talent," Leila replied, not understanding why Nalick wasn't talking about what would happen in ten years.

"That was just a good side benefit. Actually, I brought over seventy men before Gabor told me that he already knew who you were meant to be with. Anatolio's soul is as pure as yours. He's the man who you're meant to spend your life with," Nalick explained.

"I love you, not him," Leila said, not understanding. "Besides, he's just a kid."

"And I love you, but sometimes life doesn't last as long as love." Nalick looked into the gray sky and couldn't see the moon either. Leila searched his face for clues.

"Before I was even a teenager, Gabor warned me that I'd only live ten years after I got married. It didn't matter who I married, or how old I was when I did, I'd only have ten more years of life. At the same time he told me of this beautiful, smart, girl who was years younger than me that would make those ten years the happiest of my life, *if* I was able to convince her to marry me. By the time I'd meet her, her heart would be scarred, and she wouldn't be willing to accept love. But, if I tried my best, I might find the happiness that very few people actually find in life. That girl was you." Nalick cupped her chin in his hands. Tears slowly fell down her cheeks upon hearing the words she didn't wish to hear.

"I made my choice the day I first saw you. I'd rather choose ten years of complete happiness than a lifetime without you." Nalick brushed the tears away with his thumbs.

"Are you sure he can't be wrong?" Leila asked.

Nalick wiped more tears away as they continued to fall. He wanted to run away from everything with her and protect her from the future.

"Gabor is never wrong. It would be so much easier if he was, but he isn't. He has told me how I die, and I know that, no matter what, it won't change," Nalick said, pulling her close to his chest.

"And if you don't get married?" Leila asked, peeking up, her tears still on the verge of flowing over.

"Then I won't die," he replied. Leila released the breath she had been holding. Nalick didn't need to die.

"I don't fear death," he added. "It's the trade I'm making for ten years of happiness. I didn't have to ask you to marry me, but I did. And I don't regret it for one minute. I want to marry you, Leila. I want you to be my wife and the mother of my children. I want a lot of things out of life that I won't get to have, but those two things I can have."

"And there's nothing I can do?" she asked, turning her face back down to his shirt to try to hide the tears that began again.

"No, there is nothing anyone can do to stop fate. I've accepted mine and know I can't change it, but I wouldn't want to. It was that fate that brought you to me." Nalick took her hands and kissed them.

"I don't want this to make you scared or sad. I promise you we will have ten very happy years together. Our eldest son will be the best king Lior will ever have. We will have a large, happy family where everyone will feel loved and wanted. I won't, for one day, regret my decision. And you will never be alone again. That's why I found Anatolio. In ten years, he will no longer be just a kid. He will be a man, able to take care of you and our children."

"Does he know all of this?" Leila asked. Anatolio was standing out of sight, but near enough to hear them talk without Nalick noticing.

"Yes," Nalick replied. "I told him why I wanted him to follow you, and, at my prompting, Gabor told him his fate."

"And he's just willing to sit and wait for you to die?" she asked, amazed, trying to steal a glance and give away his hiding spot.

"As you said before, right now he's just a boy, and he knows this also," Nalick replied. "It's probably the reason he's such a good learner. He has had to grow up fast, and I didn't relieve the situation any. I'd have never asked you to marry me if I didn't find Anatolio. I know the pain of loneliness, and I never want you to feel that way again."

Leila rested her head against his chest as they continued to sit in the darkness. She was tired and emotionally exhausted. Everything Nalick told her was swirling in her head. Nalick put his arm around her and held onto her. He could see she was tired, but she wasn't giving the reaction he expected. There was nothing more Nalick could say to her, so he scooped her into his arms and carried her down to their bed. Leila moved close as he lay down beside her, and she rested her head on his chest. Her world was spinning, and she felt like it would not stop. As she lay there, she could hear his heartbeat as he gently stroked her head. The constant thumping calmed everything as she closed her eyes. No matter what Nalick told her about fate, at that moment, Leila could hear the beating of his heart and knew he was alive.

Leila woke the next morning with her thoughts still swirling around in her head from the night before. As she walked into the main room she could hear Nalick and Phillip talking from the balcony while having their breakfast. Leila quietly approached, but did not want to disturb them, so she stood in the archway and listened.

"Do you love her?" Phillip asked seriously.

"With all my heart," Nalick replied, and Leila smiled behind him. She understood he did and felt it every time he looked her direction. He had no reservations in marrying her, even though it was going to shorten his life.

"Then does that mean I'll have more brothers and

sisters?" Phillip asked eagerly.

Nalick laughed a booming laugh that made Leila smile even more. "Is that what you want?" Nalick asked, and Phillip nodded. "Eventually, hopefully, but you better be willing to help out. Someday when I'm gone, you will have to be the head of the family and take care of everyone. Can you do that?" Phillip nodded more.

"But that won't be for a long time right?" Phillip asked seriously.

To a twelve-year-old, ten years was a long time. "Not for a long time," Nalick promised. "I'll wait until you're at least grown-up and married, how about that."

"Good. I need someone to teach me to ride horses and fight," Phillip said.

"What about Mom?" Nalick asked.

"She can teach me how to fight, but you ride more," Phillip said. "So can we go ride before lunch?" Nalick nodded. Phillip quickly jumped up and ran back to his room to get dressed. Leila backed into the room as he passed.

"Good morning, Mom," Phillip said as he ran by.

Nalick slowly approached Leila and looked for a sign of how she felt after the previous night's talk. Leila couldn't meet his gaze and looked at the floor. She still hadn't had time to sort out how she felt about everything. She needed more time, and he quietly turned to walk past her. As soon as Nalick was close enough, Leila reached out and took his hand. He looked down on her, but she still wouldn't meet his gaze.

"I really do love you," Leila said quietly, before giving his hand a squeeze and then letting go. Nalick turned and wrapped his arms around her from behind.

"I'll always love you. I promise that will never change," Nalick whispered, before kissing her cheek. "From here or beyond."

Phillip ran back down the stairs, interrupting the

moment. "Dad, hurry up," he said, and Nalick let go of Leila.

Leila poured a cup of tea and silently walked out to her garden to sit down in the same place she was the night before. She sipped her tea and thought about everything Nalick had told her. Bittersweet thoughts ran through her mind.

Softly, Roger walked out into the garden and sat next to Leila. "Anatolio suggested we talk," he explained his presence.

"How long have you known about everything?" Leila asked, without turning to look at him.

"Well, that depends on which part. I've known who Anatolio was since the first time you told me he followed you around Lexia. I've known about Nalick's fate since before you even started to do your runs into Lior." Roger tried to gauge her reaction.

"And you didn't think that all this information might be helpful to me?" she asked.

"I didn't want you to run away from him like I knew you would if you knew every detail," Roger said. "He's a good man. If you finally gave love a chance again you might end up happy. Did I do something wrong in wanting you to be happy again?"

Leila shook her head *no*. "But now what can I do? He's not about to take no as an answer to marriage. But if I marry him, then our time will be limited."

"You're lucky child. At least you know you will get ten happy years together. It could be far less. Just think of Kay," Roger said. Kay lost her husband shortly after having Luca. Roger had lost his own wife only a few years after their third son was born.

"I know," Leila said. "It's just that I wish I knew how he will die. Then maybe I could do something to stop it."

"I don't think he will ever tell you for that exact reason. All I know from Anatolio is that Nalick will die protecting one of his children. That's not something I think you can talk him out of doing, nor is it something you can stop from happening," Roger explained.

"Don't let this make you sad. You will live a happy life. He has made sure of it." Roger was always good at finding the positive in any situation. "You can't just sit and let life pass you by. Sure, you might get hurt if you jump right in, but it's worth it." Roger patted her knee. "Love is always worth the pain it might bring. Trust an old man for once. I haven't gathered all this wisdom by getting old for you to just ignore it. Nalick will take care of you, and someday Anatolio will also, if you let him." Leila wanted to protest, but couldn't find the words to do so before they were interrupted.

"To the bath," Ruth commanded, running into the garden. Leila beamed as she stood and scooped Ruth into her arms. Roger waved good-bye as the two left down the stairs.

Anatolio approached Roger and looked up at the clouds before sighing. "Do you think she will ever see me as a man, and not a boy?"

Roger chuckled. "To her you are a boy. Don't worry. We all grow up faster than we want. Enjoy being young and having no responsibility. Someday, this will all be yours, and trust me; you will wish you were just a boy again. Life goes by so quickly."

"I feel like she will always see me as a younger brother and never as the man she's supposed to spend the rest of her life with," Anatolio added.

"Only you can change how she sees you now," Roger said. "You will know what to do when the moment is right. I wouldn't worry about it." Roger trusted Nalick and Gabor that this young man was truly Leila's match. Even Roger could see it.

CHAPTER THIRTY-TWO

The next day, Leila endured being cleaned and dressed to be presented, yet again, to another group of visiting wedding guests. Leila had been so busy with getting ready that she failed to notice that Nalick and Phillip hadn't been around all morning. Once they returned together they also hurried to get ready, and it was obvious they were up to something yet again. Seeing the happiness in his eyes when he was with Phillip, Leila smiled at Nalick as he passed by her. She wanted to interrogate the two men, but knew it would have to wait until she was finished getting ready. As soon as she got the last nod of Mauve's satisfaction, Leila quickly hurried to find Phillip. Leila found him sitting in his room already dressed.

"What were you doing all morning?" Leila asked, wanting to get to the end of the secrets in their lives.

"Nothing," Phillip replied with a smile. Leila sat down next to him and placed her arm around his shoulder. As he gasped and pulled away, she knew what they had been up to.

"Let me see," she said strictly, and Phillip reluctantly raised the back of his shirt. On the upper center portion of his back was the royal family crest, still red from it having been done the same morning. "And when were you going to tell me about this?"

"After I got my hand done also, but I think I might wait a bit longer for that. I didn't know it would hurt so much. Dad said you didn't take any pain medication when you

had yours done, so I thought I could be as tough as you."
Phillip grinned. "I was wrong. It hurt, a lot!!"

Leila rustled his hair. "Why did he tell you that I didn't use any medicine? And yes, it hurts a lot. I could have told you that."

"I did tell him that," Nalick said, standing in the doorway. "Trying to get me into trouble with Mom?" Nalick asked Phillip, who began to laugh.

"If you didn't show up, it could have worked," Phillip said, and Leila laughed with him. "Have you seen Dad's?" Phillip asked, and Leila nodded her head, trying not to blush at admitting she had seen Nalick shirtless. "It's huge. It must have hurt so much."

"We better get going," Nalick said, noticing the blush.

"This isn't going to be fun," Leila complained.

"I don't know about that. From what I hear, several of the men coming tonight, many with their wives, once asked a certain ghost courier to marry them," Nalick said quietly while they walked down the stairs.

"You didn't," she replied, and he nodded. "Isn't that a bit like gloating?"

"And why not?" Nalick responded. "We need at least a bit of entertainment." Leila playfully hit his arm. She might just enjoy the night after all.

With dinner done, and Leila tucked into bed for the night, she was relieved to only have one last dinner left. She didn't enjoy all the people, no matter how entertaining it was to greet the last set of guests.

The next day, Leila was pampered for her last formal dinner. The whole family was ushered into waiting carriages and driven to the location. Nalick offered her his hand as he led her into the market square of Lexia. Leila realized why Mauve didn't mind when Leila removed several pieces of jewelry before she left. The market was completely filled with decorated tables, and people she recognized sitting at them. They arrived from the north end of the market, and Leila could see games set up on both the east and west sides where the vendor tents normally were on market days. Waiting at their own set of tables was Leila's family.

"There are plain-clothed guards around the perimeter, and the two guards here are to watch each child," Nalick explained as the children ran to the table.

"And how many of them are watching me?" Leila teased, but he didn't answer as she set Ruth down.

"I'll stay with her," Phillip volunteered, as he took hold of his sister's hand.

Leila looked at the faces around her. Nalick had a hand in inviting the people present. Emma and her husband, along with Lady and Lord Pillas were the only nobles there for the party. Leila caught a glimpse of Nikias. He was there to watch someone, and she hoped it was Phillip. Across the way, she saw Frank and Marg, the fruit stand owner, along with their son who had worked on her arm and back. Theo, Macarius, and Theo's entire family were also nearby. Gazing around, she knew most of the faces, and recognized the rest from her trips to the market.

"When did you plan this?" Leila asked Nalick.

"Oh, it didn't take much planning," Nalick replied. "Most of the vendors in the market already wanted to throw a party for you, and I just helped them along, with the help of your family and Roger, of course."

"Where's Roger?" she asked. She quickly looked around and did not find him.

"He will be a little late with Anatolio," Nalick explained, sitting down next to one of her brothers.

Leila immediately knew then that Nikias was there, watching over her in the place of Anatolio. Tim pulled on Leila's hand, and she kneeled next to him.

"Can I play, too?" Tim asked, pointing at Phillip across the way.

"Of course," Leila replied, taking the child's hand and walking him over to his brother. Phillip easily took charge of both his brother and sister as several of his new cousins also joined them at the games.

Leila spent the evening enjoying herself with her family and friends. The dinner, dance, and games were much more relaxed, and she felt comfortable in the atmosphere. Leila was surrounded by what she considered "normal" people, and found that the stuffiness and coldness of the nobles' court and dinner was not there. Everyone there seemed truly happy for Leila and Nalick, and wanted to share in the happiness they saw between the two of them.

"So, sis," Leon said, approaching from one side, and Nael from the other on the walk back to the palace. "Are you ready for tomorrow?" Leila stared at Leon as she tried to remember the plans for the next day. Her week had been so long and every day there were plans, but everything seemed to be running together.

"And tomorrow is?" Leila asked, still not remembering.

"Your wedding," Nael replied, picking her up as Leon tapped on her head. Her brothers had always treated her like a doll because she was so much smaller than them.

"I think you'd forget your own name if left alone too long," Leon added, motioning for Nael to toss Leila to him.

"Put me down," Leila complained, before she could be tossed in the air. "It's been a long week, and I've gotten little sleep. It's okay for me to forget stuff without enough sleep," she added, pounding on her brother's chest to set her down. Nael complied and set her down.

"So you're actually going to go through with it?" Leon asked.

Leila smiled, punching him in the arm. "Of course. Some of us don't get cold feet before making a commitment."

"Just checking," Leon said, grinning. Nalick joined her and handed her the sleeping Ruth while he picked up Tim.

"I don't know how you still have the energy to fight with your brothers," Nalick said quietly.

"I don't think she has ever *not* had energy to fight with those two," Dirk added, also walking beside them. "All three have been fighting since the day she was born. Just wait until you have more children. They are not all as nicely behaved as the three you have."

After she tucked all three children into bed, Leila returned downstairs to find Anatolio and Nalick on the balcony talking. She slowly approached so that they would not know she was there. She stood just inside the doorway and listened.

"I'm sure," Anatolio replied, keeping his head bowed.

"Are you two not getting along?" Nalick asked.

"No, everything is fine. She seems to be treating me the same as before. I just feel it would be better if you have Nikias escort her tomorrow," Anatolio added.

"It won't be a problem, but she might be disappointed you won't be there," Nalick added. For his plan to work, there would have to be more between Leila and Anatolio than a teacher-student relationship in the future. Nalick was betting his life on the fact that Leila and Anatolio would end up together.

"She won't even notice," Anatolio lied. He knew better than anyone that Leila noticed everything that happened. She had never once failed to know exactly where he was in the two years that he had been following her.

"I know you're afraid of what everyone will think when I die and you take care of Leila and my family. It doesn't matter. Everyone that matters knows that I asked you to be here. I truly wish you'd come tomorrow, but I'm not going to force you." Nalick stared at the young man. Anatolio had conflicted feelings on the issue.

"Do you have enough guards to keep her protected?" Anatolio asked. Nalick nodded his head *yes*. "Then, I wish to not come." Anatolio had agreed to wait ten years, but he understood there would be times that it would be hard. Seeing Leila on her wedding day, marrying someone else, would be one of them.

Leila hurried to her room quietly and slid under the covers. She was confused. *Why did Anatiolo follow me non-stop for two months, and yet now he doesn't want to? What changed now?* Nalick didn't know either. Before long, Nalick joined her in bed, and she pretended to be asleep. She felt his hand on her back as he quietly drifted off to sleep.

The next morning, Leila yawned as she sat up next to Nalick, who had gently shaken her awake before dawn. "Is it morning already?" Leila asked, rubbing her eyes.

"Sorry," Nalick replied. "Mauve needs to start early. The first set of ceremonies begins at dawn."

As she walked into the main room, it was still dark outside, but she could see the sun was creating a light haze on the horizon. Nalick stood on the balcony, looking at the city below him. Leila approached quietly as he was deep in thought. Nalick was busy watching the few people in the city below move around. He, too, was filled with a mix of emotions; he was setting in motion the events that would lead to his own death, but he only had a single regret. He would leave Leila before they could grow old together. Nalick had made sure that she would not be alone, and that his children would have a father, but still, his death would greatly affect her life. Words weren't needed for him to understand her feelings toward him.

"Hey, you!" Leila said, startling him, as he didn't hear her approach. "Are we going to do this or not?" she teased.

Nalick turned to see Leila dressed all in white with her hair hung loose down to her waist. To him, she looked like the same wood nymph he thought she was the first time he saw her. She seemed to sparkle in the dimly-lit room. Stunned, Nalick couldn't reply. He was truly speechless at the sight of her. Leila giggled and moved closer to him.

"Do I need to slap some sense into you?" she asked, patting his face playfully. Nalick smiled and took both her hands in his. He couldn't find the words to tell her how beautiful he thought she looked, so instead, he just kissed her hands. Leila blushed at his sudden loss for words. "We better go. It will be dawn soon, and we wouldn't want to be late to the start of a very long day." They made their way to the door of their room. Leila quickly looked up at Anatolio's bedroom door and saw it was still shut.

"He's young. In ten years, he will be a man. Things will be different between you then. I'm sure he will love you," Nalick replied, and she nodded her head. At times she thought that she could see that he already loved her, but at other times, he was completely indifferent.

I can do this, she thought. Nalick took her hand and squeezed it. He could feel her nervousness, and he automatically smiled. The great ghost courier could get nervous.

CHAPTER THIRTY-THREE

The dawn ceremony lasted longer than Leila had expected, and she was happy to go back to their wing and find breakfast waiting. The children happily greeted them at the door as they arrived. Leila picked up Ruth as she moved to the table and gladly began to eat. Ruth sat on Leila's lap and began to play with her mother's loose hair.

"Why's mommy's hair this color?" Ruth asked, and everyone laughed.

"Where I come from people have all different color hair," Leila replied. "Red, yellow, brown, black."

"Can Ruth be different, too?" Ruth asked.

"But you're beautiful the way you are now," Leila replied, Ruth grinned. "You're the most beautiful princess in all of Lior." Ruth giggled and clapped her hands.

Leila's happy breakfast was short-lived. Nalick carefully kissed Leila's forehead as he whispered, "I'll see you at the amphitheater." Leila nodded; she sat Ruth on the chair and was immediately dragged away by Mauve. She was already sick of all the pampering, but it wasn't a day to complain. Leila's thoughts wandered as she sat, getting ready. As Leila started to get sad thinking about how short ten years would be, Tim ran into the dressing room and past the women, who all tried to catch him. He sat down quickly and grabbed Leila's leg.

"Mommy," Tim cried. "They're trying to make me wear girl clothes." Leila couldn't move to pick him up, so she patted her lap, and he happily hopped on it.

"Are you sure it's girls' clothes?" Tim nodded. "We should tell Dad about this," she suggested, knowing that if Tim saw what Nalick was wearing, he would change his mind.

"Mommy," Tim started, "you look pretty." Leila hugged the small child. He could cheer her up so easily. Leila hugged him again. "Should I go tell Daddy?"

"Sure," Leila replied. "He's in his office, but you better run quickly so they can't catch you." Tim nodded and hopped off her lap and ran through the main room and kitchen to Nalick's office.

"Come, come," Mauve directed Leila.

"Nikias will be here soon to escort you," Mauve explained, ushering Leila back to the dressing room.

"Just one more thing," Mauve added, carefully placing a thin gold crown on Leila's head to complete the pale blue, gold-accented ensemble Leila wore. With Leila's red hair, the crown was barely visible because it matched the golden highlights of her hair.

"Now am I ready?" Leila asked, and Mauve circled her one last time. Mauve nodded, and Leila slowly moved to the door. Leila was anxious yet scared at the same time.

Nikias was standing outside the door, diligently waiting for her. As Leila carefully opened the door, Nikias quickly bowed. He was amazed by how different she seemed than the day he first saw her. She was quieter and shyer than he ever imagine she could be. Hesitation filled her eyes and every movement. Leila was much more uncomfortable as a lady than as a warrior.

"This way," Nikias said, leading her down the stairs and to a courtyard where her ride waited for her. Leila took his arm, and he led her to the waiting carriage.

"I heard you gave Anatolio quite a bit of trouble the other day," Nikias commented, lifting her gently to the seat.

"It's kind of hard to get alone time around here. He

follows me like my own shadow." Leila yearned to pull the pins out of her head and scratch it.

"That's his job," Nikias responded with a shrug, sitting beside her. "Besides, after Seth came into the palace and he wasn't there to protect you, I think he feels guilty," Nikias replied.

"That wasn't his fault." Leila clenched her hands so as to not pull at her hair.

"You will let us know in the future if you decide to go wandering around outside the palace walls, right? There are still several kings wanting to get a hold of you. We've been sorting through reports of threats on a daily basis since you came to stay in Lexia," Nikias continued.

Leila was surprised to find how easy it was to talk to Nikias. She had not heard him talk much around her, beyond barking directions to people. Nikias lifted his arm to gracefully brace her as she slid on the seat at a turn. Leila was beginning to see that Anatolio had a good possibility of growing into a quite different man than she had pictured. Nikias was quiet, warm, enduring, and funny when alone. Leila would have never pictured this other side of him from all her previous interactions, but was happy to see beyond the dull, serious man he had become.

"Now, don't give Anatolio too hard of a time. He's still young and learning," Nikias added, as the carriage came near the amphitheater.

"But if I don't, how will I be entertained?" Leila asked, and he laughed again. Leila liked the sound of his laugh and smiled. Leila could see in Nikias the man Anatolio would be someday. "Do you know why Anatolio isn't escorting me?"

Nikias shook his head *no*. "He asked if I'd escort you. That's all I know." Nikias could see his answer was not what she wanted to hear.

"Anatolio is a shy kid," Nikias explained. "This sort of

thing is too bold for him. He would rather sit in the back of the room than on the stage. He's always been like that." She somehow didn't think Anatolio's shyness was the reason he was staying away from her.

They arrived at the ground floor of the amphitheater, and Nikias escorted Leila to the room behind the stage. As soon as she was left alone for a moment, Leila snuck to the edge of the stage and peered from around the corner. In the middle of the room were all the foreign dignitaries she had met days ago. To each side were the nobles of Lior, and the fourth and fifth sections were being filled from the people standing behind the seats. Leila was relieved to see that her family was already seated in the front rows. As she stepped back in the waiting room, she was surprised to see Roger. She hugged him immediately.

"Finally, some company," Leila said to him. "It's supposed to be the happiest day of my life, and I've been left sitting here alone."

"I just wanted to stop by quickly and give you this." He handed her a small vial.

"Anatolio explained the ceremony to me. I don't need you getting sick on me before you have to get everyone home to the North Country, as I'm using most of my resources to get your family back there tomorrow. Now, I have to get going also, otherwise there will be no seat for me." Roger hugged her and disappeared quickly.

Leila sat and looked at the small vial. She had used the stuff before, and it was quite effective at stopping a cut from bleeding. It was just like Roger to worry about a small cut. Roger tended to worry over nothing, but in his own way, he was trying his best to be useful.

When the time arrived, Nikias took her to the right side of the stage, and she waited for the ceremony to begin. Looking across the way, she noticed Nalick was waiting, also. He didn't see her laugh to herself. *Finally, at least I won't be the only one a bit lacking in clothing*, she thought, staring at Nalick, who was shirtless and obviously uncomfortable with it.

As soon as the ceremony started, Leila began to forget the world around her and the large audience that was there. Even though it lasted hours, to her, it felt like it only took a minute. As soon as she held onto Nalick's hand, she lost all the nervous, regretful feelings. Nalick was as solid as a rock. He didn't waver in his decision in the least and had no regrets. His desire to marry her outweighed the consequences of his actions. There was nothing more Nalick desired in life than to stand by her side, no matter how short their time together would be.

In the back of the room, dressed in a disguise he created with the help of Roger, Anatolio watched the ceremony. Below him, Leila nervously walked across the stage to meet Nalick. She was as beautiful as the first day he saw her. The gold lines on her arm glimmered in the few rays of sunlight that penetrated the tent ceiling of the amphitheater. Anatolio could see her nervousness fade as soon she touched Nalick's arm. This wasn't something Anatolio could have done. With just the look in his eyes, Nalick was able to calm Leila's heart. Someday, it would have to be him, but Anatolio had no idea how.

Leila was happy to see a full meal waiting for them when they returned to the palace with their children. The room was empty of servants, and Leila relished the quietness of the children laughing and enjoying their time together.

"That's it for today right?" Leila asked Nalick.

"Well, there's supposed to be a third ceremony tonight, but I thought it wasn't necessary, since..." he paused, looking at the children, and didn't finish his statement.

"They didn't tell me about a third ceremony," Leila replied, trying to remember any mention of a third ceremony. Nalick coughed to try to cover his laugh.

"Let's just say the priests didn't think the ceremony was needed tonight," Nalick added. A red-faced Leila nodded in response. "So, instead, I thought this would be a good time; we can spend just the five of us, undisturbed by anyone for the rest of tonight." The children cheered.

After a night of games and stories, all five were lying on Nalick's and Leila's bed. Ruth and Tim were the first to fall asleep. Leila watched as Phillip then fell asleep between his siblings. Leila slowly stood to move to the other side of the bed, and sat down next to Nalick, who was also falling asleep. He wrapped his arms around her and pulled her down beside him.

"If I could freeze any moment and keep it that way forever, it would be this moment," Nalick whispered. "Thank you for marrying me." Leila studied his face as he talked. She was trying to remember each detail to forever remember the moment.

"I love you, Benét Leila. I can only hope to someday make you as happy as you have made me."

Leila kissed his forehead as he dozed off to sleep.

"Silly man, you already have. I love you too, Nalick," she whispered to the sleeping man before standing and going to the balcony. Leila was also quite tired from her long day, but she didn't feel like sleeping yet. The sooner she fell asleep, the sooner the magic of the day would end.

Leila sat on the balcony in the dark and could see the last few remaining lights in the city still sparkling. The situation, for now, was exactly how she wanted it, but in time that would change. *What will life be like without him?* He made her happy for the first time since Erich died. Leila heard the door to the room quietly open, and she turned to watch Anatolio quietly creep into the room. He immediately noticed her on the balcony. Leila stared across the darkness and could not read his expression.

Little by little, he approached her, and she continued to stare at him.

"Why?" Leila simply asked as Anatolio crossed over to lean against the railing of the balcony. He didn't face her as he answered, knowing that she would try to read his expression.

"It was a day for you and Nalick," Anatolio replied.

"Along with our family and friends," Leila added. "I guess I assumed you fit in that category though, which I'm still a bit confused on."

Anatolio smiled slightly. She had always been friendly to him, but she was friendly toward everyone who wasn't an enemy. Anatolio couldn't guess her feelings toward him. He was just another young man admiring her.

"You've always been beside me, and yet today you seem to want nothing to do with me," she added, wanting to go over and pull him to face her.

"I just didn't want to be a distraction," he replied. "You had enough to worry about for the day. You didn't need some kid following you around."

"You're not a distraction," she replied. Anatolio was relieved to hear her say it.

"It just would have been nice to have you there," she said quietly. Anatolio could hear the disappointment in her voice.

Anatolio turned to leave and still did not look her in the eyes. He bowed to her as he came close, and he stopped to pick up her hand. Gently he kissed it. "You were truly beautiful today," he said, as he looked down at Leila, who smiled at him.

"Thank you," she replied, shocked that he actually had gone to the wedding without her knowing.

CHAPTER THIRTY-FOUR

Leila anxiously awaited the next three days in the palace; she couldn't wait to leave for the North Country. She already had a plan of how to get Nalick, Phillip, Tim, and Ruth there without any problems, but she had to wait for Roger to escort her family back before she could leave with her own plans. Leila was excited to finally get on a boat heading north. She had told the children about her home, but to the three children who had never set foot outside Lexia, they couldn't understand what she was describing. The children could see Leila's excitement, and so they, too, were excited. The night before they were going to leave, Leila double-checked each bag she had packed. She had more than just herself to worry about, so she didn't want to forget anything. Nalick was happy to sit and watch her hurry around, making lists in her head. In the years to come, it would be the same. When Leila was finally satisfied that everything was ready, she quickly changed into common clothes.

"Now what?" Nalick asked, noticing she was covering up the lines on her arm.

"I'm going to go check our ride," Leila replied.

"Take Anatolio with you, please," Nalick begged, seeing that she was going to leave without him.

Anatolio was standing on the stairway as he watched Leila also get ready. He didn't need Nalick to remind him to do his job and follow Leila, but she did.

Leila hurried through the calm streets of Lexia on her way to the docks. Anatolio watched her stop and talk to several men from various ships along the way. She was happy to finally not be stuck in the palace. Going home meant freedom. Anatolio recognized the ship that she stopped at was the same ship that returned them to Lior the last time they were in the North Country. Leila easily climbed on deck and searched for the captain.

"My, oh my! If it isn't Meg coming to visit," a young man said from behind her. Leila twirled around and quickly ran over to hug the man, who was barely older than herself, as he lifted her off the ground.

"I hear congratulations are in order. Marx stopped by and said he was in town for your wedding." The captain, Fred, set her back down gently.

"Marx is here?" Leila asked, looking around.

"No, as we pulled in this morning he was boarding another boat heading north. He just said he came down for a short visit, but I assumed that meant he visited you," Fred explained.

"No, as usual he just came and watched, I guess," she said, disappointed.

"So, I hear the whole country has a week vacation," Fred said, changing the subject and noticing her disappointment in missing Marx.

"Yeah, I guess so," Leila replied.

"What a time for you to go and get married. The same week as the King of Lior was getting married," Fred added. His father hadn't told him who she was marrying. "I've yet to see this new queen, but all the locals say she's the most beautiful woman they have ever seen. Compared to the locals of Lior, maybe she's the most beautiful, but no one could compare to you." Leila smiled at Fred and patted his head.

"You're here early. I thought we were to expect you tomorrow?" he said, once again changing the subject and hoping to stay out of trouble with Leila.

"I was in the area, and thought I'd stop by to check on

everything," Leila responded. "I was expecting to see your dad. Is everything all right?"

"Yes and no. He was expecting to see you, too, but my mother got sick at the last minute, and he stayed home to take care of her. The last time he saw you, Dad said that you were planning to get married. Boy did I get an earful from my mother about that." Fred's mother had been bugging him for years to ask Leila to marry him. "She won't be happy until I bring you home as my wife. So, any thoughts of reconsidering the whole marriage idea?"

"Fred," Leila said, playfully punching him in the arm. "I'm a married woman now. You shouldn't be making proposals like that."

"You wouldn't, by chance, have a sister you could lend me in your place," he added. She punched him again and they both laughed. "My mother is going to be so disappointed."

"So how many crew members do you have with you this trip?" she asked.

"I have all of Dad's regular crew. He arranged everything before I left. Roger told him you'd have some valuable, fragile items you were transporting north to Cath. Trust me, as soon as the men heard it was you that we needed to pick up, we had more men sign up for this trip than we needed. If you want, you can drop the large items off tonight," he added.

"I shouldn't do that," she replied, knowing that her items would be Nalick and the kids. Transporting human cargo was always done in secret for both the protection of the people being transported, and the shipmen doing the transporting.

"I'll bring everything tomorrow morning. What time would you want me here by?" she asked.

"If we leave around sunrise, we can make Dria by midafternoon and Cath around dinner time," he explained.

"Sounds good. We will be on time." Leila gave Fred one last hug before jumping down to the docks and catching back up to Anatolio.

"Is everything in order for tomorrow?" she asked Anatolio, not noticing his hesitation to be near her.

"Yes," Anatolio replied. "The cart is packed and waiting in the stables. Roger left two barrels and two boxes as he figured Tim and Ruth could be in the barrels with either Phillip or Elena." Leila nodded, finally noticing the distance he was keeping from her. Leila gave him a questioning look, and he just faded back into the shadows. Leila wanted to talk to him more.

Anatolio walked her back in silence. Leila joined Nalick, who was sitting outside, without a word from Anatolio.

"All done packing?" Nalick asked. She joined him and sat on the balcony overlooking the city.

"Yes, hopefully," she said, sitting beside him and trying to remember if she had forgotten anything.

"You promise this time it won't be so cold there?" Nalick asked, remembering his first visit in the snow. Leila wasn't packing any warm clothing for anyone.

"No, it's spring now, so, the trees should be starting to get leaves and the early flowers blooming," she explained. Leila paused while mentally checking her list for the tenth time. "The snow should be all gone, except for on top of the mountains, but I didn't think you wanted to do any mountain climbing on this trip," she teased.

"Do people really intentionally climb the mountains?" Nalick asked in amazement at her suggestion. Leila nodded while laughing at the question. Nalick moved his arm around her, pulling her tight to himself.

"Let's go to bed," Leila suggested, standing and pulling at his arm. "It will be a very long day tomorrow getting to my parents." Nalick stood at her prompting and quickly scooped her into his arms. Leila giggled, throwing her arms around his neck. "To bed, husband of mine," she directed, nuzzling into his chest. Nalick kissed the top of her head and carried her to their bedroom.

Leila rose early the next morning and got everyone moving on time. With all her planning, everything happened in order. She easily transported her family, hidden away, from the palace to the ship that took them north. With the help of Roger and his sons, her family made it off the ship and out of Cath without a single tracker following them. Leila was a professional, and her three months in the palace didn't dull her skills at all. After a full days' worth of traveling from before dawn until after dark, they finally arrived at her parents' place.

Leila was relieved to make it to her parents' house without a single issue and all of her family safe. Leila opened the door to her parents' house and led the way into their home with her guests. Selma and Dirk were waiting for them with supper prepared for the travelers who were still awake. Leila smiled but couldn't hug them without waking Ruth.

"We really should put them to bed," Leila said to Nalick, who was caring for Tim while he was sleeping. Selma quickly stopped them from walking to the stairs.

"Theo and Macarius can have the same rooms they used the last time," Selma said, and they both nodded, "But for you," Selma stopped talking. "I wish it were still light out so you could see it better, but we have a surprise for you."

"Can we put them to bed, first?" Leila asked her mother. Nalick pushed Leila to follow her mother. She followed her mother through the living room and out a side hallway that had never been there before. The hallway led to a new building behind her parents' home that she didn't see in the dark when they approached.

"It's not completely done yet," Dirk explained, walking beside Leila. "But it's livable. The bedrooms and living room are done, but the kitchen is not. We figure if there was one room that couldn't be finished, the kitchen would be the best bet." He was hinting at her lack of cooking skills.

Leila stepped into the living room. Several couches faced the west wall that was lined with windows and a glass door that oversaw the lake. The large stone fireplace along the same wall was burning, keeping the huge room warm. She noticed the ceiling was higher than normal. Leila could see that the staircase in the back of the living room led to a second floor and at the base of the stairs was an archway that led to what she could see was the start of a kitchen.

"There are six small bedrooms upstairs for the kids, Elena, and Anatolio," Selma explained.

"There is a larger bedroom downstairs off the kitchen for you and Nalick." Leila nodded, following her mother up the stairs. Selma opened the door to the farthest room, and it was decorated with all her old furniture from her bedroom growing up. "I figured Ruth could have this room." Selma pulled the covers down from the bed and Leila laid Ruth inside it.

"Through the kitchen is a room for you two," Selma explained, leading them back downstairs and through the closest door to the living room. Leila walked into the room and smiled. Selma had spent much time decorating the room.

"It's beautiful," Leila said while hugging her mom.

"Thank you, Mom and Dad," she said, quickly hugging her father, also. Leila looked around the room again. She could see the quilt was handmade by her mother. She gently touched it, knowing how much time her mother must have put into finishing it before they arrived.

"I know it's not as fancy as you're accustomed to now," Selma added. "But we all tried our best. Your brothers even helped out as much as your dad."

"Mom, it's wonderful," Leila tried to reassure her mother. Selma stared at her only daughter and hugged her again. It was good to have her back home, even if it were only for a week. There was no greater treasure in the world than finally seeing Leila happy after so many years of sadness.

CHAPTER THIRTY-FIVE

Leila woke the next morning before anyone else, but she lay ever so still in her bed. She could hear the birds chirping outside, and found that it was one sound she hadn't missed in the palace until now. The fresh spring scent of flowers, the birds chirping in the trees, and the cool mountain air all told her she was home. The excitement of being home woke her early. Silently, she walked around the house her family had built for her. She looked at the detail of the trim on the railing of the staircase, and the stones evenly placed to make the fireplace. Her dad must have spent every waking moment since she left, working on her new home.

Leila and the children passed the next three days being lazy and lounging around the house. Elena, on the other hand, was lost with what to do, since she wasn't needed to clean and cook. Elena was slowly adjusting, and found Phillip to be quite entertaining, as she often joined him on his many walks to the lake. Each time they would leave, Leila caught Nalick smiling.

"Why do you smile like that each time?" Leila asked Nalick.

"It just makes me happy to see they are forming a friendship," Nalick replied, picking up Tim and swinging him around, causing him to giggle louder and louder.

"What do you know?" Leila interrogated him. Nalick had told her that he had many talks with Gabor over how, not only his life, but that of everyone he cared for, especially his children, would turn out.

"I can't tell you," Nalick teased. "You don't believe in fate."

Leila pouted and Tim stopped giggling to run to her.

"Daddy, make Mommy smile," Tim told Nalick.

Nalick walked over to Leila and sat down next to her, he began to pretend he was going to tell her, but he quickly picked her up and began to tickle her. Leila couldn't help but laugh, and Tim joined in, trying to tickle her also. When they finally stopped, Leila stared at Nalick; behind the sparkle, he did know something more about Elena and Phillip.

"What would you say to someday having Elena as a daughter-in-law?" Nalick hinted.

"Really? You know that? And what about the children we will have someday?" she asked.

"There's so much I'm going to miss, but at least I know what will happen," Nalick explained, Tim began his run of the house.

"It's at least some consolation for the fate I've been dealt." Leila rested her head on his chest. It was hard to be as convinced of fate as Nalick had been to believe that everything would be okay.

"What if Anatolio decides that he doesn't want to wait ten years and finds someone else?" Leila asked without looking up at him as he stared at the top of her head.

"He won't," Nalick replied, looking into the woods.

"But how can you be so sure?" Leila asked. Nalick was still staring ahead as she tried to catch his attention. "He has been avoiding me now for days. He didn't even want to come to our wedding. In fact, I can't remember the last time he even came within two feet of me."

"He loves you as much as I do. He's not going anywhere. He will wait. He promised me that he would wait for you, and when the day comes, he will step up and take care of everybody," Nalick explained, finally looking down at her. "It was the deal we made years ago, and every day I see in his face that there is no way he would ever break that deal."

I hope so, she thought, dreading that Nalick's fate would someday be a reality quicker than either of them wanted it to be. Nalick gently stroked her head, taking in the complete serenity around them. This was the life he had always wished for. No nobles or lawmen asking for decisions, or neighboring kings and armies to deal with, just his wife and their children enjoying the spring in the mountains. Even though Nalick only had ten years with the beautiful woman in his arms, he was content and always would be.

"Two more days until the wedding," Leila said, changing the subject. "I've been half tempted to have you cleaned until you sparkle as revenge, but around here it doesn't matter as much. Besides, I don't think you could keep spotless on the walk to the church."

"That wasn't my policy," Nalick said, defending himself. "I've always liked you just the way you are. That was all Mauve's doing." Leila pulled her head up from his chest and nodded sarcastically.

That night, after the children were tucked in bed and fast asleep, Leila returned downstairs to find Nalick sitting on the hill outside their back door. Leila walked over and sat down beside him. It was chilly outside, as it was every spring. The days were warm and the flowers were in bloom, but after the sun set, there was the nice cool reminder that it wasn't yet summer. Nalick wrapped his arms around her as he looked into the sky.

"You once told me these are the same stars we see in Lexia. Are you sure? They seem so much brighter here, and there are so many more," Nalick said, breaking the silence.

"You see right over there?" Leila pointed to the left. "Those three stars; if you sit on the balcony at home and look straight up into the sky, you see them." Leila rested against him. Her heart began to race, feeling him so close, but then thoughts of their short future began to muddle her happy feelings.

"Tell me what our life together will be like," she said with a childlike innocence. The sadness was building within her again. Leila needed Nalick to rescue her from the part of her new life she now dreaded.

"We will be happier than any other person in the whole world," Nalick began.

"In a year, we will have our first son. He will luckily have your brains and beauty along with my strength. He will have your kindness and your eyes, so that everyone in Lior won't fear him as they do me. He will learn the most from you, and everyone will again praise my choice in asking you to marry me. But don't worry. After him we will have a daughter who, unfortunately, will have many of my characteristics." Leila smiled and patted his hand in sympathy.

"We will come here to the mountains at least twice a year so that our children will grow up knowing what it's like to be free from the palace. Through our lives we will continue to travel, and yet still find time to be home doing everything we love. You will even help Roger from time to time, as his couriers just can't match up to your skill. The only courier that will ever come close will be Tim. Years from now, he will gladly watch over the safety of our family." Leila again nodded and rested against Nalick as he talked. His picture of the future easily calmed her sadness. "We will be happy every single moment. Our life together was always meant to be. I promise you will never regret the decision you made to stay in Lexia." Nalick wanted to hold her against him like that forever.

Leila huddled close to him in the cold as the breeze blew up from the lake. She closed her eyes. It felt like the first time she brought him home when he sat with her, looking at the stars near Roger's station. He was so cautious and timid around her, afraid she would disappear. Leila could still sense that a part of him feared losing her, but now it was for a completely different reason.

"I don't want this moment to end," Leila complained. Nalick pulled her closer and rested his head on hers. He gently stroked her hair; he too remembered their first trip. Leila held back tears.

"You don't need to worry," he said quietly. "I promise at least a hundred more of these moments to you."

Leila reached up and gently touched his cheek. There would be many more moments together, but they were limited. As they sat there longer, both knew that they needed to go to bed. Slowly, Leila stood, and Nalick followed her to bed.

It felt like she had just fallen asleep when Leila noticed a small hand tapping hers. Leila cautiously opened her eyes to find she was face-to-face with Ruth. Leila could only slightly make out from the curtains that the sun had just begun to rise, and it was indeed morning.

"How about you rest a little longer?" Leila whispered, lifting the covers.

"No, play," Ruth demanded loudly. Leila felt Nalick sit up.

"I'll take her," he said quietly. "You get more rest."

After sleeping less than an hour, she wasn't comfortable with Nalick's absence. Quietly, she walked into the living room and found Nalick in a chair with Ruth fast asleep in his right arm. Nalick was sitting and watching the sun as it hit the water on the lake below, and he did not notice Leila approaching.

"How long has she been asleep?" Leila whispered.

"Almost as soon as we got out here," he replied, pulling her onto the left side of his lap. Leila curled up in his open arm and rested her head on his shoulder, then she closed her eyes. Nalick smiled and kissed her forehead. Within moments, Nalick had a sleeping girl on each side of his lap. For once in his life, he realized how lucky he was to have found such complete happiness.

Down below their home, on one of the older trails, Roger and Anatolio approached Leila's family home. Roger stopped within sight of the home, yet was still hidden by the trees. Anatolio pulled his horse next to Roger and looked through the picture windows into the home.

"Someday, they'll be yours," Roger commented.

Anatolio nodded as he watched Leila sleep. She seemed like an angel as her eyes lightly fluttered. She felt safe and protected in Nalick's arms. Roger and Anatolio sat for some time just watching. Nalick was a great man in Anatolio's eyes, and a great husband and father as well. Anatolio inadvertently smiled as he looked again at Leila. He had spent the past days with Roger, being taught more tricks and how to better care for Leila, as she was bound to get into more trouble over the years. But they also spent a large amount of time talking. The only person who he really trusted for advice was Nikias, but on the subject of Leila, he couldn't talk with his half-brother. Roger had listened and advised him as best he could.

"Will she ever trust me like that?" Anatolio asked quietly.

"She already does," Roger replied. "I can see it in her eyes when she looks at you. Somewhere inside of her, she loves you. She might not understand those feelings, yet, but give her time."

"What about Nalick?" Anatolio asked. "Won't he be hurt once she figures this out?"

"Not in the least. We already talked about this," Roger explained.

"You asked Nalick about Leila falling in love with me?" Anatolio asked in shock. He would never be so brash with his king on the topic of another man's wife.

"Yes, and why not? I wanted to know where he stood on it. And, actually, he hopes that one day he can see you both fall in love. Then, at least, he can be reassured that when he dies, things will be all right." Anatolio stared now at Nalick and not Leila. Again, Anatolio was impressed, and he wondered if he would ever be good enough to replace Nalick.

"He's leaving you not only Leila, but also his family. I hope you're up for the task."

CHAPTER THIRTY-SIX

The next day, Leila was left alone as she got ready for her second wedding. Elena had dressed the children, who were busy helping their grandparents with the decorations. Her brothers had set up a large tent near the lake, and chairs for all the guests were in place. All the women were busy helping Kay prepare food for everyone. Leila's mother and father watched all their grandchildren as they each tried to help as much as possible. Before Leila got dressed, she quietly slipped through all the chaos to see the wedding tent before the guests arrived. Leila silently walked down the middle aisle and stopped every now and then to touch a ribbon or smell a flower. She had gone through with one wedding already, but she remembered very little as she was exhausted from the week leading up to it. Leila seriously tried to take in every little piece she saw and commit it to memory. She turned quickly as someone coughed in the back of the tent.

"Not getting ready yet?" a familiar voice asked. Leila smiled at Roger and hurried to hug him.

"It's not for a few hours," she replied.

"Your mother figured you had run off again and since Nalick couldn't come look for you, I figured I should," Roger explained. "Anatolio is worried about you."

"I'm fine, just a little sad," Leila replied, knowing it was no use lying to him.

"This is your wedding day. You can't be sad. You should be happy," Roger explained. Leila nodded, but did not smile.

"Come on kid, I'll walk you back to the house. Your mother left your dress for you on your bed." Roger put his arm around her and began to walk her back up to the house. "Ten years is a long time. There's no need to worry about it now. Just think, it hasn't even been ten years since you chased Erich home, and yet, it feels like a lifetime has passed."

As they neared the house, Leila quickly hugged him again before opening the door. It felt like she had known Roger forever; but it had only been eight years. He was right that ten years would be a long time. Roger waved as she shut the door and went to her room. Lying on the bed was a long, off-white dress that had been sewn by her mother. Leila smiled, picking up the delicately-made dress.

Slowly, Leila slipped into her wedding dress. She could remember when she was ten and her oldest brother got married. She complained for hours that her mother was making her wear a dress, but as soon as she put it on, it all changed. Leila spent hours twirling in the dress, watching the hem swirl around her. As Leila slipped into the dress her mother made, she again could feel the magic of it. It lifted her spirits as she looked at every detail her mother had included. Leila noticed the small purple flowers on the hem. This was her real wedding.

Leila was ready long before the guests started to arrive. She sat and tried her best to occupy herself with anything she could find, but her thoughts continued to drift back to Nalick and what her life would be like without him. As she continued to wait, she climbed upstairs into the room Ruth had been sleeping in. She could see every detail of her old room was completely mimicked, even down to where the windows were. Leila walked to the nearest window and slowly felt the lace on the curtains. They were the original curtains from her room, just freshly washed. While sitting on the bed, Leila stared at the pattern the quilt pieces made. As she lay on the bed she felt lost as to why she couldn't be happy on her wedding day, she wished she could see Erich, if even for just a moment, just to be reassured she was making the correct choice.

Leila was interrupted from her thoughts as she heard Anatolio calling her name. She stood and walked to the staircase. As she took one step, she stopped as tears began to trickle down her cheeks. *I can't do this*, she thought. *If I marry him, then I agree to let him die.* The tears continued to trickle. She had finally found love again, only to find it was temporary. *Ten years isn't enough time. I can't do this again. I can't lose my love.* Leila leaned against the wall, searching in her mind for alternatives.

At the bottom of the stairwell Anatolio stood, watching her. Tears flowed freely down her face. Slowly, he approached her and stopped on the step below her so that he stood eye-to-eye with her.

"I can't do this," she said to him in barely even a whisper. "By marrying him, I sign his death warrant."

"This was never your choice," Anatolio explained.

Leila began to cry more. "How could he do this to me? I don't want to be alone again." She began crying harder. "If I just stay here," she started, but she stopped as Anatolio gently took her face in his hands. Ever so gently, he leaned close to her face. His lips gently touched hers.

"You will never be alone again," Anatolio promised, staring into her eyes while wrapping his arms around her. Anatolio couldn't contain the love he already felt for her and held onto her tightly. "I'll always be there for you."

Leila looked deep into his eyes. The boy she normally saw was gone. In his place stood a man. For the first time,

Leila could see him for who he was. With his tight grip around her, Leila realized Anatolio was right. He had not left her alone since the day she first entered Lexia. Anatolio gently wiped her tears away as he regretfully let go. She had stopped crying, and he could see the change in her eyes.

"We need to get you to your wedding before you're late, my queen," Anatolio said, adding a bow.

"Nalick would understand if I told him I got lost on the way," she joked. He smiled and took her hand to lead her down the stairs and outside. Her hand fit perfectly in his.

Anatolio and Leila walked in silence to the tent by the lake that was filled with her family and friends. As she neared the open doorway, Anatolio stopped. Leila turned to him, and he smiled as Ruth ran to greet her. Ruth handed Leila flowers as Anatolio quietly slipped into the tent before she could protest. Ruth led the way between the seated guests. Her parents proudly watched her walk their way. Leila smiled as Anatolio moved and stood beside Nalick. Leila stopped near the front of the tent, and Nalick turned to greet her at Anatolio's prompting. Leila slowly moved near Nalick and as he took her hands in his she gazed intently up at him. She could see no fear or regret in his eyes—just complete happiness. Leila knew then, that even though her life wasn't going to be exactly how she wished, she was certain, as everyone had promised, she would be happy.

EPILOGUE

A week and ten years after their wedding in the North Country, Nalick woke early for his trip with Phillip to Dria. They had been planning the trip for months, and Phillip was eager to leave the palace for some peace and quiet after the birth of his first son. Nalick carefully checked his desk before having breakfast. The letter he had written Leila was still waiting there. Everything was in order to transfer power to Leila for the next five years, until Connor reached his fourteenth birthday and could claim the throne. Nalick ate before walking upstairs to sadly say good-bye to his sleeping children.

The first door he opened had an unmade empty bed in it, as Nalick had expected. Tim was always up before everyone else, training as hard as he could so that Leila would allow him to take easy runs from Roger's courier station. The next room was that of Connor, the heir to the throne of Lior. Connor was nestled between his covers, quietly sleeping. Nalick sat beside him and watched the lids of his eyes flicker. To an outside observer, they would see Connor as Nalick's child, but beyond his head of dark hair, there was little resemblance. Every day, Nalick could see more and more that Connor was growing into the person Gabor had promised Nalick he would be, even before he was born. Nalick had no reservations leaving his country to him, knowing that Connor would live up to every expectation. Nalick kissed him before checking on each of his other children: Isabella, Jeffrey, Nathanial, and Ava. Except for the youngest, they all had his dark hair and tan skin, though they all displayed a mixture of his and Leila's personalities.

Somberly, Nalick returned downstairs to Leila, still in bed asleep. She had asked him to wake her before he left, but he just couldn't do so. If he did, Leila would be able to read his eyes and know what was going to happen. He sat for over an hour watching her sleep. Every now and then Nalick would gently stroke her face or hair, trying to will himself to stand and leave her for one last time. He gently touched her stomach, knowing she was pregnant with the one child he would never meet. Nalick wiped the tears from his eyes as he again tried to stand.

"Good-bye, my love," Nalick said silently to Leila and his unborn child. He gently kissed her forehead before he forced himself to stand. He wasn't afraid of dying, and had accepted his fate the day he first saw her, but it was difficult to give her one last good-bye. Leila was everything he could have ever hoped for in life. He could have never found someone as bright, loving, and caring as she was. Even after he was gone, she would still be the bright light that their children depended on. Leila was the best wife and mother, and Nalick was proud to have married her.

"You will never be alone," he added, slowly walking away.

As he stopped at the door to their wing of the palace, Nalick gave one last look around. It had been his home his entire life, but it never really felt like a home until he had found Leila. The calm around him was in stark contrast to the normal chaos of six children, aged three to fifteen, running around. Nalick sighed, he could hear Phillip down the hallway. He quietly closed the doors, hoping that in future years, his children would still remember him. Nalick hastily made an attempt to be more cheerful, so that Phillip would not notice.

Leila woke from her sleep to find Nalick had already left. She sat and yawned leisurely. She had asked him to wake her before leaving but he had forgotten again. Leila slowly stood and wrapped her robe around herself, walking to the kitchen to get a cup of tea. It would still be an hour or two before any of the children beyond Tim would be awake. Unlike her normal morning, which she spent in the garden, for some reason Leila felt like sitting on the balcony. Leila stood by the rail and looked down below at Nalick and Phillip checking the cart filled with their supplies for their trip. Phillip noticed his mom and eagerly waved to her. Leila waited for Nalick to turn to her also, but he did not.

Leila's hands began to shake, and she set her tea down on the seat. She knew what this meant. She had been waiting since their anniversary the week before. Leila continued to watch, but he didn't look up. Leila was so caught up in the thoughts racing through her mind she didn't hear Tim and Anatolio approaching from inside their home. Tim joined his mom and watched his dad below.

"He's not coming back," Tim said, the same thought that was running wild in Leila's mind.

"No," she replied quietly. "He's not."

Anatolio moved to Leila's right while Tim stood on her left. Anatolio placed his arm around her hip, and Tim placed his around her shoulder. The two men supported Leila while she was doing her best not to break down. Below, as the cart moved to the gate, Nalick turned and glanced one last time at his home and wife. Above, Leila stood with Tim on one side and Anatolio on the other. Nalick was sad to see her one last time, but happy to see she wasn't alone. His plan had worked; he had made sure of it. Leila would never be alone again. Nalick had seen the future, and in time she would be happy with Anatolio. Nalick didn't regret his choice, to stand beside her.

❖ ACKNOWLEDGMENTS ❖

As with any work of fiction, there are many people to thank along the way.

First off- to you the reader. Thank you for taking the time to read this story. I've been writing as long as I can remember, but you are the first to actually read my works. If you liked it please leave a review at your favorite retailer and on social media. The greatest help you can provide to keep a writer going is supporting them through spreading the word about their books and leaving them with a few encouraging words.

Secondly, and not any less important, I'd like to thank my husband who has pushed me to finally let other people read my works. This novel was written over five years ago; while he was at work on Saturday mornings, I was at home with nothing to do but write (we only had one car at the time). So I set out to see if I could write a novel. Five weeks and 180,000 words later, I had done it. Thanks to his encouragement, I have continuously edited to make it to the point I am at today and finally have the courage to publish it. Thanks hubby for all the encouragement and nudging along the way.

Third on my list are my "finishing touch" people: cover artist, beta readers, and editors that have made my novel a better read for all that followed. Thank you Kathy of Kat's Eye editing for giving this the edit it deserved. A special thanks to my editors Morissa Schwartz, David Calver, and Eric Boler. Thank you for all your help making the story better and catching all those oops moments. Thank you Wicked Cover Designs for a wonderful cover and making this process feel so much more real.

Last is my family and kids that take time to let mommy write and edit as an ongoing hobby that has now resulted in a published book. Thanks to my mom and dad, my husband, and my kiddos AK and KB.

ABOUT THE AUTHOR

Originally from Wisconsin, B. Kristin currently resides in Ohio with her husband, two small children, and three cats. When not doing the mom *thing* of chasing kids, baking cookies, and playing outside, she is using her PhD in Biology working as a scientist. In her free time she is hard at work on multiple novels; as each day passes, she has more ideas for both current and future novels.

For more information on upcoming novels, please visit www.bkristinmcmichael.com